21.53

P. D. James was born in Oxford in 1920. She is the author of fifteen crime novels and two non-fiction books. For thirty years she was engaged in public service, first as an administrator in the National Health Service and then in the Home Office, from which she retired in 1979. She is a Fellow of the Royal Society of Literature and of the Royal Society of Arts. From 1988 to 1993 she was a Governor of the BBC and a member of the Board of the British Council. From 1988 to 1992 she served on the Arts Council and was Chairman of its Literary Advisory Panel. She has won awards for crime writing from Britain, America, Italy and Scandinavia and has received honorary doctorates from six British universities. In 1983 she was appointed an OBE and was created a life peer in 1991. In 1997 she was elected President of the Society of Authors.

Harriet Harvey Wood read English and Medieval Studies at the University of Edinburgh and was an orchestral manager before joining the British Council in 1973. From 1980 until 1994 she was head of its literature department. She was a judge of the Booker Prize for Fiction in 1992 and was appointed an OBE in 1993.

SIGHTLINES

Published to promote and support the work of the Royal National Institute for the Blind's Talking Books, SIGHTLINES includes pieces from many of Britain's foremost writers, all of whom have contributed their work without fee. Introduced by Sue Townsend, who recently lost her sight, Sightlines includes many hitherto unpublished stories, essays and poems by leading contemporary authors such as Louis de Bernières, Antonia Fraser, Frederick Forsyth, Doris Lessing, A. S. Byatt, Malcolm Bradbury, David Lodge, Andrew Motion and Reginald Hill, among many others.

Edited By
P. D. JAMES
AND
HARRIET HARVEY WOOD

◆

SIGHTLINES

Complete and Unabridged

CHARNWOOD
Leicester

First published in Great Britain in 2001 by
Vintage
London

First Charnwood Edition
published 2002
by arrangement with
Vintage, a division of
The Random House Group Limited
London

The moral right of the editors and contributors
has been asserted

British Library CIP Data

Sightlines.—Large print ed.
  Charnwood library series
  1. English literature—20th century
  2. Large type books
  I. James, P. D. (Phyllis Dorothy), *1920 –*
  II. Harvey Wood, Harriet, *1934 –*
  820.8'00914

  ISBN 0–7089–9353–2

Published by
F. A. Thorpe (Publishing)
Anstey, Leicestershire

Set by Words & Graphics Ltd.
Anstey, Leicestershire
Printed and bound in Great Britain by
T. J. International Ltd., Padstow, Cornwall

This book is printed on acid-free paper

Contents

Introduction *P. D. James and
Harriet Harvey Wood*   ix
Foreword *Sue Townsend*   1

Sandy and her Beautiful Sisters
  Antonia Fraser   5
Old Smokeytoes *Louis de Bernières*   25
Hush and Lupins *Lavinia Greenlaw*   32
Solitude so Far *Brian Aldiss*   35
Ogres and Augurs *Maureen Duffy*   45
The Call-Out Fee *Candia McWilliam*   47
Seeing in the Mind *Nina Bawden*   54
Isolating Madison *Nicola Barker*   57
Thirteen Ways of Curing a Headache
  and Cathedral Limerick *Wendy Cope*   82
Lebensraum *Tim Parks*   84
Moth *Rose Tremain*   117
Flowers *Dannie Abse*   130
The Death of Diana *David Lodge*   132
Injury Time *D. J. Enright*   149
Listed for Trial *Tibor Fischer*   157
Dasvidanye: the Russian for Goodbye
  Craig Raine   182
The Photograph *Romesh Gunesekera*   187
The Things You Know *Julian Barnes*   194
A Seme from Safaga *John Fowles*   212
A Note to the Milkman *Simon Brett*   224
Home from the Hill *Philip Kerr*   226

Convergence *Malcolm Bradbury*   233
Sestina *and* A Photo of Roger
   Dorothy Nimmo   249
In a Small Circus *Julia O'Faolain*   252
History *Andrew Motion*   273
The Party Upstairs *Philip Hensher*   274
John Brown's Body *Reginald Hill*   279
How to Behave *and* For Kettle
   Anthony Thwaite   311
Early Ghost *and* Like Crossing a Room
   in the Dark *Lawrence Sail*   313
Nay, Ivy, Nay *Shena Mackay*   317
The Passing of Humpy *Frederick Forsyth*   328
For Don, on his Birthday *Ruth Rendell*   338
Beulah Berlin: an A to Z *William Boyd*   341
Odours Savours Sweet . . . *A. S. Byatt*   358
Buxtehude's Daughter *David Malouf*   374
Look *Adam Thorpe*   383
Loner *Elizabeth Berridge*   385
How We Met *Brian Thompson*   396
The Mourning *William Trevor*   406
The Sweetest Dream *Doris Lessing*   434
In Paradisum *and* Old Friends *Peter Porter* 442
Off Vico *Keith Ridgway*   446
On My Bedside Table *Joanna Trollope*   469
Heaven *John Burnside*   475
The House of the Blind *Douglas Dunn*   486
Sardines *Michèle Roberts*   490
Dreaming, Sailing, Writing *Richard Holmes* 510
Eyes in the Dark *Fay Weldon*   526
When I am Blind I Shall *and* When I am
   Blind I Shall Not *Susan Wicks*   534

Introduction

For those of us who from childhood have found in books one of life's most lasting joys and consolations, there are few fears more terrible than that of losing our sight. Many of us have relations or friends facing this personal calamity. So that, when we were asked by the Royal National Institute for the Blind to edit an anthology of contemporary writing in support of their Talking Books Appeal and to help raise awareness of their work, we saw the task as both a privilege and a pleasure. And so it has proved to be.

One of the aims of the Appeal is to modernise and extend the provision of Talking Books, and for lovers of the written word there can be no more valued service which RNIB provides. The books are selected to cover a wide variety of tastes, and the readers are experienced and carefully chosen for each particular work. Talking Books bring the pleasure, stimulus, entertainment and life-enhancing joy of literature to thousands of deeply appreciative listeners. Without them people with sight difficulties, already isolated in so many ways, would be denied one of the pleasures of literature: the discussion of new discoveries with friends and the stimulus of social interaction which this can bring. It is not surprising that, when we invited contributions for the anthology in February 2000, the Appeal met with a generous response and we are grateful to all the contributors; grateful, too, to Vintage who have undertaken publication of the anthology without charge.

It was left entirely to the writers approached to decide whether their contributions should be fiction, non-fiction or poetry, and this has led to a few surprising results: some writers, more familiar in the world of fiction, have sent in poems, some poets have contributed fiction. It was also not intended that the subject matter should necessarily relate to blindness, though some of it does. We have, however, included passages, both poetry and prose, about the loss of sight from sources as widely varied in time as the Bible and modern fiction.

We hope that this anthology, which includes many of the most distinguished British writers, will both make a significant contribution to the RNIB Appeal and give pleasure to those who, by buying it, are helping to make life easier for the thousands whose eyes are unable to scan these pages.

P. D. James
Harriet Harvey Wood

Sue Townsend

FOREWORD

The card came in the post in a cheap brown envelope. I didn't open it for a few days; it looked like the newsagent's bill. When I finally opened it, I found a pink laminated card inside. It said, 'This is to certify that Mrs Susan Townsend of Holmfield Road, Leicester, has been certified as eligible for registration as a partially sighted person under the National Assistance Act, 1948; by Mr ... (Consultant Ophthalmologist) and agreed to be registered on 22/7/1999.' On the other side of the card, in larger, bolder print, it said: 'Partially-sighted person's registration card.' There was no covering letter. There was nothing to soften the blow.

When I was a child I *noticed* things: the exact pattern of the bark on a tree, the colour of a wet pavement, the elegant curve of peeling paint as it drew away from a gatepost. The twice-daily trudge to school was made bearable by such visual delights. I used to watch the way the sun moved across the sky, and changed the look of my world as it did so. I soon learned not to share my observations with other children. They seemed not to be interested in such things. I began to think instead, and this thinking turned into a constant interior monologue, and without

1

realising it I became a writer. Though I didn't dare write anything down until I was fourteen.

I know what it is like to be regarded as stupid. I was eight and a half before I could read the simplest words. Mrs Ralph's reading lessons became an ordeal. For almost three years I sat with the same reading book open on the desk mouthing words I could not read. 'Look Janet. Look, see the ball. Look John, see the dog.' Mrs Ralph's ferocious temper terrified me. To be chosen by her to read aloud in class became my greatest fear. I dreaded going to school. If we small children made a mistake of any kind she would exert a strange punishment. After a tirade of shouted sarcasm she would order the offending children to stand on their hands, and then, while upside down resting their feet against the classroom wall, she would then slap our thighs with the flat of her hand. For us girls this was a double ordeal. All girls wore skirts in the 1950s, and when we were upside down our skirts fell over our heads, blinding us. This combination of pain, humiliation and darkness is used by evil regimes throughout the world to intimidate and bully the powerless and the weak. Since I was a child I have rarely slept in darkness. I suppose I fear the dark.

My sight has deteriorated further since I received that curt pink card. I am now technically blind. I have protected myself very well from the reality of my situation. I call myself a 'blinkie' or 'Mrs Magoo'. I push negative or pessimistic thoughts out of my mind as soon as they surface, but very occasionally reality rears up and slaps me in the face.

The plain truth is that nothing can compensate for sight. I mourn the lack of detail. I can of course remember a hundred thousands details, but I am still hungry for more. I have always written in block letters in thick black ink on lined paper (as recommended by the RNIB). The difference now is that on this day, 16 November, I cannot read the writing I have written without a huge magnifying glass; and after a retinal haemorrhage I throw my words into the dark and can only hope that the words are reproduced faithfully.

On more than a few occasions I have felt sorry for myself and cried hot fat tears. The first time I failed to tell the difference between a daffodil and a tulip without touching them was a bad day. The garden was sunny at the time. Sunshine is the enemy of those of us with diabetic retinopathy. We welcome that grey English light that makes sighted people melancholy. Dawn and twilight are our friends.

The pity of people is sometimes hard to bear. A woman approached me recently after I had made a slightly stumbling public appearance in a blindingly sunny room. She gushed, 'I just want to say that I think you're very, very brave.' I felt a surge of anger towards her, and wanted to shout, 'I'm not brave, you fool, I have no bloody choice but to carry on.'

But of course I didn't.

There is a lot of sentimental nonsense talked about blindness. But oh! it is so painful to look and look at your garden, and still not be able to see it. And it makes you want to shout violent cruel words to the people who suggest that one day you will be content to touch and to smell, instead of seeing your precious plants. I still want to see the exquisite elegance of a lily, and the vibrant green of an acer.

I was being driven through a tiny hamlet in Leicestershire last year, when I remarked to my husband on the surprising preponderance of Asian and black people on the streets. My husband informed me kindly that all the people on the street were white. So there are some compensations. I now live in a melting-pot world where everyone has the same colour skin.

There are certain privileges that partially-sighted and blind people enjoy. The Talking Books Service is one. I recently listened to 27½ hours of John Updike's *Rabbit* masterpiece. And, being a fundamentally lazy person, I was glad to be relieved of all that dreary page-turning. Instead I lay in bed and was told a story, and it was a total delight.

Since being diagnosed I have written a six-part TV series. In January I begin a new novel, *A Lump in the Bed*, I plan to replant my garden with those loud vibrant-coloured flowers I had previously disliked. And perhaps I flatter myself, but I think I can still see ever so slightly more than most people with perfect sight.

Antonia Fraser

SANDY AND HER BEAUTIFUL SISTERS

A Modern Fairy Tale

Once upon a time there were three sisters, two of whom were beautiful. That was the way Sandy used to begin the story of her family.

Mainly, however, she told the story to herself. Sandy (for Alexandra) was far too fond of Harriet and Helena (names never shortened) to wish to say that kind of thing aloud. She was also far too grateful to them for their evident efforts to protect her, promote her, one might almost say, since both of them worked in different aspects of public relations. Such a sentiment — uttered out loud — would not only have hurt her two elder sisters' feelings, but implied some kind of resentment which Sandy was very far from harbouring.

After all it was not the fault of Harriet and Helena that they were long-legged goddesses with the kind of narrow hips and slender thighs which looked good in the most testing kind of athletic gear (as Sandy could see for herself since Harriet and Helena were forever getting ready for some sporting activity or other). Sandy on the other hand was the sort of person whom designers of swimwear apparently envisaged being tactful enough never to take off their clothes, so absurd did she look in any kind of costume you could buy in a shop. No, it was not the elder girls' fault: merely the result of a tall, lean, rather hawk-faced father marrying a short but adorably pretty mother, and the genes getting, as it were, shaken, but not stirred. All the same it was true: once upon a time there were three sisters, two of whom were beautiful.

The age gap between all three sisters was not, as a matter of fact, very great. Harriet was twelve months older than Helena who was two and a half years older than Sandy. But the fact that Sandy was so plump — go on, why not say it? it was the truth — made her, oddly enough, look younger than she was. The trim goddesses, tanned calves rising in such a shapely fashion above the trainer shoes in which they frequently jogged to the office, were into their thirties and in a glorious, triumphant way, looked it. Sandy, on the verge of being thirty herself, could have passed for twenty-one or two.

'Not plump, Sandy,' cried Harriet, as she gazed into the mirror, twisting some crazy yet curiously becoming bandeau round her cropped streaky blonde hair — for what? wondered Sandy. Squash with Mike? The gym? Her dance class? 'And never ever fat, please,' went on Harriet, leaning forward and rubbing some fascinating new cream with a strange green tinge to it into her perfect almost unlined throat. Improvement? Protection? 'Why put yourself down, Sandy? Rounded is the preferred word, I think, or maybe curved, though that's rather overdone. Full? I think not. It's got an old feel to it. What did you say, Sandy? Ample? For God's sake, Sandy, *ample*! I mean, why not something a little more positive — cuddly for example, Yes, I like it. Cuddly.'

'Cuddly. Definitely. I like it,' called out Helena, who was also at her dressing table, tweezering out some invisible imperfection from her high dark arched eyebrows (Helena's eyelashes were so naturally thick and black that her headmistress had once crossly ordered her to remove her make-up). The elder girls had the two large intercommunicating rooms at the front of the Fulham flat they all three shared and Sandy had the smaller — much smaller — room at the back. That might seem unfair but actually Sandy preferred it like that and had herself suggested the arrangement when they moved in. For one thing Harriet and Helena wore the same kind of make-up and clothes, frequently stealing/borrowing from each other in a jocular competitive kind of way. In fact they hardly ever shut the doors between their two rooms — in the daytime and early evening, that is. Nobody ever wanted to borrow Sandy's clothes, let alone her make-up, of which she possessed very little, for obvious reasons. And then Sandy had a view over the garden — the garden she herself looked after, once again by choice.

Nights were of course different. All doors were shut. Another kind of athleticism took over then, Sandy supposed, demanding another kind of wardrobe — those minute heart-shaped panties, for example, wisps of black lace, which she sometimes found overlooked in the washing machine when she unloaded it, along with the tracksuits and T-shirts. Sandy always unloaded the machine, and generally loaded it too — which again might seem unfair except that Harriet and Helena were always in such a hurry to set off for their offices (in the sense that they needed to leave enough time to jog, rather than take taxis). In the same way they were always in a hurry to reach the various health clubs to which they belonged.

'I'm meeting Mike at six. Christ, look at the time,' Harriet would groan. 'Sandy, can you see that tank top, the funny striped one I got in New York. Try Helena's top drawer . . . '

The slow rumbling pace of the washing machine, Sandy sometimes thought, was more suited to her own ruminative nature than the high-flying temperament of her elder sisters. (She loved cooking and planned new recipes in her head to the noise of the clothes turning.) It was when Sandy found Helena kicking the machine because it refused to wash her new white tracksuit fast enough that Sandy offered to take over the washing entirely. After that there were clean tracksuits in abundance. Not of course that Sandy would have dared wear such a thing herself; even her positive-thinking sisters had not encouraged her to go that far.

Harriet's current boyfriend, Mike, was an amusing fellow; at least Harriet seemed to think so. Sandy herself was not quite sure about him as yet: he was an executive in a television company, and far more lively — so far as conversation at breakfast was concerned — than Harriet's previous boyfriend, Danny. Indeed, Sandy was only just getting used, after six months, to providing Mike's breakfast (coffee, black and strong, muesli) instead of Danny's (tea, toast and marmalade, and two boiled eggs, four minutes). She still tended automatically to start the eggs boiling and then had to eat them herself to prevent Mike's feelings being hurt. Perhaps it was the question of the eggs which made Sandy secretly miss Danny, since it was certainly more rewarding to boil eggs for someone than to pour muesli out of a packet. Or perhaps it was the fact that Danny's kind of employment, sporadic but mainly in publishing (where he had met Harriet, then a publicity director in the same firm), seemed to allow him to take a more leisurely breakfast than Mike.

Sandy herself earned a modest (compared to her sisters) but perfectly satisfactory living going out to cook for office lunches and private dinner parties, via an agency. She too therefore had no urgent need to hurry in the morning, as she reasoned to herself with regard to these breakfasts. Mrs Fairey, who ran the agency for which Sandy worked, a wizened little woman of uncertain origin, at whose age no one dared to guess, was the only person forthright enough to express disgust at these arrangements. When she learned that Sandy regularly cooked her sisters' breakfasts before tackling her own work, even did their washing, she exploded.

'So this is the famous modern career girl for you, Sandy,' she hissed. 'I can tell you that they are using you like a slave, my child. What are these offices, these clubs, these games of which you talk? Why should you have to make their lives easy? These are not men who will look after you when you are old, in return for some good food now — Sandy, my dear child, your food is *very* good, make no mistake, just as I make no mistake when I say something like that. I *know*!' With the gaze of Mrs Fairey's fine little eyes upon her, very blue beneath silvery hair rinsed to almost the same colour, Sandy did not confess that she also cooked her sisters' boyfriends' breakfasts on occasion. But she had a horrible feeling that Mrs Fairey, who was alarmingly percipient, could see right through her to the truth.

Danny had been gentle and rather sad — even before Harriet swapped him for the more obstreperous Mike. Sandy liked his soft eyes, generally hidden behind unfashionable horn-rimmed glasses, but visible from time to time at breakfast when he forgot to bring them to the table. Danny still came round sometimes to the flat, ringing the bell — generally answered by Sandy — and standing there on the mat with a rather bewildered air like a dog whose owners had moved away, but had somehow managed to find his way back to his original home.

If Harriet and Helena were both out, Sandy formed the habit of asking Danny in, and after a drink or two (whatever the girls had left over) he would weep a bit and touch Sandy's long thick fair curly hair, her best feature, her sisters constantly assured her. They had on many different occasions forbidden Sandy to cut it, although Sandy found its tangled mass quite a nuisance, particularly cooking in the recent hot summers. She did not envy her sisters their beauty, nor indeed their richly variegated love lives — but deep down she did rather envy them their dashing short haircuts. Helena's colouring was altogether darker than Harriet's; yet their sharp, clean features were surprisingly similar, jaws which just missed being a little square, set on necks which were in contrast almost too long. This similarity meant that Harriet and Helena did from time to time attract the same man — something which then had to be sorted out between the two girls, generally according to whose need was considered to be greatest at the time.

'Short hair just wouldn't be your thing, Sandy,' said Helena, when Sandy broached the subject yet again that same evening, emboldened perhaps just a bit by Mrs Fairey's remarks — and conscious also that she had defended her sisters loyally. 'Besides, your hair is absolutely lovely in its own right,' Helena went on. 'You look just like a Botticelli when you leave it all floating about. Who was it said that about you only the other day? Someone who was here to dinner. That memorable evening you cooked the duck in three kinds of cherry — '

'Like a Botticelli? I take it he didn't mean Venus. Whoever he was.' Sandy was, frankly, quite used to tributes to her cooking — although Mrs Fairey's praise had been something special and had aroused other secret dreams in her breast — but compliments on her personal appearance, other than from her sisters, were rare indeed. Sandy smiled. Without wishing to probe too far, she wished Helena could remember exactly who had made the remark. She cast her mind over recent dinner guests of which there had been quite a few, including some new faces. Maybe her admirer would come to dinner again. She was still, as it were, smiling interiorly the next night when Mike made his awful *faux pas*.

'You can always tell a good cook by one thing,' said Mike, finishing the *boeuf bourguignon* (Sandy's special extra-tasty way of doing it) with a flourish. 'A good cook is never ever thin. Too much tasting.' Helena covered up immediately and brilliantly, but all the same the smile was wiped from Sandy's interior being. It was Harriet who came to her room later — Sandy had not joined them after she did the washing-up.

'Well, he's never coming here again,' Harriet said fiercely. There was no need for further explanation — as a matter of fact Sandy had the impression there might be someone new on Harriet's horizon in any case — but at that moment Helena also joined them in the small back room.

'You've got a beautiful body, Sandy.' Helena was equally angry. 'A lovely womanly body. Some day some man is really going to appreciate you. Plenty of men are looking for someone just like you.'

At this a totally new thought flashed into Sandy's mind. This was that she did not particularly wish to attract the sort of man who was looking for someone like her. In a perverse way, she wanted to attract the sort of person who was specifically looking for beauty. (Once upon a time there were three sisters, two of them were beautiful, the third was the most beautiful of them all.) It was Sandy's first stirring of rebellion. Shortly after that, she decided on a three-point plan for the future. First, she would deliberately shut her ears to her sisters' compliments — however well meant. Secondly, she would embark on a campaign to get thin, or at least thinner. Thirdly, when Danny next called round, she would allow him to make love to her. For practice, as it were. Getting ready for the prince who would come along and sweep the new her, the new thin beautiful Sandy, off her feet.

But this is a modern fairy tale, not an old-fashioned one, reflected Sandy bitterly afterwards. For almost immediately steps two and three cancelled each other: that is to say, Sandy, as a result of a brief, not particularly satisfactory dalliance with Danny, became pregnant — so that it was goodbye almost at once to her new figure, the figure which had only just begun to emerge owing to a strict non-tasting diet.

'You generous woman,' Danny would groan after making love to her, putting his head on her soft full white breasts (which, as a matter of fact, really were her best feature). 'There's more womanly generosity in your little finger than in the whole of your sister's beautiful body — ' But

13

Sandy always stopped Danny at that point.

Things got worse after that. Or rather, the atmosphere in the flat changed for the worse. The announcement of Sandy's pregnancy did not, as she had perhaps rather naively hoped, find Harriet and Helena at their encouraging best. It was true that no one was foolish enough to suggest that Sandy should marry poor Danny. Currently unemployed (the publishers who were his main source of freelance income had been taken over by the big Prince group of companies), without even a flat of his own, he remained a slightly woebegone bystander to the whole affair, talking sometimes of his sister with a farm in Wales, at other times of a friend he knew who lived near Canterbury.

Since the sisters irritably brushed him aside — Danny had really failed in every way to live up to that promise Harriet had once discerned in him — it was never clear whether Danny was proposing adoption, baby farming, or some herbalist with a more trenchant remedy for the whole matter. In any case Sandy herself, when anyone listened to her, made it absolutely plain that she had no intention of marrying Danny. (Danny! who couldn't even make love to her without comparing her body to Harriet's!)

Once again, to their credit, the sisters put no pressure whatsoever upon Sandy on the subject of abortion once Sandy had made it clear that this too was not an option she was prepared to consider. Before this point was reached, the girls had also done their duty generously — or offered to do so — by flying into action and discovering the best, the very best, the latest, the very latest way in which such things were managed, much as they wore the latest fashions, the newest sports shoes, and for that matter changed their public relations' jobs regularly to the newest and chic-est companies available. As to the support of Sandy and her baby, it was taken for granted that this would somehow be absorbed into that of the household generally, Sandy looking after the baby in much the same efficient manner as she bought the food, cooked it, did the washing and tended the little garden.

No, the change of atmosphere was due to something else. It was as though Harriet and Helena were, for the first time, rather bewildered by their youngest sister. Had she in some way stolen a march on them with this baby? Impossible, the very thought, the very phrase, 'stealing a march', was inconceivable associated with sweet, adorable, helpless, helpful Sandy . . . Yet Sandy herself noticed that articles in newspapers and magazines in the flat on 'the biological clock' in particular, and the declining fertility of women over thirty-five in general (Harriet had just turned thirty-four), tended to be increasingly well-thumbed.

It was also an unfortunate coincidence that Harriet and Helena had recently embarked on one of their periodic episodes of rivalry over a new suitor. The man in question was Sam Prince, the heavily handsome silver-haired tycoon, middle-aged, to be kind, whose group had recently taken over Danny's publishing company. But there was more to Sam Prince than a successful — a very successful — business career. He had inherited money, as well as made it, and maybe it was this sense of obligation to the past (his mother had been a German newspaper heiress) which made Sam Prince treat his women so generously when he abandoned them. He had been married four times — that photograph of Sam Prince, dark glasses not quite hiding a lugubrious expression, leaving a registry office yet again, was one with which all readers of tabloids were familiar. One did not see Sam Prince leaving the divorce courts; nevertheless, the world knew that all the former Mrs Princes had been handsomely recompensed for their departure.

All in all, it was hardly surprising that the presence of Sam Prince in her life, combined with that birthday and Sandy's pregnancy, should arouse a vague feeling of the possibility of yet another change of career in Harriet's breast. The trouble was that Helena (who claimed to have met Sam first and was dissatisfied with her latest P R job — her fourth in three years, Helena choosing to move in each case) was experiencing something of the same kind of yearning. Sam Prince tended to take the girls out alternately, and eat in the flat on the third evening. And even Sandy could see the charm of Sam Prince, not only because he was mad about her cooking (although he did not stay for breakfast), but because it turned out to be Sam Prince who had described her as a Botticelli. Sandy still treasured the memory even though with pregnancy her Botticelli days were long past.

It was Mrs Fairey, however, of all the members of Sandy's circle, who was both the most supportive and the most forthright in her approach. Mrs Fairey, who had surely never heard of the biological clock, let alone the endless prohibitions concerning pregnancy related rather bossily by Sandy's sisters — 'this dangerous time' — dosed Sandy with a number of fortifying potions of her own. To prevent sickness, she said, and sure enough Sandy's health and strength remained untouched by her condition. Or maybe Sandy felt so well all the time because Mrs Fairey assured her that her job was safe, she could work as long, or as little as she liked, and return to work as soon, or once again, as late as she liked after the birth of the baby. Although on the whole Mrs Fairey recommended working as long as Sandy felt up to it; unlike Sandy's sisters, Mrs Fairey regarded pregnancy as a natural state.

'Women have always cooked when having babies,' declared Mrs Fairey robustly. 'Who else feeds the men? Does the man not eat simply because the woman is having a baby? As for my agency, you are far too good to lose, such a cook, so imaginative, so creative, your special recipes — '

All of this Sandy enjoyed. It was when Mrs Fairey moved on to her second piece of advice that Sandy found herself shrinking back once more from well-meant kindness.

'But you do need a man, my child, a father for this baby. Those sisters of yours, no, it is not at all the same thing. When they have their own homes, where will you be, after all that work you

17

have done for them?'

Reluctantly Sandy admitted to Mrs Fairey that marriage did seem to be rather in the air at the Fulham Road flat. It was always difficult to keep things from Mrs Fairey, so Sandy went further and described the visits of Sam Prince. 'To be quite honest, I'm not absolutely sure which one of them he's courting — '

Mrs Fairey's little blue eyes gleamed with fierce excitement. 'Sam!' she exclaimed, clapping her hands and interrupting Sandy. 'The very person. You shall have a father for your baby. Trust me. You shall have Sam Prince. He'd make the most wonderful father — well, at least, we don't know he *won't* make a wonderful father, as he's never had any children by any of his wives. I shall arrange it immediately. What an inspiration, I shall call him at once — let me see, dinner tomorrow night, I think, at his house, that great big barn of a place which he fancies is like a Renaissance palace. Now Sandy, I shall send a car for you — '

'But Mrs Fairey,' cried Sandy, 'I can't, I mean he doesn't want me. He did once call me a Botticelli, but look at me now, it's out of the question, anyway I've got nothing to wear, Mrs Fairey, please — ' Then as Mrs Fairey appeared to be paying no attention, Sandy became even more desperate. 'You don't even know him, he'll have something better to do — '

'Of course I know him,' Mrs Fairey spoke rather coldly. 'And since I know him, I know that Sam will certainly chuck any engagement he may have if I arouse his curiosity sufficiently. And I

18

know how to do that too. You see, my child, I was married to Sam once,' she went on in a kindlier tone. 'Second or third? My third and his second, or was it the other way round? I forget, it depends whether he married the Mexican or not. The money I got from the experience — which was, incidentally, by no means all unpleasant — helped me to found my agency — '

Sandy, seeing Mrs Fairey's good humour restored, made a last effort. 'I've still got nothing to wear.'

'Don't cry, child,' said Mrs Fairey in her sweetest tone. 'What does it matter what you wear? Nothing after all shows under a cook's apron.'

As Sandy remained lost for words — but her tears had stopped — Mrs Fairey explained: 'You see, Sandy, you're not going to eat at the dinner table; a complete waste of time like most dinner parties, to be honest. You're going to *cook* for Sam, cook such divine magic things, I will teach you one or two of them myself, and then there are your special recipes. He'll fall in love with you, marry you and never let you go, and if he does, of course, he will make you a handsome settlement. All this and a name for your baby. He's incredibly greedy, you know. No wonder the only good books he publishes are cookery books, because they are the only books he actually reads.'

So Mrs Fairey went on spinning her webs, and Sandy, increasingly thoughtful, dried her tears.

It was the night after Mrs Fairey's impromptu dinner party at Sam Prince's vast house somewhere in North London — Sandy had no idea of the precise address since she had been whisked there and back by chauffeur-driven limousine. At the Fulham Road flat Harriet and Helena were tense and jumpy, both evidently waiting for the telephone to ring: Sam had not rung either of them all day, no calls from the secretary to anticipate the call from the car to anticipate the dinner, the theatre. Sam had also failed to take Helena out to dinner the night before on some rather bizarre excuse about a former wife in trouble. Only the sight of Harriet sitting at home, equally at a loss, had cheered Helena up for the lonely evening without him. Then there had been no good hot food for either of them, since Sandy, quite uncharacteristically, had gone out for the evening to some baby class.

'Do you really think you ought to go out, in your condition?' Harriet had queried automatically. But Sandy had gone out, without answering, and had stayed out surprisingly late for one at a baby class.

'Was that midnight striking as you got back?' asked Helena, but without much true curiosity.

'I thought I saw a big car out of the window, some other house, I suppose.' Harriet was at heart equally uninterested.

Yet Sandy too seemed to be waiting for something; she did go into the kitchen to prepare a little ragout with herbs, but kept popping her head round the door as though anticipating an interruption. To all three sisters, then, the loud ring at the doorbell came as a welcome relief; the sight of Sam Prince's chauffeur, bearing a vast basket of roses, freesias and lilies, only added to the excitement. And there was a card, prominently displayed, attached to the flowers.

For a moment — just a moment — Harriet and Helena lost all grace as they struggled towards the chauffeur, knocking into each other as they ran. Before the chauffeur could stop Harriet, she had ripped open the card and before Harriet could stop Helena, she had seized it from Harriet and read it aloud:

'For the most beautiful . . . ' she read and with a little smile, hugged the card to her breast; because if Harriet was just slightly cleverer than Helena, Helena was just slightly more beautiful than Harriet.

Harriet lunged and grabbed back the card. Sam Prince's large handwriting filled one side of the card; there was no signature. Harriet turned it over.

' . . . cook in the world.' Harriet read the words uncomprehendingly. Then she turned the card back and forward. 'For the most beautiful cook in the world. From your Prince,' she read out. The two sisters gazed at each other in astonished silence. Neither of them had, to their knowledge, boiled so much as an egg for years.

'I think it's meant for me.' Sandy spoke as modestly as possible — she really did not want to annoy her sisters now that she was on the point of leaving them; she had so much for which to be grateful to them.

Sandy took the card from Harriet's hand.

'But it's from Sam, our Sam,' stuttered Harriet, suddenly looking quite drawn compared to the golden flourishing looks of her youngest sister.

'Yes, I'm going to live with him. We fixed it up last night.'

'*Live* with him?' Helena's voice, generally so well modulated, was approaching a screech.

'But you're having a baby! You can't do that,' cried Harriet. 'Does he know? And when you say live with him — '

'Well he could hardly miss it, could he? The baby. But in answer to your question, no, I'm not going to live with him in that sense. He's making me a flat in the house on the garden floor — perfect for the baby — and in return I shall cook when he wants, do dinner parties, that sort of thing, he's also out a great deal — ' Sandy paused.

'I think maybe he would have liked — ' she went on, choosing her words carefully. 'But never mind, that's not what I want at all. I explained to him that what I really want is to earn my own living, have my independence, and work on my cookery book. Sam loved that idea, of course, so he really quite forgot the other plan, whatever it was.' In this way Sandy felt that she had dealt truthfully, if not altogether candidly, with what had been for one moment quite a difficult scene with Mrs Fairey.

Really Mrs Fairey's ideas of security were so old-fashioned! But then after all, she was of quite an age, and nobody, nobody, had ever been kinder to Sandy . . . a real fairy godmother, just as Sam, in his own way, was a real Prince Charming. So charming was he, in fact, that

22

Sandy had readily agreed to compromise on one small detail: she would not after all cut her long golden hair, hair which reminded Sam of his first love (but not, absolutely not, of either Harriet or Helena) who had been a Hungarian girl working in his mother's kitchen. He had pleaded with her in such a humble and courteous fashion . . .

Sandy turned back to her sisters. 'And when it's finished Sam will publish the cookery book,' she ended triumphantly. 'So you see all my wishes have come true.'

Harriet and Helena, discussing the whole thing afterwards, both agreed they should not really have said what they now did say: 'But Sandy,' they cried in unison, 'what will happen to us?'

Sandy, however, was not listening. Once upon a time, she was thinking happily, there were three sisters: two of them were beautiful and the third had everything she wanted out of life.

∾

Cyriack, this three years' day these eyes,
though clear
To outward view of blemish or of spot,
Bereft of light, their seeing have forgot;
Nor to their idle orbs doth sight appear
Of sun, or moon, or star, throughout the
year,
Or man, or woman. Yet I argue not
Against Heaven's hand or will, nor bate a
jot

Of heart or hope, but still bear up and
  steer
Right onward. What supports me, dost
  thou ask?
The conscience, Friend, to have lost them
  overplied
In Liberty's defence, my noble task,
Of which all Europe talks from side to
  side.
This thought might lead me through the
  world's vain mask,
Content, though blind, had I no better
  guide.

John Milton

Louis de Bernières

OLD SMOKEYTOES

I dreamed recently that I was a highly successful person, but that someone had placed a kipper beneath my toupé as I slept, so that for months everybody avoided me as though I were a bearer of the plague. I cannot explain the desperation of my loneliness and incomprehension, for I was unable to detect the rank stench owing to the fact that my nose had disingenuously adapted itself to detect every aroma except my own. 'Why didn't you feel the decaying fish under your wig?' I hear you enquire, and 'Didn't you see it when you took your hairpiece off?' and I reply 'For God's sake, this was a dream, and dreams don't have to make much sense.' It's enough that they're erotic, or terrifying, or arrestingly peculiar. They have their own perverse logic, and that is why I did not appreciate that there was a fish under my toupé until I woke up. I sat up in my bed and clutched at my head in an ecstasy of humiliation and embarrassment, only to realise abruptly that I wasn't bald and had never worn a toupé in my life. There was therefore no possibility of a smoked herring finding itself on or about my person. Nonetheless, it took some moments before my heart settled down and my panic subsided. I suppose that I might have dreamed about kippers because my slumbering and snorting spouse takes spoonfuls of cod liver oil after our bath and before our bed, gleefully aware, one presumes, that the resulting halitosis is an excellent prophylactic against amorous advances. They say that no man is respected by his valet, and equally I might add that no dictator is respected by his wife. Hence the unregrettable necessity of mistresses.

There is probably some elaborate Freudian explanation for this dream, but I must suppose that in fact it merely lays bare my eternal suspicion that I was born to fail even though I appear to be at the apogee of perpetual success. Great men have always born inside them the germ of their own destruction, and in my case it would appear to consist of a fatal lack of complete confidence in myself. I have always given the impression of perfectly crisp command and lucid clarity of purpose but, even when I am on the balcony and below me a delirious crowd applauds my every word, I have never been able to forget that I am merely mortal and that one day I might make a mistake. I feel that perhaps I have failed to develop that sense of personal godhead which so sustained Hitler, or the Roman emperors.

One cannot, however, become a dictator without developing an acute sense of mortality. Common people detest success, and would conspire to bring one down even if one gave them their hearts' desire on a daily and ever more generous basis, and moreover one gathers enemies as a squirrel gathers nuts. I trod on a large number of sensitive toes in order to come to rule this country, and I have had to stove in a lot of hard skulls in order to preserve my position.

In one sense it was ludicrously easy. All you have to do is stir up nationalism, and cultivate a frenzy of hatred against any group of people that takes your fancy. I decided against Jews, because that was old hat, and went for blacks instead. I know that this was not very original either, and nowadays I most poignantly wish that I had picked something a little more startling, perhaps even a little whimsical. Cat-lovers, homosexual poets, post-modernists, that kind of thing.

But blacks it was, and of course I do not need to go into the details of the things I did, because they are already world-famous, or notorious, depending upon your point of view. So famous, or notorious, that I became automatically and *de rigueur* the target of black and integrationist assassination plots from all around the world. This is one reason why I sometimes wish I had not chosen blacks; I cannot imagine cat-lovers sending me gifts of exploding cigars, or homosexual poets springing from the palace rhododendrons armed with a machete. I especially cannot imagine a post-modernist being capable of coming up with anything interesting.

For a while the attempted assassinations greatly increased my popularity with the general population, so much so that fairly regularly I had them faked, but I have to say that eventually they began to fray my nerves. I would jump out of my skin every time a door slammed, and many of life's mundane pleasures lost their charm. For example, if an admirer sent me a chocolate cake, I would not be able to eat it in case it was poisoned. My staff would guzzle it, of course, and afterwards I would be left feeling quite wistful. I began to feel persecuted, and to realise why so many great dictators finally became paranoid. One might as well dress up as an antelope and invite a pride of lions to dinner; it is an entirely thankless task, except when one is thanked by a sycophant, whose thanks one would rather not have had in any case.

But now I have very real grounds for paranoia, and I can see that finally I am going to have to go.

It is not merely that I lost the lower parts of both legs in the explosion. That was certainly bad enough, and I still wonder how I managed to run the country from my sickbed when I was either wild with pain or sedated up to my eyebrows. Moreover I had recurrent night-mares, even while wide awake, in which I stood once again upon the podium addressing the Mothers of the National Purification, only to be launched suddenly upon a terrifyingly bewildering and seemingly endless parabola. I crash abruptly back to earth amid a painful storm of planks and splinters, and when I attempt to stand, discover that I no longer have the means to do so. I experience all over again the sensation of perfect horror that leaves the stomach aching like a void, and I hear the wails and shrieks of the assembled Mothers, whose faces are blackened by soot and whose respectable but anachronistic hats are missing or askew.

It is certainly true that, just as was trumpeted by the national press, the transplant was a complete success. Indeed, the nation now sees its leader striding about as if nothing had ever happened, a wonderful tribute both to the supreme skill of the surgeons and my own fabled toughness. 'The Indestructible' was added to my imposing list of titles, honorifics and sobriquets.

Unfortunately 'The Refuted' should have been added as well, for I am now not only three centimetres taller, but I am also a black man from both knees downwards. For weeks I was told by the surgeon that this was simply post-operational trauma and bruising that would eventually disappear, and by the time that the appalling truth finally sank in, the new parts were perfectly fused into position and the surgical team had fled joyously to France, where the story had been sold to *Paris Match* for a most considerable sum.

It appeared that the black man whose lower legs were now my own means of transport had been the victim of one of my Experimentation and Extermination Squads, and that his fresh remains had been delivered in ice to the hospital. The surgeons had discovered that the tissue was a perfect match with mine, and it had occurred to them that it would be fabulously and amusingly apposite to prove upon my own person that my racial doctrines were absolutely false. After all, every schoolboy knows that the tissue of differing species cannot possibly be grafted together.

I had known perfectly well, and all along, that my propaganda was balderdash, and I had only propounded it in order to consolidate the nation behind me. I admit to a certain cynicism; cynicism is a prerequisite of intelligent dictatorship. But I had not expected to be so dramatically and ironically confounded, nor so publicly, for it was quite impossible for me to prevent the news from spreading like wildfire from France. In the modern world communications are regrettably instantaneous and uncontrollable. As is humour; it was not long before every public lavatory in the land was covered with cartoons of me in my uniform with the trouser legs rolled up, and the feet and shins shaded in black. The country rapidly became ungovernable, and Intelligence sources revealed that my nickname had been changed from an affectionate 'The Old Man' to a derisive 'Old Smokeytoes'. It took no great acuity to perceive that even my wife and my own most loyal staff were sniggering behind my back, and I began to receive invitations from swimming clubs and naturist colonies.

I have decided that the nation's gift to me upon my unexpected retirement early tomorrow shall be a nice little island in the Adriatic. I have already bought it with funds diverted from the Ministry of Racial Harmony.

It has just occurred to me that the kipper in my recurring nightmare probably symbolises my negro legs. I suppose that the toupé must

30

symbolise my trousers. But what was the stench that everyone but myself could smell?

~

You are pleased to mock my blindness.
   Have you eyes
And do not see your own damnation?
   Eyes,
And cannot see what company you keep?
Whose son are you? I tell you, you have
   sinned —
And do not know it — against your own
   on earth
And in the grave. A swift and two-edged
   sword,
Your mother's and your father's curse,
   shall sweep you
Out of this land. Those now clear-seeing
   eyes
Shall then be darkened, then no place be
   deaf,
No corner of Cithaeron echoless
To your loud crying, when you learn the
   truth.

Tiresias to Oedipus, Sophocles,
Oedipus Rex.

Lavinia Greenlaw

HUSH: THE MAPPIN TERRACES (1913)

The timber frame of a helter-skelter
smoothed over like the scandal
of the imperial wireless contract
the ministers insisted Marconi won.

A concrete cover-up
to make a mole hill of a mountain.
Gandhi was arrested. The King's horse
fell on Emily Davidson.

Each bear prowled its slice of hill
as if it were inside a wheel, as if to stay
    still
would be to backslide or sidestep
(everyone was doing the foxtrot).

Dancers, anglers, children's friends,
fractious, wary, teeth and claws
extracted. The Lords tried twice
to stop the Irish Home Rule Bill.

The last horsedrawn omnibus in Paris
failed to make it through the winter.
There were no bears in the Armory Show,
no bears in *Sons and Lovers* or *Le Grand
    Meaulnes*.

LUPINS

'That girl's uncomfortable just being inside
her own skin.' Wolves comforted me.
I grew up within earshot.

Their howls would climb the hill
like tall spikes of blue flowers,
as if the zoo's iron railings

had unfurled beneath their spell.
Traffic gets up across the canal.
Some slip through lights

like baby golden tamarin monkeys.
Others wait, like baffled clownfish,
behind glass.

∽

*I found Victor in bed in the garden, his pale
fingers lethargically exploring a big book of
Braille. His head was still copiously bandaged,
and one brown eye, impotently open, stared
glassily into fathomless blackness. If I had not
been looking for him I should not have known
him; his face seemed to have emptied and
diminished until what was visible of it was
almost devoid of expression. 'Hallo, Tah!' I said,
as casually as I could, self-consciously anxious to
keep the shock of his appearance out of my
voice.*

*He did not answer, but stiffened all over like a
dog suddenly hearing its master's call in the
distance; the drooping lethargy disappeared, and*

his mouth curved into the old listening look of half-cynical intelligence. 'Do you know who it is, Tah?' I asked him, putting my hand on his.

'Tah!' he repeated, hesitating, expectant — and then all at once, with a ring of unmistakable joy in his voice, 'Why — it's Vera!'

Vera Brittain, Testament of Youth

Brian Aldiss

SOLITUDE SO FAR

Who is your favourite cartoon character? Is it Bugs Bunny? Tom or Jerry? The ubiquitous mouse of Disneyland? Or one of the female warrior creatures who battle so bravely through computer games?

A remarkable tide in public opinion has so far gone unremarked. Until, let's say, the sixties, the belief that life might exist elsewhere in the galaxy or even in the solar system was held only by a few forward-looking eccentrics. Then a change in public opinion took place. Now, at the end of the century, it appears that almost everyone believes in alien life. Governments investigate UFO phenomena, major films depict visits between planets, where exist strange bipeds, either harmless or, more likely, well armed. A consensus has been reached — without referenda.

Non-human life is the irregular verb of the human mind. We are drawn in love and fear — and always have been — towards something living but not quite like us. There is a phylogenetic reason for this trait: deep in the brain is buried a memory of when we as a species were hardly apart from other sub-species or even animals, and dressed ourselves in their skins; before the invention of the gun, the human/animal relationship was closer than city-dwellers ever imagine. Palaeoanthropologists also remind us that time was when our species lived in a world populated also by similar but differing species — and this only some 700,000 to 125,000 years ago. Did, I wonder, *H.sapiens* ever talk to *H.erectus*? Was it only a matter of clubbing each other, or was there conversation, possibly copulation?

As we know, there remains much of the ape in us. Regrettably, I am now too old to climb trees. That early pleasure was undoubtedly a part of phylogeny, just as what passes as cute is the atavism whereby parents dress their babies in hoods with ears, turning them into mice, rabbits, or bears — or other mammals which have accompanied us along the evolutionary ladder. Our constant invention of the Unknown, the Other, has deep roots.

Those roots tap into the mental soil, presumably before the dawning of human consciousness. With the subject of consciousness now under scrutiny, we see how slowly such awareness has developed from a pre-human ancestry. One might ask if the human species has yet achieved full consciousness; using the analogy of a light bulb, we can wonder if it has yet reached highest wattage. For many of us, it is easier to fantasise than to think constructively. Education is the painful means whereby we attempt to turn up the wick a little.

One of the overriding fantasies we all share is this persistent vision of the alien, of something which lives close, but not as we do.

It is chastening to run over a partial list of beings patently without existence, in which nevertheless humanity has believed at one time or another, often for decades, even centuries. We find ourselves at once bewildered by a population explosion of persons with goat feet, persons half-human half-bull, persons with snakes growing out of their heads, fairies, elves, goblins, gnomes, trolls, leprechauns, skeletons, the walking dead, ghosts of various sorts, demons, devils, angels, spirits, sprites, *doppelgangers*, dragons, werewolves, and vampires. Like Jesus Christ, vampires have a life after death.

Every nation, every tribe, has its own particular spook. In our house when I was a boy hung a wooden plaque, on which was inscribed:

> From ghoulies and ghosties
> And long-legged beasties
> And things that go bump in the night
> Good Lord deliver us

This strange apotropaic device, executed in pokerwork, might be found in almost every house two generations ago — before, let's say, the wholesale introduction of electricity and central heating into every home, after the Second World War. It was electric light, rather than philosophy, which shook a tenacious belief in ghosts.

The list of such uncomfortable supernatural things is almost endless. The phantoms came out of the sky, the sea, the woodwork. Most of those listed above could not speak (an indication that they emerged from the limbic brain that knew only images, not language) — at least until the talkies came in and gave Dracula a voice.

But these were only minor league conjurations of alien life. Ranking above them, and above humanity, came a more troublesome cast of imaginary non-humans: the gods and goddesses which have plagued the lives of people throughout the ages.

Why, here's old Silenus with his satyrs and attendant woodland deities. Bacchus, god of wine, is popular. In the north, in Scandinavia, there was Ymin, god of numbing cold, and Thor, whose name lives on in our weekdays and Marvel Comics. Mithras, stony-faced soldiers' god. Ishtar, the terrifying Babylonian goddess of fertility. Hindu gods aplenty, such as Shiva, the destroyer, and his icing-pink wife, Parvati, dancing on her lotus leaf. Seth, embodiment of evil. Countless more swarming deities, the law-givers, the punishers, the handsome, the horrendous. Some of these deities come adorned with skulls and serpents, or armed with lightning bolts and swords. Some have an elephant head, or the skull of an ibis. Many wield impossible rules for human conduct.

Wars were fought, human and animal blood flowed for this imagined lot! Some sprout long white beards, some change shape and form, some are blue in the face, some black of body. Some take the form of bulls, or are presided over by cobras. Some consort with smartly dressed hyenas. Almost commonplace are extra arms, breasts, heads, lingams. And people much like us worshipped them, died for them.

If we now — in this 'modern age' — accord them no belief, then we must enquire where they have come from. All of them have emanated from a porridgy substance shaped almost like a giant walnut — the human brain, with its neoteric consciousness, the very petrol that runs the engine. What a ghastly crew these images make! But there is no fun in blaspheming against a dead god, against Baal, or the great god Pan, or even the astonishing Isis, who is now merely a river flowing through Oxford. Only against current gods, Allah, God the Father, Marx, L. Ron Hubbard, does blasphemy have meaning.

Like many of my generation now hurdling the old 'three score year and ten' edict, I was brought up within the whole rigmarole of Heaven and Hell. Like Graham Greene, I developed a serious belief in Hell. Damnation was taught every Sunday from the pulpit, and every evening at family prayers. Things certainly went 'bump' in my nightmares. But we must rid our minds of cant, as Samuel Johnson advised us to do, when we are adult.

We can take comfort from the words of a Buddhist priest in Kyoto, who puts the whole matter in a nutshell: 'God is an invention of Man. So the nature of God is only a shallow mystery. The deep mystery is the nature of Man.'

Suppose that we and electricity and the Internet have between us rid ourselves of all these categories of anoetic monstrosities . . . But then why do we talk to our cats and dogs as if they were just weird variants of the human shape? Why dress our kids to look like animals? Why, for that matter, do our kids behave like animals? Why are favourite cartoon characters all talking animals (Mr Magoo never won great popularity . . .)?

Perhaps the secret lies in the amygdala. The amygdala is that undiscovered country from whose bourne many memories, including the old and painful, come. It sits like an old witch on top of the brain stem, beneath later layers of cranial developments, to be seen only occasionally when the surgeon's scalpel uncovers it, following a serious accident affecting the head. The weapons of science have revealed it and some of its workings, but perhaps the amygdala is mightier than the sword.

The latest gang of imaginary unthinkables to be visited upon us are undoubtedly aliens. We watch them on our various-sized screens. They may come from Special Effects, but their true home is the brain, the amygdala, or elsewhere in that crowning glory we carry with us.

Many sensible people would claim that there is scientific reason for aliens. Well, a few years ago there were supposedly 'scientific reasons' for believing in little green men from Mars. But the science was false, the reasoning was wrong, and the little green men were terminated.

When flying saucers came into fashion in the 1950s, they were at first believed to be piloted by the aforesaid little green men. It 'seemed reasonable'. We now have ufologists among us, reasonable men; we hope they prosper like astrologists. My contention — reasonable enough — is that UFOs are simply a later version of those imaginary unthinkables we have been looking at; elder gods and godlets have been brought up to date, to be clad in the benefits of modern technology.

Promptly in 1951, Fox studios brought out *The Day the Earth Stood Still*, a science fiction film in which a flying saucer lands in Washington, and the aliens who crew it order Earth to cease her development of nuclear weapons or else. *Jehovah redivivus!*

Since the saucers have not yet blasted any of our major cities — though they are reported to have destroyed a caravan in Alabama — a general consensus regards them as benevolent. Carl Jung spoke of UFOs as a cargo cult, implying an erroneous faith in a superior power. This verdict seems to apply to the welter of aliens which have descended on us ever since, some for reasons of morality, some just for entertainment (i.e., bloodletting and destruction).

So it is that (*pace* Pooh) aliens and dinosaurs have become the kiddie favourites. However, the scientific standing of aliens and dinosaurs is by no means equal. Dr Gideon Mantell's young wife took a walk in 1822 and found a fossil tooth, later identified by her husband as belonging to an iguanadon. Painstaking investigations by experts over the past two centuries have firmly established the existence of the giant reptiles of the Jurassic, within the context of Earth's history.

But *aliens*? The scientific argument for the existence of aliens is a statistical one. Our galaxy contains some 1,000,000,000,000 stars. Many or most of them must support planetary systems, as does our sun. Most or some of those planets must support life of some kind. Some at least of that life must have acquired consciousness and intelligence. Therefore, even by a strict accounting, the galaxy must be teeming with intelligent life.

This is a popular line of argument. However, *as yet*, no other planet has been sighted which is at all likely to support life, certainly not life comparable with us bipeds. This includes Mars and the other planets of our own system of ten planets (ten, that is, if we include the recently detected mystery object, orbiting the sun at a distance of 0.5 light years).

When we start looking at our own chequered evolutionary path, other reservations emerge. It is chance that we are here, in our present shape, reading the *New Statesman* and the *Sun*. A whole number of chances. The earth just happens to move in a zone of comfort at a fortunate distance from the *Sun* — Venus is too near, Mars too far.

There's the curious fact that the solid state of water — ice — is lighter than its liquid state, contradicting what seems to be natural law; were it otherwise, the oceans would be covered by ice, filling up from the bottom. There's the curious accident whereby the eukaryotic cell was formed, of which most plants and animals are built. Among external factors, the development of grass may be mentioned. Grass grows from under ground, not from the tip of the blade. So it can be cropped and still grow; sheep may safely graze — until they get eaten by mankind. Sheep provide not only meat but wool for clothes.

Then there's that long painful pause between single-celled and multi-celled life. Those cells had to conspire into bones and organs — and brains. Consciousness had a tardy dawn.

Antonio Damasio, in his recent book *The Feeling of What Happens*, distinguishes between core consciousness and extended consciousness. We share core consciousness with some other animals, whose intelligence is imprisoned in the here and now. Only extended consciousness grants us the ability to travel mentally into the past and future. Have the findings of the last century and this given us a kind of intoxication?

It may be this intoxication which has unleashed the multiplicity of aliens upon us. They're fine as fiction; but — as reality? However, reality is changing fast. It seems that even the shape of our cosy old solar system has changed, if the recent hypothetical discovery of a tenth planet is to be believed. The fact remains that there is as yet no proof of any other life anywhere in the galaxy.

So what if humanity is alone? What if this Earth, with all its teeming phyla, happens by some cosmic accident to be the sole refuge of life and consciousness? We seem, in that case, to have got ourselves elected as the consciousness of the galaxy, maybe of the universe. It is a devastating honour for a species that believes in fairies!

It is an infinitely more challenging prospect than its opposite, a galaxy already bubbling over with aliens, with ancient wisdoms of which we may know nothing. It certainly means that we have to improve our behaviour before we start to move into outer space. Or even to set foot on Mars.

For a start, we could clear our minds of cant.

Maureen Duffy

OGRES AND AUGURS

Now when I really need her the tooth
    fairy
doesn't come any more to leave a thrup-
    penny joey
or bright tanner under my pillow
augur of a sharp ivory wedge chiselling its
    way
up from the bone. Instead those childhood
    ogres
Snaggletooth and Gummy Adams beckon
    from the shadows.
My sibilants shush like dragged feet
    through leaf mast
or the tide going out over shingle.
By the time I'm one with Yorick there'll be
hardly a peg for the archaeologists
to hang a date on. My imagination cries
    'Pah!'
Yet I've done half as well again as my
    mother
whose new National Health dentures I
    gummed
to her forty-year-old jaw with a well-meant
toffee. Yesterday in the news I saw
a mugged man my age dubbed elderly.

But how can that be when I'm reading
    Goethe
for the first time and this morning, leaving
    you,
I drove between hills sugared with rime
and hollows brimming with mist white as
    milk teeth.

Candia McWilliam

THE CALL-OUT FEE

When Amelia woke up in the night for the fourth time, she turned on her bedside light. The preceding three times she had not given in to the desire to read, knowing that it would make the return to sleep ever less likely.

But this fourth time, she knew from the frothing in her mind that sleep was receding and might very well escape her until some time — inconvenient, tempting, luxurious — during the next afternoon, when she would be at work, where nothing smelt fresh and the carpet was bristly with electric shocks.

She reached out for the light, got her hand up inside its stiff little shade, and pressed, anticipating the flood of blessed light that would allow her to pick up the safety of her book.

There was an instant's light, swift as a good idea, and as surely quashed by the officious descending darkness, attended by a nervous sound between tinkle and pop. Amelia knew that a fuse had blown.

So she lay in her bed in her room in her flat in the town until the dawn began to relieve the night. A flight of geese went over in the sky, honking. Every morning at this time she heard them, and would have felt bereft if she had not. She had begun to impose human routines upon

47

them, and was once shocked and then shocked at having been shocked, to hear them busy on a Sunday.

As soon as there was enough light, Amelia made her way to the fusebox by the hall door, in a cupboard where she also kept her collapsible umbrella and several jamjars, that she washed out when the jam was all scraped out to use as vases. Amelia acquired flowers from places where the flowers that no one owns grow, even in a town, under hedges at the edges of playgrounds, by drains where dandelions often button themselves in, and tired sprigs moulted from hanging baskets.

It was clear, thanks to the neat pianistic layout of a modern fusebox, exactly which fuse had blown, and Amelia simply tripped the switch, as the last electrician she had been driven to call out had shown her. She had been shamefaced at the time, embarrassed more by the smallness of the job she was asking the man to perform than by her own ignorance.

After all, she had until recently not been alone. There had been someone there who knew fuseboxes, who could read the habits of the flat as a doctor takes a patient's blood pressure.

She had learned though not to talk of this recent loss to those people whom she had — regrettably, extravagantly — to call out when such things as Jack had attended to required fixing. If she commenced to talk of Jack, it was sometimes understood not as a tribute but a plea.

Not that there had been more than a minute,

nevertheless undesired, advance in familiarity on these occasions, but that had been enough, an awful revelation to Amelia, in the request for biscuits, the assessing look around, the question, 'So what do you do then?' of her own unclothed loneliness.

After she had replaced the jamjars and the stubby brolly in the hall cupboard, there were perhaps three minutes of lighted peace before the dimming pop came again.

★ ★ ★

Amelia repeated her routine, like a mother bird feeding a chick that has hatched but then expired.

But she could not reillumine the veins of her flat. At nine o'clock, already late for work, she telephoned her employers to explain. Used to the lies by which their less significant employees sheltered their idleness, their hangovers, their irresponsibility, her superiors consulted, acceded to her certain late arrival, and noted Amelia as one lacking conscientiousness at best, ambition at worst.

She had worked within the firm, at very slightly rising levels, for fourteen years.

In the *Yellow Pages* were hundreds of advertisements clamouring for her attention. She knew that a well-regulated housewife would have an electrician's telephone number to hand, not be reduced to this grabbing of costly assistance like one eating take-away food rather than nutritious long-cooked casseroles.

She settled on a firm whose advertisement displayed large lightning bolts. 'No job too small', her favourite reassurance when it concerned tradesmen, the advertisement said. 'John Ottaway and Son, Lightning repairs.' So perhaps she would be in at work sooner than she feared.

'Mr Ottaway?' said Amelia, when the telephone was answered.

'No, son. Dad's in hospital.'

'Oh, I'm so sorry,' said Amelia. 'I hope it is not serious?' She knew she was wrong on every score to ask, that she had asked automatically, from exhaustion, politeness and nerves, that the man at the other end would think her intrusive, insincere, and, come to that, a soft touch. And she knew that it *would* be something bad the father had.

The younger Mr Ottaway let Amelia off every hook.

'Not perfect,' he said, relieving her of many obligations to express emotions that could not but be general rather than particular. 'But what is?'

He asked the doctor's question. 'What seems to be the trouble?'

'The electricity,' Amelia said idiotically. 'It keeps going. I've got to get to work.'

'And you don't want to get in to a dark house tonight.'

Already she felt the unwanted familiarity she was not ready for.

She made her voice cold, superior, as she heard all day the voices of her colleagues go gelid

50

when it was required.

They ran through what had happened, what the likely causes were, the particularities of Amelia's address and payment arrangements.

'I'll buck up and be over your part of town by ten,' the voice of the younger Mr Ottaway assured her. 'It's sixty pounds for the first hour or part of an hour, a hundred an hour after that.'

Stunned, Amelia heard the telephone go down at the other end. Did this mean that five minutes were to cost her sixty pounds? What if the job took sixty-three minutes? Was fusewire made of gold? Did fusewire exist? Why was she not an electrical engineer? But she knew the question was a facetious one to ask herself.

She could not face the invisibility of electricity, its moods and potentialities, its cousinship to fire. It was like money. Both touched places in her she would rather, through ignorance in the one case, through dedicated modesty and thrift in the other, avoid. She feared the glare of money that was summed up for her by those heated colourful slippery magazines that she saw people fall on as though thirsty for simple stories, full of photographs in high shadelessness and very few, godlessly optimistic, words.

The doorbell did not go, for it too of course had died, but Amelia saw the lightning-painted yellow van draw up and park illegally on the double yellow lines outside the building. She felt dizzy. Why not add a parking ticket to the day's inevitable high-living?

She noticed that Mr Ottaway was handsome. She was worried by such men, not knowing whether to become with them even more withdrawn than was her habit.

There was nothing for it but to go downstairs and let him in. He had eyes the depth and shaded shape of brown eyes, but they were blue. His overalls were covered in paint.

She led the way up the stairs to her flat, forgetting the lift, then feeling her own shrivelled electricity supply had perhaps compromised its function.

Amelia showed the man the fusebox. It was the time of day when people drink tea or coffee, but she did not want to waste time, although there was an hour of it — sixty pounds! — to waste.

'Which fitting set it off?' asked Mr Ottaway.

Amelia was in such a state she hated to reply. Everything seemed capable of misconstruction. She felt that somehow this man who could read currents and wiring would read some message she held, deeply encrypted, within herself.

She led on to the bedroom, a cube of neatness that contained just the one photograph of Jack, put so that she could see it every time she woke. She indicated the tricky bedside light.

There was no allusion by the electrician to anything beyond his function and the reason for his being here. He did not need to be shown where to find the fusebox. Amelia realised that anyway her kettle would not work, nor the hot water, nor the heating, nor the radio that came with her everywhere. She felt light, a sensation of swooning she knew from the few occasions on which she had spent more than she could afford, the purchase of her wedding suit, the deposit on their last holiday, the repeated awful buying of her season ticket.

Later, after the electrician had found and righted the fault, a series of acts that took him under fifteen costly minutes, she found herself saying, 'Would you like some coffee? Or tea?'

'I'd like that,' said the young man. 'I've been painting the kitchen. Thirsty work. For a surprise when Dad gets back. If.'

She had lost that comforting spar of resentment and suspicion, somewhere during those extravagant minutes when a stranger had restored to her not just heat and light and music and words, but the priceless thing, the sense of being normal. She felt almost sick with being alive, even well.

On the tray she set, Amelia put biscuits. She then looked at the electric kitchen clock, which had stopped all those hours before, and, reckless, her sense of time lost, said, 'Would you like toast and jam?'

She was once more a person with a future, in which, not soon, but this year certainly, she would wash out this newly begun jamjar and contemplate hunting down free flowers to pick and put in it.

Nina Bawden

SEEING IN THE MIND

I have only once written a book, not to order, exactly, but to please a particular audience; a girl of seven who was, as she put it, 'a little bit blind'.

We had gone on holiday with her family, friends who had children much the same age as ours, renting an old manse on the side of a loch on the island of Mull. Janey — that is the name I gave her in the book I wrote for her — was the youngest of four children. The older two were perfectly sighted. The third child, a boy, had been born with infantile glaucoma. He could see out of one eye, the other was glass; a useful prop for a boy with a mischievous nature. The first time I bathed him, along with my son the same age, I steeled myself to take his eye out and wash it as I had seen his mother do, intending to be absolutely *casual* about it as she was. But I was secretly terrified. And he knew it . . .

He called my bluff. He took the eye out himself, hopped out of the bath, and chased me round the bathroom with it. Serve me right.

Janey had less sight than her brother. She could only see a little light and shade. One day the other children decided to climb to a particularly enticing cave they had spotted on the face of a cliff that was too steep for Janey — and for me, too, since I was going through a vertiginous period. So she and I walked round the loch instead and talked about the old story the locals had told us about the Lake Horse, a great horse that was to be seen sometimes, galloping on the surface of the loch, a greedy creature of mist and terror that took human souls to keep it company in the deep water. Janey and I decided that this was just a story to frighten children and keep them away from the dangerous loch. Then she sighed. 'They won't let me do dangerous things,' she said.

She had wanted to climb to the cave with my children and her brothers and sister. She sighed again. Then she said, 'I wish you'd write a book about a blind girl, Nina.'

'What sort of book?'

She said, very promptly, 'A book about jewel thieves and caves. And a blind girl who does something brave.'

We discussed what a blind girl could do that was special; something a sighted person would find difficult. Then, that night in the creaky old manse, we were given the answer. There was a storm and all the lights in the house went out. (We were an improvident lot and had neglected to buy candles. Or perhaps they were provided and we had simply not seen them.) The manse was full of crooked corridors and unexpected stairs. The only person who was able to find her way around, the necessary guide when one of us wanted to go to the lavatory, was seven years old. 'I can see how to go in my mind,' Janey said.

She could find her way in the dark. So, in my story, the children — Janey and her brother and

Perdita, the witch's daughter, are abandoned by the wicked jewel thieves in a dark cave and Janey leads them out to daylight and safety. *The Witch's Daughter* is a conventional adventure story, and I hope Janey enjoyed it, but writing it, trying to imagine what she could 'see in her mind' was the real adventure for me.

Not, alas, for everyone. A couple of years ago an American company made a film of the novel. I was well paid but not consulted. This happens sometimes and I was not particularly dismayed, merely interested to see what they had made of it. And when I finally saw the film I could hardly believe it. It was quite well done, my thirteen-year-old granddaughter caught her breath and sobbed in the right places. But they had left out the blind girl. No Janey! One of my grandsons said, 'It was like making *Hamlet* without Hamlet!'

'I'm not Shakespeare,' I said. But I took his point.

Nicola Barker

ISOLATING MADISON

'Have you ever seen a worm tie itself into a knot?' Madison enquired, pulling fast a loose bow on her bootlace, and then, in the same fluid motion, yanking up her beautifully girlish *broderie anglaise* blouse to reveal two staggeringly colossal breasts. She was fully corseted. Larry could almost hear it creaking. It was antique, a pure black and very plain. Madison's pride and joy. Boned, of course.

Through the wall of glass that separated their tiny L-shaped rooms, Larry espied Madison's ghostly white bosom (how could he help himself?) and was struck by its resemblance to two hugely burgeoning field mushrooms peeking from a voluptuously dark hourglass of filthy compost.

Dr Mackle, who stood before her — separated from Madison and her corsetry only by thin air and his indomitable professionalism — was also, nevertheless, greatly impressed by Madison's *décolletage* (although strictly in a medical sense), and had been on countless previous occasions.

'I don't believe,' he said kindly, fingering his stethoscope out of sheer instinct, 'that I ever *have* seen such a thing . . . nor do I . . . ' he added regretfully, 'happen to require immediate access to your chest. It's only your arm I'm after.'

Patently unruffled, Madison unhanded her shirt. 'Well, I've seen two,' she swanked.

'Two? You jest, surely,' Dr Mackle turned towards the intercom situated on Madison's bedside table, pressed a button and then spoke clearly into it. 'I can only imagine, Larry,' he remarked encouragingly, 'considering your well-developed interest in insect life, that you must've observed the strange phenomenon Madison here is describing many times over.' (In a brief aside to Madison, he whispered, 'Larry will have been following the flow of our conversation as a matter of course. He does voluntary work with the deaf.')

Larry did indeed work voluntarily with the deaf, and had in fact been assiduously surveying the various interactions between Dr Mackle and Madison through his thickly prohibitive half inch of glass. To have been blatantly apprehended doing so would, in general, have been enough to reduce him to a state of painful agitation, but as luck would have it, his mind was as yet still so intoxicatingly fuzzed-up by an overwhelmingly erotic crush of multifarious fungi — *toadstools, chanterelles, oysters, buttons* — that he found himself neatly side-stepping his embarrassment with all the finesse of a hungry cat playing skittles with its owner's heels.

On being interrupted by the intercom's pernicious crackle, instead of faltering or flushing he paused and then frowned as if unsure whether he was actually expected to take Dr

58

Mackle's question seriously. 'Never,' he managed eventually (on finding himself suddenly the object of Madison's stern but copiously liquid-eyelinered gaze) before adding — his voice an exquisite mixture of the compliant and the dismissive — 'but then worms aren't really my field.'

'We've met before,' Madison muttered thickly, not raising her own voice even an iota to aid the antiquated technology which facilitated their communications.

'I think we may well have,' Larry concurred, nodding in what he hoped was a businesslike manner (for the past three years, the first two weeks of July, without fail, you ludicrous raven-haired bitch, he was thinking).

'Although I don't think we've enjoyed the privilege of sharing adjoining cubicles until now . . . ' Madison revealed a fine line of white teeth but not necessarily in the form of a smile. 'Last year I used my time here very constructively,' she continued, innocently inspecting a small chip on her blood-red nail polish, 'by teaching myself Latin the first week, and then passing my O level the next.'

'Without even a *trace* of a symptom!' Dr Mackle interrupted joyfully. 'And in the face of several rather nasty common cold viruses.'

'What grade?' Larry asked.

Madison paused. 'B.'

'A creditable try, then,' Larry smirked.

'The year before that I taught myself bridge up to championship level, and this year,' Madison continued haughtily, 'I am memorising three books. I have a photographic memory. I'm attempting the world record.'

'Which world record?' Larry asked.

'The memory world record.'

'Which books?' Larry queried.

Madison picked up a thick volume from the bed beside her and read directly from the cover. 'Uh, three volumes of C.S. Forester's *Captain Hornblower* series. I find it doesn't do to be too interested in the books you select. It's not an intellectual process, by and large.'

'Although it might be a good idea,' Larry muttered, 'to memorise the title, to be going on with.'

Madison's smooth forehead strained to fight off the ugly furrows of a scowl.

'Tell me about the worm,' Dr Mackle interrupted soothingly, reaching into his compact briefcase and carefully selecting a phial.

'Two worms,' Madison averred, her forehead smoothening, 'and it's not so much the worms tying themselves into knots which fascinates me as how they go about *untying* themselves . . . '

'Single or double?' Larry mused out loud.

'Single or double what?' The threatened scowl finally overwhelmed Madison's carefully pansticked visage with all the giddy ferocity of a gang of starlings assaulting a tomato patch.

'Knot.'

Before she could enjoy the satisfaction of responding ('A *double* knot? Fuck off!') and while Dr Mackle painstakingly apportioned the contents of his phial into two syringes, Larry scuttled off into the furthest reaches of his room.

Madison craned her neck to try and keep abreast of his activities, but discovered it would be impossible to do so without standing (and she was damned if she'd give this ridiculous shrimp of a man the satisfaction).

While Madison was unquestionably biased, the truth was that Larry — in *any* light, bright or dim — could still reasonably be considered a strange-looking proposition: he was short and scraggy, with wayward dark hair, a tiny nose, thick glasses and nimble fingers. Presumably — way back — of Chinese extraction. He didn't radiate good health, but he seemed solid: with his small hips, non-existent arse, unexpectedly wide shoulders, and an imbecilic sprout of facial hair, a thin strip of beard, which progressed the short distance between the centre of his bottom lip and the middle of his chin, forming a tiny hirsute walkway between his mouth and his jaw. It was downright stupid, Madison felt; a useless tuft.

She clicked her two petite, patent-leather-booted feet together in a fit of ill-concealed disquiet. 'Did he happen to bring his ant farm with him, Dr Mackle?' she enquired softly, a slightly jealous sneer entering her voice. 'Or did he think better of it this time around?'

'Ah, the legendary ant farm!' Dr Mackle cooed. 'Larry's infallible talisman.'

'Almost infallible,' Madison corrected him.

'The ant farm is perfectly well established on the desk in the far corner of my room,' Larry's voice rang out piously as the top of his head rematerialised just within Madison's sightline.

61

'In case you didn't happen to notice.'

'I didn't, but if you'd prefer it,' Madison spoke carefully, 'I'd have absolutely no objection to you placing it on the shelf in front of the glass here. The light is probably much better there and I might even find it moderately diverting from my side.'

Larry delivered an unexpectedly maniacal cackle. 'It's fine where it is!' he bellowed. Madison's grape-coloured lips puckered and then shifted to the left in an adorably bunnyish twitch.

'Arm,' Dr Mackle instructed. Madison rolled up her sleeve, adjusted her elbow to a perfect angle and clenched her hand into a fist.

'Don't do that,' Dr Mackle implored. 'It makes me feel like I'm trapped inside a dingy television drama.'

'Sorry,' Madison sighed, loosening up a little. 'Old *habits*, eh, Doctor?' For Larry's benefit she pronounced the second word with undue emphasis.

'Habits?' Larry (a lamb to the slaughter) meditated quizzically. Madison glanced up. 'Yup. Heroin habit. 1987 to 1992. That's five years. I now have almost zero immunity. Which is why, as I think Dr Mackle will testify, my astonishing ability to ward off common infections using only the force of my will is generally perceived as something of a medical phenomenon.'

Dr Mackle said nothing, merely pushed the air bubble out of Madison's syringe with a showy squirt and a flourish. 'I have always loved needles,' she added breathily. 'They are a passion.'

'Why do you think that might be?' Dr Mackle enquired, giving the inside of Madison's pale arm a nasty little slap before jabbing in the syringe.

'Yip!' Madison exclaimed, and then continued speaking, but in an enervated and somewhat abbreviated form. 'Stood on a drawing pin as a kid . . . went right into my heel . . . received huge amounts of attention . . . as a consequence.'

Dr Mackle removed the needle.

'Is that small episode,' he wondered, 'in any way connected to your diligent cultivation of such a remarkably vampyric image?' He peeled the back off a plaster and then tenderly applied it.

'No, I am a Goth, and Goth is a belief system which goes way beyond either accident or appearance . . . '

(At this juncture, Larry could be heard next door, snorting derisively. Madison, her pinna tingling, shoved a stiff clump of black, backcombed hair away from her face, her eyelashes flickering like agitated sea anemones.)

' . . . For me, Goth encapsulates both a way of life and a general philosophy,' she continued, quite emphatically but with a twinkle. 'I dress mainly in black. I collect Victoriana. I wear too much make-up. I am cynical and dissolute. I am feminine. I am ghostly. I eschew modernity. I am dark. I have great nails.'

Madison fluttered her nails at Dr Mackle seductively (he was an old man, he was happily married, he had huge earlobes, but Jesus H. Christ how she admired him), then at Larry. Larry winced, visibly, as if the nails had torn at him in some way. Perhaps intimately.

'Oh Madison!' Dr Mackle groaned, fumbling ineffectually over the catch on his briefcase. 'You'll be delighted to know that you have reduced me, yet again, to a state of absolute sixes and sevens.'

Madison flashed her eyes. 'Well, if you ask me nicely, Doctor,' she chuckled, all deep and witchily, 'I might let you play with my abacus.'

★ ★ ★

Was it black magic? Larry was horribly aware of Madison's impeccable record. Three years, without fail, in residence at the Cold Centre and not even a wheeze or a sniffle to show for it. Before Madison he alone had held that record.

Didn't matter what they'd injected him with. Three straight years as right as rain, and then, in his fourth year — Madison's first — the sudden, ghastly appearance of a cold sore on his upper lip; Madison's second — his fifth — a relentless four-day nasal drip; last year (the dreaded Latin escapade), almost a head cold. *Almost.* Before Madison, Larry and his infallible antibodies had reigned indomitably. And since? Disarray! Humiliation! *Chaos!*

Subsequent to Dr Mackle's brief visit to each of their Spartan accommodations (and then his subsequent retreat) neither Larry nor Madison had felt easy, somehow, in being the first to turn off the intercom — which flowed and gurgled like an icy aural stream between them — or better still, in drawing their blinds.

I have nothing to hide, Larry told himself, then gnawed neurotically on an apple — the core, the seeds, even the stalk — as he struggled valiantly to believe it. Madison seemed oblivious, sitting cross-legged on her bed, swigging at a bottle of alcoholic lemonade, changing her nail polish and singing obscure lyrics by Goth troubadours, Bauhaus:

> The bats have left the belltower;
> The victims have been bled,
> Red velvet lines the black box,
> Bela Lugosi's DEAD!

She had a terrible voice. He noted — under his breath — that her singing sounded like a live bat being stapled to a wall. But it's early days yet, Larry lad, he told himself, battling to maintain his equilibrium, and succeeding, eventually, by a stealthy retreat into the furthest reaches of his quarters where he pulled out a chair, sat down, cradled his chin in his hands, and silently communed with his ants.

They were Pharaohs: the common house ant, in other words, although in Larry's view they were anything but common; originating, as a species, from ancient Egypt, they had voyaged forth from their parched homeland (approximately 200 years ago) and had set about systematically travelling the world before dutifully colonising it. In doing so they proved themselves to be not only first-class ant pioneers, but also sturdy explorers and pin-headed adventurers.

As Larry's childhood hero — ant-specialist John Crompton — once so rightly observed of the Pharaohs in his classic publication, *Ways of the Ants*, 'in that small body dwelt a great spirit'. (Among the Pharaohs' proclivities which chiefly endeared them to Larry were their astonishing sense of smell, and the helpful fact — in terms of the feasibility of an artificial environment — that the queen ants had conveniently abandoned flight as a part of their mating ritual.)

The farm was established inside a large fish tank, and had been sustained by Larry since late childhood. The ants lived in a combination of rotted wood and soil. They were night creatures, by nature, but Larry had created a sophisticated lighting system so as better to facilitate his daytime observations.

The nest was his talisman. And while Larry clearly possessed astonishingly powerful antibodies — years practising various extreme forms of yoga, an organic-based macrobiotic diet, a penchant for aloe vera juice, early contact with a father who on bird-watching expeditions to Madagascar during the late sixties contracted not only typhoid and malaria, but later TB, had all seen to that — in his heart of hearts he firmly believed that his ants alone were responsible for his Cold Centre victories.

While others perceived them as merely, at best, an idiosyncratic pastime, a hobby, Larry believed that his intense closeness to the nest, his perpetual, detailed observations (scribbled into scruffy leather-bound jotters in a crazy abbreviated code), his curious combination of distance and intimacy, all contributed to inaugurating a powerful state of euphoric displacement, a kind of blissful out-of-body reverie, in the face of which no germ, no devious bacteria or malignant invader would dare to pester him.

Then came Madison. His eyes shifted — briefly — away from his inspection (the ants were busy unearthing and dissecting a small piece of apple he had recently bestowed upon them; like Larry, they too were sustained macrobiotically, although, in truth, Pharaohs have a notoriously sweet tooth) and up on to the white-painted bricks of the bare wall in front of him. While Madison could obviously not be apprehended from his present location, she was, nevertheless, distractingly audible. She was lying on her bed — the sheer volume of sound alone indicated as much — and she was turning pages.

Shhhwit! Shhhwit! Shhhhwit!

Larry grabbed his pen and his jotter. CAPTAIN HORNBLOWER!! he wrote, in an embarrassingly adolescent script, THE FIRST NIGHT AND WELL AFTER 9 PM! AH, HOW SOON THE BATTLE COMMENCETH!!

Before Madison it had been almost the perfect holiday. Two weeks in July, each year, in isolation, and paid even (if perfunctorily) for the privilege. No human interaction (nurses didn't really count, and Dr Mackle, well, he was an absolute godhead). No pressure. Just time to relax and commune with his ants. Initially he had not even considered the greater implications of his dogged and persistent non-contamination. At first he had even gone so far as to feel pangs of guilt over his resistance.

It didn't last. The gradual Morse code of admiration from other residents — neighbours, victims, blighted snot-heads and hackers on the same corridor whose parping and snivelling were sometimes repulsively audible through the long summer evenings — had eventually swelled Larry up, much in the manner of a bloated milkmaid ant (Compton called them 'living barrels of milk' in his masterwork — they were huge and distended like amiable insect udders).

Before Madison. And it wasn't just her persistent resistance. It was her lifestyle. The drinking binges, the diet consisting mainly of Cadbury's chocolate fingers, six-packs of miniature Cheddars, marshmallows and Marmite sandwiches, her refusal to eat fruit in any form, *even juiced!* Her avowed horror of vitamins. Her non-existent immunity. The Latin B grade, attained in one week.

11.30pm, following a series of coded observations — QN#2 FATTENED. EGGS? *346 SEALED, N/NW CLIPPED. A1, B1, B4, B9, GOOD — Larry then jotted: *My light has been off for over an hour. Madison recently opened her fourth alcoholic beverage. Previously the horrible page-turning, but now, WORSE!! She is halfway through memorising the opening chapter of the first book of* The Hornblower Trilogy, The Happy Return. *Captain Horatio Hornblower has been adrift in the Pacific Ocean for* seven months. In chapter one, after fearing for the lives of his crew — and taking a strangely homo-erotic naked shave in which he considers a) the parlous state of his beer belly and b) his terror of premature baldness — the Captain is delighted to hear that land has been sighted. It transpires that they are fast approaching a volcanic island.

Later, yet another note. *P.S. 3.05am. That intolerable Goth has already memorised the first chapter! Initially some hiccups over Hankey the surgeon had died of all the complications of drink and syphilis off the Horn. My theory is that Madison had trouble remembering this line on account of its clumsy, repetitive rhythm, and because, in some sense, it amused her. This fact gives me pause.*

3.25am. P.P.S. At 3.07am I was astonished to note that Madison smoked a cigar. Only eight or nine puffs, then she carefully extinguished it and secreted the long butt inside her right boot. Perhaps this is some kind of ornate Hornblower ritual? V. interesting! Already it is clear that Madison is a creature of habits. But she likes to transgress.

NB. She truly gives meaning to the ridiculous phrase 'Night owl'. Ants are nocturnal, but this is crazy. Perhaps her plan is to wear me down through lack of sleep. I do feel quite hot. Must rest well now and surprise her by rising with the larks.

* * *

Like that other incorrigible old Goth, Margaret Thatcher, Madison could, it transpired, survive quite happily on a minimum of three hours' sleep. Larry was awoken at 6.30am by an eccentric but persistent bout of gargling from her bathroom cubicle.

When Madison emerged, her chin foamy, he was shocked to note that she had not bothered to remove her make-up the night before and now resembled a gender-non-specific Gene Simmons from *Kiss*. She was attired in a white, floor-length, ribboned and pleated antique cotton nightdress. Her unexpected combination of the sluttish and the virginal made Larry feel nauseous. He sat up in bed, wearing his blue and burgundy-striped pyjamas from Littlewoods.

Madison painstakingly budded her ears, pretending not to notice him. Larry yawned. 'I wonder,' he spoke out loud, but in a dazy voice, as if cautiously peeking out from the warm confines of his dreams, 'how many days Horatio Hornblower spent at sea exactly prior to his sighting of the volcanic island?'

'Pardon?' Madison stopped budding. These were the first words Larry had spoken in many hours.

'How many days at sea, exactly? . . . Plus . . . ' he added, 'was the dead surgeon called Hankey or was he Pankey?'

Madison sniffed her earbud — with all the precision of a perfume saleswoman on a ferry ride deciding which scent to buy for her bedridden mother — and then said coldly, 'I don't know what you are talking about.'

'Perhaps he was Twankey.'

Larry collapsed back on to his pillows, smirking.

12.30pm. QWN. # SEALED. 342 BECK-ONS! N/NE* & N/NW. GD

It worked!! HA! HA! Madison tried reciting the three chapters learned yest. PM. At each point of this morrow's enquiry ie weeks at sea, incidental name of dead ship's Dr etc. falls flat! Must re-inspect book! Is enraged! Twice gets rum mixed up with whisky in 'Grog' segment. Each time I pipe up 'Rum' to correct her. She froths.

At 11.47am. Utterly convinced I saw her rub hand on nose.

* * *

Madison threw down her book. She was just completing chapter four. It was taking much longer than she'd anticipated. Larry — temporarily tiring of the Captain's adventures — had retreated into his quiet corner to interact with his ants. She stood up. Her nose felt red. Hot.

'Are ants cannibals?' she asked, spitefully.

Larry said nothing.

'I think ants must lead very tedious lives,' she continued.

Larry's back stiffened. 'Very tedious lives!' he gasped, but only internally.

'Ants are just insect-fascists,' Madison embroidered.

Larry said nothing. Madison waited patiently for a minute or so and then collapsed on to her bed, sulkily grabbing hold of *The Happy Return* again.

'By rights I should not even do you the credit,' Larry sprang up from his corner, enunciating these words with especial venom, 'of responding to such completely asinine observations . . . '

'Ah-ha!' Madison tossed her book aside, grinning.

' . . . but your astonishing ignorance with regard to ant behaviour and mores demands it.'

He came barrelling into view. His eyes were blazing. He was yanking at his tiny beard. He seemed agitated.

'I wouldn't call it stupid,' Madison interrupted him, 'to presume that a strictly hierarchical society such as the ants' would be organised along totalitarian lines.'

Larry shook his head, his rage in danger of turning into pity at the sheer extent of Madison's ignorance. 'I could tell many tales,' he said, 'about the common ant, which would both confound and amaze you.'

'Be my guest.' Madison leaned back on her elbows and crossed her legs. From where he stood, Larry idly noticed that he could see her stocking tops. At this precise moment he felt his sinuses tingle.

'Well,' he took a deep breath, 'did you know, for example, that among particular species of ant a certain level of degeneracy is actively tolerated among the ranks?'

'Pah!'

Larry's eyes widened. 'I'm perfectly serious. Some ants may accidentally fall prey to a particularly vicious internal parasite which lodges in their stomach and gives them the feeling of constant hunger. Such an ant refuses to do any work, instead spending all of its time pestering other ants for food. These ants become troublesome and demanding, sometimes collecting together into little gangs and wreaking havoc . . . '

'Then what?'

'Nothing. Unless the colony is under intolerable strife, such behaviour is tolerated. The ants are indulged.'

'You rock my world, Larry.'

Madison did not look impressed. Larry pushed his glasses up his nose. 'Ants are also irrepressible ticklers,' he said.

'Pardon?'

'Ants are irrepressible ticklers. They tickle beetles. They tickle caterpillars. They tickle and fondle their queen. They tickle each other. They are also very fond of body massages.'

Against her better judgement, Madison found herself smiling.

'Some ants live up to ten years,' Larry continued.

'That's a lot of tickling,' Madison chuckled. As she did so, she noticed a slight loosening in her nasal membranes.

'Yup!' Larry nodded benignly.

'Explain to me,' Madison continued, in exactly the same kittenish tone as before, 'the logic of that ridiculous beard.'

Larry stopped nodding. 'What do you mean, *logic*?' he snarled. 'How can a beard be logical?'

73

'All I need to understand,' Madison reiterated, 'is the point of it.'

'And this from a woman who makes Nosferatu look like he's just back from two weeks in Ibiza.'

'Beard,' Madison meditated, 'is a slight exaggeration, really. Beards are, after all, supposed to be manly things.'

'Your nose looks a little red,' Larry observed.

'Last night at approximately 3.34 am I believe I heard you sneeze.'

'Perhaps it was your cigar smoke.'

Madison was suddenly on her mettle. 'You know as well as I do,' she hissed, 'that no air can be exchanged between these two rooms.'

Larry shrugged. 'Perhaps I should confirm that fact with the lovely Dr Mackle?'

Madison sat bolt upright. 'Do that, Larry,' she said, 'and you will regret it.'

* * *

Dr Mackle shook the thermometer. 'You'll be pleased to know,' he smiled, 'that you're still only three degrees above normal.'

Larry sighed his relief.

'He sneezed last night,' Madison chimed in furiously. Her temperature had been a whole five degrees higher.

'Did he?' Dr Mackle looked diverted.

'Yes siree.'

'Perhaps it was Madison's cigar,' Larry butted in.

At first Dr Mackle said nothing, but he scowled as he put his thermometer away. 'I

would have thought it was pretty obvious, Larry,'
he finally intoned, and gruffly, 'that there can be
absolutely no exchange of air between different
rooms. And Madison knows very well that
smoking contravenes Cold Centre policy. I must
say,' he continued, 'that I find myself very
disappointed by this kind of tittle-tattle. I placed
the two of you in adjoining rooms because I
honestly believed you might find it beneficial. We
are working together here for a common goal,
are we not?'

'Of course we are, Doctor,' Madison
wheedled.

'And it *is* beneficial,' Larry concurred. 'We
absolutely *love* being next to each other, don't
we, Madison?'

Madison's eyebrows rose a fraction. 'Larry,
what's *not* to love?' she rallied.

★   ★   ★

Timing was of the essence, and even then it was
all pretty risky. Madison had observed the basic
parameters of Larry's ant-feeding ritual (by dint
of the clever use of a compact mirror) the
previous evening. He would turn the lighting in
the tank on full, wait for the ants to return to the
nest, open a small hatch in the plastic roof and
then gently pop in the edibles.

It was at this exact point, on night two, that
Madison emitted a high-pitched scream and
collapsed with much ado on to the tiled floor just
beyond her shower cubicle. She wore — Larry
observed, having hot-footed it to the window

75

— only a small, damp, scarlet teddy and one stocking.

'Are you all right?'

Madison tried pathetically to clamber to her feet. She could not.

'Shall I ring for a nurse?'

'Yes,' Madison gurgled and then, just as he was about to do so, 'no! I'll be fine. Just stay with me a while.'

'Are you sure?' Larry watched, in some agitation, as Madison crawled laboriously on to her bed and curled into the foetal position.

'Oh Larry!' she whimpered. 'Tell me something to ease my mind. Tell me about the ants again.'

'Pardon?'

'Tell me about the tickling.'

Larry frowned suspiciously. 'There isn't really all that much more to say on the matter.'

'You know,' Madison scratched lethargically at her upper thigh (Larry found the resultant weals mesmerising), 'we both have a passion for insect life. I once kept a pet tarantula called Dixon.'

'Really?'

'In the seventies. I was still a child, obviously.'

'What did you feed him?'

'Crickets, mostly.'

'Ah.'

Madison nuzzled her own shoulder. Larry noticed idly that his nose felt warm and that his hand was on the glass.

★   ★   ★

76

They spent the night reading Book Two: *A Ship of the Line* and discussing the various ramifications of Hornblower's sexism.

'If you ask me,' Madison said, clearing her throat a little, then clearing it again, 'his attitudes are still just as prevalent today in large segments of the armed forces.'

'I think you're being harsh,' Larry countered, mopping his forehead with his shirt sleeve. 'Anyway, in book one, chapter nine, when he meets Lady Barbara Wellesley for the first time, his attitude indicates fear rather than loathing.'

Madison picked up the book and reappraised the segment, smiling to herself all the while. Her compact indicated that the ants had discovered their exit and were making the most of it. Larry, watching her smile, couldn't help indulging himself just a little.

* * *

'I am sorry,' Dr Mackle spoke, his tone worryingly unapologetic, 'but under the circumstances, I'm finding it rather difficult to believe that there has been no *actual physical contact* between the two of you. The symptoms you're both exhibiting indicate some kind of mutual contamination, but not, I'm afraid, to the particular virus with which I so recently injected you.'

'I haven't touched him!' Madison wailed. 'After three good years! And with that beard! How could you think it?'

77

Larry lay in his bed feeling deathly. 'Will you deny it, Larry?' Mackle asked, carefully inspecting his copious hand-prints on the glass.

'Neither of us has left the confines of our chambers,' he croaked. 'Honestly.'

'Science rarely lies,' Dr Mackle's ears glowed enragedly, 'and if I don't feel like I can trust the two of you, then I have no alternative but to ask you both to pack up and leave.'

'While we might not in fact be contaminated with the right kind of bacteria,' Madison spoke slowly, 'I'm afraid there *is* actually some free access between these two areas . . . ' Her eyes widened beguilingly.

'Impossible!'

'It's just . . . ' Madison pointed ' . . . if there isn't, how on earth did Larry's ants get into my marshmallows?'

A thin but resolute line of Pharaohs was marching in a heroic diagonal across Madison's floor tiles.

Dr Mackle did a double take. Madison sniffed mournfully and drew up her knees. Larry sat bolt upright in bed, gasped and then unleashed an almighty *Ahhh-chooh!*

⋆ ⋆ ⋆

'Now what, Doctor?'

Nurse Bancroft peered over his shoulder as he tweaked at his venetians. Outside he could see Madison and Larry fighting over a mini-cab, their cheeks flaming, their noses dripping. He seemed to find it a gratifying sight.

78

'Who would believe,' he chuckled, 'that I injected them both with placebos?'

'Do they know?'

'What the heck do you take me for!' Dr Mackle guffawed. 'An imbecile?'

'If you don't mind my saying,' the nurse observed frankly, 'your methods are somewhat unorthodox. And the ants,' she continued, 'are presently occupying the entire left wing.'

'There's nothing like the bitter taste of disgrace,' Dr Mackle muttered, 'to bring folk together and render even the most obstinate types obliging.'

'Meaning?'

'Any child these two produce will be medically fascinating.'

The nurse shook her head. Dr Mackle waved his hand regally. 'Get on to Environmental Health,' he instructed her 'Pharaoh ants are apparently indomitable. We're moving up, Nurse Bancroft. Cold Cures are yesterday's news. I'm getting into genetics, *dammit*! That's where the smart money is.'

★ ★ ★

'Is it legal,' Madison pondered, 'to turn down a fare on the grounds of possible contamination?'

'If you hadn't tried to steal it from me in the first place,' Larry gurgled enragedly, 'I don't imagine he'd have had time to notice.'

'My suitcase is so heavy!' Madison groaned, picking it up and struggling to carry it. 'And my nose is chapping.'

79

'Where on earth are you going?'

'I'm walking to the main road. We won't see another cab here for ages.'

Larry peered after her. 'Perhaps we could share?' he yelled. 'Where do you live exactly?'

'Barnes.'

'Barnes? That's the other side of London. Hold on a minute!'

Larry ran after her. When he caught up, Madison paused and eyed him suspiciously. 'Now what?'

'Give me your case,' he panted. 'You may well have noticed I'm travelling rather light now that my ants are free-wheeling it.'

Madison handed him her case. They walked for a while.

'Do you really work voluntarily with the deaf?' she asked.

'I do.' He paused. 'Are Goths honestly all interested in Victoriana?' Madison nodded.

'They are.'

'It's strange,' Larry pondered, 'hearing your voice without amplification. It's nice. You have a slight lisp.'

'It's an affectation actually,' Madison confessed. 'I'm sorry about the ants,' she added. 'Do you think Dr Mackle will ever forgive us?'

'Of course. Given enough space and time and the services of a high-class exterminator.'

'Right.'

'So tell me about the worm,' he said eventually, by way of accepting her apology.

'The worm?' Madison's eyes turned on him.

'Tell me about how they untie themselves.'

80

'Well, it's an incredible thing,' she sniffed, 'but they do it — I don't know if you can fully imagine without *physically* seeing it — but they actually do it by remaining still but then moving just their tail-end forward. It's a complex process . . . hold on a second . . . '

Madison stopped walking and then illustrated the curious writhing motion with her two hands as a juggernaut roared past. In the blast of noise and dirt and fumes that enveloped them both as he watched her, Larry couldn't help thinking that Madison suddenly and effortlessly resembled the ebony-haired Queen of all Egypt, Cleopatra: strong and pale and proud and beautiful. Playing silly-buggers with the asp.

∾

*Love looks not with the eye, but with the
  mind,
And therefore is wing'd Cupid painted
  blind.*

Shakespeare,
A Midsummer Night's Dream

Wendy Cope

THIRTEEN WAYS OF CURING
A HEADACHE

1. Let me massage your head.
2. Let me massage your neck and shoulders.
3. Let me massage your ovaries.
4. What you need is reflexology.
5. Rub your palms together for half a minute. Then, when they are full of energy, place them over your eyes.
6. Describe the shape of your headache. Exaggerate it. Then change the shape in your mind, until the headache is better.
7. Just sit here and relax while I focus your energy points.
8. Just lie here while I work on your aura.
9. Drink this herbal tea. There is a lot of fire in you.
10. Drink *this* herbal tea. There is a lot of confused air in you.
11. Rub this menthol block over your forehead.
12. Stand on your head for at least three minutes.
13. Take two paracetamol.

CATHEDRAL LIMERICK

The choir sings, 'Grant us thy salvay-see-oan'
And I am assailed by temptay-see-oan —
Seized by the idea
For this limerick, I fear.
Lord, grant me improved concentray-see-oan.

Tim Parks

LEBENSRAUM

They announced their arrival, bridges long burnt, from Newport Pagnell Service Station. 'Of course you're welcome,' Kate knew to say. An hour later they turned into the Close just as freezing twilight was stiffening into fog. The evening was suddenly a huge milky whiteness, though fouled here and there by the urine yellow of streetlamps.

'What a furry hat, Mum!' Kate greeted Mrs Taylor as the woman had to use her shoulder to force open the passenger door.

'Old age. Your hat gets furrier and your pussy goes bald.' Hook-nosed, imperious, yet oddly raffish in her jumble-sale-salvaged coat and hat, Vi Taylor laughed with a sort of raucous cynicism. Climbing out of the opposite door, visibly exhausted by his long drive, a small squat man sent his daughter a look of pained resignation over the damp roof of the Fiesta. The women were embracing. Then the children came running through the surreal light of the fog. 'Have you got anything for me, Granny, Grandad? Come and see my new garage. Come on, come with me. No, me!' Their small fingers clutched and tugged at coats. A fat red smile on his face, Grandad Taylor had already opened the back of the car and was pulling out packages.

'Are you mad, Rupert? For heaven's sake, they'll freeze to death if they start fiddling with their presents out here. Put them in my bag.' The group walked up the path to the small block where the Langleys had their flat. Halfway up the stairs Mark Langley appeared. 'Got a lot of work to do, I'm afraid,' were his first words, not out of character. Nevertheless he seemed pleased to see his in-laws and embraced them both warmly, though winking at his wife over the old woman's shoulder. 'To what do we owe the pleasure?' he enquired.

'The ants in his bloody pants,' Vi Taylor said with grim mirth. 'If he doesn't do a thousand miles a week he gets fretful. Because at home of course there are only a million and one things need doing he'll never lift a finger to sort out.'

'Single-handedly supporting the whole Middle Eastern economy,' Kate suggested, but now grandmother had been kidnapped by children determined to be spoilt.

Walking back to the car to help with the luggage, Mark facetiously suggested that Rupert Taylor could write to Ford and offer his vehicle with its almost 200,000 miles on the clock for some advertisement on the reliability of their products.

Stout Rupert said nothing. Apparently impervious to the freezing fog wreathed about the salmon pink of his bald scalp he leaned on the car and found cigarettes and matches in his jacket. It seemed he was in no hurry to get back to the warm company of the flat. Then he said, 'I was thinking. I'm seventy-one next month, I could buy a new Escort on the never-never, minimum down payment, and I'll be dead before I've repaid the half of it. They can come and repossess the thing for all I care. Vi won't want it.'

In the back Mark found the usual orange box full of home-made jams. There was also a narrow roll of old carpet, a child's bicycle covered in rust, and a small bathroom cabinet perhaps produced in the late 1950s. Together with the Taylors' huge old tin suitcase.

'I couldn't stop her,' the old man remarked. 'As far as I'm concerned you're perfectly welcome to bung everything in the bin the moment we're gone.'

Mark began to carry things back to the flat, leaving his father-in-law to smoke in peace. But was then overtaken on the path by a now urgently scurrying Mr Taylor. The old man tossed his cigarette into the white gloom of a winter garden. 'You want to bet,' he panted, 'you just want to bet she'll be giving the kids their presents while I'm not there.' He staggered on up the stairs, presumably putting considerable strain on his heart.

★ ★ ★

The following morning, Saturday, towards seven, or perhaps it was nearer six-thirty, Kate and Mark, who had a child wheezing and sniffling between them, heard Grandfather Taylor cross the living room, where he and Mrs Taylor were sleeping on the sofa bed, and pad to the phone in the hall.

'Larry? Good. Sorry, I just wanted to be sure of catching you before you went out.'

Kate had to quickly stuff two knuckles in her mouth to stop herself from giggling. On a Saturday morning her brother was unlikely to be awake if he could help it before nine and gone.

'Yes, we're at Kate and Mark's. They'd like you to come over for lunch.'

'Oh, thanks for the info,' Mark muttered.

'No, today. We've got to get down to Salisbury tomorrow. It doesn't matter why. Well, bring Sabine with you if she's there.'

'Oh, not fucking Sabine,' Kate muttered, apparently in no danger of laughing now.

There was a fairly long silence, after which Mr Taylor said, 'Of course I understand. Just that I would have imagined that when it was a question of your father and mother you might have seen your way to changing your arrangements a bit.'

'Hang on in there, Larry boy,' Mark encouraged in the dark of their bedroom.

'Yes, I know, but we only decided to come at the last minute. Well, because that's how your mother is. It's hopeless asking her to plan anything.'

'He'll give in,' Kate announced gloomily. 'He's worried about his inheritance. And I'll have to spend the whole morning shopping and cooking.'

'Anyway,' Rupert Taylor was saying, 'Sabine may as well get used to the family if she's going to become a part of it.'

87

This brought low groans from the married couple. So much so that their child, alarmed, began to cry and had to be hushed. Otherwise they would have lost what the old man was saying.

'And then it's little Sylvia's birthday. Yes, Kate was saying you'd have forgotten. Just tell them you can't. It's not work after all, is it? I could understand if it was work. Speaking of which, I've got to talk to you about a little problem I've got. I was wondering if maybe you could arrange for a few tests. I've been going to the toilet a lot at night.'

Mark and Kate had hardly got over the surprise of hearing it was their daughter's birthday, before they were offered this juicy tit-bit. Again the whining child was hushed.

'You think so? It's not fatal is it?'

'Every time he had a stomach ache he was convinced he was going to die,' Kate whispered.

'You see! Tell Sabine she probably won't have to put up with us for much longer, so she may as well get the benefit of our wisdom now.'

'Oh Christ,' Mark said.

'See you around one then. Don't forget to bring a couple of bottles of wine.'

There was the sound of an old man scratching at flesh under pyjamas, then padding back to the sitting room.

'Dad?'

He retreated a couple of paces to appear at their door, paunchie in pale pyjamas. 'I got Larry to come for lunch,' he announced brightly. 'He's bringing Sabine.'

'But you know it's not Sylvia's birthday for another couple of weeks.'

'I don't see why that should stop us having a little party today.' The fat old man was clearly cheerful and proud of having managed to twist his son's arm. He moved away whistling softly.

However, a moment later there came the sound of raised voices from the living room.

'Mother doesn't want to see our German friend,' Kate commented.

'Who does?'

Mrs Taylor was shouting: 'The girl is bad for him. He shouldn't be encouraged to think we think he's doing the right thing!'

'Nobody,' her husband was impassive, 'ever thought you thought they were doing the right thing. And least of all did they care.' At eight o'clock he went out into a bleak morning, ostensibly to pick up a newspaper, though Vi Taylor said it would be pointless expecting him back before ten at the earliest.

The other adults were now eating breakfast.

'But where does he actually go?' Mark enquired of his mother-in-law. For this was the kind of entertainment that compensated for the hassle of their visits.

'God knows.' The old woman had a habit of laughing over things she obviously didn't find at all funny. 'He says he needs his *lebensraum*. You know how he likes to use words like that, thinking I won't know what they mean. I said, what I want to know is when *I'm* ever going to have any, thank you very much.'

'Take some,' Kate suggested.

'I have. I've stopped cooking for him.'

'Really?'

'We go and eat in a transport place every day.'

'You're joking.'

'No. I said, if, now that you've finally retired, you're still too lazy to mend the roof that's been . . .'

But the children arrived and this conversation had to be interrupted while slippers were found and milk warmed.

'I better get weaving then,' Mark said, and stood up. He was referring to an article he had told his wife had to be ready for four o'clock that afternoon. He would have to take it in personally. And if there was to be a big family lunch . . .

'Oh go. Do please go.' Kate raised her voice in sudden exasperation, though without turning to look at him. 'Off to your room, go on. Work. Kiddies, say bye-bye to Daddy now. He's going to lock himself up in his room and work on a Saturday morning.'

His two small children, four and two, turned to look at him from wide, surprised eyes.

'Kate, look, I can't quite see what I've done to deserve this. Somebody has to produce the . . .'

'While I look after two kids and shop and cook for eight.'

'But we've been over this before. Anyway, you've got your mum. Come on, let's not argue in front of . . .'

'Just don't be surprised,' Kate was almost shouting, 'don't be bloody surprised if I start taking myself a bit of *lebensraum* in future. Okay?'

'And what's that supposed to mean?'

Mrs Taylor, however, was making all kinds of mute gestures for Mark not to worry but go off and work. 'You should be lucky,' she interrupted to tell her daughter, 'that you've got a husband who wants to work at all. I wish Rupert would. Maybe we wouldn't still be driving that filthy old car and visiting jumble sales.'

'You love jumble sales,' Kate snapped.

Mark stood uncertainly for a moment, but then, unable to get any further change from his wife, retreated down the passage where the Taylors' threadbare carpet had now been laid. In his tiny study, sitting at his desk, he pressed his thumbs into his eyes. He listened through the thin modern walls to his wife telling Philip not to do his Nazi salute when Auntie Sabine came. He heard his mother-in-law objecting strongly to his wife's use of the word 'auntie', heard his wife reply that she couldn't see why her mother expected her son to marry any more intelligently than either she or her daughter had; heard the mother saying that at least she had been a good wife to Rupert, kept house and brought up children for him, whereas sulky Sabine only thought about her own career; heard his son Philip announcing he needed a poo, his wife telling her mother Sabine was right, his daughter Sylvia saying she wanted a glass of chocolate milk, his mother-in-law saying that hundreds of young English girls would be happy to marry a doctor and wait on him hand and foot, his wife urging his son to hurry up and get to the loo before he dirtied his pants, and telling her mother what stupidly old-fashioned ideas she had, nobody wanted to wait hand and foot on anyone these days, least of all on their husbands. Then while mother and son were in the loo, grandmother began to teach granddaughter 'Little Tommy Tucker'. Her rich old voice moved up and down in warbly nursery-rhyme cadences until she finished: 'How shall he cut it without a knife, how shall he marry without a wife.'

Odd rhyme, Mark thought, and carefully inserted fresh earplugs. Immediately the room, although still oppressively small and with only a lavatory-size square of window, was nevertheless freed of the oppression of sound, might even, since the window was frosted and let in only a dim glow, have been floating in some silent outer space. He looked at his watch: seven hours till paradise.

Towards mid-morning this struggling freelance journalist turned off the processor, removed earplugs and listened attentively. Given that his wife and mother-in-law, not to mention the dear children, were notoriously incapable of making anything less than an unholy racket about 100 per cent of the time, it was reasonable to suppose the coast was clear. He walked confidently down the passage, planning to treat himself to a phone call, but then had the good sense to glance in the kitchen first, where unfortunately he found Mr Taylor poring over copies of the *Sun*, the *Independent*, *The Economist*.

'Just grabbing a lightning coffee,' he explained.

The old man nodded. 'Have you seen about this character wants it to be illegal for you to hit your children?' Short fat legs wide apart, elbows propped on the paper on the table, double chin in hands, Mr Taylor communicated an impression of quiet, adult enjoyment.

'Must live in a bigger bloody house than we do.'

'Claims it teaches them to be violent.'

'I can think of no more useful education.'

The two men laughed together very cosily and with what both recognised these days as an antique male solidarity. Indeed Mark was aware that this might be one reason why his father-in-law liked to visit. The kettle whined for attention.

'Carpet in the passage blocks the living room door,' the younger man remarked.

'Talk to Vi about it.'

'Of course it's nice of her to bring things. I mean, the thought.'

The old man laughed: 'Lack of it rather.'

Hazarding, with what was on his mind, rather more than he had in the past, Mark said: 'You know, given that you and Vi are always, well, often arguing, I was wondering, didn't it ever occur to you that maybe it might have been wiser, er, I don't know, to separate or even divorce years ago.'

Mr Taylor was reading an editorial in the *Independent* and at the same time licking his fingers clean of something he had presumably just finished eating. 'Divorce?' he said mildly, without looking up. 'I should have bloody well killed her.'

★ ★ ★

Yet all was sweetness and light a couple of hours later when Mark again emerged from his room, having picked up, in his muffled, ear-plugged world, the booming voice of brother-in-law Larry. And sure enough the big boy, for it was hard to think of him as a man and even less as a doctor, stood in the passage by the front door, beaming greetings and holding high a cake box to keep it above the greedy assaults of the children. Handsome, tall, with full mouth and laughing eyes, Larry radiated vitality and ingenuous good will, kissing and calling to everybody. Beside him, small and rather plain, glum Sabine unbuckled her raincoat.

Mark called hello, then went through to the kitchen where Kate was preparing an elaborate lunch. 'Oh, who are you?' she demanded of her husband who stood dazed by the winter sunlight that found its way into this part of the flat. 'Pulitzer Prize-winning article on refuse collection in Haringey?'

'And Hornsey,' he corrected. 'Can I help?'

'I imagine,' Kate said, 'that when they've cleaned the last corpse away from Armageddon, you'll arrive offering your valuable assistance.'

'I imagine,' Mark mimicked, 'that having claimed you hate cooking, you are now slaving to produce the unnecessarily elaborate cordon bleu fare, *n'est ce pas?*'

'I don't see why I should be taken for granted just because I take pride in what I do.'

He was opening his mouth to snap back the usual reasoned male objections to unreasoned female resentment (why was his wife like this?) when Grandmother Taylor, in high spirits with having had the children all morning, pushed into the room and told him not to think badly of her daughter. She had always been like that. 'Haven't you, Kate?' It was just her character. She meant no harm and loved him very much really, otherwise she would never have stuck with him so long. 'No need to argue,' she said. And wasn't it good the children could play in the passage now there was a carpet. She went to the cupboard to pull out some of the home-made jams for her best boy Lawrence.

Finding a smile, Mark took steaming dishes from his wife and began trying to get the children to the table. In the sitting room Larry could be heard telling his father that his problem might be anything from a banal urinary infection to cancer of the prostate and imminent death. Rupert Taylor seemed gratified by both possibilities.

'But the most normal diagnostic profile would be a slight hardening of prostate tissue accompanied, if not exacerbated, by weakening of the bladder and sensitivity of the lower urethral tract.'

The speaker, in a monotone, was Sabine. 'Chronic and incurable,' she added in an English as impeccable as it was forced and painful.

95

'Perhaps mitigable to a certain extent by mild tranquillisers.'

'Private consultation. Cost you thirty quid.' Larry said, stooping to squeeze the girl affectionately and help her off with her coat. 'She'll examine you later if you like. Did we bring any gloves, darling?'

Vi Taylor in the kitchen pulled a face that meant to say, 'Listen to her! Is that any talk for a woman?' The children laughed and spluttered food. And now their grandmother was saying: 'Yes, Mark, you know, just the way Rupert and I have always loved each other despite the fact that he's a presumptuous fool. Haven't we, Rupert?' As the mild, balding man came into the kitchen, she went over and embraced him warmly. Although the look on Mr Taylor's face was one of weary condescension, he nevertheless returned the hug with obvious pleasure at this animal contact and promising lunchtime atmosphere of détente. The two swayed a moment together as if they might fall over. Sabine of serious face took the opportunity to stand on tiptoe and whisper something in her boyfriend's ear. He told her reassuringly not to worry.

'Aren't you going to kiss Grandad who bought you your new transformer?' Mr Taylor broke off one embrace and was sentimentally looking for another. What was family for after all?

Little Philip said: 'But Granny gave it me.'

There was general laughter. From where he was spooning food into daughter Sylvia, Mark shouted to his brother-in-law to open the

Frascati in the fridge and very soon six adults and two children seemed to be rather enjoying themselves. The little folks were fed and chased off to their room with threats and promises and the small kitchen table was extended, covered with a red table cloth, and extravagantly laid with porcelain white plates and side plates, paper serviettes, water tumblers and crystal wine glasses. The guests, though none had been invited by the hosts and two had come only in response to third-degree coercion, sat down in excellent spirits, while Mark served what the inexplicably aggrieved Kate was so expertly preparing.

An opening course of vol-au-vents was thus suitably ooh-ed and ah-ed over. Fat Mr Taylor was particularly appreciative of his daughter's cooking. It was one reason why he liked to come, he said. Sabine likewise ate with a gusto one wouldn't have expected from her diffident air and teutonically clipped speech. Only Mrs Taylor seemed less than engrossed in her food, while Kate didn't eat at all but went on working at the oven.

'Not going to sit down with us?' Larry shouted to her.

She shook her head. 'I'd be fat in a second if I touched that stuff. I just make it and watch you lot eat it.'

The trim young woman made no attempt to hide bitterness and even a certain note of criticism here, as if dissociating herself from the delicious food she had made and those carefree enough to be eating it.

'Oh come on. When all the family are together. Just this once.'

Mark made a face to his brother-in-law which meant, 'Don't bother, it's not worth it, she's always like this.'

But the good-hearted Larry insisted, 'It just feels wrong, us eating while you're working.'

'Oh, if it makes you feel guilty I'm sure you must have your reasons for being so. Anyway, I thought guilt was supposed to spice things up.' Mark concentrated very seriously on his food. Then his wife added, 'I take after Father, that's my lot. Hereditary. I'd be a barrel if I ate that stuff.'

From another room came the sound of the older child bossing the younger. The little girl was playing something, 'the wrong way'.

'Whereas your father here has never missed a single meal in his life, nor ever forgotten to ask for seconds.' Mrs Taylor voiced her own mixture of contempt and merriness. 'Not a place we go but he doesn't tell whoever it is they're the best cook in the world and yes, he'll treat himself to a little bit more just this once.'

'Actually, it's called politeness,' her husband remarked.

'And you know why he gets up in the middle of the night? You know why? Not to go to the loo at all. He thinks it's to go to the loo, he likes to think he's ill so he can curry some sympathy, but really he gets up to go and look in the fridge. A glass of milk at one o'clock, a ham sandwich at two o'clock, a boiled egg at four o'clock.' She mimicked the gesture of someone peering into a fridge, frowning and pulling things out to eat. 'A yoghurt at five o'clock. A piece of apple pie at six o'clock. By the time I arrive in the morning there's nothing left. So you know what the first thing I say to him in the morning is? I say, 'Rupert dear, Rupert my darling, have you said good morning to the fridge yet, Rupert? Have you asked Fridgie if he's feeling well today?' Because every time I turn round he has his big nose in there, doesn't he?'

A plump little darling in short pigtails appeared at the kitchen door weeping. 'Philip won't let me play with his train,' she wailed. 'He pushed me.' An older but shriller voice shrieked, 'There's not enough room for both of us.' A door could be heard slamming.

Swallowing vol-au-vent, Mark told her kindly: 'Well you go back and tell him he's a very naughty boy and if he doesn't open the door and let you play I'll give him the worst spanking he's ever had.'

Apparently reassured, the girl toddled off. The group sat in silence a moment to hear the baby voice in another room comically relaying her father's threat. Sabine who had discussed this at length with Mark on previous occasions said abruptly that in her experience if someone actually went and talked to the children there would be no need to keep threatening violence. Mark seemed pleased she had brought up the issue: 'At least I didn't say I'd beat the living daylights out of him,' he smiled.

My Taylor explained: 'The fact is that eating is really the only pleasure that remains to me.

Presumably Kate has other sources of satisfaction, otherwise she'd be guzzling here with the rest of us.'

'The only pleasure!' his wife protested. 'Oh that's good! And the other?'

'Oh come on, Mum,' Larry was laughing with a full mouth. 'Give us a break.'

'Just three hundred and sixty-five times a year,' she insisted. 'No, honestly, I'm not joking. There's nothing wrong with his prostate, I'm telling you. He nudges my leg and it's . . . '

A pained look crossed fat Mr Taylor's face: 'Do we have to? Isn't there some rugby on telly this afternoon?'

'I can't think of any other satisfactions at all,' Kate said. 'Mark and I gave up sex when Sylvia arrived.' She walked to the table for a moment to pour out the last of the first bottle of wine and, diet or no, drank it at a gulp.

'Don't exaggerate,' Mark said defensively.

'Oh don't worry,' Kate said. 'Nobody's questioning your libido. I blame it all on my frigidity.' But then she bent and kissed him with mock passion on an ear.

In her tone of somebody used to killing conversations quite dead, Sabine announced: 'Surveys showing mean frequencies of intercourse are known to give misleadingly inflated results. People tend to . . . '

'Mean?' Mrs Taylor interrupted. 'There's nothing mean about his frequencies!' She laughed immoderately and was obviously drunk on a single glass of wine.

Again there came the sound of squabbling

100

from the other room.

'I'd better go and spank the both of them,' Mark said and pushed back his chair, smiling deliberately at Sabine.

'It's always fun when you actually get here,' Larry confided to his girlfriend. Sitting tall and square beside his fat and shrunken father, the athletic young doctor stretched an arm around him: 'Listen Dad, when I'm on casualty, you know how many old blokes I get coming in who've had heart attacks trying to get it on? You wouldn't believe it. And almost all of them overweight. So if you want to stay on the job you'll have to cut down on your eating. They're mutually exclusive pleasures.'

'Oh, if you believe the half of what your mother says, you're more of a fool than I took you for.'

Poor Sabine said: 'He is not a fool. He got one of the best degrees they've ever given at the London School.'

Kate explained wrily: 'Freedom of calumny is one of the tenets of the Taylor household. You'll have to get used to it.'

'In the absence of *lebensraum*,' Mrs Taylor giggled with thoughtless wisdom, draining a second glass of wine.

'I beg your pardon?' enquired Larry.

But Sabine felt this could be nothing less than a below-the-belt jab at her origins. 'I can't see,' she said with sudden acrimony, 'what concepts like that have got to do with it at all. I don't . . . '

'It means,' Kate placated, 'that not being able to get away from one another, they take delight in making hell for each other.'

The German girl glared. 'It seems to me *lebensraum* is a culturally specific term and I think it would be better if it wasn't mentioned.'

Larry hadn't understood, as indeed he understood little that wasn't strictly to do with urogenital functions. 'The truth is though,' he said, 'that Mum and Dad really love each other, don't you Mum? The arguing's all a show to keep themselves on their toes. Right?'

'I love him very much,' Mrs Taylor said with sudden alcohol-aided solemnity.

'Pass,' Mr Taylor said wearily. 'And can somebody please get another bottle out.'

'For example, I was perfectly happy to give up my career to wash and cook for Rupert. When we first moved into the place in Drummond Road and there wasn't enough . . . '

There was a danger that the party would now have to hear a long account of the older woman's sacrifices, which were indeed many. But Sabine abruptly interrupted to offer the kind of hard information she was never short of: 'Statistically, married people live longer than single people. So there must be some advantages.'

'Determination to outlive the other and have a few years' peace,' Rupert Taylor had no difficulty explaining.

Returning from the children's room, Mark stopped off briefly in the bedroom, opened a drawer and slipped something into his wallet. Arriving in the kitchen just as Kate was serving a dish of veal escalopes with *champignons* sautéed in red wine, he found the room steamily cosy

102

and a fresh glass of wine by his place. Suddenly elated by these luxuries and the spirited company, not to mention what was to come later that afternoon, he decided to go to his father-in-law's aid at once, as if the man had somehow been stuck there with his back to the wall all the time his son-in-law was out of the room. Rubbing his hands over his food, he said brightly, 'It seems to me perfectly reasonable and healthy that Dad should want a little action every day. To make up for all those lost years in Saudi. I'd take it as a compliment if I were you, Mother.'

Mrs Taylor snorted: 'If it wasn't me it'd be someone else. And when he was away in Saudi, no doubt it was someone else. Or some others rather.'

Mr Taylor wanted to know, 'Can't we have a quiet lunch for once?' though he didn't appear to be suffering greatly.

'He just never wants the truth to come out,' Mrs Taylor told Sabine, briefly forgetting that the girl was an enemy. 'Not that there's much danger of him recognising it if it did, he's got such a high opinion of himself.'

Rupert Taylor may indeed have wanted a quiet lunch, but was nevertheless incapable of remaining passive in the face of such naked aggression. He broke off chewing his veal to remark acidly: 'The truth about my going to Saudi, for those who have eyes to see it, is that finding myself condemned to spend my life with an argumentative ignorant woman who just would not understand where my or her own responsibilities lay, I chose, what? To leave her in the lurch as any normal man would? — no, simply to work overseas for a few years so as to avoid insanity or suicide or worse, sending 90 per cent and I repeat nine-zero per cent of my salary back to her. Any objections?'

Larry clapped as if applauding two combatants. 'Atta-boy,' he remarked. But Sabine, who was new to all this, seemed appalled. She said: 'If you'd kept your job, Mrs Taylor, you wouldn't have needed the money and you could have split up if you wanted to.'

'He wouldn't let me keep my job,' Mrs Taylor muttered grimly. 'You obviously don't know Mr All Important I Can Manage Everything, My Wife's Not Going To Work, Leave It All To Me.'

'Rubbish,' Rupert Taylor helped himself to more wine. 'She couldn't wait to stop work and have kids. And quite right too.'

'You did say, Mum,' Kate remarked, eating a spartan piece of meat with no sauce and only a few leaves of plain salad, 'that you willingly gave up your job to be a good wife.'

Mrs Vi Taylor suddenly changed tone, became jolly, almost coquettish. 'Well, I had my illusions then, didn't I, Rupert dear. I was in love. I thought he was right. I respected him.'

Pressing her point, and with a wink at her father, Kate said: 'So given that you admit yourself that it was an illusion, why complain about the fact that Sabine wants to work?'

'I never complained about Sabine,' Mrs Taylor lied with enviably fluency. 'I only said life might be difficult if they were both working.'

'When has life not been difficult?' Mr Taylor enquired rhetorically, sensing a consensus in his favour.

It was a characteristic of these conversations, however, that the youngsters would mercilessly keep the ball in motion at the expense of their elders, who anyway appeared to take pleasure in a gladiatorial performance that had begun almost forty years before. So after a moment's pause now, Mark said archly: 'You are just concerned for their welfare, right, Mother?'

Mrs Taylor pouted. Although her body still seemed solid and trim, her face had a sort of savage, haggard dignity about it which only age could confer, hook-nosed and bluishly gaunt to her husband's rosy mellow chubbiness: 'No,' she said, 'the point is, it's *right* for a woman to have illusions when she marries. I didn't know I'd married a fraud. In Larry's case it's different, and I just think with all respect to Sabine that as a doctor he would be better off married to somebody who would stay at home and cook for him.'

Sabine rather surprisingly said: 'So do I.' With what she had been drinking her accent was creeping out, so that 'so' became a rather ominous 'zo'. 'Naturally it would be better for him. But I am not like that. I want to work and I don't want children.'

Mr Taylor was signalling to his daughter to bring him another helping of veal. 'You insist on holding contradictory positions,' Kate needled her mother, standing up. 'You can't say your life has been a disaster and then expect everybody else to repeat it.'

Mark promptly came to the old woman's aid. 'It's just that your mother has a sense of the ideal, a vision of how things might be in the best of best possible worlds. That's why you never wanted to split up even when things were bad, right Mum?'

Mrs Taylor nodded vigorously. 'You're the only one who ever understands me,' she said to her pleasantly smirking son-in-law. 'A sense of the ideal is what it is.'

'And no sense of reality.' Mr Taylor's policy, having said his piece, now seemed to be to keep out of the spotlight and just toss in a grenade from time to time.

'You what?' Mrs Taylor shrilled, perhaps more theatrically than from real shock. 'Me got no sense of reality? Who washed and cooked and slaved for forty years? While somebody else we know hasn't even got the time and energy to fix a leaking roof, has to jump into the car and go gallivanting off to see friends and relatives every time he can't think of a better excuse.'

Larry said ingenuously, 'Well, I'd much rather have a wife with a career. So please don't anyone worry about us,' and he turned to Sabine and kissed the graceless young woman on the lips. 'I don't want my wife at home.'

'More fool you,' Mr Taylor came out at his driest.

'You see!' his wife shouted.

'In marriages where both partners work, the divorce rate is much higher.' Kate cheerfully took a leaf out of the German girl's book. 'I saw it on telly.'

'So be it,' Sabine said. 'We divorce then. Why is everybody so scared of that?'

'Just do it before you have any children,' Kate said sincerely.

'But I told you: I don't want any children. No problem.'

'When I was thirteen' — Kate found it hard to keep a note of condescension out of her voice when talking to her brother's girlfriend — 'I wanted to be a film star. When I was twenty-four I was quite a good radio producer. Now I'm a housewife.'

Sabine didn't seem to appreciate the point of this.

'She'd always sworn she'd keep working,' Mark explained to Larry, 'otherwise I'd have found a job that took me out of the house.'

At which somebody observed that the children had been screaming loudly for some minutes now, so once again Mark went off to sort them out. Returning, he stopped in the bathroom and examined himself in the mirror. Was his skin smooth enough, or did he need another shave?

When he returned Mr and Mrs Taylor were arguing, presumably after careful prompting from Kate and Larry, about some event of twenty and more years ago when Mr Taylor had walked out of the house one Saturday, apparently to get cigarettes, and had not come back until two days later. Mr Taylor was vigorously denying this scenario. It merely indicated how little his wife had ever listened to what he said. Because in fact he had been going to a conference and had told her so. But then as an afterthought he remarked that if he had ever thus walked out in desperation, which of course he hadn't, then rather than just getting hysterical about it, his wife might have done worse than to ask herself why a man to all intents and purposes so sensible and responsible should have done such a thing.

Kate innocently enquired whether this had occurred before or after the introduction of decimal currency.

In response to a question from Larry, Sabine claimed that her parents never argued, though her mother had a fetish about bathrooms; she would only ever use her own bathroom in her own house, which meant that she refused to travel, so that once a year her father, who loved travelling, went on holiday on his own.

'Excellent arrangement,' Mr Taylor thought.

Mrs Taylor weighed in that having shared a bathroom for forty years with a man who didn't even know the seat could be lifted up, for her the toilet was one of the pleasanter aspects of travel.

'If it's any comfort, they'll be giving me a colostomy bag soon,' Mr Taylor came back.

The battle smouldered on. It was pushing three o'clock now. The windows were definitively steamed over and anyway the winter light was already fading. The family gathering had eaten their apple crumble and were now enjoying whisky in their coffee, and out of it too in the case of Mr Taylor. There was, on their six faces, the glow of people having a good time eating and

108

drinking and merrily exorcising all the little irritations that made living together so heroic.

Inspired by the bathroom conversation of a moment before, Larry now launched into an enthusiastic account of a man brought into urology in the small hours a couple of nights back with a severe bite on his genitals which he had ludicrously tried to pass off as the result of a toilet seat falling while he was urinating. Sabine abruptly interrupted to ask why Mr and Mrs Taylor were going off home in such a hurry. Wouldn't it be nice perhaps to go to a restaurant tomorrow, Sunday evening?

Whether the German girl found what her fiancé was saying distasteful, or whether she was deliberately trying to win the favour of her in-laws, or merely thought that such invitations were the 'done thing', the suggestion came as a surprise, if not a shock. The atmosphere in the little suburban kitchen grew suddenly tense.

Mark said quite cheerfully that he was on for it, knowing as he spoke that his wife would immediately trot out the excellent excuse of the children.

She did.

'Just with Larry and me then,' Sabine said. 'You're not on call, are you?'

'I second the motion,' Mr Taylor raised his hand with a provocative light in his eyes. 'As long as it's a good restaurant and expensive. To my daughter-in-law, Sabine,' he added, raising his whisky glass.

Sabine beamed. 'Larry and I will offer, won't we, Larry?'

'No,' Mrs Taylor said. 'Rupert, we've got to get to Salisbury tomorrow.'

'Why?' Kate asked. 'Who's in Salisbury?' And she said: 'You did get that they're offering to pay, Mum?'

'Go on,' Mr Taylor said, 'tell them, Vi. Listen to this everybody. This is the real reason things don't get done around the house. Not my mythical laziness.' And he poured himself a second full glass of whisky, at which his son protested: 'Dad, it'll kill you.'

'We have to go and see a very dear friend of mine.' Mrs Taylor was dramatically tight-lipped and solemn.

'Who she has neither thought of, spoken about, nor in any way communicated with for twenty years.'

'Who is it though?' asked Kate.

'The woman who taught dressmaking with me after the war in Manchester. Valerie.'

'But can't it wait till Monday, so you could eat together tomorrow? Seeing as you've made all the effort to drive down here.'

'She's dying,' Rupert Taylor explained drily. 'Last week it was someone called Hannah in Glasgow who I'd never heard of before, a month ago somebody else in Preston, not to mention the endless visits to the Leeds Infirmary to visit every declining pensioner within a five-mile catchment area.'

'Valerie's an old friend. We had good times together,' Mrs Taylor insisted. 'It was her birthday party we first met at.'

'We met at Talbot Road bus station,' Mr Taylor

corrected. 'And you wouldn't even have known she was ill if you hadn't run into a friend of a friend who has kept in touch.'

'We had such laughs together,' old Vi Taylor repeated. For a moment it seemed as if she might cry. Her eyes watered. 'Anyway, I would have kept in touch with all sorts of people if somebody had given me the kind of life where I had time.'

Mr Taylor lit a cigarette.

Mark said nostalgia seemed a perfectly legitimate reason for visiting people.

'Maybe one day you'll feel that way about me,' Kate said.

For some reason Larry laughed quite immoderately at this.

Mark said, 'Hardly.'

Becoming unusually aggressive, Mr Taylor said that it wasn't nostalgia. It wasn't nostalgia at all. It was just a morbid bloody desire to bury one's contemporaries and savour one's own imminent end into the bargain, an occasion to be at once smug and self-pitying. Because Vi never went to see somebody unless they were condemned. It was like the kiss of death when old Vi came to see you. You knew you'd be in your box before the week was out. She was a stupid insensitive woman.

Scathing and loud, Rupert Taylor appeared to be losing control.

Mrs Taylor said quietly: 'Rupert's just scared.' Then she said: 'More often than not he naps in the car while I go in, because it upsets him to see people who are ill. He can't face death.'

111

'You could refuse to drive,' Mark suggested to his father-in-law. 'After all, it's dangerous in this weather. What with the fog we've been having.'

'I like driving,' Mr Taylor snapped. 'I hope to die in a car accident. That's how scared I am. At least I won't have to suffer her ministrations in some miserable hospital.'

The fat old man so obviously meant this that the jovial veneer of enthusiasm and banter at last went out of the conversation. There was silence. Unless it was just that the soporific and depressive effects of the alcohol were now replacing the initial sense of exhilaration. One or two people sighed. Larry yawned, smiled: 'God, I feel good. Haven't eaten so well in years.' But nobody responded. The verbal carnival was over. They were tired after eating and drinking; the grey twilight through misted kitchen windows contributed to a general Lenten feeling.

Then Mark said: 'Oh shit, I've got to get that article in. I'll be late.' He jumped up from his seat.

'Here we go again. The busy man only has time to sit and eat,' Kate said. Then she shouted far too loudly: 'Come and say goodbye to Daddy, kiddies. Off he goes out to work on Saturday afternoon!'

'I hate you,' Mark informed her in a tone that might have been suited to a purchase over a post office counter.

Larry was the only one who could still laugh at this charade. Sabine said a polite goodbye. Mark took a last look at himself in the mirror in the bathroom and escaped.

112

When he returned it was almost midnight. Unusually, his wife was up waiting for him.

'Sorry, they dragged me in for editing,' he said. The flat was quiet, so that a faint swish of traffic on the High Road could be heard. 'Garry was off sick.'

'Oh really?'

'Yes, what a bore. Except they'll have to pay of course. Which is nice.'

'Just that I've been phoning all evening,' she said quietly. 'And you weren't there.'

There was no interruption in the flow of Mark's movements as he slipped off his coat. Nor did his expression betray even a flicker of concern. He had already decided long ago, and in this he was taking a leaf out of his father-in-law's book, that whatever came to light, whenever, and however damning, he would brazen it out to the end.

Offhand, unwinding a scarf, he complained: 'Give me a break. If you'd phoned, which I can't remember you ever doing before, they would have called me, wouldn't they? And then why on earth should you phone all evening?'

'Oh, only that Mother killed Father,' she said.

This thin woman, his wife, was sitting cross-legged and stony-faced on the sofa.

Mark, holding his wet overcoat, didn't believe her.

'They had an argument. I don't know. About who had wanted to sell the place in Kirby and move to Broughton Street. It would have been funny. Until suddenly he lost his head: why would she never never let be, etc. etc., why wouldn't she let him breathe, and he hit her.' Kate paused. She spoke quietly, almost crisply. 'They started hitting each other. I tried to stop them. The kids were terrified. Then she gave him a big push. He fell backwards over the coffee table and banged his head on the corner of the cabinet. The next thing we knew he was dead. The doctor said it was a heart attack.'

Mark sat down in a green upholstered armchair.

'Jesus,' he said. 'And your Mother?'

'They took her to hospital with him. Naturally she was desperate, saying how much she loved him and never wished him any harm. I phoned for Larry to go and be with her.'

As so often before Mark couldn't help feeling his wife had flint in her heart. So unlike the woman he should have married. And all the time, while trying to take in his in-laws' tragedy, for he had always felt a very deep affection for the old couple, his mind was nevertheless racing against time to find answers to the questions she would be asking any moment now.

'So I phoned you up,' she said, 'only about ten or fifteen times, so that you could come and look after the kids and I could go and be with my mother. And you weren't there.' She paused. 'And now you come back and you say you were there.'

Boyish Mark looked at the woman he had married. He remembered that ten years ago they had been very much in love, very much, so that

114

a confrontation like this would have been unimaginable.

Kate had aged more markedly than he. Above all, her features had dried and hardened around their handsomeness.

'Well?' she demanded.

Fortunately, at this very moment a little boy came scuffling into the room. 'I had a bad dream,' he wailed and went straight to his mother.

'What about?'

'I don't know,' the boy said, trembling. 'But it was horrible.' Then he said: 'Sylvia was a horrible monster.'

He clung to his mother. She kissed him softly, and her hard features smoothed a little. The father watched. For a moment there was the satisfying intimacy of a family dealing capably with the classic traumas, bringing the children through.

Mark said: 'Listen Kate.'

She didn't look up.

'Kate, listen, we're going to have enough on our plates the next few days, sorting everything out, aren't we?'

'And so?'

'Well, so I was thinking: can't we, maybe, I don't know, let this argument wait?' Raising his eyebrows, he managed to half laugh in an attractive winsome way. 'I mean, wait thirty years or so. Row about it when the kids invite us to lunch some time.'

'I can't imagine we'll make it thirty years,' she said.

'It seems people do though,' he said. 'You know, Kate? We could bring it up over twenty-first-century vol-au-vent. We wouldn't even be sure we'd remembered it right. It'd feel like it didn't matter at all.' After a moment's silence he added, 'The way your father goes out to a café every morning, for his *lebensraum*.'

She lifted her dark eyes to look at him now, the child wriggling on her lap. Very coldly, she sized him up.

'Used to go,' she said tonelessly. Then began to cry, rocking back and forth with her child, shivering silently. 'Now he's got all the room he needs,' she sobbed.

'Kate,' he said, but was afraid to go and comfort her. The little boy burrowed into her breasts and clutched.

❧

Does it matter? — losing your sight? . . .
There's such splendid work for the blind;
And people will always be kind,
As you sit on the terrace remembering
And turning your face to the light.

Siegfried Sassoon, 'Does it Matter?'

116

Rose Tremain

MOTH

I was her new neighbour on the Sunny Lawns
Trailer Park, that's all. The park was a mile or
two out of Knoxville in some nice country with a
lake and a cluster of live oaks.

Everybody called her Pete. I dunno what name
she got at her baptism. That's her secret. She was
Pete to us all. Nobody said okay but what's your
real name?

She was on her own with two kids, a girl and
then a boy who was just a baby. The thing she
loved to do was called *appliqué*. She'd learned it
from some sewing magazine. You cut up shapes
of fabric preferably shiny and you machine them
on to things to make patterns. That's *appliqué*. If
you get tired of making patterns, you can make
pictures like a girl in a bonnet or a bluebird. Day
and night, night and day Pete sat in her trailer
doing her *appliqué*. Her sewing machine got so
hot it wouldn't let itself be touched. She made
laundry bags and cushion covers and aprons and
sold them up in the Smokey Mountains
somewhere, in a craft village. There was a
flaked-out hippie in that village who had a thing
for her. He made rustic fencing and his hair was
grey as a waterfall. Pete and he lay on the floor of
his cabin lit by oil lamps, but she wouldn't let
him do it to her. When I imagine this scene, I put

117

a poster of Yoko Ono on the wall above, wearing her dark glasses.

The father of her kids used to work for the Fire Service. Still does, I guess. You could dial 911 in Knoxville and still get him to fight your fire. His name was Chester and he had an appetite so big, he used to snatch food off Pete's plate and stick it in his own mouth. He weighed down the trailer. And his shit wouldn't flush away, it was that huge. Apparently. Pete would have to take a hoe and break it up like you break up the dirt of the yard after the winter frost.

Yet I guess she loved him. That's one of the odd things about it all. She loved Chester and never minded breaking up his shit with a hoe or letting him grab the bacon off her plate. But then he left her for a girl of twenty-two and this she did mind. That's when she took up the *appliqué*. If I'd been her, I would have imagined I was sewing Chester's foreskin on to his face, stitching up all his lying orifices, but I don't know what her reason was precisely. All she said about it was, Annie never again will I put my trust in one single thing.

★　★　★

Her little girl, Lisa, was five and as good as gold. She came to visit me and we'd make popcorn and Lisa'd hold tight to the long-handled pan and say Wow! She had a whispery laugh like the wind in the grasses at the edge of the lake and her favourite singer was Mary Chapin Carpenter. She never mentioned her Daddy. I guess

118

Pete told her not to think about him any more because he didn't seem to figure in her mind at all. Whenever she slept over at my trailer — when Pete went to sell her *appliqué* and get fondled by the mountain hippie — Lisa would say her prayers and leave the cheatin' ole firefighter out of them completely. *God bless Mom and Baby Ricky and All the Poor People everywhere, Amen.* And then she'd sing herself to sleep with the words of Country songs. Her little thin arms would wave around in the cot in time to the beat and then suddenly she'd go quiet and never wake till morning. She was the only human being I've met who could go to sleep with her arms sticking straight up in the air. Sometimes I'd lay them down by her sides or sometimes I'd just leave them the way they were.

★   ★   ★

Baby Ricky was different from Lisa right from the start. Pete told me when he was born he weighed so heavy the scales emitted a bleep like a warning. He was Chester's boy. Pete tried to suckle him as she'd suckled Lisa, but she told me I couldn't go on with it, Annie, Ricky'd pull at the nipple so hard. So I weaned him and put him on a full bottle; he'd fill his diapers and soon as I'd changed him he'd yell out for more and some days I had to feed him twenty times in twenty-four hours and all I got of sleep was a few minutes here and there.

She got him on solid food and he quietened down. That's when Chester left — in one of those quiet times when Baby Ricky was full of food and lying in his pram staring at the ceiling of his trailer home and Pete was dead asleep. Who knows if he looked at Baby Ricky one last time and said 'see ya' or if he was just in such a sweat to get out of there that he never gave his son a glance. It makes no difference. It's just a habit I have, trying to imagine the details of things, like I put that Yoko Ono poster in the hippie's cabin. Anyway, Chester was gone, leaving Pete with those two kids, Lisa and Baby Ricky and her sewing machine. And it was soon after that I moved into the trailer next door to them and Pete and I became friends.

I was on my own. I worked in a dry-cleaners called Secco's where all the bagged-up clean stuff on its hangers got rotated round the back room on a moving rail and all the employees got rotated round the different machines to keep them alert. Some days I stood in the back window operating the presser and watching the Tennessee spring bust out of the redbud trees and out of the earth. A lot of the clothes I pressed had moth holes or scorchmarks in them and weren't worth cleaning. I day-dreamed I'd write a book before I was forty. I guess the heat from the presser and the scent from the frothy redbuds mingled together to give me this grand illusion because now my fortieth has come and gone and there's no sign of my book, only this true story about Pete and Lisa and Baby Ricky and the things that happened.

★ ★ ★

120

I guess Ricky was about nine or ten months old when Pete said to me Annie, there's something wrong when I lay Ricky down because he kicks and screams like he's in pain, but I don't know why. I said take him to the doctor's, Pete, but she said no, she wouldn't yet, she hated going there and waiting in line and breathing the germ-filled air and anyway doctors these days didn't know shit. I had to agree with her.

So I helped her to examine Ricky. We put him on a blanket and undressed him and held him up like a Sumo wrestler and looked at him limb by limb. He wouldn't keep still. He wanted to be on his knees crawling around among the scraps of satin under the *appliqué* table. His body felt hot and there was a glisten of sweat in the fold of his neck, but his eyes were bright as tin and his skin was rosy and there was no bruise or scratch on him. But then we tried to lay him on his back and when his shoulders touched the floor he screamed so loud Lisa came running in from the dusty yard and stood in the doorway watching.

Pete picked him up and real gently, trying to make my hands as soft as gloves, I touched his back and then I said to Pete I can feel something here, Pete, where his shoulder blades are, I can feel two lumps there.

Jesus Christ! said Pete. Lumps? Where?

I showed her and she pressed them with her fingers and Ricky screamed.

Couldn't be cancer, said Pete. One on either side that like. Couldn't be, could it?

No, I said.

Guess I'd better take him by the surgery, had I?

Or you could wait. See if they just go.

Yeah. They could go. Could be the way he keeps trying to pull himself up with his arms has made his muscles swell, could it?

Dunno, I said. I never studied anatomy.

★   ★   ★

Then one night I was lying asleep after my long day at Secco's when Pete came thumping on my trailer door. Annie, she said, come quick. Ricky's on the ceiling.

I said what did she mean 'on the ceiling' and she said come and see.

I got into my dressing gown and followed Pete into the room where the two kids slept. Lisa was awake and sitting on her bed, staring up. And just as Pete had said, there was Ricky, wearing a diaper but nothing else looking down on us from on high. It was like he was full of helium and had floated up there like a balloon. He wasn't holding on to anything and he wasn't one bit afraid. He was gurgling with happiness and little gobs of his spittle plopped down on to our heads like rain. It was the weirdest thing I'd seen in thirty-nine years of living.

Lisa said I want to go up on the ceiling too, so I said sweetheart hold on a minute because we don't know how Ricky got there and the ceiling ain't that good a place to be.

Pete said Annie, since Chester left, I jes'

dunno what in the world is going on and I said well Pete, maybe Ricky's practising being a fireman, but no one laughed.

Then I got a chair and climbed up on to the old teak wardrobe where the kids kept their things. I didn't feel that safe up there. I felt too heavy for the furniture. I wasn't far from where Ricky was, so I steadied myself and reached for him, but no sooner had my hand touched him than he spun away from me, going in a zig-zag towards the light fixture.

Jesus Christ! said Pete.

Ricky's flying! said Lisa.

And we could hear a miniature sound as he moved, a kind of whirring like from a portable plastic fan you can buy to keep your face cool on a June day.

We had to move the wardrobe three times before I could get Ricky because he didn't want to be got. He wanted to go on zooming around up there out of everyone's reach. But I caught him in the end and handed him down to Pete and he began screaming louder than we'd ever heard him scream before. He tried to struggle out of Pete's arms, but Pete held on to him and wouldn't let him go and that's when she started swearing Jesus Christ Jesus Christ and went real pale and Lisa stuck her thumb in her mouth and I climbed down and knelt by the side of them.

Growing out of Ricky's shoulder blades in the place where I'd found the lumps were a pair of wings. They were the colour of Ricky's pink flesh and there was blood on them and they were bedraggled and small, but they were wings all

123

right and after a long struggle with Pete, Ricky got them palpitating fast like the wings of a humming bird and he flew out of the bedroom door into the bright watery light of the kitchen.

★ ★ ★

I said to Pete we oughta let someone look at these wings, like a surgeon, but Pete said no way, we're keeping them hid and pray they drop off.

Then a few days later I said listen Pete, you know this is a phenomenon unique in the world, the Flying Baby. All you gotta do is advertise and charge for entry and let Ricky fly around the trailer park and in one month you'll be a billionaire.

This got her thinking. Instead of keeping Ricky's wings folded away all the time inside his clothes, she let him use them to fly round the trailer. He liked to hover near the ceiling and he got dirty from all the dust and grease up there, but you could tell he was happy. Except he was lousy at landings. He had to fall down and roll over like a parachutist and this crushed his wings every time and there seemed to be no way to soothe the pain he felt. We tried putting witch hazel on his feathers, but it didn't do anything and soon after that Pete said to me Annie, for nine-tenths of his life that child's in mortal agony.

Pete was still considering becoming a billionaire with my Flying Baby idea, but she said she was going off it because really she couldn't believe — after what happened with Chester

— that any human plan could turn out right. She said Annie, why can't everything just be safe and ordinary like it was before?

We were in Kroger's supermarket in Knoxville when she said this, with Ricky in our shopping cart and Lisa trailing along with a little carton of mango juice. Pete and I were examining the thirteen different kinds of salad leaves you could buy at Kroger's, looking at all their names like arugula and radicchio and lollo rosso that never used to be part of life on earth.

We were so caught up with the arugula that we forgot about Ricky for one entire minute and when we looked round at him, he'd tugged off his T-shirt and was pulling himself up and before we could grab hold of him he'd started his humming-bird thing and lifted off above the vegetable display. He hovered there for a moment, then went flying away down the supermarket aisles. We just stood there. We couldn't think what else to do. And we saw all the shoppers struck dumb one by one and stand stock still, gawping and pointing. In his usual way, Ricky had gone up to the ceiling which, in Kroger's, was chequered with big panels of light. And I shall never as long as I live forget the sight of him crossing those light panels and casting sudden little shadows across the store. I know a lot of people in Kroger's that day just didn't believe what they were seeing. They thought Ricky was an electric baby, operated by remote control.

We waited and watched and there was no sign of Ricky coming down. He was in his element up there. So I went to the manager and said Sir, what I suggest is you switch off the overhead lights and then maybe he'll decide to land. So in a moment or two the store went dark except for the fluorescent tubes above the the food counters and we all called to Ricky and held out our arms and in a while he came circling down and landed in a box of apples.

Now, the local press and then the national press and then the international press crammed into the trailer park. You couldn't go out or come in because of all the ladders and tripods and people. Pete and I and Lisa sat in the dark of Pete's trailer pretending we weren't there and reading the offers of money from the media that were stuck under the door. You were right, Annie, said Pete. I guess I could get rich now.

She was about to come to a deal with ABC News to let them film Ricky flying round the trailer ceiling when Chester arrived. He barged his way through the journalists and cooed at Pete through the window, saying honey I love you and I was wrong to leave, so let me in, doll, because I want to come back to you. I said Pete, don't listen, all he wants is Ricky. But the sight of Chester's huge face at the window seemed to be more than she could resist so she opened the door and in he came, all two hundred and fifty pounds of him, and he took her to him and stuck his tongue in her mouth and held her arse in his fat hand. Then he saw me. Who's this? he said and Pete said no one, just Annie. Tell her to get out, he said and take Lisa. We need some privacy here.

I know what happened next, but I dunno if I've got everything in the right order. I guess Chester screwed Pete so hard that afternoon that her brain stopped functioning. I guess she let him make any deal that came into his mind provided he swore he'd never leave her again.

Press guys came and went from Pete's trailer. I held on to Lisa and we made a salad that was five colours of red and green. Towards evening, Chester came out, holding Ricky in his arms, the proud father, and all the photographers went flash flash and Chester held Ricky up to the TV cameras to show the world his feathers.

Then they followed him and Ricky down to the cluster of live oaks at the north corner of the park. It was getting near to sunset, so they got some big lamps and shone them up into the trees. Pete was there, but hanging back out of sight. Lisa and I tried to get to her, but we were cut off by the crush of people and cameras so I said to Lisa don't worry sweetheart, I guess everybody just wants to see Ricky flying around under the oaks and then they'll be satisfied and go home and things will get back to normal.

She said what if he won't come down, Annie? and I said don't worry kid, Ricky came down in Kroger's, remember, he came towards the light. And I guess we were both thinking about the way Ricky had landed in among the fruit when we saw him go. The crowd gave a gasp like they do at a NASA launch and there he was, flying higher and higher and I could see insects in the

127

light beams fluttering upwards, like they wanted to join him on his journey to the dusty trees.

★ ★ ★

That was in summer and it's winter now and the bare branches of the redbuds are grey with frost.

Lisa refuses to go to school, so she comes with me to Secco's where it's warm and the manager, Mr Borzoni, lets her help sort out the clothes by colour and fetch water for the steam presser. It's lucky he's Italian and has compassion. I bring him chocolates out of gratitude.

He knows the story. Everyone round here does. What no one knows, including me, is what was in Ricky's little heart that evening when, instead of flying near the tree ceiling, he made for the open sky and disappeared from view. I think it must have been that he saw the shimmer of the lake. The light was almost gone, but even at dusk there's some brilliance left on the water and Ricky flew towards that and no one ever saw him again. They sent frogmen down into the depths to search for his body with its baby wings, but that lake is deep and they never could find it.

So I guess what Pete said to herself was that if no one could bring him back to her, she'd just go and try to be wherever he was. I dunno. I've stopped trying to guess what was in her exhausted mind. Chester was gone too, back to the young girl's bed with his bank account stuffed with media dollars. So perhaps she killed herself because of this and not because of Ricky.

I'll never know. All she said to me by way of warning was Annie, if anything happens to me, take care of Lisa and don't let Chester take her away.

They dredged Pete up. She had her sewing machine roped to her waist. We had a little ceremony for her and some of the TV people came, but fewer than those who came to see Ricky the Flying Baby.

Lisa cries for her. I stroke her hair and hold her close and call her my angel. My angel falls asleep with her arms sticking straight up in the air and gently I lay them down.

Dannie Abse

FLOWERS

For my wife white freesias.
Mid-day, in a vase, their shadows flew
to the serenity of a blank wall
when the fitful sun barged in, came
   through.

To my doubting father,
the hymns of bluebells, companionable.
What greater silences than these?
Nothing better could be his tutor.

To my pious mother,
blithe daffodils from beneath the trees,
emblems of sighing Spring. What else
could I do? Bitter, she was dying.

For my elder daughter,
a fortune-telling chain of daisies.
Demure flirts, unbuttoned and bold,
so fresh with the dew of the garden.

For my younger daughter,
a buttercup with its golden ray
turned on, to hold beneath the chin.
What good husband will give her butter?

For my little son enthralled,
Time's zany token of renascence
and decay — a dandelion clock
to puff at, puff at, and blow it all away.

David Lodge

THE DEATH OF DIANA

[This is an edited version of an essay written two or three weeks after the death of Princess Diana on August 31 1997. I wrote it 'on spec', mainly because I wanted to record my own impressions of and thoughts about the event and its aftermath while they were still fresh in my mind. I vaguely hoped to place it in an American or foreign journal, but by the time it was finished the international press was sated with articles on this subject, and I soon abandoned the attempt. Later I made some use of the material in a stage play and novella entitled Home Truths. *I have shortened the original essay considerably, but have left its reflections as they were expressed in September 1997. I would not substantially revise them in the light of subsequent developments and revelations.]*

*　*　*

I heard the news relatively late, because we don't listen to the radio at home in the mornings, and there was nothing about it in the Sunday papers delivered to our provincial doorstep, printed the night before. I was in the kitchen making mid-morning coffee, timed for the return of my wife from attending mass at our parish church.

Usually I accompany her, but on this occasion I hadn't. Mary came in at about half past ten, frowning. 'Have you heard that Princess Diana has died?' she said. 'There were prayers for her at mass.' I think I said, 'Oh no!' — something like that, anyway. I remember feeling an unexpectedly sharp pang of real regret, quite different from what one usually feels about the death of a well-known but remote public figure. 'How?' was my first question. Mary didn't know. She hadn't lingered at the church because we were going out.

We turned on the television and acquainted ourselves with the basic facts about the accident in Paris. We watched and listened to the Prime Minister speaking live outside his parish church in County Durham. He looked genuinely shocked and grief-stricken. The reporters and presenters on TV also seemed exceptionally moved by what they were reporting, real feeling threatening to overwhelm their professionalism. Martyn Lewis's voice broke once and it seemed to me that his cheeks were wet. This struck me as extraordinary and unprecedented. But there didn't seem to be any immediate prospect of additional hard news, only speculation and hand-wringing. We decided to go ahead with our expedition, but we talked over the tragedy in the car, and during the rest of the outing. Again and again one's thoughts kept reverting to it. My predominant reaction, after that initial, surprising pang of personal regret, the simple wish that it hadn't happened, was to reflect on the extraordinarily *literary* quality of the manner and timing of Diana's death. No novelist or scriptwriter could have improved on its ironies and symmetries: the legendary princess cut down in her prime, together with the man recently acknowledged as the love of her life, apparently hounded to death by the lackeys of the very media which had made her famous. The day was dark and rainy, and we drove home in the early afternoon in a ferocious thunderstorm, as if nature was doing its best to encourage the pathetic fallacy. I thought of *Julius Caesar*: 'When beggars die there are no comets seen./The heavens themselves blaze forth the death of princes.'

As soon as we got indoors I switched on the television, just in time to see Prince Charles arriving at the Paris hospital with Diana's two shocked-looking sisters. From then onwards it was hard to keep away from the television. I had never met the Princess, or seen her in the flesh; I had never thought about her unless she was prominently in the news (which admittedly was quite often, especially over the last few weeks) and I had always regarded her as a flawed human being — more sinned against than sinning, certainly, but at least partly responsible for her own misfortunes, and excessively concerned with her own public image. And yet I felt that a light had gone out of the world. I was not alone. It soon became clear that the whole nation, or a very large part of it, was swamped by an extraordinarily powerful tidal wave of emotion, in which grief predominated.

Diana's death and the events of the week following surely constituted one of the most remarkable public dramas of the century, a collective catharsis that climaxed at the funeral — especially at that moment, beyond the daring of any script-writer's imagination, when applause on the streets of London for Earl Spencer's broadcast eulogy, with its implicit criticism of the Royal Family, surged through the open doors of the Abbey and was taken up by the congregation. In Hyde Park, more than a hundred thousand people who were watching the funeral service on giant TV screens, many in tears, leapt to their feet and clapped their hands. A friend of mine who was present said it was an electrifying experience. 'I understood for the first time the nature of a revolutionary crowd,' he said. 'If somebody had told us to march against Buckingham Palace, we would have marched.' But those commentators who dismissed the whole thing as a product of mass hysteria or media manipulation seem to me to have completely misread it. It was authentic.

Literally millions of blossoms — weighing some ten thousand tons in all, it is estimated — have been gathered and laid upon the ground in Diana's memory. A charitable fund opened in her name has already attracted over a hundred million pounds in donations. Her place of burial is expected to become a popular shrine. There is talk of constructing a 'pilgrimage walk' through the London parks connecting landmarks associated with her life. Hardbitten journalists have

135

apologised in print for the snide articles they wrote about her in the past. My wife, summarising one such *mea culpa* to me at breakfast, suddenly burst into tears, surprising herself as much as me. Three Scottish professional footballers, a social group not renowned for emotional sensitivity, flatly refused to play for their country in an international match scheduled for the day of Diana's funeral, and forced the Scottish Football Association to change the date of the fixture. My tennis club closed for the morning of the funeral, but reopened at 2pm. The organiser of social tennis, a down-to-earth fortysomething Birmingham businessman, sent a message that he was 'too upset' to attend. A man told a national phone-in radio programme that he had lost his wife through cancer last April; they had been happily married for forty-four years and he loved her dearly, but he had shed more tears for Diana than for his wife. These are just a few representative facts and anecdotes culled from thousands.

Whether the effects of Diana's death prove to be lasting or ephemeral, the public and private reaction to it, not only in Britain but around the world, was still extraordinary, and the question remains: why? Many theories have been advanced in the last few weeks. None of them can explain the phenomenon alone; but perhaps if we put them together they begin to suggest an answer to the question. We can list them as versions of Diana and interpretations of her 'meaning'.

1. The Star

'She was a star.' The word was used again and again in the immediate aftermath of her death. Once restricted to the film industry, it is now applied to celebrities of all kinds. In the secularised modern world, stars are the nearest thing we have to the pagan deities of the classical age, after one of whom Diana herself was named. Stars are like us, and sometimes they visit our mundane world and touch our lives, but mostly they inhabit another plane of existence, a world of luxury, glamour, mobility and excess, which we can only glimpse through the media. Nobody is born a star, but some achieve stardom and some have it thrust upon them. Diana belonged to the latter category. What propelled her from obscurity to fame was of course her engagement and marriage to the heir to the British throne. It was, as people said at the time, a fairy-tale wedding, a modern Cinderella story. Her good fortune seemed to demonstrate that the wish-fulfilment of romance need not be confined to the world of fiction; it could actually happen. In fact Diana belonged to a rich and aristocratic family, and had had the conventional upbringing of a girl of her class. But at the time of her engagement she *seemed* like the girl next door — pretty, shy, unaffected and unpretentious, earning her living in a humble job (assistant at a crèche) and sharing a flat with other working girls. She was seen as a catalyst that would modernise and humanise the monarchy.

As we all know, that hope was dashed, and the fairy tale turned into something more melodramatic and more ironic: the royal soap opera. It is important to remember, amid the posthumous adulation she is receiving, that public opinion was always divided about Diana's part in the deterioration and collapse of her marriage to Charles, and about her behaviour after they separated and divorced. If she had lived to marry her Dodi, she would undoubtedly have attracted a good deal of criticism for so doing. Controversy didn't make her any less of a star — on the contrary — but it was only in death that she achieved apotheosis, that immortal stardom which very few attain (e.g. Marilyn Monroe, Eva Peron, Elvis Presley — and none of them so quickly or on the same global scale). Diana's death instantly edited out all her faults and follies in public consciousness. It was only her virtues, her good works, her suffering and her beauty that were remembered. In the days following her death we were frequently told that she had been the most famous woman in the world, and it seemed obviously true, but I can't recall anyone saying it before her death.

2. *The Icon*

It is hardly necessary to state that Diana would never have achieved her quasi-mythical status if she hadn't been beautiful, but it is worth considering what kind of beauty it was, and how it was mediated. It was not flawless (her nose, for

138

instance, was too long and the wrong shape for classical perfection) but it was highly photogenic. In the days following her death we were reminded again and again of the stunning visual impact of her appearance in photographs and on film. To use a film industry cliché, the camera loved her; while, as an article in the *Independent* newspaper shrewdly observed, portrait painters generally failed to convey any sense of her exceptional physical presence. She could have been a model — she had the tall, lissom figure for it, and the natural grace of movement, and a passion for clothes. Though she suffered from and resented the attentions of the paparazzi, she clearly enjoyed posing for the camera on her own terms.

Cynics will say that Diana's fame was precisely an illusion, a trick performed by the media, who exploited her iconic potential for their own materialistic ends; and that the demonstration of public grief at her death was also largely generated and manipulated by the media. Undoubtedly the myth of Diana both before and after her death would never have developed as it did before the age of the mass media. It was through the media that she imprinted her image on our consciousness, more deeply than we realised until she was dead. But the media are such an all-pervasive part of modern life that it is vain to suppose we can find some other, more authentic ground for public, collective experience. Although there was certainly something contagious about the grieving for Diana which television, in particular, encouraged, there was nothing hysterical about the behaviour of the people who queued to write in the books of condolence, or lined the streets of Diana's funeral route. And the saturation coverage of the event does not explain, or explain away, the small private pang of sorrow which most people felt when they first heard the news.

3. *The Madonna of the Charities*

The media which were so pruriently fascinated by Diana's marital and emotional problems in life have focused since her death on her devotion to her two sons, and on her work for charity and good causes like the abolition of anti-personnel mines. This is all part of the ongoing secular canonisation of Diana, against which the Earl Spencer gently warned in his funeral address, when he pointed out that her high-profile charitable work was in part an effort to overcome a lack of self-esteem. This is not to say that it was simply a calculated polishing of her public image. On the contrary it is clear that she often did good by stealth, and that when she did it publicly she genuinely saw this as a way of turning her media celebrity to positive account. However, it was, again, her beauty, her effortless physical grace, which made her such a potent figure in the fund-raising, consciousness-raising business. The images we saw replayed and reprinted again and again in the last week or so, of Diana touching an AIDS patient, of Diana walking through a minefield, and above all of Diana hugging, cradling and holding on her lap children and infants suffering from all kinds of dreadful disease, mutilation and malnutrition, were intensely moving precisely because she never seemed to be straining for effect. She didn't need to.

4. *The Culture Heroine*

I first encountered this term in Richard Chase's classic 1948 essay, 'The Bröntes, or Myth Domesticated':

> *Rochester and Heathcliff are portrayed as being at once godlike and satanic. In them the universal enemies may be set at war by a culture-heroine. Then if the Devil is overcome, a higher state of society will have been achieved. The tyrannical Father-God will have been displaced.*

Chase argued that the Brönte sisters, or their fictional heroines, ultimately backed away from the achievement of this mission, settling for domesticity, bourgeois marriage and Christian orthodoxy; but he gave them credit for challenging their patriarchal society in such ambitious terms, thus anticipating much later feminist criticism.

Modern feminist writers have been ambivalent about Diana, especially Diana the star, Diana the icon, for obvious reasons; but many women in Britain today, and in other countries, have seen her struggle for personal fulfilment against the

141

restrictions imposed on her by a monarchy whose values are essentially patriarchal (even though the present monarch is a queen), and her experience of emotional neglect, marital breakdown, depression, eating disorders, and single parenthood, as an epic version of their own trials and tribulations. The key to the astonishing reaction to Diana's death, according to the psychiatrist Oliver James, writing in the *Independent*, 'was the way that the agonies of her particular plotline mirrored the real suffering of the populace, particularly women and young people ... Above all, the scale of the reaction is caused by a massive undercurrent of misery that afflicts women throughout the developed world today and for which Diana's death is a conduit.' It is crucial to this interpretation that Diana was killed at the very moment when she seemed to have triumphed over the repressive patriarchal forces ranged against her. If she had married Dodi and spent the rest of her life swanning happily about the world in luxury yachts and private planes from one exclusive fleshpot to another, she would have failed as a culture heroine even more spectacularly than Chase thought the Brönte heroines failed.

This is not merely a feminist issue. Much has been read by political commentators into the mass identification with Diana in her death by people of all races, creeds, classes and regions in British society, and their success in forcing a full-scale ceremony of public mourning upon a reluctant Royal Family. It has been dubbed the

'Floral Revolution' by Martin Jacques, formerly editor of *Marxism Today*. Jacques was one of the first British Marxist intellectuals to recognise that the Thatcher era had banished old-fashioned socialism from British political life for good, and that New Labour's version of a market economy human- ised by a corporate state was the Left's best hope for the future. Connections have been drawn between Tony Blair's landslide victory last May and the surge of popular feeling over the death of Diana, reinforced by the Prime Minister's faultless handling of the latter event, publicly and behind the scenes.

The General Election result and the popular reaction to Diana's death were both unprecedented and totally unexpected in *scale*; and both were motivated by sentiment rather than ideology. The occurrence of two such massive convulsions in such a short space of time has prompted specula- tion that British society really has changed; that the old patriarchal code of the stiff upper lip, emotional reticence, respect for authority, tradi- tion and social precedence, which used to characterise us as a nation, has gone for ever, along with the cynicism, individualism and greed which flour- ished in the Thatcher years, to be replaced by a much more open, flexible and compassionate and feminised ethos. Well, we shall see.

5. *The Victim*

The first instinctive reaction to Diana's death was to see her as the victim of a degenerate press, and this remains an important element in the more complex web of emotion and interpretation that now surrounds the event. It would have been deeply satisfying to the general public if early reports that the paparazzi directly caused the fatal accident by buzzing her car on their motorcycles had been confirmed. It now seems clear that the main cause was that the driver Henri Paul was drunk (and using pharmaceutical drugs prescribed for depression and alcoholism) and driving the vehicle at reckless speed. Indirectly, however, the paparazzi were responsible for the tragedy. Their relentless pursuit of Diana and Dodi, which had been going on for weeks, had reached a pitch of hysteria on both sides by the day of the fatal crash. An article in the London *Sunday Times* for 7 September, which reconstructed the last day of Diana and Dodi in meticulous detail, revealed that the couple changed their plans several times in a vain effort to throw the photographers off their trail. And the well-attested reports of the paparazzi clustered round the crushed Mercedes like carrion crows, shooting photos of the dead and dying occupants through the windows instead of giving assistance, aroused widespread anger and disgust. Here, at the scene of her death, the various images of Diana — the divinity, the icon, the culture heroine, the victim — were violently forced together. Earl Spencer noted in his tribute the irony that his sister, named after the goddess of hunting, was herself the most hunted of human beings. But another legend associated with the goddess — the story of Acteon surprising her bathing — portrays her as the object of male voyeurism. The paparazzi, toting their gross telescopic lenses like swollen phalluses, are the very embodiment of commercialised voyeurism. There have been calls for new laws and codes of practice to restrict their activities, and promises by contrite editors not to use their services in future. But I fear this will be the most transitory effect of Diana's death.

6. *The Departed Soul*

If Richard Dawkins has publicly commented on the death of Diana and its aftermath, I missed it. I would dearly like to know what he, or Daniel Dennett, or any other of our fashionable neo-Darwinian scientists and philosophers, made of it. They must be exasperated. For years they have been telling us in well-written, well-argued, well-researched books and articles and lectures and TV documentaries that there is no such thing as the immortal soul, no ghost in the machine; that individual self-consciousness is a product of the brain capacity we happen to have surplus to our evolutionary requirements, and ceases when our brain activity ceases; that human beings are disposable vehicles for the transmission of genes, the only true immortals. Then a beautiful young woman dies in a car crash and all over the world people are consumed with grief, and seek consolation in behaviour that, however vulgar and improvised,

145

has its roots in religious ritual and language and assumes the immortality of the individual soul. Anyone who had stood up in Hyde Park on Saturday 6 September and declared that the person called Diana, Princess of Wales was extinguished utterly and for ever would have been seriously endangering their health. 'DIANA WE LOVE YOU' read a banner held up during the minute's silence at an international football match between England and Moldova ten days after her death. Not 'loved' but 'love'. Diana lives.

But is this a manifestation of unsuspected reservoirs of faith, or a release of suppressed anxiety and dread? Britain today is a largely secular country, with a small and diminishing number of regular churchgoers. And among the latter many, like myself, unwilling to sever their links with that long and rich tradition of scripture, liturgy and ethical discourse which has contributed so much to human civilisation, will readily admit that for them it only makes a kind of metaphorical sense, expressing a yearning for, rather than a belief in, transcendence. The scientific materialists are much more confident, and more plausible. We fear they may be right. Science has not deprived us of awe and wonder at the nature of the universe — quite the contrary; but it has made the idea of a personal God who intervenes in human history, and numbers every hair of our individual heads, desperately difficult to believe for all except fundamentalists. Immortality seems impossible; but extinction seems unbearable. That is the metaphysical double bind in which we find ourselves.

The man, or woman, in the street does not perhaps reflect on these matters in such abstract terms, but the same unresolved contradiction gnaws away at their peace of mind, as they pursue the materialistic good life which capitalism and modern technology have made increasingly accessible. We all live in secret fear of the positive biopsy, the unsurvivable air crash, the fatal road accident, that interrupts and renders irrelevant our quotidian desires, anxieties and satisfactions. When we hear about such things happening to strangers, or read about them in the newspapers, or see them on the TV news, our compassion is mingled with relief that the tragedy didn't happen to us, or anyone near and dear to us, and with the dread knowledge that one day it will, in one form or another. We quickly suppress these intimations of mortality, and get on with our lives. But when the tragedy happens to a star, a goddess, an icon, a culture heroine, a figure uniquely loaded with meanings for a vast number of people, who seemed to move on a different plane from ordinary mortals, but succumbed to the most banal and unnecessary of violent deaths, then it is not surprising if all that repressed emotion should erupt in an explosion of collective grief and quasi-religious feeling. The man who wept more for Diana than for his wife was perhaps only weeping deferred tears for his spouse, and proleptic tears for his own inevitable end.

147

Margaret, are you grieving
Over Goldengrove unleaving?

Thus begins Gerard Manley Hopkins's poem, 'Spring and Fall', addressed to a young child moved to tears by the sad beauty of the autumn leaves. It ends:

> *It is the blight man was born for,*
> *It is Margaret you mourn for.*

In the last analysis it was not Diana, but ourselves, that we mourned for.

I am trying to strike a balance between presenting a text which is immediately readable and one which is faithful to the original manuscript, aims which do not always coalesce.

∾

One of the problems I face is that, never having actually seen print, I am not quite sure what constitutes a good-looking page lay-out.

Paul Jarman, a young blind scholar.

D. J. Enright

INJURY TIME: A NOTEBOOK

An extract from work in progress

THE ELECTRONIC NOTICEBOARD reads 'WELCOME TO ACCIDENT AND EMERGENCY'. Below: 'WAITING TIME MAJOR INJURIES FOUR HOURS . . . MINOR INJURIES FOUR HOURS', followed by running information, broken by occasional lacunae, about the more serious cases being treated before the less, and on how to procure food and drink while waiting and a taxi to take one home. The Coca-Cola dispensers are built like tanks; some of the foam-rubber seats have suffered major injury.

In fact there isn't a long wait. The electronic notice-board was on the blink.

'Welcome to Accident and Emergency.' One might wish to respond with the Psalmist's words: 'Give ear unto my cry, for I am a stranger with thee, and a sojourner. O spare me, that I may recover strength, before I go hence, and be no more.'

No trouble with the hospital computer this time, no vain search for an Enwright. Thanks no doubt to the BBC's Dublin reporter, Leo Enright, whose genial face, subtitled by his name, is often seen on television these days. I was pleased that Anthony Burgess spelt the name

149

correctly in his novel, *Earthly Powers*. Even though he gave it to a catamite.

* * *

'Great physical languor, especially in the morning. It is Calvary to get out of bed and shoulder the day's burden.

'What's been the matter?' they ask.

'Oh! senile decay — general histolysis of the tissues,' I say, fencing.' (Barbellion, 1914, *aetat*. 25.)

At my age, every trivial twinge seems a harbinger of dissolution. Yet there is safety in numbers. Variety is the spice of life? More certainly, variety is the spice of death.

* * *

Optician discovers cataract in one eye and glaucoma in both. Six months later, hospital ophthalmologist tells me that cataracts in both eyes are due to wear and tear, and there's nothing to be done about them, while the glaucoma doesn't exist. Apparently the device used by opticians to detect glaucoma — a puff of air in the eye — creates the pressure it is meant to reveal. Another self-fulfilling prophecy. What interesting medical times we live in!

Nothing to be done . . . Someone says, you should tell them you're a writer, you need your eyes. But who doesn't need his or her eyes? If you want personal treatment (this person is a writer, or whatever) you should make a personal payment to a professional person who operates privately. Money talks, but 'wear and tear' is not in its vocabulary, and he will listen respectfully.

There's a charity that runs a factory in which blind people make bookmarks. Something striking, something fine about this, a noble irony. More refined than turning out white sticks or dark glasses. The bookmark keeps reminding you how lucky you are.

★ ★ ★

Creative misunderstanding. 'The very deaf, as I am, hear the most astounding things all around them, which have not, in fact, been said. This enlivens my replies until, through mishearing, a new level of communication is reached': Henry Green, during an interview for *The Paris Review*, 1958.

In his early years Peter Vansittart was an avid reader, not unduly bothered about whether or not he truly understood what he was reading. The author of *The Scarlet Pimpernel*, could 'Baroness' be her Christian name? The expression 'Master of the Horse' intrigued him — was there only one horse? And a chapter heading, 'Louis Napoleon flees from Ham', came alive when he thought of school meals. It may have occurred to him that getting things wrong was less hazardous than getting them right: when a question was asked in class and he came up with the correct answer, 'Jesus', the master misheard it as 'Jeeves', and he was beaten for irreverence.

In that same interview, Henry Green was

asked what he thought of the idea that his work was 'too subtle' for American readers.

INTERVIEWER: How about 'subtle'?

MR GREEN: I don't follow. Suttee, as I understand it, is the suicide — now forbidden — of a Hindu wife on her husband's flaming bier. I don't want my wife to do that when my time comes — and with great respect, as I know her, she won't.

INTERVIEWER: I'm sorry, you misheard me; I said, 'subtle' — that the message was too subtle.

MR GREEN: Oh, *subtle*. How dull!

★   ★   ★

Pyjamas might be reasonable garb for a cystoscopy, but my wife reminds me that I am on my way to the eye clinic at Bolingbroke Hospital, not the urological clinic at St George's. I've got the dates mixed. Ought to feel relieved, but don't. At the eye clinic my pyjamas are found out of place, and I am dressed in a pair of velvety trunks. Unfortunately there don't seem to be any eye specialists available. I wait, though there's nowhere to wait. The hospital is much darker than I remember it, more like a stage castle falling into ruin. I drift into a large room, comfortable, well lit, full of armchairs, where an ophthalmologist is giving a lecture to an audience of ophthalmologists, and am firmly ejected. A mournful ageing nurse kindly takes me for a spin in her car to pass the time, and confides a long tedious story of how her first love

152

went wrong and she has never loved since.

Back at the hospital, and a small plump man pops up, takes a quick look at me, and mutters, 'It is not well.' He must be a foreigner. He holds up a sheet of paper, and tells me to read off the letters. It appears to be a restaurant menu, with the dishes written in swirling ornate script, and I can't make out a thing. It's not fair! I grab at the sheet . . .

But I am exhausted. So exhausted that I wake up, in a sweat. Having pulled myself together, I reach for the morning paper, and read about a coffin wrapped in brown paper and bearing the legend, 'Return to Sender'. This makes me feel better.

   '*Half Price Memory': advertisement*
What do you want for half the price,
Half the nasty, half the nice?
At your age passion's best aborted,
The full-strength fact can't be afforded.
'Was £99.99. Now £49.99',
Joys indistinct, griefs anodyne.
A temperate tear, a low-pitched laugh,
Suffice to form the better half.
Yet who can tell what you may access,
Some small beauty spot, some large abscess?
Let the trained conscience known to Nietzsche
Be your memories' tender teacher,
So they kiss you while they bite —
Then you'll know the price is right.

'*Please read this leaflet carefully. Keep it since you may want to read it again.*

You should not take the tablets if you are pregnant or planning to become pregnant, or breastfeeding, or have had reactions to similar medicines such as difficulty in breathing or swallowing, swelling of the hands, feet, face, lips, tongue or throat, or if a member of your family has had a similar reaction for any other reason. You should consult your doctor if you have problems with your liver or kidneys, are on a low-salt diet, or are suffering from diabetes, loose bowels, vomiting, or low blood pressure (characterised by fainting and dizziness), or are receiving treatment for an allergy to bee or wasp stings. The tablets may affect your ability to drive a car or operate machinery, so you should not perform such tasks until you know whether or not you are able to do so.

'Like all medicines, your tablets can have unwanted effects, among them light-headedness, dry mouth, rashes (with or without itching), psoriasis, sensitivity to sunlight, joint and muscle pains, pins and needles, abdominal bloating, ringing in the ears, diarrhoea, constipation, sleepiness, inability to sleep, strange dreams, running nose, wheezing, the production of no or less urine, black stools, heartburn, jaundice, hair loss, weight gain, changes in the way things taste, impotence, confusion, decrease in mental agility.

'Do not be alarmed at this list. For more exhaustive answers to your questions concerning your condition, free booklets are available from the address given below.'

To sum up: If a way to the better there be, it exacts a full look at the worst.

A truly remarkable, praiseworthy instrument. The flexible tube bends this way and that, peering into every nook and cranny of the bladder. At its further end are a camera, an intense light, and a device for making and retrieving small removals. The operator sees all through an attached monocular, and may choose to distract the patient (who needs to be distracted) by displaying the glorious multicoloured turbulence on a screen above his head. All this is blessedly achieved without surgical intervention. The only snag — and that too is remarkable in its way, and no doubt aptly chastening — is getting the instrument into the bladder. A small, a transitory price to pay.

Still, as Santayana said: 'Nothing can so pierce the soul as the uttermost sigh of the body.' And Marvell's Soul: 'I feel, that cannot feel, the pain.'

★ ★ ★

An old grey-faced man in the ward, in a dreadful state, wouldn't or couldn't say a word to his wordless wife when she visited, a trial to the nurses hunting for the bloodstained pyjamas he had hidden, he moaned throughout the night.

A tall black orderly on the ward, standing upright, silent, staring into space, as if he had just arrived in a strange country, speaking to nobody, nobody speaking to him, he seemed to have no duties.

Seen early one morning, the orderly, stock-still, expressionless, hugging the sick old man, quiet now, tightly against his chest, time passing, not a word passing between them. So that was what he was there for.

ॐ

When I consider how my light is spent
Ere half my days in this dark world and
    wide,
And that one talent which is death to hide
Lodged with me useless, though my soul
    more bent
To serve therewith my Maker, and present
My true account, lest He returning chide;
'Doth God exact day-labour, light denied?'
I fondly ask. But Patience, to prevent
That murmur, soon replies, 'God doth not
    need
Either man's work or his own gifts. Who
    best
Bear his mild yoke, they serve him best.
    His state
Is Kingly. Thousands at his bidding speed,
And post o'er land and ocean without rest:
They also serve who only stand and wait.'

John Milton

Tibor Fischer

LISTED FOR TRIAL

He didn't like attending County Hall. Too far from the railway station, especially when it was raining.

Tutty didn't make it any more attractive. Going to County Hall for Tutty. Now that was something Guy could live without. He had tried to get out of it, but there had been no one else. He had had Tutty all the way, probably precisely because he had said to Gareth something such as, 'Try and keep me away from Tutty, will you?'

It was money. Money he really did need, since although he had made a point of sleeping with his landlady on the last two slow Sunday afternoons (when there wasn't anything good on television), she had remarked pointedly afterwards: 'Guy, don't think this changes a thing.' Still, she was already going easy on him.

If a landlady had never rented to an actor, it could get you some indulgence. Actors were sometimes considered interesting by people who hadn't had much to do with them. Mother Art's kids. Naturally, if a landperson had had an actor on the premises before, you weren't getting in anyhow. They could be very vindictive. There was one still chasing him from four years ago over a question of a collapsed roof.

It was quarter past ten, that was cutting it fine.

But Tutty, if he had arrived, could wait for once. Guy shoved his reflection in the glass door out of the way. He really did look like a lawyer. Amazing.

Admittedly, he didn't have an ironed shirt. Suit and tie yes, but he hadn't bothered to iron the shirt. Because he had been hoping to get out of it and because, well, some people weren't worth ironing shirts for. Cf. Tutty. He had to wear the suit and tie because otherwise the judge might fuss. But even at Kingston the judges couldn't be eagle-eyed enough to spot the rumples in his collar.

He looked round. Since there were only two courts at County Hall, you couldn't miss anyone. No Tutty.

He would have been surprised if he had been there. Tutty's only reliable quality was his infallibility in irritating. He was the Pope of wrong-way-rubbing. He should have been there at ten. Guy should have as well, but then he wasn't looking at five years. It was a pity you couldn't go down to your nearest turf accountant to load a tenner on Tutty not showing. In a way he was pleased Tutty was absent — the only drawback was that if Tutty didn't show it was down to him to do something about it. Not that there was much he could do.

★　★　★

When he had started as an outdoor clerk, Guy had been apprehensive, as what he knew about the law was, well, it existed. He'd never been to court. However minor his part, he'd been anxious about being involved in deciding someone's freedom or imprisonment. He'd been worried that if he wasn't looking properly, if his writing wasn't legible or he mislaid a paper, whoops, someone could go down for twenty years. Now he found himself praying that clients *would* disappear for twenty years. Take Tutty.

But in practice being an outdoor clerk required next to no knowledge. The only real qualification you needed was owning a suit. The suit did the work of suggesting professional competence. Otherwise you didn't do much. You carried the file to court. Wrote down the gist of what was going on. You could chase things, make phone calls. You saved counsel the use of his feet by shuttling back and forth between him and the client. You obtained cigarettes for the def if he was on remand.

The clients expected some knowledge of course. But this was where the suit earned its money. And you quickly picked up enough to keep the clients spinning, to camouflage yourself. They asked two questions. Number One: 'Am I going to get off?' Number Two: 'How long will I get if I go down?'

The answer to the first was to point to the evidence the prosecution had and watch the client wince, and then say something like 'We've got a chance,' even if you hadn't any rational grounds for saying so. The answer to the second was to say, 'It's not a science,' explain that the judge's diet was an important factor and then give the client the maximum sentence and watch

159

him wince — because if he got off he might even go as far as thanking you, and if he didn't he felt he'd had fair warning.

Guy had only taken the work because he thought it would nicely cover a month till he got a beer commercial. That had been eighteen months ago. As his agent had repeatedly assured him, 'You've got beer-drinker's face.' Guy had looked forward to complaining to his chums about having to drink beer for thirty takes and getting thousands of quid for it. But the commercial had kept on treading water a month away as the seasons seasoned. His agent had kept saying, 'They're coming. The hops are on the hop,' until finally Guy had said to him: 'Look I don't care what you tell me. Tell me I'll never work again, but don't ever tell me that the hops are on the hop.'

★   ★   ★

Guy flipped through the file, making sure everything was in its right place. He glanced through the medical report. They had sent Tutty to a head doctor. The report was double spaced, covering four sheets. The doctor hadn't called Tutty a lying shitbag because that wasn't a recognised medical term and because if you actually spelt something like that out you were unlikely to be consulted again by solicitors bearing fees that would help put down some more paving stones outside your villa in Tuscany. For anyone who had seen reports before the judgement was clear. But the doc had earned his

160

money by helpfully saying that just because there was no evidence that Tutty was epileptic, that didn't mean he wasn't. And as Xavier had pointed out when he had advised getting the report: 'We don't like it, we don't use it.' Checking his watch, Guy went to look for counsel.

He went into the robing room, an unheated space that had all the atmosphere of a shoebox. Wigs were being broken out. Collars were done up with a dreamy expression, minds wallowing in fantasies of big fraud trials with endless refreshers. The thing about everyday criminal work was hardly anybody really wanted to be there.

Xavier was seated, looking relaxed, the papers all bound up crimsonly. He knew it all by heart since this was the fourth occasion the matter had risked coming to trial. Xavier was wearing a suit that was certainly worth more than Tutty's accumulated wealth, worth probably more than everything Guy owned. It had to be one of the ten most expensive suits in the country. You just wanted to go up and stroke it. And it fitted him perfectly, spiritually as well as girthily.

It wasn't that Xavier was so well off; he just liked to invest his money in clothes. To Xavier it didn't make any difference that it was Tuesday morning, that it was Kingston; you could hear the halves of air hit the ground as he cut through. The other barristers felt and looked dowdy compared with Xavier. At six-two, he could probably walk into a job as a male model if the briefs ran out. Though he had doubtless been out a.m.-ing in a casino or club, he was fresh.

'Have you got our man?' Xavier asked.

'No sign.'

'I really am going to have a word with him this time,' he said testily. This was surely the greatest indictment for Tutty. Xavier never lost his good humour. People whom you could happily describe as scum, scorbutic armed robbers, child murderers, stinky drug addicts who raped old-age pensioners, he greeted them all with a chuckle like long-lost friends. Everyone wanted to work with Xavier. While the prosecution or judge was summing up, he'd be entertaining you. Judge to jury: 'While I direct you on the law, you, and you alone, are the judges of the evidence . . . ' Xavier to Guy: 'The doctor says to him, there's good news and bad news. 'What's the bad news?' 'You've got AIDS.' 'And the good news?' 'You've also got Alzheimer's so you'll have forgotten all about this by the time you leave the room.' ' But he missed nothing, he was as quick on the draw with an appeal as anyone. People, you felt, almost went out to commit offences to be represented by Xavier.

'I'll go and have another sweep,' Guy offered.

Tutty didn't know how lucky he was to have Xavier.

Certainly word spread among the more alert offenders. 'I want that Mr Rawlings,' would be the request of sweaty individuals in police cells. Chambers cruised him up because having a black brief got you Hampstead points and was supposed to soothe the black clients. But Xavier was big all round with everyone from skinheads

162

to Yardies. Skins up on race charges wanted Xavier because it was like having a living testimony to their tolerance, an endorsement on two legs. And he got them off. The British National Party sent him Christmas cards which he showed everybody before wiping his feet on them and tearing them up.

And the Jamaicans all forgave him for coming from St Lucia. They liked him because he spoke bad bwoy. And he got them off. Nearly always. And if he didn't, well, a trial with Xavier was fun, and you knew you'd had a good roll of the dice.

★ ★ ★

'Are you effective?' enquired the court usher, peering round the door. Xavier took her to one side to recount their difficulty.

It was twenty-five past ten. Tutty could, of course, just be a little late. But he had been told to be there for ten and his previous attempts at punctuality didn't encourage optimism. He could be a little late, Guy repeated to himself, but found it impossible to sound convincing.

This was after all one of the barcodes of those that ended up in the system. Time-blindness. Date-deafness. Appointment-deficiency. It was as if policemen walked up to people in the street and asked them: 'Do you know what time it is?' If the answer was 'No idea,' they'd be taken in.

The other common feature was guilt. Either amoralists with beer guts of culpability, or unfortunates splashed with misdemeanour. But uninnocent. The plods weren't much cop at doing their job, but it had to be said that the bodies that ended up at the cop shop were usually the right bodies.

There had been only one client whom Guy had felt was innocent: Yusuf, the Somalian paratrooper who had got political asylum because he hadn't felt like killing women and children and had ended up on a housing estate in Peckham no less civil wary. He had been coming home from his night shift at a yoghurt factory when someone twice his size (unemployed, history of assault) who had been waiting for him (convinced that Yusuf had been molesting his sister) smashed him in the face. Yusuf burst his assailant like a bubble with a couple of stabs from a pointed screwdriver. If you don't get beaten up, you get charged. Yusuf was charged with malicious wounding, despite the sister giving evidence making it clear Yusuf hadn't been bothering her. Yusuf went down. Too nice, that was probably his mistake. He was begging for it. He turned up for his appointments and said things like thank you.

There had been a few other cases where Guy hadn't been sure, until the clients had gone for a guilty on a deal. James, for instance, one of the Frontline's leading sinsemillia retailers, had been picked up on a smash and grab on a corner shop in the early hours of the morning. The haul was three teddy bears.

Bearing in mind James could buy as many corner shops as he wanted, and his usual legal problems were mysterious strangers leaving Uzis

164

in his car boot, it didn't look right. James had been arrested urinating against a wall, with the three bears next to him.

At the nick, James had been total in his denial. However, when the Crown hinted at handling rather than burglary, he dived with both hands. Even distinguished businessmen went out, got newted and did stupid things on Saturday night.

★ ★ ★

Guy walked outside to see if Tutty was wandering there, unable to work out how to cross the road. Back inside he found another brief complaining to Xavier about the failures of his clients to appear for conferences. 'We might as well start double-booking them.'

Tutty had missed his first appointment with Xavier. That wasn't unusual. He had also missed his second. You might think that looking at a few years inside would be an incentive to filling in your counsel as to why you are innocent. Especially as it didn't cost you anything. Legal Aid. But even missing two wasn't unique. Guy wouldn't have minded that much normally but he had had to sit in the office for forty minutes assessing Tutty's non-appearance and dwelling on the lift from two Australian girls to a party in Ipswich he was missing. 'Who're you waiting for?' Gareth had asked.

'Tutty.'

'Ah,' he had said, walking off, 'arsehole.' Confirmation from the boss. Gareth had developed a sort of shorthand for his firm's clients, which rather dismayed his fellow solicitors who felt he was letting the side down by being so brusque, though he noticed most of them couldn't argue very forcefully he was wrong. Most solicitors liked to look concerned, solicitous about their clients' welfare. They talked a lot about justice, deprivation and stuff like that. Gareth just filed them away: 'Charge it up. Charge it up.' His thoughts always got airtime and he was always developing systems of classification.

'The Baddies. The Maddies. The Saddies . . . Plus the Paddies.' He'd pick up some files from the enormous stacks on his desk, and would shuffle them like a deck of cards, commenting as he went. 'Toe-rag.' 'Nutter.' 'Arch toe-rag.' 'Chancer.' Etc. Guy had worked for another firm where the earnestness had been like air freshener. Saving the planet expressions. Whether it was his Welsh voice that made him seem more relaxed and detached than he was, Gareth might be caustic but never tired. He had come from the Welsh valleys to Brixton in the mid-seventies to ceaselessly mine the deep seams of iniquity in the inner city, arriving in the quiet days before it had been colonised by gays, hacks and slightly successful rock stars, and before they had even had any interesting riots. His card was carried all over South London. He got them off.

★   ★   ★

And Gareth never fizzled. Guy admired him for that and wished he could borrow some of his

166

poise. Tutty really wore you down. Tutty was the original inert client. He never replied to letters. He never phoned despite being strongly urged to do so, since staying in contact with your solicitors might help prolong your liberty. It would probably be simpler to follow him around all week, dress him in the morning and have a taxi standing by to take him to court.

Then Tutty got upset when he was picked up on a warrant not backed for bail. He saw his arrest as your failure. 'I give you good business, you're getting your money,' he said when Guy had gone to deal with him at the police station, 'and I don't get anything. I'm jacking you next time.' He had been hoping Tutty would jack them then, but he hadn't. Generally the ones that talked about it most didn't. They saw this as a brilliant tactic to get service, they saw the bloated lawyers fearing for their piles of gold bullion. Gareth only made money because he had arrived when you could buy a street in Brixton for a couple of cartons of cigarettes. But a lot of the clients thought you'd be down a Swiss chalet if they switched to another company, not appreciating that one file more or less would make no difference to Jones & Keita. What was one less turd in the sewer?

Moreover Tutty had threatened him (just before asking him if he'd care to stand surety for him and trying to ponce some bus fare — doubtless some ovum was waiting): 'Yeah, maybe see you on your own walking down the road one day, you know.' It had taken Guy a moment to realise this was Tuttyspeak for promise of violence. This was infuriating because it was rather outrageous going to a lot of trouble for someone who was threatening you and who had been stupid, and not just once or twice — someone who had never unclenched his stupid-muscle.

★ ★ ★

Tutty's warning was also insulting because Tutty didn't have the mandate to threaten him. Plenty of clients were frightening, but not Tutty. He was disgusting, and the idea of physical contact with him was alarming in that sense, but he was too runty.

His skill in carving up pregnant women shouldn't let him think he could try his hand at outdoor clerks. It was the suit, of course. The suit marked you out as belonging to a docile, drone caste that was there to be robbed, begged from, taxed, burgled and hit. It would be unprofessional, but Guy had promised himself — since he fancied a new job — that if Tutty tried getting menacey again, he would give a big smile, adjust his tie and kick him in the balls. He had promised himself that.

He phoned the office from the one payphone. It was a curious thing how in courts they seemed to go to great lengths not to provide phones. Gareth answered. 'Any news from Tutty?' Guy asked.

'Tutty? Any news from Tutty? A man who is in the running for arsehole of the year? Do you think he'd blow it by contacting us? No, the wise

168

money's on our Mr Tutty. No, Mr Tutty is a man who knows how to make the taxpayer pay. I can hear the jingle of paying taxpayers behind you.'

He certainly could. They were there. The jury. The witnesses. The police officers. The barristers. The court staff. As before. Though to be fair to Tutty, the previous failures had not been his fault. He had been late for the first trial but that hadn't gone ahead because the arresting police officer had been hospitalised. The victim herself, Ms Grant, had gone immaterial on the next two occasions. It was clear she wasn't happy about giving evidence, but once the system got hold of you, well . . .

There she was, flanked by concerned individuals from the Domestic Violence Unit, Guy presumed. That was the problem for both Ms Grant and Tutty — theirs was fashionable stuff. And however much they wanted to forget about it, the Unit wanted a result. Ms Grant had been unhappy about giving evidence against Tutty, they knew, because she had written to them as well as to the Crown Prosecution Service explaining that she would like to carry on with Tutty because she was carrying Tutty's child, and their domestic bliss was being marred by legal proceedings.

He had heard that Ms Grant had had a credit-card fraud outstanding which had somehow quietly ended up in the shredder. Whether this was the main motivation for her attendance, or whether it was the discovery that Tutty now had another blastula on the go in another young lady, they weren't going to find out.

Xavier appeared bewigged. Guy shook his head. 'They're going to stick in some pleas. He had better have something inventive and interesting to say if he turns up. But he'll probably go for some rubbish about the trains.'

'So what do we do?'

'You carry on waiting. You're a natural, you know that? You wait better than anyone I know. I'll be having a coffee.'

Of course they never said they forgot. They never said they couldn't be bothered to get out of bed. And it was never their fault. Amid all the tardiness, Guy had never heard once the simple, 'Sorry I'm late.' If he ever heard that he'd buy the utterer a drink. Usually it was Jones & Keita's fault.

Tutty had been very vexed about the letter they had sent to his address, the address he had given them. The address he was bailed to. He had been in fact on the other side of London busy on an impregnation. It seemed to be that those who had the least reason for reproducing themselves went to the greatest trouble to do so. Tutty procreated like other people doodled. 'I've moved,' Tutty had said, as if somehow that was their fault too. 'And our team of psychic monitors didn't spot that? I can't understand what went wrong.' Guy had been hoping this would offend Tutty or annoy him, but sarcasm didn't seem to get through to him any more than anything else they said.

Perhaps Tutty had some work. He was a

plasterer. Few clients had a trade, but when you pondered how builders disregarded the clock, you realised their intrinsically criminal nature. And it had to be said the building profession was always well represented in matters of violence, notably vicious domestics, as in the case of Mr Tutty.

★ ★ ★

Guy was realising more and more that it wasn't just hard to put yourself in another's mind, but nearly impossible, although that was supposedly part of the acting profession. The truth was that you absorbed traits rather than mentality. In plays and scripts you always had the tracks of cause and effect. But in life if you were dealing with people who didn't come from your own patch you weren't going to get it right. The answers came haphazardly, from the spinning wheel of a roulette table.

Take Ms Grant. He really couldn't understand how she could have ended up in such proximity to Tutty, living with him. You could understand how in life you might have to pass someone like Tutty in the street, but the healthy reaction to the prospect of further intimacy was to reach for an automatic weapon with a full magazine.

You very rarely got to escort a client all the way through the legal process, but Guy had been with Tutty from the first evening in Battersea police station. When Guy had started outdoor clerking, he had thought he might get some useful material to act with, but it was no use trying to trade places. The things they came out with, you couldn't concoct.

Tutty was up on GBH and assault on one of the officers who had wanted to arrest him when the blood-drenched Ms Grant had been found huddled up, clutching her young daughter. Tutty wasn't worried about the GBH. 'She won't give evidence,' he had said, the expert's assessment. And the assault on the policeman? 'A technicality,' he had said. A technicality?

Tutty had been wrong. It was the assault on the policeman that had been dropped. It hadn't been much of an assault, even the police surgeon's report had only spoken of slight swelling. Guy heard from the CPS that the police officer had got a place on an advanced driving course he had been waiting for for six years, and couldn't be bothered to hang around court to nail Tutty. They didn't usually drop stuff like that, but the plods obviously reckoned they had Tutty banged to rights for GBH anyway, and that he would be spending many a night sniffing his own shit, H.M.P.-ing somewhere.

So Tutty had been wrong about Ms Grant. Which was odd because you would have thought that Tutty was the sort of client you could count on to have Ms Grant tied up, whimpering in a basement somewhere. If she hadn't shown, the case would have folded. He was vicious, but he couldn't even be vicious in his own interest. If you said to Tutty, you push this button, all your problems will be over and you'll get a million quid to boot, he wouldn't make it.

Perhaps he had gone on the run. That was

sound. Let the witnesses move, disappear, die. The Crown offers no evidence. And nothing much happened if you were caught — but you probably wouldn't be if you could be bothered to move three miles from where you had lived. Police investigations consisted of ringing the doorbell at your last known address; if you had someone to answer the door and say you weren't there you could even carry on watching television.

Having phoned the office again for word of Tutty, they had gone in to explain to the judge they were having client trouble. Judge Foxx didn't look too happy. He had been told by the usher what was going on, but judges like to get counsel up on their feet to hear it from them. If they were going to have a difficult morning, so could counsel.

Tutty, B. Trial, KCC, 11.05 a.m. Court 6. Judge Foxx. Counsel: X. Rawlings. Clerk: G. Gavett, he wrote on his pad. Foxx wasn't really vicious, but he didn't see his job as making life easier for counsel. He liked to ask questions and watch them squirm. Foxx wasn't tolerant of the shortcomings of the system, in the way that some others were. The shrug of the shoulders was becoming a common sight on the bench. He could be quite a turn too.

When Potts had gone down for threats to kill and breach of probation, he had been standing quietly in a boozy haze (he had sneaked out at lunchtime for a session at the pub) when the dock officer had wanted to take him down to the cells. Suddenly, as if he had just noticed he was

173

in a courtroom and going down for the two-year count, he started bawling at Foxx; 'You cunt! You fucking cunt!' They bundled Potts below, but Foxx indicated he should be brought back when he had cooled. Everyone was anticipating that he was going to top up Potts's sentence.

'Mr Potts, let me tell you a few things. I'm going home in a few minutes. Then I'll put my feet up, read a paper. Have a nice hot bath. Chat with my wife while she makes supper. Then I'll relax. Watch television. Have a brandy. Maybe not. Phone a friend or two. Maybe not. But it's up to me. You on the other hand are going to Brixton prison. Now, Mr Potts, on reflection, you tell me who's the cunt?'

Foxx suggested a review in three-quarters of an hour. There was no doubt that if Tutty was going down, he was really going all the way.

★ ★ ★

Guy re-examined his newspaper, but he had consumed all the interest on the train. Returning the paper to his bag, he got up and strolled over to the staircase.

Tutty. He could see him on the ground floor approaching the staircase, slowly, like he'd never seen a staircase before. You couldn't be seen doing anything like concern. It was eleven-forty.

But he looked a bit twitchy. That was Tutty. Arsehole with just a hint of nuttiness. Not the sort of solid, twenty-four hour insanity that would get you stamped padded-cell fodder, or the sort of sad obsessional behaviour that could earn some sympathy. Just the jumps every now and then. And bad luck if Tutty had the carving knife and you didn't.

Tutty was carrying a beery force field. You got clients who were double-barrelled trouble: nuts and drunk. Out of their head anyway and eager to erect another barricade to the return of good sense. 'Whoa, Mr Tutty,' you felt like saying, 'don't have another drink, you're disgusting enough already.' If the police could manage to arrest everyone who didn't know what time it was and who drank Tennent's, the crime figures would really slump.

'You do know you're late?' Guy opened. Tutty looked quizzical.

'It was eleven-fifteen last time,' he replied stonily.

'Didn't you get the lexigram?'

'It was eleven-fifteen last time,' he repeated, which obviously in Tuttyland counted as a clear explanation. And he was right. It had been eleven-fifteen last time. Tutty was dressed as if auditioning for the part of a felon. You gave advice to clients about how to dress from time to time; there was no need to overdo it and get a cummerbund, but there was no doubt that clothes acted as ambassadors and Tutty's were succinctly saying up yours. He had a pair of headphones around his neck which were broadcasting the message: I had to bring some music because you're all boring me so much.

Despite his sunglasses, Tutty was visibly tense. A tension which rapidly gained ground when he saw Ms Grant across the hall. For whatever

175

reason, he obviously hadn't been counting on her appearance. He must have been hoping, as Guy had been, for a no Ms Grant, no trial morning.

They all got sweaty. Some could stay loose until the verdict, but then, no matter how hard they were, they all got gulpy. Because that was the moment you realised that the silly-looking sod in a wig opposite you, who had probably spent his youth train-spotting, could drop you into a place where you'd be eating cold mashed potato, where brushing your teeth would be huge excitement and where you'd be sharing a cell with someone so reeky it would take an entire perfume department to swamp it. And it didn't matter how unlikely that was. Even Guy got nervous when the verdict came.

Xavier appeared, shook hands with Tutty and moved off after minimum courtesy to inform the court that Tutty was ready. Child molesters even got more than that, a slap on the back.

He sat with Tutty going through the file as if he were looking for something important, doing his job. Any measure to dissuade conversation. He flicked through the transcript of the interview Tutty had given at the police station. Tutty had done the selective memory number. He had talked co-operatively with the police. He had talked so freely that the interviewing officer had had to break in repeatedly to try and steer him back to the chargey bit. Your real vet never veered from no comment. Right to silence. An interesting one the lawyers had smuggled through.

Normally officers liked them to ramble on because they nearly always blotted themselves; the more they talked the more chance there was of them tripping. But after fifteen minutes of Tutty's intro on the history of his domestic relations with Ms Grant, Guy had been itching to say, yeah but what about the stabbing? Just tell us about that so we can go home. But there was more about how they liked to go out and look for carpets together and how they had been discussing what colour the kitchen should be painted. Tutty went through the afternoon of that day in real-time detail.

He skilfully related how the argument had started because Ms Grant had been angry about the behaviour of Tutty's son by a previous liaison. Tutty had been angry about the behaviour of Ms Grant's daughter by a previous relationship. Various observations were traded on the brattiness of the offspring. Cases cited. Tutty was lavish on that. The detective had to change tape. Observations were exchanged on the likely behaviour patterns of the unborn child Ms Grant was carrying depending on which parent it might most resemble. Ms Grant decided that their relationship had reached the end of the road and announced her intention to leave.

Here Tutty owned up to hitting her. Nice touch. An admission of veniality. Man under pressure after carpet-hunting and smears on his son. But Mr Memory ran out of steam.

No, he didn't remember stabbing her seven times. That's it, Guy had thought, when it comes to explaining something tricky, wholesale denial or just go for the blank. Don't wobble. The detective tried to elicit something from him, fished around in Tutty's mnemonic black hole. Yes, Ms Grant had obviously been stabbed, he remembered the ambulance coming, the police arriving, but not the stabbing.

The tapes were a great help to the police. Apparently they hadn't been very keen on their introduction, but they were very useful for dealing with people who couldn't make their minds up about their guilt. They loved it now. They taped everyone. Of course, just because you confessed on tape to something didn't mean you couldn't deny it later when you had considered (on remand) that putting your hands up wasn't in your best interests. It was uphill work for counsel, but it could be done: They said if I told them I did that they'd let me go home/give me some cigarettes/wouldn't charge me with a rape.

★　★　★

Guy glanced over at Tutty who had that preoccupied look that people have when they begin to imagine a five-year sentence. Even some of the arseholes you could feel sorry for, but not Tutty. Some you felt really sorry for. Because while it was true that many of the clients were people whose imprisonment made you sleep better at night, there were also a lot who had had no chance. Like Tutty's kids. Clients in the making.

Tutty was wilting now. He had his head in his hands. Clearly Ms Grant's presence had had a

178

cataclysmic effect on his morale. 'Don't want to go to jail,' he said, which was fair enough.

Guy felt professionally bound to try and be encouraging. 'You've got no form for GBH' (Tutty had form for plenty else); 'You won't necessarily get a custodial.'

More head-holding from Tutty. 'It wasn't no GBH.'

Guy nodded sympathetically because he was paid to. Not enough, but it was his job. Although it was hard to see what else it could be apart from GBH. Had Ms Grant mutilated herself to frame Tutty? Had passing Martians beamed her up for a spot of vivisection, leaving Tutty to take the can?

'Wasn't GBH,' Tutty reiterated. Another sympathetic nod. Across the hall, it had to be said, Ms Grant too didn't look happy.

Tutty glanced over. 'She knows it wasn't GBH. At least not me.' Guy felt Tutty had received his portion of sympathetic nods. Tutty shook his head powerfully as if trying to shake off his irritation. 'You know all I want is a wife and kids. Just to be left in peace to get on with my life.' It was a reasonable request. 'She's pregnant, you know. Tell the judge that.'

'If it comes to that we will,' Guy said, thinking that for so many of the clients children stood for mitigation.

He looked at his watch. No one else was around him and the woeful Tutty. No one in earshot.

'I've got to tell you something,' said Tutty, 'on a private basis. This ain't how it looks.' Guy tried to appear attentive.

'I didn't attack her. Three guys came round.

179

Drug dealers. They tried to rob us. One of them cut Hilary up.' Yes, when you needed walk-on villains, drug dealers were your men. For on-tap scum, you can't beat drug dealers. Their union should do something about it.

'I killed one of them.' This was said quietly, but unfortunately audibly.

'I don't want to know,' came out of Guy faster than he thought possible, because actually he didn't want to know. 'I didn't hear that.' He didn't really know what to do, a client confessing to a killing. Be professional.

'Do you want to change your instructions? Do you want to change your instructions to us?' he asked. Tutty looked really tortured. If this was a put on, Tutty should consider a career change from plastering to acting. As a dissimulation technician Guy couldn't fault it. Tutty breathed heavily.

'Nah,' he said finally. But just as he was calming down, Tutty continued: 'I buried the body. I'm sure they're going to find it. I listen to the news all the time. I keep listening 'cause I'm sure they'll find it.'

★　★　★

Guy got up and walked hurriedly to the phone. He misdialled the number twice, before forcing himself to do it so slowly he couldn't get it wrong. The thing was, ostensibly, the story fitted. Knowing what was on file, there was nothing which prevented the idea of three men coming in, having a go at Grant, one getting killed and Tutty just having time to dispose of the body before the police turned up, alerted by neighbours. The call had been made earlier, forty minutes before the police turned up. Had he stuck the body out back? Would the police have checked? Called to a domestic, finding a gory woman, why check the garden, or anywhere else where Tutty might have stashed the corpse? And in her statement Ms Grant had been rather unremembering about the knifings.

'Gareth, look, Tutty's just told me he's killed someone.'

'What, just one? We could really do with a serial killer.' Guy repeated Tutty's revelations.

'Well, I think he's making it up,' Gareth pronounced.

'Shouldn't we tell someone?'

'No. We can't. It's the confessional — we have to respect the confidence. Get him to endorse the instructions in writing. Otherwise, if he sticks with them, there's nothing else we can do.' Who was he to care? Probably Tutty was inventing the whole business out of some rogue logic — in the belief his smiting the drug dealer would win him a round of applause instead of some bird. Nevertheless, Guy found his guts looping the loop as he went upstairs and saw the usher emerging from the court to call: 'Mr Tutty?'

In they all went.

~

I have only one eye, — I have a right to be blind sometimes . . . I really do not see the signal.

Nelson at the Battle of Copenhagen

181

Craig Raine

DASVIDANYE:
THE RUSSIAN FOR GOODBYE

At 6 in the morning,
the telephone tells us you are dead.

Instead of mourning,
I prefer to think of you alive —

tortoise mouth, orange peel pores,
your legs like bolsters.

The dottoressa, giving us pause,
years ago: new hairstyle already wilted,

your evening gown a comfit,
enrobed in hundreds and thousands,

your medical medal kitsch, no comfort,
a decorative decoration — singular

in all its encrusted splendour,
and impossible to arrange satisfactorily.

It was semi-precious plunder,
a giant suspender only just

clinging to your steep chest,
the slippery slope where talc curdled

between each chaste
braced breast. You were drenched

and the bathroom looked like a cement works.
The beau monde, fashionable life —

basking in black tie, socialite sharks —
bored you and scared you to death.

That August heat. A mechanic's chest
like a Jackson Pollock. The tilda's heatwave.

Roadside rocks in veils. Heat. He checks
the oil, like a matador. Dry heat.

★ ★ ★

Last Easter, we hoped you were dying.
You were bed-ridden, gaga, unable to move,

so Li decided it was time to fly in
and say goodbye at your bedside, to sit

in silence, just holding your hand.
In fact, you pushed her hand away.

Repeatedly. You needed the bed pan.
In private. A tiny sign you were there.

The nurse came. Li left the room,
then returned to sit in the stench.

But she had come with a gift, a *rhume*,
so that her nose was blocked. To shit or scent.

Your right ear was swollen and sore
where you tended to tilt your head.

Your right eye saw what it saw
through the saline tail

from the tear duct
into the opposite, encrusted corner.

The left eye saw nothing, ducked
nothing, a blue unblinking circle.

At the edge of your face and hairline,
bran-coloured coins, little blotches,

like cabin windows on an airliner.
Otherwise your skin was sallow and clear.

Not toothless, but no bottom set,
so your face had collapsed.

It wasn't the silence. Li was upset
by your unwavering

stare at the ceiling, and she said:
'how is it you don't blink?'

And immediately you answered
by closing your eyes.

And after another hour,
you spoke one word in Russian:

Dura. A last drop from a dusty ewer.
Which means 'idiot' in English.

Shaking her head, Li said 'no',
when she was able to speak.

'I'm the Lisa you know,
who loves you very much.' Silence.

But then you pressed
her hand, made your mouth make a kiss.

Its laminates compressed,
the bow was strung with waxed cord.

Atoms on the inside were crushed,
outside atoms were lonely.

Released, they rushed
away and together.

And the arrow found the flesh
ready to sheathe its sharpness.

Sschuu. Its arrow flash
a sneeze. Eros and Azrael one.

Dasvidanye — you said. Like an Afrit
you were gone. Carried away. Swept off your
feet.

★ ★ ★

~

It was in 1978 that I became totally blind . . . In the summer . . . my eye became infected and irritable. I consulted my doctor who prescribed an antibiotic, but as it did not clear up the trouble, I was sent for further examination at a Marylebone hospital specialising in eye diseases. It turned out that there was, in fact, no sight remaining in my left eye. I was quite unaware of this deterioration because the imagination creates what it thinks it should see. If I were standing on the kerb waiting to cross and I heard a bus coming I would 'see' that bus. This effect is not generally understood.

John Heath-Stubbs, *Hindsights*

Romesh Gunesekera

THE PHOTOGRAPH

'Trouble?' a voice burbled behind me. 'You have trouble?'

A small grey head appeared above a textile parapet. A table piled high with T-shirts and packeted cloth: batik lengths, sarongs, bedspreads and cushion covers.

I nodded.

'I can help.' He extended a thin brown hand through a gap. 'I know cameras. I know something about these little machines.'

I gave him my electronic bundle of plastic and fish-eyed glass.

'Sit,' he said. 'Sit down a minute.'

There was a small milking stool by the table. I sat down. It was hot. I was tired and fed up. Nothing worked that was mine, although all around me Singapore buzzed with efficiency.

He stepped out of his alcove and turned my camera in the sun. He removed the lens and lowered the body; he peered at the mirror inside. I caught a glimpse of an eye descending, a flash of sunlight cupped in his cracked hands. 'I dealt in cameras once,' he said, 'years ago.' He made a sound that reminded me of my father's chuckle, a sound he made in his last months when the sheer futility of living against time became a source of humour for him. 'But in those days you

187

could tell when a part was broken. Mechanical, no? The trouble now is that everything just stops.' He squeezed a button, pipped a pip, then held the camera a little further away from his eyes and squinted at it.

He had a little patch of grey stubble on his chin, as if he had missed a spot while shaving in the dark. He twisted his mouth to one side when he spoke, almost coyly, rhyming the crook of his lips to his eyelids. It made him seem much younger than he clearly was.

'You sold cameras?' I asked.

'Everything,' he said. 'I sold everything.'

'And now?'

He shrugged. 'Now you can see, no?'

His little stall was set against the wall of a municipal market place designed like a theme park: a miniature Disney India. The three square metres of his space was packed with hundreds of pieces of cloth wrapped in crisp cellophane; a dazzling array of threads waiting to be loosed upon the world.

'Where are you from?' I asked. Some childhood memory of Sindbad and his merchants ferrying their bales in search of new markets stirred in me a need to know more, to find a story explaining where he came from to help me discover where I was heading.

He smiled sweetly, showing a gap in his upper teeth. 'A little place,' he said.

'Where?'

'India, you know. A small place there,' he said, 'in India.' Like a dark peninsula of dodol-cake in his mouth; a taste, a sweetness slowly dissolving

188

with each year, decade, that passed leaving in him only a figment to conjure with: a gap in his head, decaying memory. 'I come from a little place,' he smiled, effortlessly dismissing the grander views of more imperial surveyors, the juggernauts of a compressed country. 'When I was thirteen I was already bumping my head. Even our doorway was little. I left in 1946. There was nothing back there then. There was no future for me. I smelled the sea. I followed the sea. Only the sea, for years.' He stroked the top edge of the camera as though it was real satin, driftwood polished by the ocean. 'But fifty years is a long time in any life.'

'You have not been back?'

'Where?' His eyes were slightly out of focus, as though a memory had flitted behind one but not the other. A memory that failed to survive; a small disintegrating meteorite. His eyes were closer together than one expected. He blinked.

I asked if he had family in this new adopted place. The island he had stopped at finally: his gilded landfall.

He put the reassembled camera down on a pile of T-shirts. 'I married my wife here. I changed my custom and married here, in this place. I learned to sell. Yes, to sell and buy. To give and take, to live in a market.' He had one son and one daughter. The son had gone to sea, like him, and had not been seen again. The daughter had her own family, and her own business. She followed in his other footsteps. 'But now I live in her house,' he said. 'My daughter has a house with a big doorway. I can

189

go in and out without bending,' he chuckled. He reached under the table and groped for something. 'You like Coca-Cola?' A red can appeared in his hand. I shook my head. I had no intention of buying anything; I was simply drawn to that familiar chuckle in his throat, the echo of my father's last smile. 'Take,' he said. 'It is nothing. Every day I sit here and only talk about the price of cloth. Today you have asked me about my life. Take.'

There was one shelf behind him that was not packed with textiles. It had a small radio and next to it two photograph albums, an incense holder and a wooden fan. 'When I had a big shop, I used to take photos, you know. Try out the merchandise — the cameras. *Nikon, Canon, Yashica*.' He stepped back into his alcove and reached for the two albums. 'You like to see?'

The first small album had a picture of a slender, delicate woman; her head and half her face covered in green cloth. She was sewing. There was a close-up of her hands, moving towards each other like fish lost in a stream. 'My wife. She did not like photos.'

On the next page there was a picture of a faintly familiar, handsome young man. 'Self-portrait,' he said proudly. A study in that charmed studio light of all those older than ourselves who were once on the brink of happiness, and were always captured without the shadows of the past or the future falling upon them.

'This is my daughter. Married. With

husband.' His hand trembled as he smoothed the wrinkles on the next page with its single photograph of a sturdy, truculent boy. 'My son.' He quickly closed that album and opened the other. 'The year we opened our big shop. You see the cameras? Strong cameras. They used metal in those days.' But some of the photos had slipped out of place under their plastic film; the adhesive had lost its grip. There was a woman, veiled, opening a curtain.

'Your wife?'

'No.' He turned to more photos of the shop blossoming. A neon light. A party. I asked what happened to the shop. He did not say anything for a moment. Instead he looked at me as if he was searching for something. Then he shrugged. 'You know, my son was seventeen when he went away. He said the shop was suffocating. Even though we had so many things coming in from all over the world. Customers from everywhere.' Even in his little stall now he had batik from Indonesia, silk from Thailand and cotton that could only have come from his India. Some small corner somewhere. 'In 1976 he went. He is out there somewhere still. He doesn't even know his mother died.' I imagined him, like me, in a bazaar of some other port looking for nothing in particular, or perhaps everything that must lie ahead.

'My daughter is in the business now. I had to stop. At my age I wanted something simpler. Here I can sit and wait.' He folded a length of batik someone had opened earlier. It fell neatly back into one small red tablet with an intricate border of gold and blue. 'Everybody comes here some time, to this little place.'

I could see a line of tourists making their way in stops and starts down the row of stalls: brass and sandalwood junk, a grilled Bollywood outlet, bric-a-brac, garlands and pan. Beyond them a food court. A brightly lit speckless hall circumscribed by the regional tastes of a boundless fantasy of India: counters offering Mughal, Bengali, tandoori, Gujerati and even, in a cross-border leap, Sri Lankan cooking.

'This is my world now,' he said. 'You like it?'

Inside my head my memories also seemed to shrink.

He picked up my camera again. 'But the trouble with these machines is that they make you think that what is gone is still here. They do not tell the truth, you know. What is gone is gone. The replica is not the same thing. The vital ingredient is no longer there.' He looked at the machine as if at a recalcitrant child. 'But then, maybe it does not matter in the end.' He tapped the back of the camera with a crooked finger: a hard tap, as if he was knocking on a door, wanting to be let in. There was whirr. A smile shifted the side of his mouth. He gave me back the camera, pleased. 'Try it, now try it.' He clicked his tongue, beaming. 'Manual override.'

I pointed it at him and pushed the button, wanting somehow to anchor his world to mine.

As a poet, I have found that blindness actually tends to stimulate the visual imagination. T. S. Eliot's essay on Milton is in many ways misleading. Eliot was obviously influenced by his own acquaintance with James Joyce, who was almost blind for a large part of his life. Joyce was exceptionally aurally orientated, but, even so, visual imagery is very important to him, as in the famous image of the 'snot green sea' in Ulysses

John Heath-Stubbs, *Hindsights*

Julian Barnes

THE THINGS YOU KNOW

I

'Coffee, ladies?'

They both looked up at the waiter, but he was already advancing the flask towards Merrill's cup. When he'd finished pouring, he moved his eyes, not to Janice, but to Janice's cup. She covered it with her hand. Even after all these years, she didn't understand why Americans wanted coffee immediately the waiter arrived. They drank hot coffee, then cold orange juice, then more coffee. It didn't make sense at all.

'No coffee?' the waiter asked, as if her gesture could have been ambiguous. He wore a green linen apron and his hair was so gelled that you could see every comb mark.

'I'll have tea. Later.'

'English Breakfast, Orange Pekoe, Earl Grey?'

'English Breakfast. But later.'

The waiter moved off as though offended, and still without making eye contact. Janice wasn't surprised, let alone hurt. They were two elderly ladies and he was probably a homosexual. It seemed to her that American waiters were becoming more and more homosexual, or at least more and more openly so. Perhaps they always had been. It must, after all, be a good way

194

to meet lonely businessmen. Assuming that lonely businessmen were themselves homo-sexual, which wasn't, she admitted, necessarily the case.

'I like the look of the poached egg,' said Merrill.

'Poached egg sounds nice.' But Janice's agreement didn't mean she'd be ordering it. She thought poached egg was lunch, not breakfast. There were a lot of things on this menu that weren't breakfast either in her book: waffles, home-style pancakes, Arctic halibut. Fish for breakfast? That had never made sense to her. Bill used to like kippers, but she would only let him have them when they were staying at a hotel. They stank the kitchen out, she'd tell him. And they repeated all day. Which was largely, though not entirely, his problem, but still. It had been a matter of some contention between them.

'Bill used to love a kipper,' she said fondly.

Merrill looked at her as if there were some logical step in the conversation she must have missed.

'Of course, you never knew Bill,' said Janice, as if it had been a solecism on Bill's part — one for which she was now apologising — to have died before he could meet Merrill.

'My dear,' said Merrill, 'with me it's Tom this, Tom that, you have to stop me or I'm off and running.'

They settled down with the menu again, as if the terms on which breakfast was to be conducted had been somehow agreed.

'We went to see *The Thin Red Line*,' said

195

Janice. 'We enjoyed it very much.'

Merrill wondered who 'we' might be. 'We' must have meant 'Bill and I' at one time. Who did it mean now? Or was it just a habit? Perhaps Janice, even after three years of widowhood, couldn't bear to slip back into 'I'.

'I didn't like it,' said Merrill.

'Oh.' Janice gave a sidelong glance to her menu, as if looking for a prompt. 'We thought it was very well filmed.'

'Yes,' said Merrill. 'But I found it, well, boring.'

'We didn't like *Little Voice*,' said Janice, as an offering.

'Oh, I *loved* it.'

'To tell you the truth, we only went for Michael Caine.'

'Oh, I *loved* it.'

'Do you think he's won an Oscar?'

'Michael Caine? For *Little Voice*?'

'No, I mean — generally.'

'Generally? I should think so. After all this time.'

'After all this time, yes. He must be nearly as old as us by now.'

'Do you think so?' In Merrill's opinion, Janice talked far too much about getting old, or at least older. It must be on account of being so European.

'Or if not now, he soon will be,' said Janice. They both thought about this, and then laughed. Not that Merrill agreed, even allowing for the joke. That was the thing about movie stars, they managed not to age at the normal rate. Nothing to do with the surgery either. They somehow remained the age they were when you first saw them. Even when they started playing maturer characters, you didn't really believe it; you still thought of them as young, but acting old — and often not very convincingly.

Merrill was fond of Janice, but always found her a little dowdy. She did insist on greys and pale greens and beiges, and she'd let her hair go streaky-grey which didn't help. It was so natural it looked false. Even that big scarf, pinned across one shoulder in some kind of a gesture, was greeny-grey, for God's sake. And it certainly didn't call for pants, or at least, not pants like those. A pity. She might have been a pretty thing once. Never a beauty, of course. But pretty. Nice eyes. Well, nice enough. Not that she did anything to draw attention to them.

'It's terrible what's happening in the Balkans,' said Janice.

'Yes.' Merrill had long ago stopped reading those pages of the newspaper.

'Milosevic must be taught a lesson.'

'I don't know what to think.'

'The Serbs never change their spots.'

'I don't know what to think,' repeated Merrill.

'I remember Munich.'

That seemed to clinch the discussion. Janice had been saying 'I remember Munich' a lot lately; though in truth what she meant was that she must, in early childhood, have heard grown-ups referring to Munich as a shameful betrayal of recent occurrence. But this wasn't worth explaining; it would only take away from the authority of the statement.

'I might just have the granola and some wholewheat toast.'

'It's what you always have,' Merrill pointed out, though without impatience, more as a matter of indulgent fact.

'Yes, but I like to think I might have something else.' Also, every time she had the granola she had to remember that shaky molar.

'Well, I guess I'll have the poached egg.'

'It's what you always have,' Janice replied. Eggs were binding, kippers repeated, waffles weren't breakfast.

'Will you make the sign for him?'

That was just like Merrill. She always arrived first and chose the seat from which you couldn't catch the waiter's eye without getting a crick in your neck. Which left Janice to flap her hand a few times and try not to get embarrassed when the waiter displayed other priorities. It was as bad as trying to hail a taxi. They just didn't notice you nowadays, she thought.

II

They met here, in the breakfast room of the Harborview, among the hurrying businessmen and lounging vacationers, on the first Tuesday of every month. Come rain or shine, they said. Come hell or high water. Actually, it was more, come Janice's knee operation and come Merrill's ill-advised trip to Mexico with her daughter. Apart from that, they'd made it a regular date these last three years.

'I'm ready for my tea now,' said Janice.

'English Breakfast, Orange Pekoe, Earl Grey?'

'English Breakfast.' She said it with a nervous crispness which made the waiter stop checking the table. An indeterminate nod was as near as he came to an apology. 'Coming right up,' he said, as he was already moving off.

'Do you think he's a pansy?' For some reason unknown to her, Janice had deliberately avoided a modern word, though the effect was, if anything, more pointed.

'I couldn't care less,' said Merrill.

'I couldn't care less either,' said Janice. 'Especially not at my age. Anyway, they make very good waiters.' This didn't seem right either, so she added, 'That's what Bill used to say.' Bill hadn't said anything of the kind, as far as she could remember, but his posthumous authority was useful when she got flustered.

She looked across at Merrill, who was wearing a burgundy jacket over a purple skirt. On her lapel was a gilt brooch large enough to be a small sculpture. Her hair, cut short, was an improbable bright straw, and seemed not to care that it was unconvincing; instead, it merely said, this is to remind you that I was once a blonde — some sort of blonde, anyway. More an aide-memoire than a hair-colouring, thought Janice. It was a pity about Merrill: she didn't seem to understand that after a certain age women should no longer pretend to be what they had once been. They should submit to time. Neutrality, discretion, dignity were called for. Merrill's

199

refusal must be something to do with being American.

What the two of them had in common, apart from widowhood, were flat suede shoes with special gripper soles. Janice had found them in a mail-order catalogue, and Merrill had surprised her by asking for a pair too. They were very good on wet pavements, as Janice still called them, and it did rain an awful lot up here in the Pacific North-West. People constantly told her it must remind her of England, and she always said Yes, always meaning No.

'I mean, he didn't think they ought to be allowed in the armed forces, but he wasn't prejudiced.'

In response, Merrill stabbed her egg. 'Everyone was a darned sight more discreet about their private business when I was young.'

'Me too,' said Janice hastily. 'I mean, when I was too. Which would have been at about the same time.' Merrill glanced at her, and Janice, reading a reproof, added, 'Though of course in a different part of the world.'

'Tom always said you could tell from the way they walked. Not that it bothers me.' Yet Merrill did seem a little bothered.

'How do they walk?' In asking the question, Janice felt transported back into adolescence, back before marriage.

'Oh, you know,' said Merrill.

Janice watched Merrill eat a mouthful of poached egg. If she was being given a hint, she couldn't imagine what it might be. She hadn't noticed how their waiter walked. 'I don't,' she said, feeling her ignorance as culpable, almost infantile.

'With their hands out,' Merrill wanted to say. Instead, uncharacteristically, she turned her head and shouted, 'Coffee,' surprising both Janice and the waiter. Perhaps she was calling for a demonstration.

When she turned back, she was composed again. 'Tom was in Korea,' she said. 'Oak leaves and clusters.'

'My Bill did his National Service. Well, everyone had to then.'

'It was so cold, if you put your tea on the ground, it turned to a mug of brown ice.'

'He missed Suez. He was in the reserves but they didn't call him up.'

'It was so cold you had to tip your razor out of its case into warm water before you could use it.'

'He quite enjoyed it. He was a good mixer, Bill.'

'It was so cold, if you put your hand on the side of a tank, your skin came away.'

'Probably a better mixer than me, if the truth be known.'

'Even the gas froze solid. The *gas*.'

'There was a very cold winter back in England. Just after the war. Forty-six, I think, or maybe it was forty-seven.'

Merrill felt suddenly impatient. What did her Tom's suffering have to do with a cold spell in Europe? Really. 'How's your granola?' she asked.

'Hard on the teeth. I've got this molar.' Janice picked a hazelnut out of her bowl and tapped it on the side. 'Looks a bit like a tooth, doesn't it?'

She giggled, in a way that further annoyed Merrill. 'What do you think about these implant things?'

'Tom had every tooth in his head when he died.'

'So did Bill.' This wasn't, in fact, true, but it would be letting him down to say anything less.

'They couldn't get a shovel into the ground to bury their dead.'

'Who couldn't?' Under Merrill's stare, Janice worked it out. 'Yes, of course.' She felt herself beginning to panic. 'Well, I suppose it didn't matter in a way.'

'In what way?'

'Oh, nothing.'

'In what way?' Merrill liked to say — to herself and to others — that while she didn't believe in disagreement and unpleasantness, she did believe in saying things straight out.

'In . . . well, the . . . people they were waiting to bury . . . if it was that cold . . . you know what I mean.'

Merrill did, but chose to remain implacable. 'A true soldier always buries his dead. You should know that.'

'Yes,' said Janice, remembering *The Thin Red Line* but not liking to mention it. Odd how Merrill chose to comport herself like some high falutin military widow. Janice knew that Tom had been drafted. Janice knew a thing or two more about him, for that matter. What they said on campus. What she'd seen with her own eyes.

'Of course, I never met your husband, but everyone spoke so highly of him.'

'Tom was wonderful,' said Merrill. 'It was a love match.'

'He was very popular, they all told me.'

'Popular?' Merrill repeated the word as if it were peculiarly inadequate in the circumstances.

'That's what people said.'

'You just have to face the future,' said Merrill. 'Look it full in the face. That's the only way.' Tom had told her this when he was dying.

Better to face the future than the past, thought Janice. Did she really have no idea? Janice remembered a sudden view from a bathroom window, down behind a hedge, a red-faced man unzipping, an argument in dumbshow as the party's noise swirled below her, the man slapping the woman across the top of the head, a cameo of lust and rage in twenty seconds, the couple parting, the war hero and love match and famous campus groper zipping himself up again, someone rattling the handle of the bathroom, Janice finding her way downstairs and asking Bill to take her home immediately, Bill commenting on her colour and speculating about that extra glass or two she must have downed when he wasn't looking, Janice snapping at him in the car and then apologising. Over the years, she had forced herself to forget this scene, pushing it to the back of her mind as if it were about Bill and herself in some way. Then, after Bill had died, and she had met Merrill, there was another reason for trying to forget it.

'People said I would never get over him.' Merrill's manner seemed to Janice monstrously complacent. 'That's the truth. I shall never get over him. It was a love match.'

Janice buttered some toast. At least here they didn't give you your toast already buttered, as they did at some other places. That was another American habit she couldn't get used to. She tried to unscrew the lid of a small pot of honey, but her wrist wasn't strong enough. Then she tried the bramble jelly, with equal lack of success. Merrill seemed not to notice. Janice put a triangle of ungarnished toast into her mouth.

'Bill never looked at another woman in thirty years.' Aggression had risen in her like a burp. She preferred to agree with other people in conversation, and she tried to please, but sometimes the pressure of doing this made her say things which surprised her. Not the thing itself, but the fact that she said it. And when Merrill failed to respond, it made her insist.

'Bill never looked at another woman in thirty years.'

'I'm sure you're right, my dear.'

'When he died, I was bereft. Quite bereft. I felt my life had come to an end. Well it has. I try not to feel sorry for myself, I keep myself entertained, no, I suppose distracted is more the word, but I know that's my lot, really. I've had my life, and now I've buried it.'

'Tom used to tell me that just seeing me across a room made his heart lift.'

'Bill never forgot a wedding anniversary. Not once in thirty years.'

'Tom used to do this wonderfully romantic thing. We'd go away for the weekend, up into the mountains, and he'd book us into the lodge under a false name. We'd be Tom and Merrill Humphreys, or Tom and Merrill Carpenter, or Tom and Merrill Delivio, and we'd keep it up all weekend, and he'd pay in cash when we left. It made it . . . exciting.'

'Bill pretended to forget one year. No flowers in the morning, and he told me he'd be working late so he'd grab a bite at his desk. I tried not to think about it, but it made me a bit down, and then in the middle of the afternoon I got a call from the car company to check they were to pick me up at seven thirty and bring me to the French House. Can you imagine? He'd even thought it out so that they gave me a few hours' warning. And he'd managed to smuggle his best suit into work without me noticing so that he could change into it. *Such* an evening. Ah.'

'I always made an effort before I went to the hospital. I said to myself, Merrill, no matter how darned sorry you feel for yourself, you make sure he sees you looking like something worth living for. I even bought new clothes. He'd say, 'Honey, I haven't seen that before, have I?' and give me his smile.'

Janice nodded, imagining the scene differently: the campus groper, on his deathbed, seeing his wife spend money on new clothes to please his successor. As soon as the thought occurred, she felt ashamed of it, and hurried on. 'Bill said that if there was a way to send me a message — afterwards — then he'd find one. He'd get through to me somehow.'

'The doctors told me they'd never seen anyone hang in there that long. They said, the

205

courage of the man. I said, oak leaves and clusters.'

'But I guess even if he was trying to send me a message, I might not be able to recognise the form in which it came. I comfort myself with that. Though the thought of Bill trying to get through and seeing me not understand is unbearable.'

Next she'll be into that reincarnation crap again, thought Merrill. How we all come back as squirrels. Listen, kid, your husband is not only dead, but when he was alive he walked with his hands out, know what I mean? No, she probably wouldn't get it. Your husband was known on campus as that little limey fag in administration — that any clearer? He was a teabag, OK? Not that she would ever actually tell Janice. Far too delicate. She'd just crumble to bits.

It was odd. Knowing this gave Merrill a sense of superiority, but not of power. It made her think, someone's got to look out for her now that little fag husband of hers is gone, and you seem to have volunteered for the job, Merrill. She may irritate the hell out of you from time to time, but Tom would have wanted you to see this one through.

'More coffee, ladies?'

'I'd like some fresh tea, please.'

Janice expected to be offered yet again the choice of English Breakfast, Orange Pekoe or Earl Grey. But the waiter merely took away the miniature, one-cup pot which Americans mysteriously judged sufficient for morning tea.

'How's the knee?' Merrill asked.

'Oh, much easier now. I'm so glad I had it done.'

When the waiter returned, Janice looked at the pot and said sharply, 'I wanted fresh.'

'I'm sorry?'

'I said I wanted fresh. I didn't ask just for more hot water.'

'I'm sorry?'

'This,' said Janice, reaching for the yellow label which dangled from the lid of the pot, 'is the same old *teabag*.' She glared at the supercilious young man. She really was cross.

Afterwards, she wondered why he had got all huffy, and why Merrill had suddenly burst into manic laughter, raised her coffee mug, and said, 'Here's to you, my dear.'

Janice raised her own empty cup, and with a dull, unechoing chink, they toasted one another.

III

'He's the man to go to for knees. She was driving again in two days.'

'That's quick,' said Merrill.

'I saw Steve the other day.'

'And?'

'Not good.'

'It's heart, isn't it?'

'And he's far too overweight.'

'Never a good idea.'

'Do you think there's a connection between the heart and the heart?'

Merrill gave a smiling shake of the head. She

was such a funny little thing, Janice. You never knew which way she would jump. 'I'm not with you there, Janice.'

'Oh, do you think you can get a heart attack from being in love?'

'I don't know.' She gave it some thought. 'I know something else you can get a heart attack from though.' Janice looked puzzled. 'Nelson Rockefeller.'

'What's he got to do with it?'

'That's how he died.'

'What's how he died?'

'They said he was working late on an art book. Well, I never believed that for a minute.' She waited until it was certain Janice had got the point.

'The things you know, Merrill.' And the things I know too.

'Yes, the things I know.'

Janice pushed her breakfast away to make room for her elbows. Half a bowl of granola and a round of toast. Two cups of tea. Liquids went through her so fast nowadays. She looked across at Merrill, at her beaky face and flat, unconvincing hair. She was a friend. And because she was a friend, Janice would protect her from what she knew about that awful husband of hers. It was just as well they had met only as widows; Bill would have loathed Tom.

Yes, she was a friend. And yet . . . Was it more that she was an ally? Like it had been back at the beginning. When you were a child, you thought you had friends, but in fact you had only allies — people on your side who would see you

208

through until you were grown up. Then — in her case — they fell away, and there was being grown-up, and Bill, and the children, and the children leaving, and Bill dying. And then? Then you needed allies again, people to see you through until the end. Allies who remembered Munich, who remembered the old films, which were still the best, even if you tried to like the new ones. Allies who helped you to understand a tax form and open little pots of jam. Allies who worried just as much about money, even if you suspected that some of them had more of it than they let on.

'Did you hear,' Merrill said, 'that Stanhope's deposit has doubled?'

'No, what is it now?'

'A thousand a year. Up from five hundred.'

'Well, it's certainly nice. But the rooms are very small.'

'They're small everywhere.'

'And I shall need two bedrooms. I've got to have two bedrooms.'

'Everyone needs two bedrooms.'

'The rooms at Norton are big. And it's downtown.'

'But the other people are boring, I've heard.'

'Me too.'

'I don't like Wallingford.'

'I don't like Wallingford either.'

'It may have to be Stanhope.'

'If they double the deposit like that you can't be sure they won't double the charges just after you move in.'

'They've got a good scheme where Steve is.

They ask you to post a notice saying what you can do to help — like if you can drive someone to hospital or put up a shelf or change a bulb or know about tax forms.'

'That's a good idea.'

'As long as it doesn't make you too reliant on others.'

'That's a bad idea.'

'I don't like Wallingford.'

'I don't like Wallingford.'

They looked at one another harmoniously.

'Waiter, would you divide this check?'

'Oh, we can divide it ourselves, Merrill.'

'But I had the egg.'

'Oh, stuff and nonsense.' Janice held out a ten-dollar bill. 'Will that do it?'

'Well, it's twelve if we're sharing.'

Typical Merrill. Typical bloody Merrill. With the money the campus groper left her. A thousand dollars a year just to stay on the waiting list is small change to her. *And* she had the juice as well as the egg. But Janice merely unsnapped her purse, took out two dollar notes, and said, 'Yes, we're sharing.'

∾

A Blind Man

I do not know what face is looking back
whenever I look at the face in the mirror;
I do not know what old face seeks its image
in silent and already weary anger.
Slow in my blindness, with my hand I feel

210

the contours of my face. A flash of light
gets through to me. I have made out your hair,
colour of ash and at the same time, gold.
I say again that I have lost no more
than the inconsequential skin of things.
These wise words come from Milton, and are
    noble,
but then I think of letters and of roses.
I think, too, that if I could see my features,
I would know who I am, this precious
afternoon.

Jorge Luis Borges, The Book of Sand

John Fowles

A SEME FROM SAFAGA

A Seme is an old-fashioned term from the new discipline of deconstruction. It means any element of meaning, any symbol or sign; effectively, any message. Safaga is a small port in Egypt, opposite Jeddah and Mecca across the Red Sea in Saudi Arabia. We, Sarah my wife and I, went in November on a wander between the two great religions, Christianity and Islam, of this part of our planet. I hoped to attack, or more accurately diminish, both faiths. I had long decided or felt it was time to ask humanity to face the two great questions in all our existences. Is there a god? And linked to it, is there an afterlife, a guaranteed entry into heaven? Indeed, is there a heaven one may enter, apart from the memory of our own lives?

Sarah and I arrived by air in Damascus on 12 November. That was salutary as it immediately made us aware of a key word in Doughty's *Arabia Deserta* (1888), the great guide to the area. The word descended through a tangled forest of Romance languages. It is *mesquin* in French and originally issues from Arabic itself. A local guide to the old village of Salt near Amman puts it neatly: ' . . . The place looks as if it were only put together in the last twenty years.' Not to have caught up with time is very meskin. Its implications are almost all, in the usual European way, contemptuous or racist. Meskin or meskeen signifies mean- or small-minded, paltry, puny; in Arabic simply poor. Used more sympathetically, it evokes that aspect of the nomadic Bedouin, so many English — most famously T. E. Lawrence — admiring of their courage and pride, and their primitive codes of generosity and hospitality, have fallen in love with. You can't travel in the Levant without feeling and sensing this word. It is ubiquitous, even though embarrassingly reminiscent of the way we British once looked on West Indians, Pakistanis and Indians. That is a deficiency that, as we now realise, we have unfortunately not yet remedied in ourselves.

We began by visiting one of the great shrines of very early Christianity. That was Maalala, near Damascus itself, a village where they still spoke Christ's own language, Aramaic. The chapel itself in spite of all its vulgar tourist bric-à-brac moved me emotionally and I immediately felt the cost of a lifetime of having been brainwashed into Christianity. It was then that I first realised what a difficult task, in dismissing all this, I had undertaken. No god, no afterlife; the lack of these dynamited millions. So much age, such accreted veneration: in not seeing it, I began to suspect that I was meskin myself. I was to have this reaction again and again. My motives were shabby in themselves, like so many of the buildings and sites we were to see during the next month. There was something distinctly second-rate in trying to harass this poor old ghost, just to prove there is neither a god, nor an afterlife.

One thing I decided from the beginning was that I would not try to go into competition with any of the formidable present batch of English travel-writers. Now I felt I had a far more important task. I am, or would be, pre-eminently a novelist, deeply believing, as the Greeks said, that fiction is woven into everything. I have for instance long believed that Charles Darwin was the greatest scientist and thinker of the former century and was clearly at heart another novelist. He had gained most of his great insight thereby. Years ago I gained a pat on the back from the Cambridge primatologist and psychologist Nicholas Humphrey. He persuaded me to see myself — though outwardly a storyteller in love with all narrative — as a kind of shaman (one of those semi-magicians in South America that hold the mysteries and knowledges of their tribes, and most of their secrets). In other words I had a duty, like any animal, to warn other members of my species that we might have taken a very wrong road or turning in our past. This is really, of course, electing myself as a sort of priest, a function that many medieval writers — even the very greatest ones, such as Rabelais — granted themselves.

Before we left, Sarah and I made a little list of the books we thought we'd like to have with us. The most important was the very acute *Arabia Deserta* by Charles Doughty. This masterpiece I read throughout in intermittent snatches. The next was Victoria Glendinning's *Jonathan Swift*.

His rough sarcasms and flashes of acerbic wit have always much appealed to something in me. Another book I would certainly have brought if I could was J. T. Fraser's *Time, Conflict and Human Values*, but I didn't receive that until we had returned from the Levant. Julius Fraser founded the invaluable International Society for the Study of Time. I first attended it years ago at Bellagio in Italy, along with a whole gaggle of Nobel prizewinners, mainly physicists. I hadn't forgotten either them or him. There is one other book we took, but that may wait.

As a novelist perhaps I may begin with an imagined fragment of Pinteresque dialogue between Sarah and myself. I am sorry (but not very) if I may seem to be introducing a note of flippancy. Having crawled our way down from Damascus through Syria and Jordan, we came one afternoon to an imposing fortress called Al Karak (Kerak) where I heard something that saddened me and seemed only too familiar in that cruelly rugged landscape. There had a few centuries ago been a garrison commander of Kerak — I think Turkish, but that hardly surprises. It is cruel how sunk into sadism all these lands are. The commandant's habit was to throw prisoners off one of the beetling cliffs surrounding the fortress. Realising that in so doing he risked losing the exquisite pleasure of watching them in their last agonies, he had before each huge drop carefully caused wooden cages to be built round their skulls. This seemed a completely gratuitous cruelty, even by the barbarous standards of the region, indeed very

215

close to what was eventually done to poor Jesus of Nazareth.

I'd been parked on a wall to spare my arthritis, while Sarah went on a tour of the fortress. Seeing her put a book aside I looked, as I do sometimes, schoolmasterly and reproving.

John: You'll be punished for that — not finishing a book.
Sarah: I don't care. It bores me.
John: Do you know what the commandant here used to do?
(*Sarah shakes her head. He tells her.*)
Sarah: Ugh!
John: He was probably a Turk, or a Crusader.
Sarah: That's no excuse.
John: He knew the mindless cruelty of existence.
Sarah: That's still no excuse.
John: T.E. Lawrence once said it was not the pain, but learning to stand it.
Sarah: To hell with Lawrence.
John: Shame on you.
Sarah: Why don't you believe in God? Not even in Allah!
John: Because I knew, I still know, that commandant.
Sarah: You're not a sadistic brute — except occasionally.
John: But a thinking one.
Sarah: You're a monster.
John: I'm a human . . . the same thing.
Sarah: You're impossible.

John: It's also why I have no belief in either Christ or Allah.
Sarah: You're quite impossible.
John: No argument.
        Sarah shrugs with contempt.
        Now you're doing what you did to that book — dodging the issue.
Sarah: Kiss me.
John: You're still dodging it.

Sarah, by the way, works in advertising in London. Two years ago she worked on a poster for Messrs Heineken that amused me. We are shown an ancient desert, tribal people, of a kind we had frequently been seeing in recent days. A man whom we recognise as Joseph raises his arms like an exultant father. He speech-bubbles to a waiting crowd: 'It's a girl!' The poster had to be taken down after two days in New York because it was deemed offensive. It seemed to me a classic example of chicken-heartedness, a fear, as old as the pyramids of Egypt, of outraging convention. Sarah and her colleagues swallowed it, which made me mistrust her trade. She has countless amenable qualities and I am very much, almost blindly, in love with her.

Safaga. Now we are near the end of our peregrination. We are enclosed behind a jagged indigo range of scarps that protect a coastal plain. I walk around the deserted afterdeck, where we usually eat, and stand at the rail over the oily green of the harbour waters. The temptation to jump is great . . . childish. Half the cruise, the other passengers, have left us, touring

217

Luxor and the Nile across the waste of sand. Sarah and I don't, having been before. We are both minimalists in our fashion. Sarah likes the starkness of these landscapes, though she more than I, who really only like them because they so nakedly reject.

Tomorrow we shall cross the Red Sea to Jeddah, liquid gold and queues of tankers. It's only a short way on to Mecca. I know I shall detest it. It'll be a hideous concrete showcase to illustrate the Saudi contempt — poor fellow! — for everything feminine. So it is, and I shall duly detest.

I had often thought on a previous cruise of just such a suicide, an obliteration in salt, as this at Safaga; yet always rejected it in the past. I accept here that I am quite certainly godless and infinitely alone into the bargain. I feel unhappy in this wretched little Egyptian port, yet not in complete despair. I won't just feebly kill myself, to end this dull existence. The dark water beckons, the jagged range waits; I will be patient, bear it — and life — a little longer.

Now to business: which is openly to declare my profound lack of belief. In a series of works in the latter part of my life I have repeatedly claimed I cannot be judged or known except through my, or a, love of nature. It is only by that love and affection that my other work, my poems and novels, may begin to be understood. The other day I bought a secondhand copy of Buffon, that great French categoriser of life, who effectively first laid all nature out for inspection. This primary importance was greatly helped by his Swedish friend, Linnaeus, whose contribution was his brilliant realisation of how it might be simply named and categorised. More of the modern science of natural history is based on Linnaeus and Buffon than we realise. At least, I have seen that Buffon's huge work is the equivalent of an early Bible, a fundamental aspect of all the knowledge we then possessed, indeed an enormous step forward.

Science tries to discover the nature of all knowledge, both in general and in detail. This comparative and quite sudden (since 1780) throwing open of the doors of reality is a kind of miracle, an exuberant leap and, of course, it has been paralleled by the similar miracle of communication. We have comparatively quickly acquired a vast treasury of hitherto unknown knowledge. We constantly know it does not reach deep enough. Our facile ability to communicate is something whose revolutionary nature we too little comprehend. As one with the intelligence of one of our most gifted tribes drily says, almost as if to a creator, 'Why should we be so lucky?' This tribe, the Jewish, shares with us British one very great advantage in the ongoing battles of evolution. That is a sense of humour, and a skill with irony; to take nothing, least of all life, quite seriously. It provides the very opposite of the meskin view of life. All this knowing completely changes our reason for being on this globe; in other words it changes the whole purpose and input of evolution. In many ways we are (we eternally continue to be) further up the grand staircase than we sometimes imagine, or feel we may one day be able to master. It is the astounding onwardness of time that hurtles us on. It often leaves us dizzy and breathless, as little as many of us sense we are now.

Another feature of modern life is something I once called the *keraunos*: that is the existence of pure chance. This tyrant governs all life. It breaks all the rules. It is never foreseeable or calculable. It consists largely of complete flukes, the whole eight draws, what we call 'sheer luck'. Its occurrence can, in our personal terms, be either good or bad. We see it not only in the petty circumstances of our lives, but the very great ones also. The *keraunos* occurs both in science and the arts, it comes in what we call brainwaves or strokes of genius. The *keraunos* (from the classical Greek), and its total unpredictability, explain countless human drives and activities. Betting and gambling, insuring, encouraging and despairing, hoping and fearing are all affected by this mysterious constituent in our lives. We depend on it for most of our pleasures and depressions, we would hate to live without it. It causes many of the things that terrify us; the recent earthquakes in Turkey, the abominable follies of Kosovo, the merciless floods in India and Venezuela are all due to it. Trying to find a science to combat it has given birth to what we now call the laws of chaos. It occurs to me even now as I write, for I have long known that I am unimaginably dependent on pure hazard.

I deeply despise the whole concept of millennarianism, or the importance of the millennium, of numbers. It seems to me that our belief in it really dates back, as with so many other things, to the Stone Age. The present manias about it seem faintly ridiculous except that this is obviously a good time to make us laugh and think, to mark both where we are and what we are. We realise we are, like our simian ancestors, exceptionally ingenious. A clever TV programme (*The 1900 House*) involving a 1999 family recently and vividly reminded us of that ingenuity. It gave a list of all the gadgets and inventions discovered since that year. We would now count ourselves uncivilised or unhappy 'barbarians' if we lacked them. Of course most of us are without these inventions in reality. It gave us all a shock, to be shown we had so totally forgotten so much. Ingenuity is being always able to imagine answers. There are so many things we just don't know (and perhaps never will in the foreseeable future). What is remarkable, and what we must accept and act on, is this great explosion of knowing. Its existence dominates our actions and determines our moods. We should be proud to be a member of our species. I begin to appreciate the constant reasons for our depressions and for our discrediting ourselves. It is as if we need a name for this vast new change in being. And finally gain an understanding of it, even though we know that the *keraunos* with its alternatives will always bring trouble as well as many better things. A nice Irish woman I met on our journey, Maura, has just sent me after our return a new book on an Irish writer I have always particularly liked: Flann O'Brien. His humour is very nearly sublime. Nowhere is the *keraunos* better evoked.

★   ★   ★

Fujeira, Oman. We're at the end of our journey, completely mixologised (look it up!), miscegenated and miskenified, whatever the word is that I'm looking for. We are in a very crowded Omani souk, as busy as an alarmed ant heap. Sharp-eyed Sarah has found us a little souvenir for our trip. It is a garish apple-green plastic model of a mosque that also serves as an alarm clock, though this one doesn't ring a bell; here an ayatollah wails a fervent muezzin call. I love it, as I'm sure (were he alive) Flann O'Brien would also.

I mentioned that there was one other book I was pleased we had on our wanderings. It won the Booker prize last season and for once I think the judges chose well. It was by the South African J.M. Coetzee, and is called *Disgrace*. It gives a marvellous indication, under its guise of dealing with an academic's selfish career, of how we might find a way ahead through the Age of Hazard. *Disgrace* is especially wise in advising us how to treat other kinds of life on this planet. Above all it raises that other huge enigma of why we have any sort of conscience at all. Where does it come from? Most people who are variously the followers of the famous religions would claim to know the answer. It is expressed and hoped for from every minaret, in every parish church.

So often we know what we would and should do were the world kinder. We touch the most important and extraordinary discovery of our short existences in this vast cosmos. It is that we know we both have a conscience and yet so often cannot hear it. In this cleft situation we can only wish ourselves Bon Voyage!

∾

O say! What is that Thing call'd Light,
Which I can ne'er enjoy;
What is the Blessing of the Sight,
O tell your poor Blind Boy!

You talk of wond'rous Things you see,
You say the Sun shines bright;
I feel him warm, but how can he
Then make it Day or Night?

My Day or Night myself I make,
Whene'er I wake or play,
And cou'd I ever keep awake,
It wou'd be always Day.

With heavy Sighs, I often hear,
You mourn my hopeless Woe;
But sure, with Patience I may bear
A loss I ne'er can know.

Then let not what I cannot have
My Chear of Mind destroy;
Whilst thus I sing, I am a King
Altho' a poor blind boy.

Colley Cibber, 'The Blind Boy'

Simon Brett

A NOTE TO THE MILKMAN

after Alexander Pope

God, when creating Man, at once decreed
That ample diet should supply our need,
And proper eating, fed by proper food,
Should sickness from our mortal lives exclude.
He also, in His Perfect Plan, decrees
That thou shouldst carry forth thy milk and
    cheese.
For thee to come unto my door with cream
Is but a part of His Eternal Scheme.
So three pints, prithee, of thy lacteous flood,
Which willing udders yield to brace our blood;
And of that cheese, whose fame is widely
    known,
Whose secret only Cheddar's sons do own
(Made from the richness of emulsive fats
And churned e'en richer in their ligneous
    vats),
A half-pound, prithee; and of yellow cream
A half-pint, pray — but not that watery stream
Men know as 'single' — no, the 'double' sort
That can be whipped to pinnacles for sport,
As when the mighty waves, by Boreas lash'd
Rise up in fury, till the rocks be splash'd
And fearful mariners, that con the sky,
Do shake their head and wink their weather-eye,

All fearful to outface the furious storm,
While quick waves break, and then, as quick,
  reform,
And trembling sailors can be heard to utter —
Oh, I forgot — add half a pound of butter!

Philip Kerr

HOME FROM THE HILL

Sometimes, the strangest stories that concern Edinburgh are the ones that begin on the other side of the world . . .

About fifteen years ago, before I enjoyed a certain literary celebrity, I went travelling in the South Seas and, being from Edinburgh and an aspiring, albeit unsuccessful, writer, naturally I visited Samoa which was where Scotland's greatest novelist, Robert Louis Stevenson, had died, in 1894.

The islands — there are two: American Samoa, where there is a naval base, and Western Samoa, comprising Savai'i and Upolu, where Stevenson's house is to be found — don't have much of a tourist industry, which is hardly surprising given how difficult it is to reach them, the frequent cyclones, the lack of decent beaches, and the few hotels. Arriving in Apia harbour off a container ship from New Zealand that was bound for the Panama Canal, and then Florida, I stayed at the Tusitala, which was what the locals had called Stevenson. The name means, the teller of tales. I don't know what the Samoans would have thought of this particular tale. These days the locals are more interested in rugby than they are in literature.

After his death, Stevenson's house, Vailima,

was sold as a working plantation, but it was currently under the management of the government of Western Samoa. Hence, like many other publicly owned buildings on the island, the largely wooden house was in a poor state of repair; and it would be several more years before Vailima would benefit from the management of some dedicated American Mormons. Nevertheless the house enjoyed an enviable location on a beautiful plateau with dramatic sea views and I was not surprised to learn that nearby there were several smart villas that were considered the best on the island.

That was my second day on Samoa. On the third I had resolved to visit the summit of Mount Vaea, and was advised by the owner of the Tusitala Hotel to leave before six the next morning, for he told me the climb was a difficult one. He did not exaggerate, for although the first part of the climb seemed no more challenging than a walk up Arthur's Seat in Edinburgh, the second part, which was through tropical rainforest along a so-called trail that was often blocked by fallen trees, or boulders, did not appear to have been used in years. For a while I even thought I was lost, and by the time I emerged from the silent forest, on to the little clearing where the grave was located, I was lathered with sweat.

The grave itself was larger than I had expected. Made of stone and painted white it most resembled a long house of the kind that could still be seen in certain parts of the island, and was covered with various inscriptions,

227

including the famous verse by Stevenson himself:

> *Under the wide and starry sky,*
> *Dig the grave and let me lie,*
> *Glad did I live and gladly die,*
> *And I laid me down with a will.*
>
> *This be the verse you grave for me,*
> *'Here he lies where he longed to be,*
> *Home is the sailor, home from the sea*
> *And the hunter home from the hill.'*

But any surprise I might have felt on finding that this epitaph included a simple mistake — 'home from the sea' instead of 'home from sea' — was overcome by the discovery that, despite the still comparatively early hour, someone had beaten me up the trail to the summit and to the grave. I had intended that I might be alone with the spirit of Stevenson. And so I was irritated to find that someone else was already there; moreover that he should be another Scot.

Finsbury was a tall, cadaverous and faintly sinister-looking man, with a droopy moustache and a rather fashionable-looking tropical suit. He did not look like much company. But after only a few minutes conversation, it was soon clear to me that he was a much more devoted fan of RLS than I had ever been, for he possessed such a strong acquaintance with Stevenson's work that he was able to quote from even the most esoteric of the essays and poems; and, despite my early reservations, I soon found that Finsbury was able to provide me with a fascinating insight into the tragically short life of Samoa's most famous former resident.

'You know a lot about RLS,' I told Finsbury as finally we left the graveside and began to make our way back down the hill towards Vailima.

'I've made a special study of him,' admitted Finsbury, tugging nervously at his moustache.

'Are you planning a book?'

'God no, although I know a lot that isn't even in the standard biographies.'

'Such as?'

'Such as the pact Stevenson made with the devil when he was still living in Edinburgh,' said Finsbury, lighting a marijuana cigarette.

'Really? What evidence is there for such a thing?'

'There's the evidence of the stories, for a start. *The Bottle Imp. Doctor Jekyll and Mister Hyde. The Suicide Club. The Master of Ballantrae.* All demonstrate a preoccupation with Man's inner demons. Then there's Stevenson's travelling. Have you ever wondered why he tried to put so much distance between himself and Edinburgh?'

'I assumed for health reasons. He had TB, didn't he?'

'Most people make that assumption. Yes, he had TB. But the simple fact of the matter is that he was afraid. He was trying to get away from something. From someone.'

'You're not serious.'

Finsbury smiled. 'Maybe. But since you say you're a writer yourself and you're from

Edinburgh, I'd be more than happy to show you the pact. I think it will interest you. Come to my house and I'll show it to you.'

'You live on Samoa?'

'Yes,' Finsbury said wistfully. 'I'd like to go back home to Edinburgh, but I'm stuck here for the present. So I visit Stevenson's house almost every other day. Or sometimes the grave. In a way it makes me feel closer to home, somehow.'

Over a few whiskies and some more dope at Finsbury's handsome house — he lived in one of the handsome and desirable villas near Vailima — he showed me a black morocco leather volume in which all but the first six of its sixty-six vellum pages were blank. I cannot answer for the handwriting, but immediately I recognised the Vailima bookplate of Stevenson's own design.

'Is this an unpublished story?' I asked, having read the pages: the wording was unmistakably Faustian. 'Or perhaps the notes for a work he left unfinished?'

'Something like that,' said Finsbury.

'But this manuscript must be worth thousands.'

'Probably.'

I looked around Finsbury's well-appointed house and felt a pang of envy.

'You seem to have everything. A fine house. Lots of wonderful books. Plenty of money.'

'Are you interested in money?'

'Who isn't interested in money?'

'Nobody who's from Edinburgh,' remarked Finsbury. 'Would *you* like to make some money?'

Finsbury seemed to be reading my mind. After the expense of my trip aboard the container ship from New Zealand, I was down to my last five hundred dollars.

'Sure. Who doesn't?'

'I need someone to take something to Edinburgh for me.'

'What kind of something?'

'The best-not-ask-any-questions kind. It's worth five grand to you.'

'Jesus.'

I told Finsbury I'd think about it. But later, when he showed me the package, the risk seemed negligible. The package was no bigger than a paperback. On the wrapping was an address in Edinburgh's New Town. Perhaps it was the familiarity of the destination that made the job seem easy. And so I agreed.

Of course, I guessed it must be drugs. Heroin, probably, at the price I was being paid. A grand up front and the balance on delivery. But it *was* easy. Even easier than I had expected. I almost forgot I even had the package until I arrived in the UK again. I know that sounds strange. But it's true. Even by the time I was back on a boat to New Zealand, it was almost like my meeting with Finsbury had never happened.

About four weeks later, when I was back in Scotland, I went to the address on the label and handed over the package to a handsome-looking man with a goatee beard who seemed very surprised to see me. But he asked me inside and agreed to pay my fee without demur.

I waited for a while in a comfortable room

with an enormous window and a clifftop view of the Dean Village that would have given an eagle pause for thought.

'Will you sign for this?' he asked, suddenly reappearing and handing me my cash.

'Sure,' I said, eager to pocket the money and be off. And it was a minute or two before I realised what I had signed.

'Is this a joke?' I asked.

'Rather an expensive joke, wouldn't you say?'

'But what was in the parcel?'

'You're looking at it.'

I stared at the same black morocco leather book Finsbury had shown me in Samoa, and in which I had just signed my name. Strangely there was now no mention of RLS in the book at all.

'How is Stevenson?' asked the bearded man. 'Or Finsbury, as I suppose you must know him?'

I stayed silent, astonished by this turn of events.

'Look,' said the man, 'you can tear up that little agreement if you want. But think about it first. Think about getting a novel published. Being famous. Hollywood film deals. Making a shit load of money. Think about all that. And then decide. I think you'll find I can help. You'd be surprised how much.'

'But who are you?'

'Who am I? That's a difficult one, Philip. May I call you Philip? I feel I know you so well already. Look, for the moment why don't you just think of me as a kind of agent?'

Malcolm Bradbury

CONVERGENCE

1

Aloha! This word means welcome in our islands. Perhaps you have already experienced some of our traditional warm hospitality. People who come here always seem to enjoy to be greeted with the *lei*, our necklace of tropical flowers. This is one of many customs from our old days that still survive. Especially here at the airport.

Maybe you know our islands have a very varied history. They were discovered by Captain James Cook, a very famous Britisher who made a tour of the Pacific in the eighteenth century and discovered many things. Of course he didn't really discover the islands. They were here a long time before that, as everyone who lived here knew already. Captain Cook was a very famous navigator and he was received here with the *lei*, and other great demonstrations of astonishment and delight. It is very sad he was killed here a little while after, simply because of a misunderstanding over a canoe. But our chiefs made an idol of his bones, and they worshipped him, until our all idols and tattoos were abolished by the Christian missionaries. Cook gave these islands a name, the Sandwich Islands. Don't think this is because of what we eat here. They were named

233

after a British earl who liked fast food. In history these islands used to have their own kings, who have been depicted on the postage stamps. For a long time we were part of the famous British Empire, and in those days the islands had two names. Then we became a territory of the United States, and now we are a very proud state of the union. Of course we like being American very much better. By the way, the name Sandwich Islands is no longer used.

(When I first learned to stand on my head, says the girl, I got so excited I wanted to do it wherever I went).

Many great writers have authored books about these islands. Persons as famous as Captain Cook, of course, who wrote about them before he died, and Isabella Bird, and Mark Twain the humorist, who came to the islands after a volcanic eruption and wrote some letters about his experiences which helped to make him very famous. Of course I don't need to mention the famous name of James A. Michener, who wrote the biggest and most famous book of all, which I expect all of you have read. If anybody likes history, you might like to look at a book called *A Portrait of a Sandwich Islander*, which is all about the old days. By the way, the map in it is no longer used.

Because they are located right here in the middle of the Pacific Ocean, these islands may seem very remote to some of you. That does not mean they have not played an important part in history. For example without these islands we might never have had World War 2. Who remembers the date of 7 December 1941? That was the day the Japanese air force took off from their carriers and bombed the American fleet over at Pearl Harbor. That made President Roosevelt declare war on them and that was the start of World War 2. You can visit the site today and see a floating museum and memorial to this effect, with some of the real wrecked ships and a video presentation.

(Do you jog at all? asks the girl. I jog twenty minutes at least every day. If I miss more than three days I know my muscles are going to fall to pieces).

But here on the islands we like to think all these things are way in the past. We like to think here all persons of all races can get along with one another just fine. We like to think maybe we're the real hub of the whole Pacific Rim. Most peoples from everywhere come through here these days, because we're a great stopover, and so our population has every kind of ethnic source. Successive waves have placed many nationalities here, including Chinese, Taiwanese, Japanese, Filipino, Indonesian, Portuguese, Hawaiian and of course mainland American, all living in happiness together. Many languages are spoken in the islands, including pidgin. One of the great attractions of the islands is that you can eat here in all sorts of ways, and dress any way you like.

Someone once called these islands Paradise, and we think those guys really knew a thing or two. Except did you know there are no snakes in the islands, so that makes it even better than paradise, right? At least, there are two snakes, but those are in the zoo, and they're both male. This is required by federal legislation. One important fact about the islands is they have very little wildlife, and that's because they're isolated and volcanic in origin. A marvel of nature, they rose from the deep bottom of the sea in a number of massive explosions. There are many mountains, their lower slopes all enrobed in dark forest. Altogether there are forty volcanic peaks, but don't worry, most of them are inactive. On the eastward islands eruptions can occur quite often, even as often as last year. By the way, we don't expect anything of this kind during your visit, and if we hear anything unusual we'll let you know.

(Are you interested in Rudolph Steiner at all? asks the girl).

As I said, many people have come to call these islands paradise, and you only have to look round you or stick around a little on vacation to find out why. The vegetation is lush, the air is temperate, and the sea is blue. Average daytime and night-time temperatures are available in your travel and vacation packs, complete with beach and inter-island travel information, and advice on the best hotels and rentals. I guess I don't need to tell you we got beaches and surf.

Have we got surf! I'd also like to remind you about our show, because we have a really nice little show here on the island. It's called *Invitation to Paradise*, and it's performed on selected days. A cast of 175 real islanders perform authentic folk dances, from Tahiti, Tonga, Samoa, Fiji, Maori and the old Hawaii. As the show unfolds, a fiery volcanic effect will command your attention. By the way, you'll find plenty more information about all that in your travel packs.

So again we say aloha!, and will you now make your way to the car park, where you'll find transport provided to take you to your next destination.

(It seems so weird, says the girl, being here without John. He's had to stay on in New York City. He teaches a course on the enjoyment of death).

2

Aloha. Welcome to the Hale Kokua Center. In order to make your stay more comfortable, we have designed this handy information pack, to acquaint you fully with our various services, rules and procedures.

State law forbids gaming, firearms, and solicitation on state property. There are no special quiet hours, but we request you to keep noise to a minimum in the evenings out of consideration for others. The orange arrows identify your floor. The elevators take only ten adult persons. Request a key if you stay out late. The desk provides the following services: loan of sports equipment, typewriters, hairdryers; light-bulb exchange; lost keys; messages; checkout; information. Bare feet are at your own risk.

Remember, this is an experiment in international living among different races and creeds. Be tolerant of others. Avoid embarrassment in the corridors. In an experiment in international living, most tension occurs in the bathrooms. Attached is a list which indicates the items you're supposed to receive in our room during your stay. They've already been checked by your staff, so they should be properly provided. Please sign the bottom of the sheet to show you have received them.

> Table lamp (1)
> Soap dish (1)
> Toshiba fan (1)
> Digital radio-clock (1)
> Tumblers (2)
> Pitcher (1)
> Towels (2)
> Washcloth (1)
> Personal soaps (2)

Have a good stay with us. Lock your room and your valuables away at all times. The Center is not responsible for personal loss or damage to resident possessions. Theft or suspicious person: notify the staff on duty.

Thank you!!! Wallace Yamashita, Your Staff Assistant.

*(Why don't we take a walk in the gardens? says
the girl. It helps you get over the jet lag).*

3

Japanese garden. Visitors welcome. Garden is
maintained for your viewing pleasure. Please
restrict traffic to front grassy area. No private or
commercial use. No food or animals. These are
sacred Japanese carp *(koi)*, symbols of longevity
and order. They cost a hundred dollars or more.
Please don't feed me, I'm on a fish diet. A
garden is a place of peace, and always there is
running water.

(The carp are big and solemn. They navigate
seriously under the flow. Then they jump, take
flies from the air, plop bug-eyed back into their
own element again. Their eyes seem highly attentive to the upper world. Their mouths are large,
noisy, sucking orifices. Around us underground
water jets burst into stuttering life and spray their
rainbow jetstreams over the artificial lawns.)

*(I think those Japanese fish are really lewd, says
the girl, tucking her long skirt under her thighs
on the watered and highly green grass. Well,
don't you think sucking is sexy?)*

4

Aloha! Hi! Welcome to the conference restaurant.
Attention! People with pacemakers: microwave

oven in building. This restaurant operates a serve yourself system. Please choose only one: Thousand Islands or Rocquefort. Try the local tropical fruit. Low calorie. High protein. Salt free. Use heat-resistant cups for hot drinks only. Wait until machine totalises before putting in new coin. Vending guaranteed, do not kick. Express lane: five food items or less. This fountain is for human use only. Smokers: please respect the rights of others.

(I guess I'm really a vegetarian, says the girl, but I'd like some of that).

This table can accommodate you. In our culture no part of food is wasted. Even the webbed feet of duck are dried and used. The food is allowed to have its own nature. It is fibre and semen and fat, eggy and uncooked, the raw fish, the poo poo . . .

(Hey, you must be hungry, says the girl. Wouldn't you like me to give you a proper calorie count on all of that?)

5

Aloha, everybody! The ones on the right are juices and soft drinks, these on the left are manhattan, martini and gin and tonic . . . Oh Kim, Kim, my old Korean friend, you are so far from us in Asia. So what are you doing these days, why don't you send us zen any more? . . . It

240

is my privilege on behalf of the foundation to bid you all welcome to what we all expect will be a major conference and talkfest . . . Ah, but let the Westerner always remember that for instance *Mansfield Park* is not always perfectly comprehended by our students in Japan . . . So many people, from so many countries, ensuring a meaningful dialogue . . . To take a single example, baths do not mean the same thing in every culture . . . Where better than here in these islands, the meeting place of East and West? . . . I think man-woman relationships are changing now in all the places . . . That is why so many people, writers and scholars, have been invited to come here. Where better, with such distinguished guests, to understand the multi-cultural universe of the new millennium? . . .

(Between my divorce and the AA I've had so much to do, says the girl).

6

Great! I think this has been a really excellent session. I'm sure we all of us want to thank both of you, for presenting us with that very beautiful poem and that very beautiful story. I wonder if you could explain them to us just a little?

In my poem, we have the pear blossom passing across the face of a fixed star. Then, in despair, the girl spreads the hairs in her armpit, and the wind carries her away. You must understand it does not translate very well. In our language we

241

have a phonetic syllabary and ideogrammic symbols, and we can also add the phonetics of the Chinese characters at the side. Also in my culture there is no word for 'I'. Therefore we have to manufacture a way to say it. In the poem I use a foreign character that means a private person. Now we have a rebellion against the classical, a return to the collective and moral culture. Oh, by the way, women in my culture have a different form of literature to write in. At the end of the poem the woman is speaking, and we are no longer looking at each other.

(It's a necklace I bought at the stopover in Pago Pago, says the girl).

That's great! I suggest we all discuss that.

Excuse me, in Sanskrit there is no word for conscience. You are moral and mental people, but we are metaphysical . . . Perhaps we should ask this question: why have so many Japanese novelists in recent times have committed suicide? Maybe it is because they tried to grow an unnatural foreign ego in their native souls . . . Yes, but the role of the narrative self has also been subsumed in contemporary Western, that is to say, postmodern writing. The lore of Marxism and deconstruction has been increasingly applied. In the French *nouveau roman*, as you remember Roland Barthes has once noted, language acts lexically, foregrounding the elements of text and certain tropic states of mind, to the point where perceptions of objects exceed

242

their apparent function, and conventional literary space is redefined. Of course, we all see ourselves as part of Asia in this new global age . . . Excuse me, sir, I should like to point to a falsie in your argument . . .

In the story you heard, the boy flees into the bush, pursued by the ghost of his grandfather. This is a bitter indictment of a modern world which has distorted progress. In expressing the story, the writer senses the postwar world is over at last. He makes a free stream of consciousness, using the simile of sex surrounding a person's soul like a rainbow . . .

(Have you ever tried taking a shower with a Korean? asks the girl).

7

Aloha! Welcome to the Ala Moana Shopping Center, which for a long time was the biggest shopping centre in the world. Maybe it still is. That's because the islands have always been a meeting place for international trade, a crossover place for style. Take my word, there's hardly a country in the world that isn't represented here by a store. I think you'll find there isn't a thing you need you ain't going to be able to get. You'll find Polynesian things, Japanese things, German things, Iranian things, Chinese and Taiwanese things. I'm sure our French representative will be glad to know there's a *boutique francaise*, and for our British representative an authentic British pub with Guinness. I think you'll want to take a long time looking round, so why don't we all meet again by Ben and Jerry's, right across from the McDonald's. Don't forget we have another official reception at five. And if there are any special souvenirs of our island culture you want to take back to your homes, I'll be only too glad to guide you . . .

Trees. Musak. Umbrellas, fire-eaters. Mickey Mouse, twice. Escalators up, escalators down. Screeching macaws, screeching stereos. Japanese teahouse. Hawaiian mummu store. Belgian chocolate shop. Finnish textiles. Thai ties. Xian antiques. Style booths, food booths: Korean, Polynesian, Jewish, Turkish, Polish, Armenian, Sechzuan, Mandarin, Cantonese, Russian, Filipino, junk. Yuppie, guppie. Hippie, faddie. Essential oils and aromas. Ginseng, kouskous. Edible panties. Condom of the Month club. Store after store, orifice after orifice. Level after level, flavour after flavour. Convergence.

(What kind of lifestyle are you shopping for today? asks the girl. I think I see you maybe in French silk underwear with Nike shoes and something Japanese on top).

8

Aloha. As maybe you've already discovered by now, this is the traditional native word for welcome in our islands. This is papaya juice and that is rum. I am sure now that you've seen a little of our glorious sea and our beaches you would like to know a little more about the history of our islands. Ours is an ancient Pacific civilisation with its own famous kings and queens. Most of our indigenous people were of moderate stature, with reddish-brown skin. But the chieftains and the women of their families were remarkable for their height, and four hundred pounds wasn't an unusual weight. This superiority in physique among the nobles is said to be due to a system of massage called the lomi-lomi . . .

(Oh, don't you love massage? says the girl).

As you'll have found out, there are few animals here, and there are no snakes on the island. The only reptiles are skinks and gecko. We have plenty of insects, and cockroaches and green locusts are serious pests. Owing to the nature of our origins, the proportion of endemic plants is greater here than anywhere else. The chelo berry is famous in song and story, and formerly served as a propitiatory offering to Pele. In old times, birds were protected by the native belief that messages from the Gods came to us in the form of bird cries, and also by a royal edict that forbade the killing of the species used for making feather cloaks. There are several old languages, but these are no longer used.

(I'm really starting to get kind of hungry, aren't you? says the girl).

9

Well, good evening, hi there, and how are you tonight! Welcome to Top Floor. Customers tell us we're the best restaurant west of San Francisco, and we want to show you they're right. So I'm Steve, and tonight I'll be helped in serving you by Suzie and Ya-Ya, who are at your full service. Cash is your wine waiter, and he'll come by to greet you in a minute. We want you to feel really wonderful here, and I'm ready to answer any questions you might have about our menu. The soup of the day is asparagus, and that comes with pitta croutons. Chef's choices tonight include pan-fried sturgeon, Cape Cod clams, French escargots, trout from the Maine rivers, venison and several varieties of Alaska salmon. Our produce is fresh, we have flights every day from Boston and San Francisco to make sure you get cream of the crop. If you wish to take a little longer, I'll gladly leave you for a few minutes to study our hand-printed menu and make your personal selection. Meantime duck pate is served at our pleasure. So welcome, you guys, sit back, enjoy, and have a real nice evening.

(*I just don't know which me is me any more, says the girl, the person who was back there with John or the person who's here. I just have this feeling that somewhere, somewhere everything should just come together. Converge, you know what I mean?*)

(I too have this feeling: everywhere people meeting, orifices opening, the mouths of carp snapping, the garden streaming, the water-jets juddering.)

(*Oh, and that question you never made up your mind to ask me, says the girl, I guess the answer is yes.*)

10

Manoa! We hoped you enjoyed your stay in our experiment in international living. If we've succeeded with you, please let us know. If not, just tell us on this form where we went wrong.

1. Your room was as clean and orderly as your own home, right?
    Right: —
    Wrong: —
2. Everything in your room worked, right?
    Right: —
    Wrong: —
3. Your kitchen was properly provisioned at all times, right?
    Right: —
    Wrong: —
4. Maybe it wasn't the most fantastic experience of your whole life, but it came close, right?
    Right: —
    Wrong: —

THANKS FOR YOUR HELP.
AND COME BACK, YOU ALL.

(I don't think it's such a great idea if I give you my home address, says the girl. I don't really have a fixed location, and I don't think I know who I am anyway.)

11

Manoa, everybody. I hope you had a very fruitful conference in our lovely international islands here in the middle of our beautiful Pacific ocean, and that our really fine weather helped you get together in a useful way. I hope you're all going back to your countries feeling refreshed.

In these islands we have a pleasant custom on departure. It is the *lei*, a necklace of flowers. It means welcome, of course, but also farewell. What it really means is we wish you will come back to see us because after what you have experienced you will never want to stay apart from us again. These *leis* are presented to you by the society for Eastern and Western friendship, bringing together all races and creeds. Please check with your airline to make sure your countries will accept them.

(Sometimes I'd like just to spread the hairs in my armpit and let the wind just carry me away, says the girl. And, flowers round her neck, she goes to the New York check-in, while I head for the London flight.)

Dorothy Nimmo

SESTINA

When we were young there was this game
we'd play, where the garden
ran wild to the river. Small fish
made rings in the shadow-water, light
fractured the summer-time,
clocks clicked the house towards dark.

We would sleep under our dark
duvets, tired by relentless games,
growing taller, until it was time
for us to leave the garden,
the trees, the roses, the underwater light
glinting on shoals of little fish.

Have you gone off to fish?
Do you still get up early in the dark,
creep barefoot in the thin light
while shadows strengthen? What game
are you playing now? Outside the garden
casting your line time after time after time?

Have you caught anything all this time?
Is there, after all this trouble, even one
    fish?
A tiny one? For you to carry up the garden
grinning, for me to fillet? It's too dark
now to finish this last game.
I tap the cards together, turn off the light.

But this evening, in the thin clear light,
you turn up again. For a long time,
years, I've played this esoteric game
cards flipping over, smooth like fish,
as I waited for you to come in from those
  dark
hiding-places you made in the garden.

You are outside now in the garden —
I catch that sharp whiff of ladslove the
  light
breeze carries over the lawn. It's quite
  dark.
I knew there would come a time
when you'd have caught every last fish
and there'd be no point going on with this
  game.

My old love, the game's up. It's time for
  me to walk
down in the dark to the end of the garden,
hear the fish jump, see the light fade.

A PHOTO OF ROGER

He drapes himself over his mother, says,
  No.
We just want him to behave himself,
to be a good boy. Our mouths are set,
we bribe, coax, threaten but he can't
  behave himself,
he has too much sense of himself
that he mustn't betray if it's to come to
  good.

In this space full of images of people
dressed up as people he takes himself
   away,
at the end of his tether: *What I'm going to*
   do now
is I'm going down field with my tractor
I'm going down to bring cows in,
that's what I'm going to do.

His self (his true self, full of pain and fear,
sensitive and self-centred as it must be)
is no good to us. He moves away into his
   own space,
abandons us and our own selves are full of
   pain and fear,
sensitive and self-centred as they must be.

Julia O'Faolain

IN A SMALL CIRCUS

For moments tight smiles hovered on the solicitor's lips, then expanded thinly as though on the wires of an abacus. 'Desmond Lynch,' the solicitor introduced himself, and thrust a hand across his desk. Jittery! Sean was not surprised. The late Father Tim Cronin had been Lynch's cousin.

'And you are Sean Dunne. Sean, how are you? A sad occasion.'

'Yes.' Guardedly.

'Sit down. Sit down.'

Leaning back and away from each other, the two made reticent probes. Hadn't they, each wondered, met before? Neither could quite say when. Maybe when Sean, then still in short pants, had earned tips by carrying fishing tackle to and from the landing stage? Above on the lake? Fifteen years ago, could it be?

'I'm afraid it could.'

'Back in the slow old days,' said Lynch.

'Yes.'

In Sean's memory a rowboat scored the lake's shine with a wake like a kite's tail. Bottles of lemonade, towed through those waters, stayed cool even on the hottest days, for the lake was fed by mountain streams. Churning past peat and stones, these jinked from silver to amber,

252

leaving a gauze of froth on reeds and sedge. For years Father Tim had been the parish priest in the valley, and Lynch had spent almost all his weekends in a lakeside cottage now rented to Germans.

'Tim Cronin and I were close,' said Lynch. 'Poor Tim! He was a good man!' As though startled by what he'd said, he began to talk about the will and about how, lest unforeseen claims be made against the estate, the bulk of the money could not be paid out just yet. This, he explained, was normal practice. No need for concern! He shook his head, and this time his smile lingered. Did he think Sean still needed reassurance? Sean did. He felt numb: the news gagged him. This legacy, he told himself with shamed eagerness, could change his life. Money! His mind reeled, then raced, working out that there'd be more than enough to get a phone hooked up, employ a boy full time and put his market garden on a sustainable footing! Maybe buy a refrigerated van?

'Sustainable' had been the bank manager's word, last year, when refusing Sean's request for a loan. 'I'd like to be more positive,' the man had said, 'but it's out of my hands.' A business, he had explained, must look sustainable before he could advise the bank to invest. Sean's didn't.

'My bosses like to allow no margin for error.'

'Hard men!' Sean had tried to make a joke of it, but the manager didn't return his grin.

Now though . . . In a way, Sean was just as glad there were drawbacks. They made his luck look less odd — the way silver linings weren't

253

odd when there were clouds. Well, there were plenty of those! Scads! Poor Father Tim had had a bad time at the end. It was what had given him his stroke. Massive and sudden, this had cut him down from one day to the next! A man who had never been ill! Though wasn't it queer that he'd had time . . . queer — the word tripped Sean, but he swept it aside, marvelling instead at the surprise legacy: his big chance. Manna! Come to think of it, wasn't there a lot more money coming than he'd just mentally disposed of? There was! Yes! Jesus! What would he do with the surplus? And so what if people said it was tainted and that there was a stigma attached! He didn't care. Or rather, yes, he cared greatly about poor Father Tim, but not . . . Confusion, spreading, like ink in water, darkened his mind. It could become chronic, he told himself. It could recur like one of those freak pains that are put down to wind or allergy, signals of some hidden trouble that needs to be addressed.

As if pinpointing this, his suit, unworn in years, was painfully tight. The bus ride into town had left it wrinkled; the waistband was cutting into his stomach, and his feelings were haywire. Sorrow for his dead — should he call him benefactor? — was snagged in awkwardness. He hadn't attended the funeral, so wearing the penitential dark suit today was his tribute.

He wished now that he *had* gone to the funeral. Paid his respects. Who had, he wondered? Mr Lynch must surely have, but probably nobody else from around here. It was held in Dublin. Father Cronin had been retired from parish work some time ago and put to teaching in a Dublin school. Just as well, people had murmured later, when rumours began to leak.

Sean was anxious about publicity. Would there be more, he asked, hoping the question didn't sound ungrateful, then saw that it did. Hot as metal, a flush burned his cheeks.

'Have some decency!' he told himself. 'Keep your gob shut!' Aloud he attempted to withdraw the query but heard his voice blab out of control, making things worse. 'I . . . it's not the publicity itself, but . . .' He had no idea how to ask for the enlightenment he craved.

'Well, that's not my province. However . . .' The solicitor glanced out the window, then back at Sean and paused. The will, he said at last, would have to be published in the newspaper. There was no getting around that. It was the law. When Sean asked how the case would be if he said no to the legacy, Mr Lynch noted that a refusal would not make the matter less public.

'It might make it more so!'

Mr Lynch's spectacles shone, and when he dipped his head to stare over them, his gaze doubled. 'Four eyes,' thought Sean idly. A refusal, said the lawyer, would excite comment. Busying himself with papers, he imposed another pause.

This one had a suppressed hum. It was sly: the sort you got in towns like this, in out-of-season pubs while drinkers stared into the black of their pints and dreamed up slanders. Jokes. Hurtful gossip about — never mind about what! With luck, Lynch was thinking less of slanders than of how to fend them off. That surely must be a lawyer's job, and he looked just the man to do it. Judging by this office — the glass! the pale wood! the space! — he'd got his hands on some of the money now pouring into the county thanks to the tourist boom and grants to big farmers. Sean had seen none of it. But once he got going with his market garden — an idea of Father Cronin's — he could sell with profit to those who had. Not all of Cronin's enthusiasms had been in step with the times, but this one was shrewd. Almost four years ago, while here on a flying visit, he had dropped off a stack of seed catalogues along with samples and advice that had proved spot on.

'Your farm's too small for livestock,' he'd told Sean. 'That's why your dad could never make a go of it. But have you thought of draining the lower field and putting up polythene tunnels? There are markets now for fresh vegetables.'

How had he known that? He wasn't even living here any more! He was alert. That was how! Concerned. Interested! A lovely, lively man! And look what thanks he got. Poor Father Tim! He'd put himself out for people — and come a cropper. But he'd been right about the markets. Customers *were* ready to fork out and pay fancy prices for novelties: lamb's lettuce and wild rocket. Chicory, artichokes, mangetout and fennel. Endive and radicchio. Baby marrows. Anything out of the ordinary. The plants thrived in the raised beds of rich mud which Sean had reclaimed from the lake, and already he was sending deliveries to three towns. By bus. With a van he'd be able to go further afield. Posh restaurants were springing up like mushrooms.

Poor Father Tim, who was always ready to rejoice in other people's luck, would have been pleased.

Was there a risk though, Sean worried, that spiteful talk could hurt sales? How to stop it he wondered. By sending out solicitor's letters? To whom? Best ask Lynch. Paper was plainly *his* weapon. Wedged into box files, it manned the shelves behind him while, smoothed out on the desk, thumb-worn documents, soft with creases, looked ready to split along the folds. Some, no doubt, held the sort of secrets to which lawyers were as privy as priests.

The thought wound back to Cronin and to the stacks, not of paper but of crisply porous pancakes seasoned with jam and whiskey which he had loved to cook for Sean and his mother when he came to their cottage for supper.

'Wouldn't His Reverence make someone a grand wife!' The tart joke had signalled Sean's mother's resistance. The priest, as a friend of her late husband's, had wanted Sean to go to boarding school.

'He's got the grey matter. We could get him a scholarship. Would you not think about it, Máire?'

But the widow thought only of her loneliness. Few, she argued, who left came back! Look what had happened to her poor husband, Bat.

What had happened was that Bat, being desperate for cash to stock their small, run-down farm, went to work for a North London builder, fell off a roof and died. Hopes of compensation died too when witnesses blamed the fall on Bat's having drunk too many pints on his lunch break in a pub called the Good Mixer.

'Poor Bat! Why wouldn't he drink and he far from home?'

Once tears started, talk of boarding school had to be set aside and the widow comforted with more pancakes and hot whiskey.

'*Crêpes*,' the priest called the light concoctions which he tossed with a flourish of his frying pan — he always brought his own — turning them out as thin as doilies and as lacy with air bubbles as fizzy lemonade. 'Gluttony,' he'd say, patting his troublesome paunch, 'is a safe sin and unlikely to lead to worse.' He kept the paunch more or less in order by rowing round the lake or hiking over mountain bogs to shoot snipe.

Another hobby was writing children's books which, to his amazement, made money. He was a lively man whose popularity was heightened by rumours that he had been exiled to this parish after falling foul of Rome. Cronin was a local name, so he was liked for that too; but what gave him glamour was the whisper that he had been groomed to be a high-flier, then grounded. Connoisseurs of sad balladry, the locals commiserated. The false dawn of the 1960s had misled Father Tim who, having joined the Church in its moment of exuberant reform, felt he'd been sold a pup when ex-classmates were punitively dispersed and their mentor, a liberal theologian, kicked upstairs to Rome where the Polish ecclesiastical mafia could keep tabs on him.

Cronin himself ended up in what some wag dubbed 'this Irish Siberia'.

'Remember what they say about ill winds? They've blown our own man back to us! We should be grateful!'

'We should be thanking our stars!'

Sean couldn't remember who'd said that. It could have been almost anyone, softened by pity and the pleasure of hearing Father Tim sing. For he had that talent too. Both in the gloom of the hotel bar — brown but glinty with glass cases displaying stuffed fish — and out on the lake he would always oblige with a song. And he sang well. Though no one wondered at first whether he felt drawn to riskier pleasures, the question, later, grew hard to dodge.

* * *

'The Church,' Mr Lynch assured Sean, 'has no claim on the money coming to you. It's from his children's books. Did your father read them to you? When my kids were small they loved me to read them aloud.'

Sean, who had thought the books silly, didn't say so. They were about some animal, and his father's copies had been lent or given away. Sean had been ten when his father fell from the roof, and what he remembered was the priest saying he'd try to take his place, 'until we're all together again'. Cronin had put his arms around Sean and soothed and rocked him until it felt as if his father really were in some way present. After that the priest sang a great, deep, glum but somehow comforting hymn which made Sean cry. Father Cronin had had a thrilling bass voice. Calling him 'father' was embarrassing though, so Sean wouldn't.

'Nor 'Daddy'! I can't call you that!' Half laughing, he'd licked smeared tears from his fingers.

'Call me Tim so.'

'I'm too young. People here wouldn't like it.'

'Why wouldn't they?'

'Because you're a priest.'

Father Cronin blew out an angry breath. 'Do they think I should be on the job full time? Wearing the aul' collar?'

'Collar?'

'The Roman one. It's like being on a leash. Like having a sign that says 'the wearer of this may at no time be teased, shown affection or otherwise distracted from his function'.'

Sean must have looked puzzled, for Cronin squeezed his shoulder and began to sing a song about a cowboy who was 'wrapped in white linen and going to die'. It had an Irish tune and he said that what it was really about was syphilis.

'Don't be shocked,' he told Sean. 'Stories about the pain in everyday lives hold more for us than ones about shoot-outs and bent sheriffs.'

But Cronin wouldn't have mentioned syphilis to a ten-year-old, so that must have been said years later — maybe when the priest was being obliged to leave the valley and was once again singing his sad songs. Both times he advised Sean to forget the story about his father's drinking in the Good Mixer and any notions he

260

might be harbouring of going to London to sort out the treacherous witnesses. 'That's cowboy stuff,' he warned. 'Dangerous! Indeed most dreams of justice and improvement do more harm than good.'

'Was he unhappy?' Sean asked Lynch, who said Tim might have been better off in some foreign slum or shantytown where he'd have felt needed.

'His parish here was getting depopulated, so what was there for him to do? Fish? Chat with me on the phone? Take a trip to Cork or Dublin? Mostly, there he'd be, stuck in that grim presbytery with sly young curates whom he daren't trust. Having to mind what he said. A brilliant man who'd loved company and adored children. The stories he wrote for them tell a lot! You'll remember, maybe, that they were about a seal which played so restlessly in the water that a great foam ruff formed around its neck, and people cried, 'That seal should be in a circus!' But this was the creature's downfall for it grew ambitious. Of course,' Lynch shook his head, 'it was a secret parable. The seal was Cronin himself: black with a white collar, too clever for his own good, stuck in the wrong element and yearning to be on a bigger stage. That private joke gave the stories edge.'

'It passed me by,' Sean admitted.

'It did?' Lynch looked disappointed. 'That's because you hadn't known him when he was young. I suppose you won't remember the talk of priests marrying either? Tim firmly believed for years that that reform was in the pipeline.

261

Wishful thinking, to be sure! He'd wanted kids of his own, you see. He envied me my three and desperately needed something more than he had in his life. He'd gone to Rome very young as secretary to one of the more go-ahead theologians working on the Council and found it hard, later, to simmer down. I used to tell him that the fiery haloes the old painters drew around saints' heads showed that their brains were boiling like his, and that their purgatory was going on inside them. He'd laugh and say I should have been a theologian. When I read his stories, I told him that his seal's foam ruff was a fallen halo. Ash!'

'Rome was the circus?'

'Oh, the Circus Maximus! What else?' Lynch's tone was lightly scornful. 'I suppose you read the stories *about* him too? Later. In the press? Flimsy speculation amplified by gossip! To my mind they'd not have stood up in court. Remember what was said?'

Sean nodded. How forget? It was a year now since Sergeant Breen had delivered his tip-off. The day had been clear and cool. A breeze, ruffling the lake, made it shiver like foil, and the dazzle in Sean's eye lingered long after he'd stepped, squinting, into the shade.

Broom in hand and clad in a cast-off cassock, he was busy cleaning the lakeside chapel for the May devotions when a shadow alerted him. The policeman stood in the arched doorway, blocking the light. The arch was narrow, and Breen was a burly man. The chapel, a Victorian-Gothic folly, stayed locked all winter, and Sean kept the key.

262

'Mister Dunne!'

'What can I do for you?' Sean's mock-formality matched the sergeant's. He had been to school with Breen's sons, Seamus and J.J., so being addressed as 'Mister' was either a joke or it meant something was up.

'Let's talk in my car.' As Breen's silhouette backed towards the light, the nap on his uniform glowed like filament.

Sean followed him out, then, once in the gàrda car, wished he had stopped to remove the niffy, soiled cassock. It was only good now for use as an overall when clearing out the mould and mouse droppings which collected in the chapel every winter. One year he had found bats.

'You've been a sort of volunteer sexton, have you?' Breen put the car into gear. 'Since Father Cronin's day?'

There was something about his tone.

'You know I have.' Sean tried to get the cassock off, but lacked space for manoeuvre, and the cloth tore. Rotten! At one time he had enjoyed wearing the old garment. It had carried prestige, set off his waist, and swung pleasingly when he strode. A label with a coat of arms was sewn into one seam. The young Father Cronin had had it made by a Roman tailor, and in its day it had had style. Now, well . . . Sean started to undo the buttons.

'Good thinking,' said Breen. 'Between myself and yourself, Father Mac doesn't like you wearing that.'

'Oh?'

'I thought you should know.'

'Did he ask you to tell me?' That would be like the new PP. Father MacDermot, Cronin's successor, was leery of local resentments and fond of delegating.

'In a way.' Breen drew up in a rough slot hacked out between tall rhododendrons. Once prized, these were now growing too vigorously, and foresters had turned against them. Blossoms, filtering the sunlight, threw purple patches on the grass. 'Have a read.' Breen handed Sean a folder of newspaper clippings. 'It's background. Father Mac wants you briefed before we meet the men from Dublin. They're trying to mount a case against Cronin.'

'Against Father Tim? What kind of a case? Who?'

The sergeant nodded at the folder. 'That'll help understand.'

Sean ran his eye over headlines which someone had haloed with a yellow marker. '*Roman Catholic monks,*' he read, '*to attend sex-offenders' programme. Church in disarray. Former headmaster denies assaulting boys in dormitories. Priests to resume duties after police find no basis for allegations of abuse. Teacher at St Fiachra's suspended pending ...* ' St Fiachra's was the school where Father Cronin had been teaching.

Sean handed back the file. 'What's this about?' he asked. 'I'm a gom and an innocent. Make it clear to me.'

'Buggery,' said Breen simply. 'Child abuse.' A charge, he explained, had been made by a past pupil of Father Cronin's, and was being investigated. There was no corroborative evidence, so detectives planned to look into the priest's record in this parish. 'Two are coming down this afternoon. We got a message to say they'll want statements from men who were close to Cronin when they were boys. Such as . . . ' Breen's voice wobbled, 'yourself. Mind you,' steadying, the voice soothed, 'it may all fizzle out.'

'You can't prove a negative.' Mr Lynch gave Sean a shrewd look. 'So if rumours bother you, you'd best up sticks and move. Go to Dublin. City people have no time to waste on the past. Here . . . '

'My mother . . . '

'Ah, I forgot. Bedridden, isn't she? With arthritis? So you can't leave.'

'No.'

★ ★ ★

There was probably nothing to it, concluded Breen. Cases of this sort were often either fanciful or touched off by mental trouble. But even those stirred up a stink, and no way did Father Mac or the superintendent of the local gárdaí want fall-out reaching this parish. 'I suppose that cassock was Cronin's? Best give it to me.' Getting out of the car, Breen took a plastic bin liner from the boot, folded the cassock into it and stowed the package away. Returning to his seat, he said he hoped he'd made it clear that Father Mac and the super wanted us all to mind what we said to outsiders.

That included Dublin detectives.

'Discretion is in everyone's interests. Tell them as little as you can.' The big danger, Breen warned, was the press. Sensational newspaper stories could force the hands of the gárdaí and maybe lead to cases for damages. Later. Down the road! 'Then who do you think would be left with the bill? Not Dublin! Us.' Breen's tone was weary. His message whorled like the design on a finger print.

★   ★   ★

'You weren't serious,' Lynch hoped, 'just now about maybe saying 'no' to the legacy.'

Sean blushed. 'No.'

'That's all right so. Because if you did, people would see it as a guilty verdict. That, coming from you, would be damaging.'

★   ★   ★

'There's nothing *to* tell,' Sean told Sergeant Breen. 'Father Cronin was always an innocent.'

'Good man. Stick to that.'

'It's true. He's . . . ' Sean, who had been about to say 'a lovely man', didn't, because just now the words did not sound innocent at all. Neither did 'idealist', which, he knew from Cronin himself, could be code for 'disloyal'. 'What are people saying?' he thought to ask.

'What *aren't* they saying?' Tipping his cap back on his poll, the sergeant threw up his eyes. 'Mostly,' he told the car ceiling, 'they're telling

266

jokes about priests!' Taking a last, red drag from his cigarette, he dropped it through the window, then opened the car door to stamp out the butt. As if ungagged, he began to talk angrily about priest-baiting. 'It's the new sport! People are taking revenge for the way they used to lick clerical boots. That's how it goes! The wind changes and flocks attack their pastors. Killer sheep! Anti-clerical mice! They'll turn on poor Cronin because they used to bow and scrape to him! They'll have it in for you too because they used to envy your friendship with him. Nowadays if they saw you in a cassock, they'd say you were in drag. Cassocks are out! Coats have been turned. Don't look at me like that. I'm too old to turn mine, which is why I'm giving you the benefit of what I know. Steer clear of the lickspittle who gets a chance to spit! My granda told me it was the same when the English left.'

Breen raised his big, soft policeman's palm. Wait, it signalled. 'I know we all wore clerical gear when we were kids serving mass. I did and so did Seamus and J. J. But you kept it up.'

'Jesus, Sergeant Breen!'

'Sean, I'm trying to help. I know you don't go much to pubs because of your father and all. So you mayn't know what people are like now.' The sergeant shook his head. 'They're rabid. Did you hear about the two altar boys in a parish I won't name who tried to blackmail the priest? Threatened to accuse him of abuse if he didn't pay them a hundred pounds apiece, so he denounced them from the pulpit. Guess what happened.'

'The parish wanted to lynch them?'

'Wrong! It wanted to lynch *him*.' Breen's fist thumped his palm. 'What one parishioner told the gárdaí was that most priests — note the 'most'! — only became priests so as to mess with boys. Girls were a risk, but boys were as safe as goats, and access went with the job. 'There they used to be,' says this fellow, 'rows of them with bare thighs and short pants. Choir boys, altar boys and the confirmation class. A sight more convenient than a trip to Thailand.'

Breen's snort of laughter could have been pure shock. The rhododendrons threw a purple splotch on to his already vivid face.

Sean had trouble taking all this in. 'What harm did Father Cronin do anyone?'

'Probably none.' Breen's mood had changed. Adjusting the peak of his cap, he started the engine. 'We'll do our best for him anyway. No need to tell the Dubliners that you and I talked. They asked who here had been close to him, so your name came up. You *were* close, weren't you? What's this that Vincentian used to call you? The one who came every May for the fishing? When you and our J.J. were teenagers. Cronin's 'fidus Achates', was it? What did that mean?'

'How would I know?' Sean remembered the Vincentian. Cheerful Father Jones, a demon at the dartboard. He'd been one of a succession of holiday priests whose mass Sean had served in the island chapel. 'Fidus?' Sean guessed must be like the dog's name 'Fido'. Faithful?

★ ★ ★

268

'Remember the talk of false memory syndrome?' Lynch asked.

'Of course. It showed the charges were lies.'

'Not quite. It stopped them going to court. But stories are like viruses. They mutate.'

* * *

Driving past the lake's sparkle where sharp waves tongued the shore, they reached the small cemetery whose roughly-cut tombstones reflected the sparkle. 'What's that tag about not speaking ill of the dead,' asked Breen. '*De mort . . . what?* You used to be a great one for the Latin tags.'

'I forget.'

'It's a dumb message,' said the policeman. 'It's the living we shouldn't speak ill of. What harm can slanders do the dead?'

Sean, only half listening, burned to think how he'd gloried in being called Cronin's 'fidus Achates'. He hadn't studied Latin, and the visiting priests must have thought him a parrot. No, it seemed likely now that they'd thought something worse! And Cronin let them. Hot with humiliation, Sean thought 'bastard', then told himself that no, the priest had been moved by — what? High spirits? Carelessness? Loneliness? Affection? Poor bastard! Poor Father Tim.

'*De mortuis,*' he told Breen, '*nil nisi bonum.*'

'That's it,' said the sergeant. '*Nil nisi bonum!* A pity we can't manage that for the living! Here you are home. Someone will come for you when the Dubliners get in. In the morning, maybe

269

around ten. Will that be all right?'

Sean said it would. Getting out of the car, he started up his own pathway.

'Oh, I'll forget my head yet,' the sergeant called after him. 'I meant to tell you two other things.' He lowered his voice. 'One is that the fellow accusing Father Cronin isn't suing him personally. Oh no! He's suing the diocese for negligence. That's what they do now. Go where the money is. That's what all these buckos are after! Thousands they want in compensation. Millions if you add it all up. No wonder Father Mac is worried. The other thing is this. One of St Fiachra's School yearbooks has a photo of the bloke when he was fourteen, which is when the abuse allegedly took place. He was the image of yourself at the same age.'

'Of me?' Sean stared. 'What am I to make of that?'

'No idea,' Breen told him. 'Not the foggiest. I just thought it best if you heard it from me and not one of the nosy parkers from Dublin. It might unsettle you coming from them.'

★ ★ ★

Sean's mother was in bed. Her arthritis had flared up, so he brought her tea and listened to complaints about her medication's side effects and general inadequacy. She didn't ask where he had spent the morning. Then, very gingerly, he removed the tray. Touching her painfully stretched skin and distorted bones was like handling a bag of eggs.

270

Taking a plateful of dinner with him — it was warmed-over stew — he went outside and, when he'd eaten it, used his licked fork to prick out a tray of rocket seedlings. The tines were just the right size for disentangling the fine, white, thready roots. Next, using his fingers, he pressed the sooty compost around each stem. As always, he relished feeling the grain of it ooze soothingly under his nails. He had read somewhere that humans shared genes with plants, and was reminded of a picture Father Tim had had on his wall showing a naked girl turning into a tree. Already her fingers were leaves; the whole of her was as pale and frail as seedling roots, and Father Tim had told a story explaining what had made this happen. Sean couldn't remember it. Some spell no doubt. Some enchantment.

As though the memory had caught him off guard, restraint peeled away and he began to shake. He had, he saw now, been holding himself in and down since the sergeant's shadow fell on him this morning. He hadn't allowed himself to think, even less to feel and now that he did, tears started to flow and he cried as he hadn't done since he'd cried for his dead father. That, of course, was when Cronin had taken him in his arms. Was that what those bastards meant by 'abuse'? Or was fear of the word — or of some addictive reality? — the reason why Cronin had only kissed and cuddled Sean that one time? He had soothed and stroked and held him tenderly — then stopped. Why had he stopped? And never done it again? Why? Was it Sean's fault? Sean had wondered about that, but hadn't liked to ask. How could he ask? He couldn't. His life and Cronin's were hedged in, blocked and braked like — like an arthritic's. By now tears were pouring down his cheeks. They were running into his mouth and ears.

'I think I'm jealous,' he said aloud, 'of the abuse victim. I am! I'm jealous of the bastard!' Hearing his words, he laughed in shock and covered his face with his hands. It was true though. That was the real shock.

★ ★ ★

Lynch stood up and came round his desk. It was time for Sean to leave.

'He told me,' said Lynch, 'that you wrote him a great letter. When he was going through the dark night. Sensitive. Private. A bit mad, but comforting. Naturally I never saw it. But did you know that it was after he got it that he changed his will? He wanted to open things up for you, make *your* life a bit easier. Ah, I'm sorry. I didn't mean to make you cry.'

Andrew Motion

HISTORY

The simplest things
expand and grow more astonishing:

after two years away
I have stumbled today

on this granite chip
a child Hercules sent skipping

over the Med to end
at a particular bend

of this particular track
thousands of summers back

and see (without having known
to remember this or any other stone)

it still fits exactly into its own place.
Cicada-chat. Thyme-whiff. Heat. Amazing grace.

Philip Hensher

THE PARTY UPSTAIRS

The letter lay on the table between them, like a ticking bomb. Charles was sitting in silence. Melanie decided to fold her arms too. They sat back, in the sort of unison which couples fall into, even if they don't like each other that much. It was a Saturday night, around seven o'clock.

'We could still go out,' Melanie said.

'I'm not going out,' Charles said. 'I've said. I'm not going out.'

'We quite often go out on a Saturday night anyway,' Melanie said. Or used to, she thought.

Charles sighed heavily. She could see that he had got to that point in the argument where he had turned into a man who was certain he was right.

'I don't want to go out,' he said. 'I don't feel like it. And I don't see why I should be told to leave my own house by a complete stranger.'

What the complete stranger had to do with it, Melanie couldn't say. You wouldn't do what you were told by your best friend, she thought savagely.

'It's quite a polite letter,' she said. 'And he wasn't telling you to leave your own house. He was just telling you what the situation is, and if you feel like staying in, you have been warned.'

They had lived in the flat for nearly eight years. Three years in mildly groovy sin, five years married. To Melanie, it still looked like the flat of two people who were trying to see what it would be like to live together; she could identify without too much trouble what, in the room, belonged to Charles and what to her. The boy upstairs had moved in one month before. He had seemed quite nice.

'And that's exactly what I propose to do. Stay in. He didn't post it until Wednesday,' Charles said. 'That's not enough notice. We could have been having a party ourselves. We could have asked friends round to dinner. Anything.'

Charles leaned forward and picked the letter up from the table and read it, furiously, for the fiftieth time.

Dear Charles, it said, and (sorry!) Mrs Charles, I thought I should warn you that I'm having a little party next Saturday. It won't go on beyond two or so, but I think it might prove a bit noisy for you before then. With best wishes, Jimmy (upstairs).

'Beyond two or so,' Charles said disdainfully.

'Everyone has parties,' Melanie said. 'Except us. It's not unreasonable.'

'We have parties,' Charles said. 'I don't know what you mean.'

'We don't have any friends,' Melanie said. 'Enough, I mean. And we could go to the pictures.'

'There's nothing I want to see,' Charles said. 'And I don't see why — '

'There's a Harrison Ford on at the Picture

House,' Melanie said quickly.

'You don't like Harrison Ford,' Charles said. 'And it's probably sold out by now. You hate Harrison Ford.'

'He's all right,' Melanie said.

'You can't stand Harrison Ford,' Charles said. 'Don't you remember — years ago — I took you to see *Witness* because I heard it was good. And afterwards — we went to that pizza place — '

'That pizza place — '

Melanie smiled, almost to herself. That pizza place, a million million years ago.

' — and I didn't want to say I thought it was really boring.'

'And I didn't say it was really boring — '

'Because I thought you liked it.'

'And I thought you liked him.'

'I thought you liked him.'

'But then you said that you liked the film but you didn't like him much.'

'I'd forgotten,' Melanie said. She had forgotten, it was true. There was a pizza place, and once, she was sitting there with the man who she didn't know that well, and he had taken her to a film with Harrison Ford in it, and she had sat through it, and thought whatever thoughts she had had, a million million years ago, and afterwards they had gone to eat pizza. So many decisions; so many forgotten decisions. 'No, I never liked him that much,' she said. 'I don't know why not. I suppose he's all right.'

Upstairs, the music suddenly started. Both of them looked up at the ceiling. It seemed almost to tremble with the violent hammering beat, as if the man upstairs was beating a dead rabbit against the floor.

'Hark at that,' Charles said with obvious, perverse pleasure. 'A whole evening of that.'

'We could go out,' Melanie said. 'I don't hate Harrison Ford that much. You, you're turning into your father.'

Charles let this go. 'I don't feel like going out,' he said again.

One day, Melanie thought, one day . . . One day, I'm going to come into this room, and I'm going to look at you, reading the television guide, and I'm going to say to you, put that down, and you'll look at me, and I'll say to you, I'll say to you . . .

She felt an overwhelming satisfaction at her own thought. It was like being in school and finding the way through the thickets of maths to the right answer. She felt this, even though her thought was unfinished, even though she'd thought exactly the same thing a thousand times before. One day I'll say to you, Charles Simpson, she thought, and knew that when she came to the day, she would know exactly what to say to him. And more than anything, she thought, looking at him, she hoped it wasn't going to be have to be 'Charles, I'm pregnant.'

'I'm going to be thirty next year,' Melanie said.

'And I'll be thirty-two,' Charles said. He got up and went to the window, opening the curtains.

'Starting to rain,' he said. 'Maybe nobody will come to his sodding party.'

277

But then, they could hear, the upstairs doorbell rang. Charles turned, and went to the console table. He took a bottle of whisky, opened it, and poured himself a drink.

'It's raining,' he said, taking a swig. 'I'm certainly not going out now.'

'It might not rain all night,' Melanie said.

'It might,' Charles said. He threw a savage glance up at the throbbing ceiling. Footsteps trod heavily across. 'What kind of name is Harrison anyway.'

'It's a name like any other,' Melanie said.

❧

At the violet hour, when the eyes and back
Turn upward from the desk, when the human
    engine waits
Like a taxi throbbing, waiting,
I, Tiresias, though blind, throbbing between
    two lives,
Old man with wrinkled female breasts, can see
At the violet hour, the evening hour that
    strives
Homeward, and brings the sailor home from
    sea,
The typist home at teatime, clears her break-
    fast, lights
Her stove, and lays out food in tins.

T. S. Eliot, The Waste Land, part 3

Reginald Hill

JOHN BROWN'S BODY

It's a great beach for bodies.

To the north towers the craggy height of Bale Head, the county's favourite spot for suicides whose battered corpses a decorous current lays neatly on the crescent of golden sand curving two miles south to the sharp point of Bodd Ness. Beyond this the incoming tide squeezes itself into the narrow estuary of the Bodd and rapidly becomes a bit of a bore. Most of those caught in that sudden rush (and, despite the warnings, each year brings half a dozen) are swept out on the ebb and left as testaments to folly on our sunny beach. Add to this a funnel of tides widening out into the Atlantic which, after a big storm, has brought us bodies from as far afield as the Scillies, and you've got yourself a boddicomber's dream.

What's a boddicomber? With a capital **B**, it's a native of Boddicombe, the village half a mile inland where I've been living for the past twenty years. But with a small **b,** it's a beachcomber who's found a body. Macabre? Not really, not if you live here. Here with our tides and currents, it's almost the norm, and all the regulars in the bar of the Drowned Sailor are boddicombers in both senses.

All except one, that is.

Me.

John Brown.

I suppose, having married a local lass and lived here for two decades, I can claim the capital B as an adopted son of the village. Certainly after some initial caution, quite natural when an outsider sweeps a local heiress off her feet, the denizens of the Sailor took me to their hearts and treated me as one of their own. Only one thing was needed to put the seal on the deed of adoption. But so far it hasn't happened.

For twenty years now I've been walking the beach once, sometimes twice a day, and I've never found a body.

Don't misunderstand me. They're not a morbid lot down in the Sailor. Bodies on the beach aren't a staple of conversation. But whenever another corpse is washed up, naturally this sparks off reminiscences of past tragedies with comparisons and contrasts and significant anecdotes as each discoverer in turn recalls *his* body. That's how they're identified, not by their own names, but by the boddicomber's name, as *Dick's body* or *Ernie's body*, or where the man in question has been fortunate enough to come across more than one, *Tony's second* or *Andy's third*.

It's amazing how possessive a boddicomber becomes. Every detail that can be gleaned from police investigations, coroner's inquests, newspaper reports, and any other source, is hoarded up and treasured. Sometimes their depth of background knowledge makes me wonder if some of them don't employ private detectives. I listen in dumb admiration. For that's all I can do, listen, though they've always done their best to include me, and everyone was mightily pleased when the year before last Charley Trenfold's *seventh* gave them a hook to hang their kindness on. Now as soon as Charley's *seventh* is mentioned, someone will turn to me and urge me to make my pathetic contribution. And I always do, because a man shouldn't turn his back on kindness. But oh! how the words bring back the bitter taste of *proxime accessit*, as sharp and pungent as it was on that misty morning two years ago.

I'd got up early to take a walk. To tell the truth it had been one of those nights I'd spent uncomfortably in the spare room after yet another row with Lorna. God, that mattress! Once when friendly relations were resumed after an earlier exile, I'd joked that if we were going to make a habit of this, we really ought to think about getting a more user-friendly guest bed. To which she'd replied that if I had the money to spare, that might not be a bad idea. Which rapidly led to a breach of our armistice and another bout of sleepless nights for me.

This particular morning as I strolled along the path to the beach, I wondered gloomily whether my marriage was in terminal decline. For ten years after our romantic start, things had only got better and better. Lorna had been so in love that she'd assured me there'd be no problem in leaving the lovely family house she'd inherited in Boddicombe to move into my flat in town ninety slow miles away. But I knew how much she loved

281

that house and assured her in turn that there was no need. Modern technology meant I could do my job as easily from Boddicombe as I could in company HQ, and I'd get to walk the beach nearly every day. Funny thing, love. We nearly fell out each trying to make sacrifices for the other! But I won, and for the next ten years I worked from home and as I'd forecast, there were no problems at all. Then the company fell on hard times and suddenly the flaw in my arrangement became apparent. When downsizing's in the air, it's easier to start with the faces you're not seeing every day in the executive dining room.

So I was out, but it didn't seem to matter. I'd made enough money when I was in to provide a reassuring cushion till I found a new job. Except there were no new jobs, not even when I cast my net well beyond the old ninety-mile limit.

No problem, I said. If you can't find someone to employ you, employ yourself! I already had a well-equipped home office. Now I invested what remained of my money in upgrading it to cutting-edge status, called in a few old favours, and suddenly I was an entrepreneur.

For a while it looked like it was going to work, but at best I was never more than holding my own. Slowly I ran out of favours and commissions. The e-mails fell to a trickle then dried up completely, the fax only chugged out advertising junk, the phone never rang and the postman brought nothing but bills.

Till finally I had to face up to it. I was an unemployment statistic living in his wife's house on his wife's money. Things might have been better if I hadn't felt so guilty about it. Looking back, I think I spent so much time telling Lorna what a liability I was that in the end she believed it.

But I did get a lot more time to walk the beach.

And that misty morning, as I stood on my usual high dune letting my gaze run north along the sand, I thought my luck might be on the change.

Each tide left its own signature on the beach and over the years I had grown expert at reading those scrawls of flotsam and jetsam and beached jellyfish and sea wrack, and like all the boddicombers, I was ultra-sensitive to anything whose configuration or bulk was out of the ordinary.

And this morning there was something there, right at the limit of of my view, nothing more than a dark smudge in the bluey-pink wreaths the sun's warm rays were drawing off the damp sand, but definitely *something* . . .

I took a deep breath and was just about to descend from the dune when a voice called my name.

'John! Good morning to you!'

I turned in irritation to see Maisie Palliser climbing up towards me followed by her overweight and panting pug, Samson.

I forced my features into something as close to a smile as I could manage and said, 'Good morning.'

Maisie Palliser was one of those women who

get a reputation for kindness by making unacceptable offers of help and who uses her much vaunted sympathy as a tool for getting under the defences of the vulnerable to the secrets below. She was Lorna's cousin, a couple of years older and unmarried. Not that she was physically unattractive. Indeed she and Lorna could almost have been twins. But Maisie though devious in many ways had no art to conceal her desire to dominate. There'd been a quarrel between their fathers, the two Palliser brothers, over their inheritance many years before and as they grew up, the two cousins hadn't had much to do with each other. A pity in some ways. There's nothing like a shared childhood for giving you a proper insight into character. Myself I never cared for her from the start. How Lorna felt I never enquired, but I got an impression she wasn't all that worried about the after-effects of their fathers' quarrel. But when illness and accident removed the last of the older generation a few years back, Maisie had been so assiduous in bringing about a rapprochement that Lorna's gentler nature was quite unable to resist. The big card Maisie played was that she and Lorna were the last of the Pallisers, so family feuds must give way to family solidarity. I gently mocked this *non sequitur* this sentiment, but it was no contest. Lorna was a sucker for sentiment and, perhaps unjustly, I date the beginning of the deterioration in my marital relationship not so much from the day I lost my job as from the day I first found Maisie enjoying afternoon tea in our drawing room.

After that she became a regular visitor and soon Lorna seemed happy to admit her as a confidante. She drew the line however, at welcoming Samson, the pug, who combined a delicate stomach with insatiable greed, eating anything he could get his thieving teeth on, then after just long enough for his inefficient digestive juices to render it revolting, vomiting it back up, preferably on a chair or a carpet. Lorna was usually pretty neutral about domestic animals, but in this case she made an exception. She really detested that dog, its very presence set her teeth on edge, and in her quiet way she made it absolutely clear that Samson was not welcome in her house. So whenever Maisie visited, the pug was locked in the kitchen porch where he could do no harm.

'Best part of the day this,' said Maisie now as she joined me. 'I don't see it often enough but I couldn't sleep last night. My old trouble.'

She smiled bravely. What her old trouble was nobody knew exactly, but that it was exceedingly painful and bravely borne no one could avoid knowing.

'Same with you, was it, John?' she went on.

'Doubt it, Maisie. I don't have your old trouble,' I replied.

It was bird-shot against a tank.

'How lucky you are,' she sighed. 'But I meant something must have got you out of bed early too. I sincerely hope it wasn't anything causing you physical pain.'

'No. Just fancied a stroll, that's all.'

'And you managed to steal away without

285

disturbing Lorna, I'm sure. How is the dear girl? I must call round and have a chat soon. Don't worry. I won't take up too much of her time. I know how hard the pair of you work to make your business a success. Don't forget my offer. Anything I can do to help — folding envelopes, addressing labels, even a bit of typing — I can still manage to get my fingers dancing over a keyboard even with my arthritis — all you have to do is ask, John.'

She knew damn well the business had given up the ghost just as she knew damn well Lorna and I spent more time sleeping apart than together, but how was I to tell her that without telling her that, if you see what I mean, opening the floodgates to a new torrent of useless advice and ersatz sympathy?

But I might have exploded if over her shoulder I hadn't seen the last thing I wanted to see, the familar hunched figure of Charley Trenfold dropping down to the beach from the dunes between me and that distant mist-shrouded shape.

I muttered something to Maisie, I don't know what, and set out after him. I was the younger man and got plenty of exercise to keep me fit. But old Charley was no slouch either, and by the way he was striding out, he'd clearly his *seventh* firmly in his sights. It was partly the fact that his cottage stood a little way out of the village and a lot closer to the beach that gave him his boddicombing pre-eminence, but you couldn't deny that he had a nose for it, and though the idea was never openly expressed, everyone in the

Sailor knew it was his ambition to overtake the record of the greatest boddicomber (and Boddicomber) of them all, Jacob Palliser, my wife's and Maisie's grandfather, who during the course of a long and profitable life had found a round dozen.

Fast as I moved, even breaking into a trot when I got close enough to see that the shape on the beach was undoubtedly a corpse, I couldn't overtake Charley. I couldn't even claim a dead heat. He reached the body a full step ahead, turned to look at me with a little start of surprise as if he'd been unaware of my pursuit, and said, 'Is that you, John Brown? Well, here's a sad sight for a summer's morn. Another poor soul lured by Old Nick to leap off the Head.'

I didn't doubt for one moment he'd be right. Old Charley was so familiar with the general configuration of the tides and currents and the modifying effect of specific weather conditions that he could tell with amazing accuracy the likely point of entry of any body washed up on our beach.

I looked down at the face of the man at our feet. There was a dreadful gash across his brow with splintered bone showing through, confirming Charley's judgement. Those who jumped off the Head usually died on the rocks below and lay there till the height of the tide picked them up and carried them away. I didn't recognise the face. The Head's reputation lured people from far and wide. But I knew from experience that over the next few weeks, Charley would somehow research chapter and verse of his life and background and the circumstances which brought him to this sad end. All of which would have been my task if Maisie hadn't delayed me. The bitch! She was my bird of ill omen even in this.

'Why don't you stay with him and I'll head back to the cottage and ring the police?' said Charley.

Reporting was the next important stage after finding. It got you officially into the records, established your claim, so to speak.

'No need for that,' I said. 'I'll do it from here.'

And I took out my mobile phone and dialled.

And that was how I got my footnote in the boddicombers' annals. Mobiles, already the common furniture of urban life, hadn't reached Boddicombe in any great numbers then. Now everyone in the Sailor has one. Rumour has it that Charley went out and bought one the next day. I smile whenever I see him use it, for I know it still rankles slightly that every time his seventh comes up in conversation, some kind soul, eager to bring me into things, will say, 'Aye, that's the one that John Brown reported on his mobile, isn't that right, John?' and I'll get my thirty seconds of fame.

Two years on and that was still all I could lay claim to, though I seemed to spend more time walking the beach and its environs than I did at home. *Home!* It was hardly that any more. It was simply the house where I lodged by the grudging permission of the woman who used to be my wife. Why didn't she throw me out and sue for divorce? There were several reasons, not least among them being the fact that she'd been brought up as a Boddicombe Baptist. I don't know if this term has any official standing in the religious world, but I do know that the attitude of the BBs to divorce made the Roman Catholic Church look like Club Mediterranée.

As for me, why didn't I call it a day and walk out?

Again several reasons, with large among them the fact that I had nowhere to walk to. The years of desperately seeking work had made me a man old acquaintance crossed the street to avoid. And the years of not having any work had made me a man who crossed the street to avoid old acquaintance. So I'd zig-zagged to a situation where the only place I felt at home and among friends was the bar of the Drowned Sailor. If I walked away from this, my probable destination was a cardboard box in a shop doorway. Or Bale Head. Which would at least have meant that I got my place permanently in the mythology of the Sailor. But when I thought of the satisfaction it would give Maisie Palliser, I knew it wasn't really an option.

At my blackest moments I sometimes thought that my only chance of a future better than this demeaning present lay in Lorna dying. We'd never made wills. With only the two of us to consider in those early loving days, it seemed to be tempting fate to pay someone to formalise what would happen anyway, which is to say if one of us died, the survivor would get all. Well, those loving days were long gone, though deep inside of me I still nursed a weak runt of a hope that a love as strong as ours had been couldn't altogether die. Perhaps it was our common memories rather than Lorna's religion and my fears that kept us together? Certainly I can honestly say that even in those blackest moments I stopped short of wishing her dead, and I never got close to fantasising about killing her. But words have a life of their own, and one day not long after Christmas when some minor financial irritation had melted the cold courtesy between us to molten antagonism, I exploded, 'Money, money, money, that's all you think about, isn't it? Well, I didn't marry you for your money, and as far as I'm concerned you can grow old and ugly counting it. I don't want any part of it!'

To which she replied, equally incensed, 'That's just as well, because from now on you're not getting any more. You might make me miserable but you're not going to make me bankrupt.'

And I, God forgive me, cried, 'So you're rich and miserable and I'm broke and miserable. So why don't you take a dive off Bale Head, and that would solve all our problems, wouldn't it?'

I saw the shock in her face and wished it unsaid instantly. I wanted to say I didn't mean it, that we shouldn't be surprised if two people who'd loved each other as much as we had were as extreme in their quarrels as they'd been in their passion. But the door was pushed open at that moment and Maisie was standing there, saying, 'Sorry, I rang the bell but no-one answered so I just came in.' How much she'd heard, I couldn't say. Everything, I suspected. Whatever, there was nothing for me to do now but leave with my retraction unattempted, and over the next couple of days Lorna gave me neither opportunity nor encouragement to apologise and, as is the way in these matters, I soon began to feel the fault was as much hers as mine, so why should I be the one who grovelled?

Then a few days later, returning to the house after another unproductive stroll along the beach, I heard Lorna call my name from the drawing room.

The first person I saw when I entered was Maisie, drinking tea. She gave a thin smile, which had something unpleasantly gloating in it. Once she'd been at some pains to conceal her antagonism towards me. For several weeks in the run up to Christmas, Maisie had been all sweetness and light, indeed almost likeable. I wondered if she'd found God or taken up marijuana. Then suddenly, over the holiday period, she'd done a Scrooge in reverse and emerged at the other side even more of a foul-tempered, man-hating termagant than she'd been before.

Lorna was sitting opposite her on a sofa with the lanky figure of Tim Edlington, the Palliser family solicitor by her side. He rose to shake my hand and said something conventional like 'Good to see you again, John'. But I detected a certain embarrassment in his tone which worried me. One thing I learned in business was when lawyers sound embarrassed you're really in trouble.

Lorna said brusquely, 'John, I need you to witness my signature.'

'Of course dear,' I said. 'On what?'

'On my will.'

I tried to hide my surprise. I doubt if I was successful.

'Your will?' I said. 'I didn't realise . . . I mean, isn't it illegal, for a husband I mean, to witness . . . ?'

'Only if he is a beneficiary,' said Lorna coldly.

And now I felt real shock and I didn't even bother to try to hide it. I saw at once what was happening. She must have been deeply shocked by what I'd said. I guessed she'd confided in Maisie. Indeed with Maisie having overheard my outburst, it would have been impossible for someone feeling as vulnerable as Lorna must have felt to resist her cousin's spurious sympathy and vicarious outrage. No doubt in her present anti-male mood she'd assured Lorna that all men were murdering rapists under the skin. And now I was being told loud and clear in front of witnesses that whatever else Lorna's death might do for me, it wasn't going to make me rich.

Maisie was observing me with her face set in a mask of sympathy which she didn't mind me piercing to the malicious pleasure beneath. Tim Edlington's embarrassed sympathy on the other hand was very real and he rushed in to fill the silence that followed Lorna's remark with an attempt at explanation.

'What Lorna and Maisie want to do, John, is repair the damage done to the Palliser estate, not to mention the Palliser family, by old Jacob's will.'

He glanced up at the portrait of Jacob Palliser,

292

founder of the family fortunes and grandfather to Maisie and Lorna. It was from him that Maisie inherited her need to dominate. From all accounts he had kept his sons under his thumb until he died, and even then he'd left a will cunningly constructed to leave both feeling cheated, dividing the property so that the younger son (Lorna's father) got the house and land which the elder son (Maisie's father) thought his due, while the elder got a controlling interest in the dairy products business which the younger had almost single-handedly built up. Some necessary concessions had been agreed, but effectively that malicious will had set the brothers at each other's throats for the rest of their lives.

'So,' concluded Tim, 'Lorna and Maisie have asked me to draw up mutually beneficial wills by which, when in the fullness of time one or the other of them passes on, the estate such as it now is will once more be joined together as a single entity.'

He tried to make it sound like a reasonable act of conciliation but he knew that he was talking bollocks. This wasn't about old Jacob and the estate. It was about me. And it was also about Maisie, who was potentially by far the biggest beneficiary of this new arrangement. Neither brother had made much of his inheritance, but whereas Lorna's father had hung on to a good proportion of his, Maisie had seen her prospects dwindle to the small family cottage in which she lived, and a small income to go with it. Already, it seemed to me, she was looking around that

293

handsome drawing room with a proprietary air.

I said, 'Where do I sign?'

I didn't even bother to read the wills, just countersigned the women's signatures. Tim acted as the other witness. I shook him by the hand again and left the room. As I closed the door quietly behind me, I glanced up at old Jacob's portrait.

I'd never met the old man, but now I read in those piercing black eyes the scorn of a self-made man for a failure and a weakling who had not only lost his wife's love and respect but couldn't even find a single body on our bountiful beach.

Which of course was where I headed now. To rage and brood and plot. And to look for bodies.

Does that sound crazily obsessive? I suppose it must. But somehow my failure to find a body had become a symbol of all my failures. No; it was more than a symbol. It was as if everything that had gone wrong in my life could somehow be tracked back to this one deficiency. It placed the blame fairly not on my own shoulders but on a malevolent fate or at best the vagaries of blind chance. It seemed to me that if only I could find my body and take my place as of right among the native boddicombers in the Drowned Sailor, all would be well. I could look the portrait of old Jacob straight in the eye, Lorna would regain her respect for me, her love, her energy, and her healthy bank balance would be put at my disposal, and thus armed I could renew my assault on the world of commerce, and this time I would win . . .

Yes, I continued to think like this even after the business of the will. At first it had seemed to me that for Lorna to let Maisie into the act had been a deliberate attempt to add insult to injury. She knew how much I disliked and distrusted her. But more mature consideration led me to the conclusion that far from wanting to pile on the pain, Lorna had looked for a device which would give the whole business a patina of rationality. She could just have left everything to the Boddicombe Baptists. But that would have been undisguisable as anything but a wish to cause me pain. The business of reuniting the estate was the best way she could find of softening the blow, and her general demeanour in the days that followed made me think the whole affair was making her feel guilty and gave me hope that the embers of our love might still be warm enough to melt her heart which my stupid outburst had so hardened against me.

So I continued with my secret crazy dream that things could still be turned around if only I could find that elusive body. One corpse. That wasn't much to ask. Charley Trenfold had had a great couple of years and was up to eleven now, just one short of old Jacob's record. Surely the great and generous ocean could spare a single corpse for me?

Who was it who said, be careful what you pray for because you might get it?

A couple of weeks later I came home in the gloam of an overcast February evening, slightly out of breath as I'd been hurrying.

Happily, Lorna's principles which forbade her

to divorce me also forbade her to starve me and she cooked our meal every night. A creature of habit, her menu was dictated by the day, without any reference to possible variation of appetite, and she set our meal on the table between seven and seven thirty, and started to eat regardless of whether I had arrived or not.

On nut cutlet night, I didn't much mind whether I got it hot or cold, but today was pork chop day, my favourite, so I hurried to be on time even though it meant leaving the beach half an hour before high tide. I went round to the kitchen entrance as usual. But as I kicked off my wellingtons in the covered porchway, I realised that something was missing — the mouthwatering smell of grilling pork.

Puzzled, I pushed open the kitchen door. On the table I could see assembled for cooking all the ingredients of dinner. Mushrooms, tomatoes, chipped potatoes, and a succulent chop with the kidney in, the way I liked it. But no Lorna.

I went through the house calling her name.

There was no reply.

I went out to the old barn which acted as a garage. I had declined from Jag through Mondeo to Daewoo, but finally even that had gone and now our only vehicle was the aged Land Rover which Lorna claimed was all that country dwellers needed.

It wasn't there.

Puzzled and just beginning to be worried, but not wanting to give the local gossips still more material by ringing around, I walked into the village and called at Maisie's house. There was no sign of the Land Rover, and no sign of Maisie either. Only Samson greeted me on the threshold. He looked so disconsolate that I started to bend to stroke him. Then he belched noisomely and brought up a disgusting bolus of gristle and bone which spread itself across Maisie's pristine doorstep.

I walked down the street, past the Drowned Sailor. No sign of the Land Rover in the car park. I thought of going inside, but all that that would have done was feed the local rumour machine. Increasingly anxious but still a long way from panic, I walked home by a route which took me past several outlying houses belonging to various friends of Lorna, hoping I'd see the Land Rover parked outside one of them. No luck, but as I passed the last of these, its owner, a farmer called Tony Simkin (two bodies to his credit, one of them a local politician who'd solved his problem with a corruption scandal by stepping off Bale Head) spotted me as he came out of his lambing shed.

'Evening, John,' he said. 'Fed up with the beach then?'

Meaning it was a bit unusual for me to be taking my evening stroll along these lanes.

'Change is as good as a rest,' I said.

'Could do with one myself,' he said. 'These early lambs are a pain. Thought I saw you driving that old heap of yours down the coast road earlier and I said to myself, there John and Lorna off to the movies in Lymton, lucky devils.'

The ancient cinema which had somehow contrived to survive in Lymton, twelve miles north, was our nearest source of public entertainment.

'Not me,' I said lightly.

'No?' He looked at me doubtfully. 'Could have sworn I recognised the hat. But never mind. Here you are now. Won't you step into the house for a dram? Say hello to Betsy?'

Four months earlier, Tony's wife, Betsy, had left him, taking their two children. Then at Christmas there'd been a reconciliation, and Tony was still in the honeymoon period, wanting everyone who came near to call in and see what a happy united family they were.

I wasn't in the mood for happy united families so I made an excuse, took my leave, and hastened home.

Still no sign of Lorna, but Tony's possible sighting of the Land Rover was encouraging a new and reassuring hypothesis. Probably it was as straightforward as that . . . Lorna had simply gone to the cinema . . . a last minute decision . . . someone had reminded her there was a film she was keen to see . . .

But she wouldn't have gone without leaving a note . . .

I knew there was nothing on the kitchen table but I checked as I passed through. Our other note-leaving place was against the clock on the mantelpiece in the drawing room. I'd pushed open the door and called Lorna's name into the darkened room when I'd first missed her, but I hadn't actually gone inside.

Now I stepped in and put the light on.

No note against the clock. Above it, old Jacob

sneered down at me.

I was turning away when my eye caught sight of what looked like a piece of paper on the hearth beneath the mantel. Perhaps the note had slipped. I went forward and picked it up. There was some writing on it in a familiar hand, but not Lorna's.

Mine.

It was my signature preceded by the typed words *signed by the testatrix in the presence of* . . .

The fire basket was grey with paper ash.

And as I stopped to take a closer look I saw something else.

A dark brown stain on the sharp corner of the raised stone hearth.

I touched it. It was dry. I scraped at it with my fingernail, raised the resulting powdery flakes to the light, sniffed at them.

It was blood.

I sank to the floor and squatted there, letting all the fragmented thoughts whirling around my head settle slowly into a meaningful mosaic.

I recalled the single chop on the kitchen table where there should have been two. And I recalled the bony gristly mess that Samson had vomited up on Maisie's doorstep.

Suddenly it was like putting a video in the VCR and pressing the *play* button.

Maisie had been here. Lorna had told her she'd changed her mind about the will. Maisie had protested. Lorna had been adamant. And being a woman who thought that deeds spoke louder than words, she'd produced the will and put a match to it and stooped to hold it over the fire basket. Maisie had tried to wrest it from her. Lorna, off balance, had fallen forward, crashing heavily, fatally, against the edge of the hearth.

And then . . . ?

I knew how Maisie's mind worked. The burned will, signs of a struggle, her cousin's corpse . . . even if the inquest brought in a verdict of accidental death, there would be talk for ever more. She would judge others by herself and guess that in the eyes of many she would be marked as a murderess who'd got away with it for the rest of her life. That wouldn't bother her too much perhaps if she could claim the compensation of Lorna's house and money. But the will was in the fireplace, burned beyond retrieval.

Then slowly as she sat there reviewing her options, an idea formed in her devious mind . . . an idea which at worst would clear her of any suspicion of involvement in Lorna's death and at best might result in her claiming the Palliser inheritance after all . . .

The coast road to Lymton which Tony thought he'd seen me driving along was also the road to Bale Head.

Maisie had put the body in the Land Rover, driven to the Head, and tipped Lorna over the edge.

Suicide while the balance of her mind was disturbed. I could hear Maisie at the inquest reluctantly letting herself be bullied into admitting that the wreck of our marriage and my unreasonable behaviour had brought Lorna to the edge of despair.

As for the burned will, who had lit the flame? Who benefitted most from its destruction?

I could see all eyes in the coroner's court turning towards me.

I'm sure Maisie's lawyer, especially if it wasn't Tim, could make a strong legal argument for reinstating the burned will.

But why take a chance on the uncertainties of the law when there was another more certain way?

Maisie wouldn't find it hard when talking to the police to refer 'inadvertently' to my threats against Lorna's life, threats which had included a mention of Bale Head. Indeed for all I knew she'd already told everyone in the village about them. The police would start looking for other evidence, and eventually they'd come up with Tony Simkin and anyone else who'd seen the Land Rover heading along the coast road.

Why had Tony had been so sure he'd seen me in the driving seat? He'd said something about recognising my hat . . .

I went back into the kitchen and looked at the clothes hooks behind the door.

An ancient and very distinctive old-fashioned floppy cap I often wore when driving in cold wintry conditions wasn't there. The bitch had already been thinking ahead to putting me in the frame!

I shook my head and asked myself, could even Maisie be as cunningly manipulative as that?

Of course she could! I answered. She'd know that once the police started looking closely at things, it wouldn't be long before the bloodstains in the drawing room were found, and then . . .

But even as I ran this frightening scenario through my mind, I knew that what I was really doing was attempting to block off my shock, my horror, my despair, at the prospect of admitting Lorna was dead.

Before I was finally going to lay myself open to that destructive knowledge, I would need to see her corpse.

And if my hypothesis was right, I knew exactly where I'd find it.

For the first time in many years, I headed down to the beach, praying that I wouldn't find a body.

Two hours or more had passed since I'd come away and headed home for dinner and the tide had long turned and it was its receding roar that I heard as I clambered up the dunes. The night was pitch-black, the air full of wind and sand and the smell of sea wrack and the intermittent cries of storm-disturbed birds which fell upon my ear like the desperate appeals of a lost soul. The sea itself was nothing more than a vague far-off line of dim whiteness and I could make out no horizon, sky and water blending into a single bowl of blackness. No use to stand up here on the dunes and try to pick out shapes on the beach. I needed to be down there, and even then, without a torch, it was almost going to be a matter of feeling my way along the sand.

My heart sank at the grisly prospect. Then as if in answer to my prayers, I saw a beam of light wavering towards me up the dunes.

It shone full in my face and Charley Trenfold's voice said, 'Is that you, John? God, you're keen, on a night like this!'

You too, I thought. But I was glad to see him, both for his torch and his company.

Then I recalled Charley's famous nose for a body, and I didn't feel so glad.

I said nothing except, 'Come on then. Let's get down there.'

We descended and moved forward together in silence along the wavering high tide mark.

We both saw it at the same time. I suppose what went through Charley's mind was, this could be my twelfth! This could be the night I equal old Jacob's record!

What went through my mind I have no words to tell.

I let out a cry compounded of shock, of grief, of anger, of recognition, of farewell, and, shouldering Charley aside, I ran forward, stumbling in the soft sand till I fell on my knees by Lorna's body.

She lay on her face, as if asleep. I turned her over and my straining tearful eyes saw the deep wound on her brow which I knew probably came from the corner of the hearth rather than her fall from the Head.

My grief is impossible to describe. Not for a single moment did it occur to me how damning it was going to sound when Charley described the way I shoved him aside and went rushing forward. 'And how could you be so certain that you had found your wife's body, Mr Brown? Unless of course you knew exactly where it was

303

going to be found . . . '

Then Charley arrived, saying grudgingly, 'So I suppose we'll have to call this your *first*, John Brown,' as he let the beam of his torch play full on the face cradled in my hands.

And I looked at those dear pallid features in the pool of light. And I thought what strange changes death brought about. And Charley exclaimed, 'My God! It's Maisie Palliser!'

It was like the breaking of a spell.

I blinked once, and what the darkness of the night, the tears in my eyes, and above all my fearful expectation had persuaded me was Lorna, instantly and unmistakably became Maisie.

And with equal speed the hypothesis I had programmed in my mind was reformatted. I guessed I'd been right in most particulars except one. It had been Maisie who, rushing forward in a fit of rage when she saw that Lorna really was destroying the will, had fallen and smashed her skull against the edge of the stone hearth. And it had been Lorna who, fearful of the consequences — the long drawn-out legal inquiries, the rumours and gossip, the threat to her treasured privacy and her family reputation — had untypically panicked, packed the corpse into the Land Rover, and driven up to Bale Head. My hat she'd have put on merely to disguise herself, not to masquerade as me.

Where was she now?

My heart went out to her, wherever she was. This wasn't something she should have to bear alone. I needed to find her, let her know that whatever happened, I was steadfast.

Charley was busy phoning the emergency services. My role with his *seventh*.

Finished, he said, 'Well, poor old Maisie. Anyone could see her disappointment over Tony had hit her really hard, but I never thought she'd take it this bad. At least she looks at peace now.'

And she did. In fact death had taken ten years off her face, another reason why I'd confounded her with Lorna. But these thoughts were for later. At that moment I was just trying to puzzle out what Charley was talking about.

'Sorry?' I said. 'What disappointment?'

'Didn't you know?' He sounded genuinely surprised. 'I thought everyone knew. When Betsy left Tony, Maisie was right in there. You know how she was. Anything I can do to help? Washing, cleaning, ironing, shopping . . . and is there anything else, Tony? Anything a big strong handsome man like you is missing . . . ? Well, he wasn't going to say no, was he? Not when it's there on a plate. From all accounts, Maisie got to hoping this was going to turn into something permanent, but anyone could have told her, first sniff Tony got of Betsy coming back, and goodbye Maisie! Well, that happened at Christmas. You must have noticed Maisie wasn't exactly going round wishing everyone a happy New Year!'

I listened, amazed and delighted. Wrapped up in my own affairs, I'd been stone deaf to local gossip. It certainly explained why Maisie's mood had changed from one of relative benevolence for several weeks to one of more than normal malignancy! And best of all, it provided a motive for self-slaughter which would never be allowed into the open but which would certainly be whispered in the ears of the police and the coroner.

I said, 'Charley, can I leave you to handle this by yourself? I'd like to get back and let Lorna know what's happened before someone else gets there with the story.'

'No problem,' said Charley. 'You're right. It'll be better coming from you. Poor Lorna. Last of the Pallisers now.'

'Indeed. Thanks, Charley. And by the way, sorry I rushed forward just now. No way to behave. This is clearly your body. We'd never have found it without your torch. It's your *twelfth*.'

I could see he was sorely tempted but we boddicombing Boddicombers may not have a written code, but we play things by the book.

'No,' he said regretfully but firmly. 'You were first there, John. She's yours.'

That's what I call real moral fibre.

When I got back to the house, the Land Rover was parked outside. Lorna was sitting in the kitchen, drinking a glass of whisky.

On my way back I'd been working out how to play this. If she blurted everything out straight away, so be it. I'd do everything I could to cover things up. But in the long term, I doubted if this would do anything for our marriage. Shared guilt isn't a good basis for a relationship. What she needed was my unconditional love, not my complicity. And what I needed was hers, not a sense that she was in thrall to me.

So before she could speak I said, 'I'll have one of those. I've got some bad news, I'm afraid, dear.'

I told her about finding Maisie on the beach. When I told her about Maisie and Tony Simkin, I could tell from her reaction that she'd missed this too. Boddicombers might like their gossip, but they can be as discreet as doctors when it comes to keeping things from people they don't think should know them, like family.

'So poor Maisie must have just cracked under the strain. I thought she'd been acting a bit odd lately, even for her,' I concluded.

She sat in silence for a while. She looked pale and I guessed she was nerving herself to tell me the truth. Confession followed by expiation, that was the only route for a Boddicombe Baptist. Though if we could cut straight to the expiation, and it was painful enough, we might be able to put the confession on permanent hold . . .

But what form of expiation could I offer which would do the trick? How in the space of a few seconds could I weave a hair shirt fit for a guilt-ridden baptist?

Then it came to me. Thank you God, I thought. You've got yourself a convert.

I said, 'This has been a terrible shock for you, darling. You look whacked out. Have you had anything to eat yet? Why don't I rustle up something for both of us. And then we'll go round to Maisie's.'

She looked at me in fearful alarm.

'What for . . . ? I'm not sure . . . John, there's something . . . '

'To collect Samson, of course. You know how the poor beast doted on Maisie. He's going to be desolate. Someone's got to look after him, and if you don't, who will?'

'Samson? Look after Samson?'

I knew how she hated that dog, far worse than any dislike she'd ever felt for Maisie.

'Yes. Maisie would have wanted that, don't you think? Good job you're here to do it. Maisie will rest all the easier for knowing that dear old Samson's in good hands for the rest of his days. If you aren't around to do it, then who will? No, it would be the needle, I'm afraid . . . '

I was laying it on thick. No other way when someone's in search of a sacrifice.

She said again, 'Samson . . . look after Samson . . . '

For a moment I thought the prospect was going to be too daunting. But it was probably the very horror it roused that did the trick.

She nodded vigorously, even tried a smile.

'Yes, you're right, John. You're so right. That's exactly what Maisie would have wanted.'

As hair shirts went, Samson was going to be really scratchy for me as well as Lorna, I thought as I contemplated the single pork chop and recalled viewing the remnants of its one-time partner.

'Right,' I said. 'So let's have a bite to eat then I'll collect the dear little chap. Oh, there seems to be only one chop, dear.'

'Yes. It's yours. You have it. I'm not terribly hungry.'

She smiled at me as she spoke with more affection than I'd seen in her face for a long long time.

I smiled back at her. It was a long way back, but we were taking the first steps.

It suddenly occurred to me that while Lorna's will had been burned, Maisie's presumably hadn't, which meant her cottage and income would be coming to Lorna. Knowing my wife, she would do everything in her power to renounce the inheritance.

That was going to be my next test in diplomacy. Already I was seeing a way round it.

At the height of our anger, Lorna had sworn I would never get another penny of her money, and I had vowed that even if she begged me to take it, I would throw it back in her face.

Of course in our improved relations it would be easy to go back on both of those promises. But how much easier it would be simply to agree that whatever both of us had said in the past about her money, she need feel no compunction about giving nor I about taking what had once been Maisie's.

And with that little bit of help, I could soon be back on my feet again!

Foolish overconfidence? Why so?

I was a fully fledged Boddicomber boddicomber and my luck had changed.

I took a knife and sliced the chop in half.

'No problem,' I said. 'Let's share.'

~

He walks the white hills of Egypt
Reading the map of clay —
And through his night there moves the light
Artillery of day.

Charles Causley, 'Homage to Jack Clemo'

Anthony Thwaite

HOW TO BEHAVE

Alex is almost four, and knows ways to behave.
'Being silly' is not one of them.
He knows his Grandpa shouldn't be like this.

Kicking my feet up, pulling a face,
Putting on funny voices — this is 'being silly',
And Alex hates it, wants to tell me so.

So he takes his Grann off, and says to her:
'Please let me talk to Grandpa by myself,'
He tells me what he has to say. I promise.

And so I am not silly. I know how to behave,
At least in front of Alex. How to behave
Elsewhere is something I have still to learn.

FOR KETTLE

Poor old creature, friend for eighteen years,
Your spine and ribs too sharp, your cry so
    quiet,
You lie disconsolate, and bring to mind
The lion of St Jerome in that altar-piece,
The saint's companion in this passing world,
Who now lies miserably curled
At the side of the bed which has just become a
    bier:
As if in dumb reaction to the grief

Others more piously indicate above
With praying hands, letting a devout tear
Drop in the margin of this Pietà,
You and that big cat behave
With weary instinct, imitate with grace
Something we want somehow to mark as love.

❧

And Saul, yet breathing out threatenings and slaughter against the disciples of the Lord, went unto the high Priest, and desired of him letters to Damascus, to the Synagogues, that if he found any of this way, whether they were men or women, he might bring them bound unto Jerusalem. And as he journeyed he came near Damascus, and suddenly there shined round about him a light from heaven. And he fell to the earth, and heard a voice saying unto him, Saul, Saul, why persecutest thou me? And he said, Who art thou Lord? And the Lord said. I am Jesus whom thou persecutest: It is hard for thee to kick against the pricks. And he trembling and astonished, said, Lord, what wilt thou have me to do? And the Lord said unto him, Arise, and go into the city, and it shall be told thee what thou must do. And the men which journeyed with him, stood speechless, hearing a voice, but seeing no man. And Saul arose from the earth, and when his eyes were opened, he saw no man: but they led him by the hand, and brought him into Damascus. And he was three days without sight, and neither did eat, nor drink.

Acts of Apostles, chapter IX

Lawrence Sail

EARLY GHOST

Each saturday morning, about halfway through the show, he was led out. From the shimmering dusty folds of the curtains, he was taken over to where the upright piano stood in the spotlight, a dark oblong in a bright distended circle. He walked waveringly, as if expecting a collision. He was thin and quite tall, and his jacket and trousers were loose on him. His hair, light brown, was tousled, and against the wavy curtains his crinkled shadow looked awry. He looked somehow as if he needed filling out. It would have been hard to guess his age.

A burly man held him at the elbow, helping him to find his way towards the piano. Meanwhile, a small square screen was lowered in front of the curtains. It came down quite fast, stopped abruptly and hung there, swaying slightly from side to side. Now he had reached the piano. Released from his companion, he felt his way round it, located the stool, lowered himself on to it, steadying himself with both hands.

And all this time the cheerful hubbub continued: loud chatter and laughter, the thump of seats flipping up as someone or other changed places, or went running down the aisle to the toilets, the sprung doors beneath the green

EXIT signs banging back and sending a waft of disinfectant into the auditorium.

He always waited for what seemed many minutes, leaning forward, his hands resting on the keys. He would smile, slightly: no telling whether this meant patience, or that he was pleased to hear the kids just going on being kids, and he in among them; or something else. Then the words of the songs appeared on the screen, a crescendo of wolf whistles gave way to silence and he would strike up. My bonny lying over the ocean; a long way to the sweetest girl I know; your troubles packed up in the old kit bag — they were always the same songs, and the youthful audience took them as they found them, out of any known context, singing with ragged gusto.

At the end it was always the same, too. The burly man reappearing, clapping noisily and inviting the audience to do the same: the pianist bowing vaguely, holding on to the piano with his left hand, before being led off again. Wild clapping. More wolf whistles. A few minutes later, the small screen was jerked up and out of sight, then the great globe lights dimmed to deep orange and died away, the great curtains flooding from gold to raspberry, then deep blue, then sweeping back for the second half of the show.

Half a century on, it is that pale ghost of a pianist who has lodged most firmly, even though he existed only once a week for ten minutes or so. More than Roy Rogers or Trigger, more than the invitation to take a look at life again soon, more even than Tom or Jerry, Micky or Pluto.

But why — and who was he? Does he live in the minds of everyone in that long-gone audience, like a soft infection, or as if each young filmgoer had picked up and kept a piece of a shattered hologram, with his image intact on each fragment? Is it the irony of his own situation that makes him so memorable, his own darkness pointing the darkness in which we sat, and through which the beam of the projector drove its twisting shaft of images? And why did no one ever say his name? He would not answer even if he could. The business of ghosts is simply to haunt: that is their *raison de non-être*. The questions come from us: and we must try to answer them.

Lawrence Sail

LIKE CROSSING A ROOM IN THE DARK

Something enjoys the thought of a minor
    challenge
and wants to swim in the dark, among the
    objects
that live there. It becomes a burglar's game
with rules you make yourself: not to stub
your toe, knock into chairs or tables, or
make a noise. You push off from the door,
stop to guess at shapes — your eyes can do
no better than dark purple. And to listen.
Somewhere a slow clock is lying in wait.

What is it that the room seems to expect?
Why should you think the furniture is swelling
to half its size again? You drift your arms
to feel the air ahead. You say to yourself,
I have a purpose, my own expectations.
I am crossing a room in the dark: foolish
    enough,
but harmless. On the far side there must be a
    door.
You breast the night like a dreamer, waiting to
    strike
the first giant chair, the first boulder of dust.

Shena Mackay

NAY, IVY, NAY

Once upon a time there lived a professor in a house which was so old that a forest of concrete had grown up around it. Holly House had withstood and weathered centuries before the first paving stones were ever planted there. Its solitary inhabitant was a professor of botany and his head was so full of ferns and fungi that he was quite impervious to the preoccuptions of the rest of the populace. In the short dark days and long nights of December, while some folk wrapped presents and others lagged themselves in polythene against the blast, when revellers, barrow boys and beggars took to the streets in novelty Santa Claus hats, and turkeys and conifers counted the cost, the professor's mind ran on the furtive inflorescence of dank and secret places. The eminent mycologist was tall and thin, with a voice as dry as sawdust and you might imagine that he dined like a worm on the crumbled detritus of dead foliage or bored like a beetle through the ancient volumes on his bookshelves. He proposed to spend Christmas Day working on a paper he was to deliver at the South London Botanical Institute, a treatise titled *Some Mutations of Crusted Fungi in Metropolitan Cemeteries*.

Sharp and smooth-leaved hollies, glossy, dark

317

and variegated hollies with berries of every shade of red and yellow surrounded the house and two gnarled trees had twined into a thicket over the gate, where they clutched the professor's few visitors in their prickly fingers. The high walls of the garden at the back were thick with ivy and globes of mistletoe hung in the apple boughs. A lead sundial marked the hours, there was a birdbath with a trickling fountain and here and there the silhouette of a bird clipped from laurel, privet, box and yew. It was this walled garden that held the professor's greatest treasure: a slender holly tree with a crown of waxen leaves and, threaded on milky stalks, clusters of berries whiter than snow. He loved the white holly more than anybody in this world; he had cherished her since her first tentative, astonishing leaf had pierced the mould, protected her until she was strong enough to dance in the winter wind; she was his pale darling decked in pearls.

Now, although the professor cared not a candied fig for the Christmas conventions, he was not averse to certain archaic carols and, when the fancy took him, he would creak out 'The Holly and the Ivy' in counterpoint to the garden birds' chorale or declaim in his sawdusty, sing-song voice a version of the ballad for which he had a particular fancy:

> Nay, ivy, nay,
> It shall not be, I wys,
> Let holly have the mastery
> As the manner is.

Not far from the professor's house, in the heart of the concrete forest, stood a tall tower where there lived a poor woodcutter and his wife. Her name was Ivy, his was John and they were contented, honest and hardworking, he in pruning and felling the borough's trees and she on the bakery counter of Simmington's Supermart. But late one evening, Ivy stood at her high window in the tower looking out with a heavy heart. Her sister Blanche, whom she had not seen for many years, was arriving soon from Australia with her family and, on the telephone, Blanche had instructed her, 'Don't forget now, Ivy, we're all looking forward to a white Christmas. We insist on it. We're counting on you, so don't let us down!'

There was a hard frost that night but, alas, the forecast for Christmas was damp and mild. Then, as Ivy gazed sadly down, she saw the white tree glittering in the professor's garden far below, so sharp and clear in the moonlight that it seemed as if a breath of wind would set icy music tinkling through its branches. A frozen plume rose from the birdbath and, among the statuary and topiary, was a frosted bush as round as a perfect Christmas pudding.

'If I cannot order a white Christmas out of doors,' Ivy told her husband John, 'I will create one here in our flat on the eleventh floor, a miniature world as magical as the scene inside the glass snowstorm ball that Blanche and I loved when we were children.'

'Go for it, girl,' said he.

* * *

On a foggy evening not long afterwards, the professor was enraged by a knocking at his door. He opened it to find a woman standing in his porch. Her hair was like a raven's wing, a single bead of blood as red as a berry stood out on her ivory cheek where a holly had scratched her. She carried a pair of secateurs and a white box.

'If you've come to demand figgy pudding,' said the professor, 'you've come to the wrong house. I've just seen off a couple of young scoundrels who had the effrontery to interrupt my work with their caterwauling for figgy pudding. 'Good tidings we bring to you and your *king*', indeed! I'll guarantee they won't make that mistake again!'

'It's a traditional carol,' said Ivy, 'and it's traditional for children to get the words wrong but I haven't come for figgy pudding.'

She shivered in the draught from inside the house that was colder than the air outside, and noticed a tracery of lichen on the professor's teeth.

'Who *are* you then, and what do you want? Why do you have those secateurs in your hand?'

'My name is Ivy and I have come to ask for a single spray of your white holly, which I can see from my window on the estate,' she said. 'I borrowed the secateurs from my husband who is employed by the council. My sister Blanche who is flying from Australia has set her heart on a white Christmas and as I cannot bear to disappoint her, I have transformed my flat into a

320

fairy-tale grotto with a silver Christmas tree and perspex icicles and frosted baubles and a kissing bough of artificial mistletoe. I have hung silver paper chains, sprayed snow on the windows and made a round pudding from white sugar and spices, pale sultanas and blanched almonds. A sprig of white berries would be its crowning glory.'

'How dare you!' shouted the professor. 'Have you any idea what desecration, what violation you have the temerity to suggest? You have the effrontery, *Hedera Helix Vulgaris*, to presume to stick my precious holly in your pallid pudding, to shrivel and blacken in the blue flames of your cheap cooking brandy! Leave my property at once, return to your vandal husband and the common, ignorant hooligans of your estate and never darken my door again!'

'I may be common, but I am not ignorant,' said Ivy. 'I have brought you a box of our luxury cognac mince pies. Deep-filled, with latticed lids and suitable for vegetarians. I work at Simmington's Supermart where the baking is done in store and I can vouch for all the ingredients.'

'Pah!' said the professor. 'What sort of exchange is that? My holly is beyond price and No-Frills mince pies are two a penny at Kwiksave. It is apparent that you look upon the festive season as an excuse for intemperance and gluttony. You would do well to heed the sorry example of a family by the name of Cratchit who, I recollect, gorged themselves silly on a superfattened fowl. It did for the youngest, a peevish and sickly lad, and serve him right!'

'That is a wicked lie. Everybody knows that Tiny Tim did not die. You are as cruel as dead King Herod in your hatred for little children.'

The professor laughed, like holly leaves rasping in an icy wind.

'What makes you think King Herod is dead? Do you never watch your television or open a newspaper?'

'I only wanted to make Christmas magical,' Ivy whispered.

'To make Christmas magical?' he repeated. 'You confuse the secular with the sacred, my good woman.'

'I am not your good woman, nor am I of the Druid persuasion, but my philosophy can accommodate mistletoe and miracle, Magi and magic, faith and Father Christmas. I acknowledge that I was wrong to ask for your white berries, but even as we speak, my sister Blanche is homing through the clouds in the anticipation of snow.'

The professor took the box from Ivy, and biting into a pie, spoke through a mouthful of mincemeat, 'In opting for the Antipodes your sister Blanche has forfeited her claim to snow and deserves no more than sand in her Christmas pudding. However, if you insist on humouring her, I suggest that you apply to the Clerk of the Weather.'

'I had no idea that such a person existed outside the pages of the Rupert Annual,' said Ivy, adding, 'it is evident that you never had a sister.'

'I had a sister once,' the professor told her. 'Gladdon by name, a scholar like myself, but fleet of foot and skilful at spinning yarn. She was cast under a spell by an enchanter who turned her into a dancing bear, and now she has been sold to a travelling circus.'

'Bears are not born to dance,' said Ivy. 'Why do you not enlist the services of an animal welfare agency, or force the enchanter to lift the spell?'

'That I cannot do, for the enchanter is Time himself, but I believe she is quite happy, although it is hard to tell,' the professor replied. 'She shambles and her fur is rather shabby but everybody says how kind her master is; he feeds her titbits from his own plate and the people love to see her dance in the circus ring and toss coins into her paper cup when she leads the parade.'

'I do not believe you,' said Ivy. 'I am going home now and I wish you joy of your white holly!'

So saying, she turned and walked down the path to the professor's sing-song refrain:

> Nay, Ivy, nay,
> It shall not be, I wys,
> Let Holly have the mastery,
> As the manner is.
>
> Holly stands in the hall,
> Fayre to behold;
> Ivy stands without the door,
> She is full sore a-cold.

Ivy did not look back as the mocking verses pursued her.

Holly and his merry men,
They dance and they sing;
Ivy and her maidens,
They weep and they wring.

Ivy hath a chilblain
She caught it with the cold,
So might they all have one
That with Ivy hold.

When Ivy reached the gate prickly fingers held
her captive while the professor's cawing, sawing
voice came carolling through the gloom.

Holly hath berries,
As red as any rose,
The foster and the hunter,
Keep them from the does.

Ivy hath berries
As black as any sloe,
There comes the owl,
And eats them as she goes.

Holly hath birds,
A full, fayre flock,
The nightingale, the poppinjay,
The gentle laverock.

Good Ivy, tell me,
What birds hast thou?
Only the owlet
That cries how, how!

As Ivy freed herself from the thicket, she could not imagine the professor dancing and singing with any merry men, unless they were a company of ghosts. The professor may have the mastery, she thought, or perchance the mystery, but I shall not weep and wring my chilblained hands like a poor maid consigned to the ice and muck of a medieval midden. Ivy's berries, black and green, are as lovely as any, her sweet-scented flowers are full of bees and passionate shepherds weave belts of straw and ivy buds with coral clasps and amber studs. Besides, I have always been rather partial to owls.

By midnight on Christmas Eve the professor had consumed all but two of the luxury pies.

'This mincemeat is rather rich for my digestion,' he decided, laying aside his pen. 'I shall scatter the remains where my feathered friends may find it more to their taste,' and he went out into his garden, heedless of the falling rain.

High in the nearby tower, John the woodcutter, his brother-in-law and nephews and nieces were all asleep, but Ivy and her sister Blanche still sat up talking.

'Midnight,' said Blanche. 'Let us pull up the blind and listen for sleigh bells as we used to long ago.'

The sisters stood at the window looking down. They heard church bells pealing out and from deep in the concrete forest came the first cry of a newborn child, that breaks and heals the heart in the same instant.

'Look, Ivy! Look at the magical tree!' Blanche

exclaimed. 'How luminously it shines, with moonstones glimmering among its leaves! But how weird — it may be jet lag or the white port we have been drinking — but that garden below appears to be full of flying birds, dipping in and out of the rising cascades of the fountain, and surely that's a topiaried bush but it's fluttering down from its pedestal, and there's a peacock spreading its tail! That long-legged striding figure, look, it seems to be growing taller and taller! Ivy, is it a man or a walking tree?'

'I cannot tell,' said Ivy.

And as she watched the great dark shape moving down the garden, reaching out branching arms to embrace the white holly tree, a white owl detached itself from the flock and circled upwards, soaring over black treetops and hazy streetlights, beating through the rain towards the tower on dipping snowy wings.

∾

I will relate a (doubtless fictitious) anecdote which was told me as a boy at Worcester College for the blind. I find it funny, but it is also quite brutal. It shows the kind of stories which disadvantaged people tell about themselves. There was a young girl who was, unfortunately, very short-sighted. She refused to wear glasses, doubtless subscribing to Dorothy Parker's dictum, 'men seldom make passes at girls who wear glasses'. This girl was walking out with a young man and was worried that he might discover her defective sight, and that this would

326

put him off her. *So*, one day, she proceeded to the field where she often used to take walks with her boyfriend, and stuck a pin in the bark of an oak tree. On their next country walk, she casually remarked to him: 'I have an idea that you think I don't see very well.' 'Well,' said the young man, 'I suppose I did rather think that.' 'In fact, I have unusually good sight. For example, you see that oak tree at the other end of the field? I can see that someone has stuck a pin in the bark.' 'I don't believe you,' said the young man, 'you couldn't possibly see a pin at that distance.' 'I'll prove that I'm right,' she said, and, striding out briskly across the field, walked straight into a cow.

John Heath-Stubbs, *Hindsights*

Frederick Forsyth

THE PASSING OF HUMPY

The fishing had been superb. Starting early from the marina, we had cruised due east until the dim blur of the low-lying Florida Keys slipped away into the horizon behind us and we were alone on the wide blue Gulf Stream that runs twenty miles off the coast from New England to Mexico.

During the journey out to the 'hot spot' my sons and I had idled the time on the roomy afterdeck, the fishing deck, as Greg the boatman had prepared the rods, lines, lures and baits. My sons Stuart and Shane were then thirteen and eleven and a day fishing the gulf was a great adventure.

As one rod after another was prepared for the water and stacked in the rod-holders, the MV *Otter* put her nose into the rising swell and ploughed onwards at twenty knots. High above us on the flying bridge the skipper Clyde Upchurch had the helm, constantly scanning the horizon for the tell-tale cluster of diving and wheeling seabirds that meant a school of bait fish near the surface. Such a school indicates that if the birds are above there are big predator fish circling down below.

By eight we had reached our target, a spot far out on the ocean quite unmarked by any buoy or pennon, yet which Clyde could identify with the help of his echo-sounder. From the sea floor two thousand feet below a great, single, conical mountain reared up, coming to within 409 feet of the surface. This was known as the Four-Oh-Nine or simply the Hump.

As always with such features, the underwater mountain climbed towards the light. That light meant that plants and weed could finally grow on the mountain peak, dim though the light might be. The vegetation attracted algae and small fish; they in turn brought the larger fish to hunt them; and the larger fish brought the giants: tuna, sailfish and the strong, heavy-muscled amberjack. Round them all, slow and seemingly lethargic, waiting their moment, were the oceanic sharks, white-fin and black-tip, tiger and bull.

By nine we had our first strike. One of our baited lures, hung with a fetching array of squid, had been taken by an amberjack and the struggle was on. I gave the rod to Stuart, while Shane danced around waiting for his turn. The sun climbed higher and came down on the afterdeck as hammer on anvil.

It was a good jack, fifty-five pounds of meat and muscle when a boy with aching shoulders and arms finally brought it up from four hundred feet to the side of the boat and Greg took over with his gaff to haul it over the side.

It was quickly despatched and its great body would provide an ample supply of bait-meat for the rest of the day. The rest of the catches would be for the fish market on Islamorada to defray the costs of the trip.

So it went on all morning, with Stuart, Shane and I taking turns. Sometimes two rods were on the go at the same time; the afterdeck noisy with shouts of 'strike on number three', grunts of effort, yells of triumph as a line raced away, planks slick with sea water, hazardous with the thrash of flailing tails as the fish came aboard. That is sea-angling; muscle-pain, strain, patience, excitement, blazing sun, hard brown hands on bent-over rods, screaming reels, G-string lines, the one-on-one contest of man and big fish, and final exhaustion. You either like it or you do not. We did.

By twelve noon we had nine amberjack including the now dismembered bait fish, the rest cleanly gutted and lying in the fish trunk under a mound of ice; there had been two bonito and twice something had bitten that was so big and powerful it had simply taken the line and snapped it. Almost certainly gigantic shark. Once Stuart insisted on trying for shark, with a huge hook and the entire head of the first amberjack. The bait was taken all right, but we never saw the monster who had it. Just too big to handle. There was no choice but to cut line or lose the whole rig.

The *Otter* could obviously not anchor at this depth, so all morning we had drifted on the one-knot current, engines at the idle. When we cleared the Hump on the down-tide side, we had to haul everything back up while Clyde gunned the motors and took us round to a point half a mile up-tide of the Hump and we would start the drift again. We must have done this twenty times.

By half past twelve I called for a break. The boys wanted to go on but I was already tired and Greg had worked non-stop. Clyde shut down both engines and we drifted and bobbed on the ocean while breaking open the sandwich lunches. The tide would carry us well away from the Hump during lunch, but Clyde would quickly find it again with his sounder. So we chomped the meaty 'subs' from the marina deli and slurped the welcome cold beer.

It was about one o'clock when I saw something far out to sea. I was sitting on the edge of the fish locker, staring across the water, bright under the sun even through Polaroid glasses. I was thinking of nothing in particular when I caught sight of a wheeling gull several hundred yards east of the stern. The gutting of the jacks had brought us the usual crowd of these raucous robbers, always eager and angry to snap up the sinking entrails in the water before they drifted out of reach and back to the ocean floor where they would either be caught on the way down or nestle finally in the rocks below for crab and lobster.

The gull I saw was alone but aloft, turning as if looking at something below, and uttering short angry screams. Between the gull and the sea was something else, a tiny dot that hovered just above the water. I looked again and saw it was not hovering but flying, a little bird but not a sea bird; much too small even for the tiniest tern. This was a land-based bird. But so far out? And, by the flight pattern, exhausted, at the end of its tether, seeking to avoid the dives of the gull yet not splash down in the sea and be lost for ever. More, the little fugitive was heading straight towards us, the only piece of 'land' in all that ocean. I stood up.

She was failing fast. At a hundred yards she was only a few inches above the water, rising desperately to about a foot as the rolling swell reached up, tiny wings losing the last strength to stay aloft, straining towards the taffrail of the *Otter* where I stood. At fifty yards I knew she could not make it; when she hit the sea the gull would win and have her meal. I took the gaff net on its pole and waved it high above my head, shouting at the black-headed gull.

The gull saw the movement and swerved away, torn between lust for the meal and fear of the human. At twenty yards the little flier trembled one last time, the sea reached up and she was gone. By now Stuart and Shane were beside me, watching the aerial drama so near and yet so out of reach. The gull dived towards the water. We yelled, all three; it screamed in rage and pulled away, back up into the blue sky. I shouted to Clyde, up on his flying bridge draining a Bud, asking if he could back up. He grinned, shrugged, hit one of the starter motors and an engine coughed into life. Slowly *Otter* began to back stern first through the rolling water. And there she was.

She lay quite limp on the surface of the sea, a little brown sodden thing, eyes closed, gone presumably to another and a kinder world. I

332

used the gaff net to scoop her up and signalled to Clyde to cut the engine.

She lay in my hand, little more than an ounce, and that included the salt water, quite limp and dead. But I was surprised by her appearance. Years ago I used to study birds and this was a sort of small finch or warbler, but not from North America. I was sure I had seen a picture of her like in a book called *Birds of Africa*. But how on earth had she crossed the Atlantic?

I surmised there could only be one explanation. Blown far off course above the Sahara by desert winds while on her migratory journey, she must have lost sight of the coast, lost also her bearings, and sought refuge in the rigging of an ocean tramp. Only a ship could have brought her so far from home.

Then, sensing the approach of land as the vessel neared the American coast, she must have thought she could return on the wing to her native home. But she underestimated the length of the journey still remaining, and overgauged her own strength. She was still twenty miles from shore when her little spirit failed and she went down in the sea. And even the *Otter*, her last hope, was now too late.

I was for throwing the limp body back, but Shane would have none of it. A burial was in order, when we got home. So he took the lifeless refugee into the cabin, made a pall from one of those rough towels that fishermen use to wipe faces and hands, drew the last fold of the cloth over the body and returned to the fishing deck. It was hot in the cabin, with both side windows and the doors open to catch any passing breeze, but still hot. We resumed our fishing, allowing ourselves two more hours before the hour-long journey home.

Sixty minutes later I was passing through the cabin to the heads when I saw something that stopped me in my tracks. Beneath the fold of towel something stirred. I lifted the corner of cloth with finger and thumb. A bright bead of eye was staring at me. I went out and called Shane. He was ecstatic. He shouted up to Clyde on his flying bridge, 'She's alive, the little bird is still alive.'

Clyde grinned and shouted back, 'Right on.'

Shane stared down at the sodden bird and the bird stared back.

'What shall we call her?' he asked.

'Well, we found her over the Hump. Let's call her Humpy,' said I.

Shane insisted on taking over as nurse for his new charge. He had had enough of fishing. Stuart, the angling fanatic, was still tending his rods. Shane caught a fly on a window pane in case Humpy was hungry but after examining the trophy Humpy rejected it.

A bottle cap of fresh spring water was different. After testing to make sure it was not salty, Humpy thrust her beak in, then tilted back to let the clear liquid trickle down her throat. This she did a dozen times. Thirst slaked, she began to preen. Salt water dries sticky on unoiled feathers, so it took some time. Shane and I went back outside to the rods.

Thirty minutes later Shane screamed at me

and pointed. Out to the side of the boat was Humpy — flying. But flying away.

'She's gone,' he yelled, 'she won't make it.'

She had not come past us. She had hopped off the towel, across the table to the cabin's side window and launched herself into space. As we watched, the little brown bird turned on the breeze and began to curve back. After a circle of the boat she plonked herself down on the after-rail, tilted her head to one side and looked up as if to say: 'See? Circuits.'

Then she hopped across the deck, through the doors, up to the table, across the Formica, out the window and did it again. Twenty times, and she always came back.

At four it was time to go. I looked up at Clyde and nodded. Lines up. He nodded back. Stuart, Greg and I cranked the reels until our baits came back up from four hundred feet. When they were in the holders there was no more point in staying. Cleaning the afterdeck would occupy Greg on the way home. For the rest of us, nursing shoulders, biceps, forearms and wrists that seemed to be made of aching lead was enough. Clyde hit the throttles and *Otter* punched forward, stern down, prow up, heading for the Keys and the marina. Then Shane screamed: 'She's gone. Don't leave her behind.'

But, without thinking, we had left her behind. She was not in the cabin, she was not abeam of the *Otter*, twenty yards away on one of her circuits. And the *Otter* had covered two hundred yards. I shouted at Clyde but the roar was too loud. I ran up the ladder and yelled in his ear.

He cut the engines, put them into reverse and we began to backtrack. But a fishing boat is broad-sterned and a stern is not supposed to push itself through water. It was slower, much slower. Waves formed and crashed over the rail at the back. Then we saw Humpy.

She was well astern, two hundred yards, fluttering desperately towards us. And the gull came back. We shouted and raved at the gull but he seemed to grin and the razor-beak dropped in pre-attack. With a hundred yards between Humpy and the bucking boat I thought she would still make it. Just. The gull dropped lower. At fifty yards the gull swooped. We saw the hard yellow beak take the little brown meal and it reared upwards, over us. I seized a one-pound lead weight from the tackle box, tried to recall my cricketing days and hurled it hard at the bandit above.

It did not hit the gull. That would have been a lot to ask. But its eye, that eye that could catch the glitter of a sprat in the water at a hundred feet, must have seen something coming up towards it. It opened its beak to utter an angry scream and a small feathery bundle fell free, landing barely ten yards from the boat. Again the gaff net brought her inboard.

This time it really was too late. The steel-hard bill of the predator had crushed the tiny body; the indomitable little heart had ceased to beat, the eye was dull and matt in death. Despite the wonderful day and the trunk brimming with fish we returned sadly to the marina on Islamorada.

That evening we buried Humpy in the

336

grounds of the hotel, beneath the pines, well above the high-water mark where the sea would never have her again. We begged a cigar box from the tobacco shop, made a bed of moss, dug a hole with knives from the restaurant and laid her down.

Shane was deeply miserable that our unthinking mistake had taken Humpy away. I consoled him with the thought that brave little Humpy might never fly in the skies of America, nor rest in its trees, but at least in death she had finally made her journey all the way from Africa to the New World.

Ruth Rendell

FOR DON, ON HIS BIRTHDAY

With apologies to Samuel Johnson

Oft in danger, yet alive,
You are come to forty-five,
Sharing, though in obvious way,
Attributes of Dorian Gray.
His creator tells us he
Never aged past twenty-three,
In other words, or rather,
A venerable great-grandfather,
A hoary ancient among men
To you who look no more than ten,
Or in the brilliant light of noon
As if you'll be eleven soon.
But in the evening afterglow,
Or later when the lights are low,
And people see you drinking brandy,
They say, 'That child should have a shandy
Or sip some milk, he's up too late,
Why, look at him, he's only eight!'
Dim candlelight is playing tricks,
Reducing you to under six.
At nightfall's hour, 'tis very true,
You could pass for rising two,
And later as a babe in arms,
All admire your infant charms.
The final step is evident,

Disaster without precedent.
So, growing younger at this pace,
Winning time's long steeplechase,
Put the brakes on while you may
And fix yourself at twenty, say.
Some score of years from time revoke,
Ere midnight sounds his final stroke.

The Blind Man

i

He is divested of the diverse world,
of faces, which still stay as once they were,
of the adjoining streets, now far away,
and of the concave sky, once infinite.
Of books, he keeps no more than what is left
    him
by memory, that brother of forgetting,
which keeps the formula but not the feeling
and which reflects no more than tag and
    name.
Traps lie in wait for me. My every step
might be a fall. I am a prisoner
shuffling through a time which feels like
    dream,
taking no note of mornings or of sunsets.
It is night, I am alone. In verse like this,
I must create my insipid universe.

ii

Since I was born, in 1899,
beside the concave vine and the deep cistern,

frittering time, so brief in memory,
kept taking from me all my eye-shaped world.
Both days and nights would wear away the
   profiles
of human letters and of well-loved faces.
My wasted eyes would ask their useless
   questions
of pointless libraries and lecterns.
Blue and vermilion both are now a fog,
both useless sounds. The mirror I look into
is grey. I breathe a rose across the garden,
a wistful rose, my friends, out of the twilight.
Only the shades of yellow stay with me
and I can see only to look on nightmares.

Jorge Luis Borges, *The Book of Sand*

William Boyd

BEULAH BERLIN, AN A TO Z

Angst, ennui, weltschmerz, cafard, taedium vitae, anomie — Curious how oddly beguiling these words are. I almost don't mind suffering from the conditions they describe. Some of the so-called 'beautiful diseases', perhaps. But I exaggerate: for most of my life everything was normal — I only realised I was in trouble when I went to Berlin.

★   ★   ★

Berlin gave me my name and was the making of me. Before Berlin everything was relatively straightforward: I was born, I became a child, I went to school then college (media studies), then film school — nothing about my life was particularly interesting. In film school I wanted to be an editor (I wanted control), but then changed my mind after a year and decided to become an art director (I was good at drawing but I wasn't sure I had it in me to be an artist). How do you know when your life is intrinsically uninteresting? You just do — you feel you are a slab of concrete. Some people live quietly, unhappily, with this knowledge, others do something about it.

At a film festival in Hamburg, where a short

341

film I had art-directed was being screened, I met my first husband Georg. He was an artist and, after the festival was over, I went, suddenly, spontaneously, with him to Berlin. I was twenty-two years old and I think I knew that this would be the beginning of everything. A month later we were married.

A man has just walked by leading a Great Dane and a dachshund. How peculiar. (I am writing this in Amsterdam.)

Georg and some of his friends staged an exhibition called Stunk — it should be pronounced with a German accent. They rented a floor of an office building for a month on the something-strasse and it became their art gallery. (Stunk-Kunst.) They had a spare office suite and Georg asked me to contribute something. And that was how the 'Transparent Wardrobe' happened, how Beulah Berlin came into being. After being Beulah McTurk for twenty-two years I knew that Beulah Berlin was bound to be more intriguing, altogether cooler.

★   ★   ★

Colour dominated my wardrobe in those days. I wore the brightest clothes to cover up the concrete. Now I only wear black, white and grey. At the Stunk show I hung all my garish clothes around this office on chrome rails and wore nothing but a black brassiere and panties. People could select a combination of clothes from my wardrobe, write the request on a piece of paper and I would wear whatever items they had suggested for an hour. Any combination: black stiletto and brown hiking boot; leather jacket and bikini bottom; straw sombrero and pyjama trousers. I took a Polaroid photograph of the combination and pinned it on a giant pinboard. I have to say that without Beulah Berlin and her transparent wardrobe the Stunk show would be completely forgotten. Ninety-nine per cent of the press coverage was about me and my tireless transformations. By the time the lease ran out I had over a thousand photographs: the pinboard was a huge multi-coloured collage of various Beulah Berlins. Georg never really forgave me, I now see in retrospect, and from then on our relationship went steadily to the dogs.

* * *

Dogs are wonderful animals and it's a source of endless regret to me that I've never been able to have one as a pet — because of my allergies. Who was it who said, 'The more I see of men the more I come to value dogs'? Matthew Arnold, Nietzsche? Somebody else? Certainly I place dogs higher in my estimation than my ex-husbands. Well, my first ex, definitely, not necessarily my soon-to-be second ex.

* * *

'Exudations' was the name of Georg's next show. We were still married, just, and I agreed to participate. If Stunk made me famous, Exudations made me notorious. Georg's plan was to remain indoors in our apartment for a year and to collect and preserve everything his body exuded. Everything, yes, every last drop — I don't need to go into details, suffice to say he strained his shaving water through muslin to recover the bristles. These 'exudations' bottled and boxed, hermetically sealed and carefully labelled, would then form the basis of a touring exhibition, the point being that they provided an idiosyncratic but perfect historical record of his body over one year. I managed to last three weeks in the apartment before I fell seriously ill with some potent gastro-bacteriological infection. I was hospitalised. Georg refused to leave the flat — his work was still in progress, he argued, and moreover he was in perfect health — and eventually the police had to break the doors down (neighbours were complaining also). Disinfection and fumigation followed, and Exudations was no more than a brief footnote in the history of contemporary German art. Unfortunately, I had to sue Georg for my medical bills (I was uninsured and he refused any contribution, claiming I had betrayed him). Of course, our marriage didn't survive and we were swiftly divorced. Georg went to live in a shack in Ibiza where he became something of a recluse. I haven't seen him since. I now realise that Georg was an accident waiting to happen, a faulty missile they forgot to test-fire.

★ ★ ★

Fire warmed and illuminated my early life — or, should I say, fires. Our home was in Eastbourne, on England's south coast. My father's business was the fitting and installation of gas and electric fires. In the 1980s he moved, in a small way, into the gas-coal or gas-log fire business. We lived above the shop: my father, Finlay, my mother, Irene, and my elder sister, Jayne. Just before I went to college in London my parents separated, my mother and Jayne moving west along the coast to Brighton where my mother started a surprisingly successful dance academy, as she called it: 'Irene McTurk — Academie de Danse'. My father stayed on in Eastbourne, seemingly content. I once asked him why he liked Eastbourne so.

'I hate it,' he said.

'But the people are nice.'

'I hate them.'

When he became ill I blamed it on this lifelong hatred festering in him. He should have moved away, especially when my mother and sister left. It was the place's fault, this overcrowded south-east section of our small island. The place's fault, England's.

★   ★   ★

Glands, my father later claimed, were the root cause of his lassitude and weight loss. He was in no pain but it was clear something was seriously, profoundly wrong with him. He started taking all manner of self-prescribed vitamin and health food combinations to battle his 'gland' problem.

Ginseng and cod liver oil. Nettle tea and royal jelly. Huge amounts of vitamin E and strange seaweed stews. He munched sunflower seeds all day. Nothing worked. One night a neighbour called my mother to say he had collapsed. I happened to be at home; the three of us had been out to the theatre to see a revival of a Noël Coward play (I should remember, why can't I remember what it was?). My father was emaciated and semi-conscious and when I bent over him to kiss his brow his breath smelt oddly of new-mown grass, fresh hay.

* * *

Hay fever suggests summer. Mowers in the thickening meadows and the pollens taking to the air as the grasses fall to the advancing scythe. Not in my case: for me hay fever is a spring phenomenon. Now I know why T.S. Eliot said 'April is the cruellest month' — he too must have suffered from early-season pollen allergies. When the trees begin to flower, particularly London's plane trees, my eyes itch and weep, my soft palate burns, I can sneeze sixty, eighty times in a row until I almost pass out. But now my allergies are with me all year long. I open a newspaper and my nose begins to run; a woman passes me and her perfume causes my throat to contract. I cough and cough. (Why do these women douse themselves in so much scent? Why this love of chemical odours?) At night I lie in bed and my hip bones ache as if I have arthritis. I'm not alone, I know, we're all becoming slowly poisoned, over-sensitised. We are all, in our own way, ill.

★   ★   ★

Illness casts a bright light, the rest of life retreats into the shadows beyond its refulgent glare. When my father was ill, no matter where I was, or what I was doing, I seemed to think about him a dozen times an hour. Eventually, there was nothing for it, and I moved back to Eastbourne to a bed and breakfast in the same street. He never went to hospital, district nurses used to visit him throughout the day, while I provided him with increasingly deliquescent then entirely liquid meals. Soon all he wanted was beef consommé. 'Ah,' he would say, as I brought him the steaming bowl, '*soupe du jour*.'

★   ★   ★

Journal-keeping has sustained me since I was twelve. I started a diary then and have been keeping one ever since. Over the last few years, however, I've refined the process. When I wake in the morning I write the first thing down that occurs to me and before I go to bed I write down the last thing in my mind. You should try it: it is astonishingly meaningful, not to say revelatory. Those two sentences define and plot your life in the most random yet illuminating way. I look back to 14 April 1999. Morning: 'Gianluca is a pure unreconstructed bastard.' Night: 'Put out rubbish.' 22 November 1996. Morning: 'Wintry sunlight makes my room look dirty.' Night: 'Edith Wharton is good but boring, must resist the temptation to skip.'

* * *

Kipling, Rudyard Kipling, wrote a book called *Stalky and Co.* In it there is a character called M'Turk, which I suppose is a form of McTurk (though the apostrophe is something I have never seen before). It is the only evidence I've been able to find of a McTurk in literature.

My own name, 'Beulah', comes out of a book, a book that my mother, Irene, was reading before I was born. *Knights of the Golden Horse-Shoe* by William Caruthers set in the antebellum Deep South. My mother was on a Deep South craze at the time, she loved everything about the romanticised vision of the place. I suppose it took her away from Eastbourne and my father's shop of fire. 'The Land of Beulah', she used to sigh, and thus I was named. But Beulah McTurk is all wrong. It suggests to me a plump and heavy woman, yet I am tall and very, very slim. Consequently, I was happy to become Beulah Berlin, to be named after a city. It suggests something steely, tougher, as if I surround myself with a protective forcefield, a non-stick coat of shellac, say, or Teflon.

* * *

London: too weird and wired, these days. New York: too busy. San Francisco: too healthy. Paris:

too self-conscious. Amsterdam: too relaxed. All these cities I have known well, or as well as any one person can know a city. There are times in your life, though, when relaxation is what you crave and I had to leave London, felt the panicked urge to flee. So where else would I go but Amsterdam? It drew me as a candle flame draws a moth.

* * *

Mother disapproved of my name change. She disapproved of my life as an artist, of Georg, my first husband and, I suspect, Otto, my second, though I never allowed her to meet Otto. Otto is English despite his Germanic Christian name. He's called Otto Carlyle and he repairs computers. Jayne, my big sister, met him once when she came up to London. 'He's very quiet,' she said. I told her that was why I liked him. Also he was very tall, six feet four, and after my father's death I wanted, for some vague reason, to be with a tall man. He is six foot four, I am five feet nine.

Nineteen sixty-nine. The year of my birth. 27 March 1969. That week John Lennon and Yoko Ono were doing their lie-in for peace at the Amsterdam Hilton. I am, just, a child of the Sixties, and it seems to me only apt that I should now be back in Amsterdam. Full circle, after a fashion. A near-perfect O.

* * *

Otto has just called from Dakar. Whenever he's abroad and he calls I place a photograph of him in front of me. It was taken at a beach café in Antibes when we were staying with my then gallerist, Clive Count (the 'o' is silent, I used to say later, after he dropped me). Otto is wearing surfing trunks and a baggy T-shirt, his hair is wet and sticks up in spikes — he looks like an impossibly lanky waif. I've come to hate a disembodied voice, I hate talking on the telephone, but it's never so bad when you're looking at a photo.

* * *

Photography is the art form I practise these days — I took it up seriously after I stopped touring with the Transparent Wardrobe, in fact. I travelled with the Transparent Wardrobe for some years (you could have seen my installation in galleries in Basle, Tokyo, Venice or Dusseldorf) and along with my occasional modelling work, some commercials and a small part in a TV sitcom in the USA, I managed to live comfortably enough. I taught film studies at a private university in San Francisco for two years before I began to photograph people's feet.

Of all our body parts the foot is the one we treat harshest. No other part of our body — faces included — shows with such brutal candour our individual ageing process. We stuff our feet into unsuitable shoes, we walk for miles, we barely minister to them, occasionally cutting toenails, occasionally painting said toenails. But

350

the calluses, corns, chilblains, verrucas and steady deformations alter them year on year in the most visible way. I have been photographing my own feet for over five years now and I am shocked at how they have altered. I have twenty-five subjects (friends and acquaintances, young and old) and every six months I take a photograph of their faces and feet, juxtaposed. Already two have asked to drop out, they find it too distressing, they say, as if the ticking clock of their own mortality is manifest there at the end of their legs, hidden in their shoes. Perhaps you saw my exhibition in Ghent, or the one in East Gallery East in London? I use a big old Deardorf (like Avedon) and get these fantastic 8 by 10 black and white prints with the most immaculate focus. Some people's feet look like vegetarian growths, others like eroded landscapes. Both exhibitions were great successes. Every morning before the doors opened there would be a substantial queue.

★ ★ ★

Qwertyuiop, that's what I'm going to call my child, male or female, whenever I have him or her. He or she can then make any name they want out of that combination of letters. Trey. Opi. Yute. Power. I don't care. I'm not sure, however, if I want Otto to be the father. We're meant to be separated but he has followed me over to Amsterdam and is living in this flat I have rented on the Kaisersgracht. He says that Schiphol airport is the perfect hub for his business, and it's true, he's often away. (The computers he fixes are huge and usually abroad: airports, hospitals, government departments, he was even hired by the Pentagon for two months.) In his spare time he's writing a novel called *Garden Airplane Traps* (after the painting by Max Ernst; I think Ernst has the best titles in modern art). Otto's often away doing his mysterious job and I find I miss him. Then, when he returns, I resent him. I want his presence and also his absence. When he's not at work he spends most of his time writing his novel and reading.

★　★　★

Reading is my great solace. I read a lot, but some years ago I decided, faced by the millions of books I hadn't read, to make my reading systematic. So every year I chose a theme and only read books that fall into the specific category. For example in 1995 I only read books whose titles were women's names. I read *Emma*, *Madame Bovary*, *Therese Raquin*, *Aunt Julia and the Scriptwriter*, *Clarissa*, and some others I can't remember. In 1998 I moved on to animals. I read *Kangaroo*, *Birdy*, *The Sandpiper*, *The Pope's Rhinoceros*. This year I'm on cities: *Goodbye to Berlin*, *London Fields*, *L.A. Confidential*, *Last Exit to Brooklyn*, *Is Paris Burning?*, *The Viceroy of Ouidah*. Next year it'll be abstract nouns, I have *Persuasion* and *Chaos* lined up ready to go on 1 January. More and more I find I like this way of giving your random, haphazard progress through time some sort of hidden organising factor, known only to you, only understood by you, a personal encryption. It looks normal — somebody reading a book — but underneath you alone know the significance — your life's private palimpsest.

★ ★ ★

Sestina, villanelle, sonnet. My favourite poetic forms in order of preference. It must be because I like the imposed shape, the rules, the order, the poetic matrix. I like to smoke a cigarette when I read poetry, I don't know why — I don't smoke a lot — but, with poetry, I just like to.

★ ★ ★

Tobacco is a strange drug, when you think about it. Alcohol seems more natural — we all have to drink after all. But drawing smoke into your lungs is not an instinctive process in any way. I like the smell of wood smoke, but if I see a bonfire I don't rush over to it and start inhaling the fumes. Otto smokes, he rolls his own (as do a huge number of people in Amsterdam — how curious). I prefer the perfect white cylinder of the industrially manufactured cigarettes to the thin, creased, collapsing, home-made version. Don't most people? Wouldn't you?

★ ★ ★

U-turns define life's progress, it seems to me, better than the old image of forking paths. How often in our life can its significant events be described as a U-turn? Falling out of love, for example, is a major emotional U-turn, rather than a bifurcation on life's highway. Going back to college, reeducation — there's another. When I went back to film school I was consciously and unconsciously trying to recapture something I had had before. Revisiting places. This sojourn in Amsterdam is a U-turn. I had to get out of London after my father died. Coming here is not a step forward but rather an urge to turn back down life's road and revisit a self I left behind somewhere. Otto is a bit of a U-turn too. I fell out of love, we were going to split, and now we're back together. Two U-turns there. I can't seem to make up my mind about Otto, what I truly feel about him — it's confusing. Or maybe, to use a film image, life is a series of jump-cuts. The continuity is illusory, imprecise, we just jump-cut from one sequence to another. Very *nouvelle vague*.

* * *

Vague ambitions are to be encouraged. Life should be full of half-thought-out plans for what you might like to do but haven't got the real desire for, or the energy or the time or just enough money. I vaguely want to go to Russia. I vaguely want to learn Spanish. I vaguely want to redecorate my apartment ... I cherish these vague ambitions because they seem to presuppose another existence — another life for myself — in which they might actually come about. There is the possibility of my vague ambitions becoming focused. Another Beulah Berlin, then, would go to Russia, would learn Spanish. The more vague ambitions you have the more potential lives you could lead. I explained all this once at great length to a psychiatrist (just after Georg and I had divorced) who was keen to put me on Valium. I don't think he thought I was very well.

* * *

Weltverbesserungswahn. How I love these German words. That's what my psychiatrist (he was German) said was wrong with me, what I suffered from (along with various other mental maladies). I didn't really care what it meant, I just loved the sound of the diagnosis. Then I discovered that it described a particular delusion: the delusion that the world could be better. Someone told me that Tolstoy suffered from this too. So, I'm an optimist. I was born in the Year of the Rooster, I was informed by the back of menu in a Chinese restaurant, once. We roosters are 'pioneers in spirit, devoted to work and hungry for knowledge'. We are also selfish and eccentric. Rabbits are trouble. Snakes and oxen are fine (Otto is a rabbit). I don't think that those of us who suffer from *weltverbesserungswahn* can be described as unhinged or unstable. Certainly not mad; we're not like those other sad souls, muttering or screaming from the sidewalks as human life flows on, not like those lost causes, those abject wrecks.

* * *

Xanadu is the name of the bar I work in three nights a week in Jordan. Just to keep my hand in, just to provide some steady income. I'll stop as soon as my book is ready (what do you think of *Pedal Extremities* for a title?). I met a publisher, here in Amsterdam. He said, all things being equal (curious expression), he could publish it next year.

* * *

Year of the Dragon was my dad's year. If you're a dragon, you're eccentric and your life is complex. 'You have a passionate nature and abundant health' it said on the back of that menu in the Chinese restaurant. It didn't work out like that for him. But I like to think of my dad as a dragon, a water dragon, like those Komodo Dragons, slow and solid, hauling himself out of some tropical river, climbing the bank to the lush forest beyond, scaly flanks dripping with ooze.

* * *

Zoos consoled me after my father died. I would visit them in whatever city I found myself. I never looked at the chimps however — chimps were too human with their deep malice and their crazy sense of fun. I looked for tranquillity. Not pacing lions or the other big cats. I looked for animals that seemed content with their zoo life. More and more I went to look at the rhinos. I came to love their massiveness, their heft and their effortless charisma. Rhinos have a real, immutable dignity. In my worst moments I longed to be a rhino and so I would calm myself, imagining I was a rhino in a zoo, my day an ordered round of eating, defecating and sleeping. In a zoo, but free somehow. Free from the world and its noisy demands. Free, finally, from angst.

A. S. Byatt

ODOURS SAVOURS SWEET...

Imagine a modern room, with its magic
window open on another world where
once the hearth used to be, with its wood
smoke, or its smell of hot coal with a ghost of
tar. The artificial paradises succeed each
other. Sunny glades in dappled woodland,
inviting tunnels of greenery like the
shadowed rides in Keats's 'Ode to a
Nightingale', where

> I cannot see what flowers are at my feet,
> Nor what soft incense hangs upon the
>   boughs
> But in embalmed darkness guess each
>   sweet ...

Keats lists the guessed-at flowers and grasses,

> White hawthorn and the pastoral eglantine,
> Fast fading violets covered up in leaves;
> And mid-May's eldest child,
> The coming musk-rose, full of dewy wine
> The murmurous haunt of flies on summer
>   eves.

★   ★   ★

The television screen shows branches and violets. It shows pine forests and sheets of falling white water ending in curls of clean shining spray. It shows meadows full of buttercups and pine forests full of mystery and crisp needles. It is telling you — enticing you — to recreate these atmospheres in your own home with air fresheners, with aerosol sprays of scented furniture polish, with jigging and extravagant canisters of flowery and fruity powder which will 'freshen' your stale carpets, with droplets or waxy cones which drink up the odours of tobacco smoke and shaggy dogs and damp wool and replace them with tangy fruit and flower bouquets. Think how many such smells contend for supremacy in the room with the television. The lavender polish (with its sharp aerosol undertow), the rich peachy freshener hanging in the window, the orris and attar of roses and orange peel in the carpet, the Glade, the Lavender Antiquax, the appley Pledge. Move out into the kitchen, where the floors have been washed with sugary hyacinth disinfectant, where the dishwasher is scented with lemon and honey, where there is a kind of mixed artificial flower scent in the washing machine, and perfumed paper strips making the contents of the dryer smell of essence of concentrated plums and overwhelming extract of cloves, or vanilla, or *pot pourri*, or all at once. You have seen ecstatic dancing women on your screen pressing their noses into heaps of enhanced-white towels, which do not smell of damp cotton but of lightness and freshness, you are told. Does pressing your nose into your own towels induce ecstasy?

You have a deodorising block in your refrigerator, which does not smell of nothing, but of ersatz orange or lemon or lime. Your steam iron emits aromatherapeutic steam, valerian for headaches and stomach cramps, nutmeg for digestion, neroli oil as an anti-depressant and aphrodisiac. Go out into the lavatory and your floor will smell of spring forest, your lavatory cleaner of 'pine forest' or 'aqua', which is not a smell of mussel shells and seaweed, or of froggy ponds and marsh marigolds, but another swoon-sweet mixed floral bouquet. The water-softening block in your loo tank will have its own strong sweet odour, as will the little block you hang from the rim to odorise the water in the bowl, to make it smell 'clean'. There will be air fresheners in canisters to spray high into the air from where they drop and drip in wisps of rosy or spicy or peardroppy vapour. In France even your lavatory paper will be printed with rosebuds or fleurs de lys and be 'delicatement parfumé'. Even your sanitary towels will have a florid fragrance. And the aspirins in your medicine cupboard will breathe artificial fruit at you when you dissolve them in water. Your toothpaste will smell of bananas or spearmint or raspberries. I imagine the liquid you put your false teeth in, these days, will taste of one or the other of those too.

And the people in the house will have sweet sanitised smells. Their perfume, their talc, their underarm deodorant, their shower gels and shampoos and conditioners and hair sprays will all be strong and probably intensify as they mingle on skin and hair. You will deodorise your shoes, socks and feet with things scented with strawberries and blackcurrants and mangoes. You will sit at dinner and eat your roast, or your delicate pea soup, or your rosewater sorbet and vanilla cream to the accompaniment of a candle which penetrates every fissure and fold of tablecloth and napkin and nostril with strong incense, myrrh, patchouli. If it were sounds it would be a cacophony. As with sounds, you are inured to it, and turn up the volume. Women don't wear ghosts of fragrance any more — Floris bluebells, lavender water. They assert themselves with Opium and Poison, the swooning, insistent scents of the Artificial Paradises of the Decadents. They have to, and even so, it doesn't work. The one thing all these fresheners and perfumed atmospheres have in common is a sickly over-sweetness, not honey, not the pale vanishing sweet scent of wild primroses, not the energy of burning sugar, but a thick, bland saccharine fug, like putting your head into a jar of lollipops. Or like the taste of old stomach medicines, masking the nastiness that was good for you with floury emulsions. Or like the banana or strawberry gels you gag on at the dentist's, when he takes an impression of your teeth with something slimy green or sticky pink.

What do we think of as good smells? We like roasting coffee, we like baking bread. We like the smells of cleanness — freshly starched and ironed linen, freshly shaved wood, with the sap still in it. Supermarkets now tempt in customers with the smells of baking and coffee-roasting wafted from grilles near the door, as clothes shops tempt in young customers with amplified drums and guitars. We like delicate plant smells — moss, and lavender, and witch hazel. The perfume name, White Linen, trades on our liking for clear smells, as the increasing number of shampoos and lotions that are transparent in transparent bottles advertise themselves as pure and crystalline. But inside they smell of heavy things — frangipani, lilies, attar of roses, overripe fruit. In the 1970s the makers of Johnson's baby powder appear to have discovered that many women were using the baby powder on themselves, and, instead of drawing the conclusion that we liked a faint scent of witch hazel and a plain bottle, they changed the packaging to a lurid pink and made the scent heavily floral. It is interesting that this decision was later reversed. We like outdoor smells — pine forests, lavender, herbs, but not those with an element of decay — bracken, mushrooms, which we find interesting, but would not want to wear or leave around our houses.

Bad smells are human smells, our own smells. Excrement first, but we don't like sweat, or cheesy feet, or stale or sickly breath, or other people's after-sex fish smell, or old clothes, and we don't like things that smell like our own smells, things like the rich rank fungus, *amanita phalloides*. Freud was very interested in the human nose. He believed that children crawling

362

in the nursery did not find excreta repulsive, whereas adults find the strong smell of other people's excreta disgusting. He put this down to the 'atrophy of a sense of smell (which was an inevitable result of man's assumption of an erect posture)' and he wondered whether 'the consequent organic repression of man's pleasure in smell may not have had a considerable share in his susceptibility to nervous disease'. He thought human sexual problems and the coming of repression came with bipedalism and distance from the earth. My husband remarked sagely, when told this, that he wondered if Freud had any views about the nervous state of giraffes.

Freud observed also that other animals used their sense of smell in the pursuit of their sexual lives without inhibition. Humans had invented sexual pleasures that came from overcoming distaste or disgust about the proximity of the sexual and the excretory organs. He noted that most people are happy with their own smells. We think of Leopold Bloom asquat on the cuckstool, reading his newspaper, 'seated calm above his own rising smell'. It is other people whose failure to be clean — according to Freud — 'to hide their own excreta' — is offensive, and 'shows no consideration'.

The smells that have invaded our modern lives are neither the good smells nor the bad smells, but the guilty masking smells. Smells we use to cover human smells. I remember as a girl reading Smollett's *Roderick Random* in which an old maiden lady tries to pass herself off as a marriageable girl and is detected by the 'violet cachous' she uses to perfume her breath, and to cover the odour from her decaying teeth. I was horrified by this image — which is of course a dance of death parody of the spring flower breath of pastoral maidens. I still shudder when I see small violet sweets. There is a different kind of horror in the idea of the intimate feminine sprays or delicately perfumed moistened wipes, with which my generation were urged to get rid of any female smell from their crutches and vaginas. Were we pretending to perpetual maidenhood? Or were we, as Freud supposed, uneasy about responding to bodily functions at all?

Richard Hoggart in the first book of his autobiography, *A Local Habitation*, gives an account of both the squeamish niceties and the wicked humour of his working-class background in 1920s Yorkshire. It is too good not to quote as it stands. He is writing about his aunts Ethel and Ida.

The lavatory in each of their homes reeked of one of the more heavily perfumed 'toilet deodorants'. The blend of that with the smell of an evacuation was more unpleasant than the smell of shit itself, like a rank and fetid growth concocted in a shifty laboratory, a poisonous but ersatz jungle plant. But it too, like the words for the things, and no matter how much they stepped up the deodorants, eventually said to them: 'Someone's just had a shit here.' So they took to leaving a pack of cigarettes in the lavatory and suggesting that their guests might feel like a smoke to reduce the unbecoming smell. There were then three smells: shit, heavy deodorants and cigs. Aunt Annie who had a slightly scatological side told me she would sit there puffing away like mad and the smell was something awful.

John Donne, in Elegie IV, 'The perfume', describes how his clandestine visits to his mistress were betrayed to her father by

'A loud perfume, which at my entrance cryed
Even at thy father's nose, so were wee spied'

The plain use of synaesthesia is very effective, dramatically, as smell replaces sound as a clue, and Donne suggests that his perfume was perhaps extravagant. He immediately contrasts his adorning smell with her father's basic human ones.

Had it beene some bad smell, he would have thought
That his owne feet or breath that smell had wrought.

He goes on to inveigh against perfume in general —

Base excrement of earth, which dost confound
Sense, from distinguishing the sicke from sound

cunningly characterising the perfume as the substance it is masking. He describes incense as loathsome:

> Gods, when yee fum'd on altars, were pleas'd well
> Because you were burnt, not that they lik'd your smell,

revealing an ambivalence about incense that is very common. Does the perfumed incense in churches replace the fatty smoke from burned offerings? Is it designed to confuse the senses into swooning? Or does it again conceal the smell of mortality? Modern churchmen make uneasy jokes about smells 'n bells. Browning's sensual Renaissance Bishop, ordering his tomb in St Praxed's Church, cannot imagine eternity except in terms of solid, bodily, earthbound emotions and pleasures, which include 'smelling' 'thick stupefying incense all day long'.

Perfumes were once rich, rare and exotic. When Scheherazade and Dunyazade married the two princely brothers, the Hammam was scented, according to Burton's translation of the *Arabian Nights*, with 'rose-water and willow-flower-water and pods of musk and fumigated with Kakili eaglewood and ambergris' — animal and fishy scents mingled with flower essences and barks. But the phrase 'All the perfumes of Arabia' is used by the desperate Lady Macbeth, whose dreams are haunted by the stink of blood she has resolutely kept from her waking self. 'All the perfumes of Arabia/ Will not sweeten this little hand.' Perfume masks. Smell is direct. When Gloucester tries to kiss the hand of the mad King Lear, the king says, 'Let me wipe it first. It smells of mortality.' Lear uses the Anglo-Saxon word, and faces up to the nature of his own body. We treat odours rather as we treat domesticated animals. Cows and pigs and sheep are Anglo-Saxon and embodied. Beef and pork and mutton are French-derived euphemisms for dead flesh. Smell is honest. Perfume is shifty and shady and variable. And what about 'scent'? When I was a girl perfume was a vulgar word, like dress or garment. You said 'frock' or 'scent' since you could hardly say 'smell'.

Scent also comes from the French, 'sentir', a word which means both to smell and to feel, acknowledging the primitive nature of the scenting sense. Scent is to do with our sense of our own identity, with our recognition of other people's identities and their emotions, with sex, with infant — mother bonding. It is also to do with finding things and places, with tracking prey and locating food, from mushrooms to honey. It is not an easy thing to describe at this level. I know and can remember the scent, the smell, of all my four children's hair when they were babies. There are no words to describe these unique scents. When they are very small there is something extraordinarily painful about other women picking them up and making them smell briefly of L'Air du Temps or Chanel's No. 5. Other women's children at that stage always seem to me to have a *Noli me tangere* smell — unless they are perfumed with talc and

Bounce in their babyjamas. Sheep only accept other ewes' lambs if they are rubbed with their own lambs' smells. We are losing functions — we don't recognise, we don't detect, it is all ersatz. Ants, as E.O. Wilson discovered and described, communicate and organise their complex societies with odours and pheromones. We also recognise — or used to recognise — good and bad food with our noses. I know the smell of tainted meat or fish, or mouldy sprouts — but I believe our senses are being blunted by the chemical haze we choose to live in, like living in a constant buzz of high-level interference, snow on the television screen, just-audible screeching on the radio to which we have had to become inured.

The French word 'sentier' for a footpath or way presumably comes from the primacy of the sense of smell in discovering our surroundings. Smelling out a way can be sinister — one of the most blood-chilling moments in literature is when Regan tells the blinded Gloucester he can 'smell/His way to Dover' and Tolkien's Black Riders are sinister in their snuffling shapelessness, *smelling* their human and hobbit prey, like hellhounds. Terry Pratchett's werewolf Ankh-Morpork guardswoman, Angua, who unravels all the foul smells of that richly rotting city, including fresh blood, is both perturbing, comic, and somehow indecent. She is related to Virginia Woolf's biography of Elizabeth Barrett Browning's spaniel, Flush, whose world is constructed of smells, good and bad. Woolf is concerned with the link and the difference between the human and the animal, as Kate Flint shows in her elegant introduction to the Oxford World's Classics edition. If Donne plays with synaesthesia between smell and sound, Woolf plays with synaesthesia between sight and touch and smell:

> He slept in this hot patch of sun — how sun made the stone reek! he sought that tunnel of shade — how acid shade made the stone smell! He devoured whole bunches of ripe grapes largely because of their purple smell; he chewed and spat out whatever tough relic of goat or macaroni the Italian housewife had thrown from the balcony — goat and macaroni were raucous smells, crimson smells. He followed the swooning sweetness of incense into the violet intricacies of dark cathedrals . . .

It has to be said that the smells that concern Woolf's Flush are somewhat human-interested smells, however bravura the writing. Pratchett's werewolf-woman is arguably more impressively canine. My favourite anthropomorphic-smelling animal — possibly because he is woven into my earliest reading memories — is Kenneth Grahame's Mole, coming across the cold dead scent of his abandoned home, breaking down into weeping, persuading the insouciant Rat to follow him. Grahame describes the 'summons' reaching Mole like 'an electric shock'.

'We others, who have long lost the more subtle of the physical senses, have not even proper terms to express an animal's inter-communications with his surroundings, living or otherwise, and have only the word 'smell', for instance, to include the whole range of delicate thrills which murmur in the nose of the animal night and day, summoning, warning, inciting, repelling.' The word 'murmur' here is a metaphor from sound, but muted — Grahame goes on to describe Mole's home-odour as a 'fine filament, the telegraphic current' and finally, moving from sound to touch 'those caressing appeals, those soft touches wafted through the air, those invisible little hands pulling and tugging, all one way'.

Woolf's anthropomorphism is in a way using Flush to make strange her own extreme sensitivity to the sensual world. Grahame is more straightforward. He points out what the human animal has lost or has not had, and then takes his animal characters, via the pull of little hands (but note, both rats and moles do have little hands) to a very anthropomorphic '*Dulce Domum*' complete with that most human of ritual occasions, Christmas carol-singing and punch. It works, because the primitive pleasure of humans in the smells and sounds of home and Christmas are truthfully related to the sense that animals follow their noses along remembered paths.

In gloomy moments I think we are bringing up a generation deafened by constant loud music and desensitised by constant loud and garish smells. You can't try on a dress in silence now, or sit quietly in the lobby of Broadcasting House, or travel in a mini-cab, without an encapsulating

370

environment of loud noise 'because our staff would go mad without it'. Taxis increasingly have swooning smells too, from sanitising tutti frutti to lingering pot. There is legislation against decibels, which seems to do little good, or else I am prejudiced by being too old and too accustomed to hearing myself think. I have friends who are allergic to perfumes. The effect of the delicately perfumed loo paper on sensitive tissue is better not described. I have a scientist friend whose lab door bears a notice forbidding students or visitors to enter wearing perfume as it gives her migraines. I met an elegant professor from Yale who said her husband felt she shouldn't wear perfume because it was intrusive and impolite.

There have been articles in the *New Scientist* suggesting that the pervasive additives to everything — washing and drying products, polishes, air itself, may be increasing our allergic susceptibilities. There was also a more ambivalent piece suggesting that seasonal affective disorder (SAD) might be treatable with summery smells as well as with bright artificial light. The research of Teodor Postolache suggested that depressed people and people in winter had less sensitive senses of smell — there is the case of the winter-depressed woman who couldn't smell her husband as she could in the spring. Postolache's research — on rats, humans and lemurs — suggest that the time of year affects our sense of smell as well as our mood. I suffer from SAD and find light boxes blissful. But the thought of a perpetual summer of artificial floral bouquet — or even artificial damp earth and leaf mould — casts me into an apprehensive depression, even to think of it.

There may be hope. Over-sensitive California, where I am happy in restaurants because my over-sensitised lungs and nose never meet tobacco smoke, apparently has perfume bans too. I hope they mean washing-up products as well as people-sprays. And Halifax Canada has become, apparently, the first town to ban heavily scented cosmetics in public places such as buses, schools and hospitals. It appears that the Mounties were recently called in to arrest a student whose scent made her teacher physically ill. The *New Scientist* reports objections from the Scented Products Education and Information Association, but comes down, firmly, on the side of the ban. It says that orris root is a major culprit. And adds that Halifax only introduced the ban after the local fishery had collapsed.

Where can we buy the products that are used in those blissfully clear-aired buses and hospital wards where we may again detect rotting food and enjoy the breath of human hair?

∾

Absolute blindness is rare. There's usually some suggestion of movement, some sense of light and shade. Not in my case. What I 'saw' was without texture or definition: it was constant, depthless and impenetrable. Sometimes I thought: Your eyes are closed. Open them. But they were already open. Wide open, seeing nothing. I could look straight into the sun and my pupils

372

would contract, but I wouldn't know it was the sun that I was looking at. Or I could put my head inside a cardboard box. Same thing. There were no graduations in the blankness, no fluctuations of any kind. It was what depression would look like, I thought, if you had to externalise it.

Rupert Thomson, *The Insult*

David Malouf

BUXTEHUDE'S DAUGHTER

Dedicated To Alec Bolton

In the first decade of the eighteenth century the old Hansa city of Lübeck in north Germany was the home of the finest organist in Europe, Diderick, or, as he is usually called, Dietrich Buxtehude. His greatness as a performer, but also as a composer of church chorales and concerti, had spread the name of the Marien-kirche through all the German states, so that when the time came to consider his successor, young men from all over Germany and the north, even as far as Sweden, began to appear in Lübeck to declare an interest and show their parts, though a good many of them, out of pride or professional caution, gave out that their only reason for coming was to pay their respects to the master and hear him play.

They watched one another closely, these unofficial candidates. Slipping into a pew at vespers when some rival was performing, they would sit with their head on one side, measuring their talent, assessing their chances, and then either present themselves to the Lübeck councillors or slip away. They would also take a look, but discreetly and without drawing attention to themselves, at the old man's daughter, Margarethe, since it had been decided, after some quaint old German custom that went with the gables and Gothic spires of the place, that the man who succeeded the father should also marry the daughter. Old Buxtehude had married the daughter of his predecessor, Franz Tunder, lived with her quite happily, and produced five daughters, of whom Margarethe, at this time, was the only survivor.

She was in her early thirties. Herself a talented performer, and with a high regard for music as a sacred art, she took great pride in her father's position, and it was this perhaps that saved her from what might otherwise have been merely humiliating, the little matter, which was strange in modern times, of being thrown in as it were as an extra to the main chance — or, in the darker view, which even she was forced to take on occasion, as an obligation to be assumed or hurdle to be got over. She was a strong young woman with a clear sense of her place in the world and she let the candidates, or contestants or suitors, know it, amusing herself by looking on the affair as one of those folk tales in which a penniless beggar or soldier of fortune tries for the hand of a princess, for a kingdom too, but at the risk of his head.

As time passed and the number of rejected candidates grew, it soon got about that the real stumbling block to the succession was the marriage clause. Young fellows who had no doubt as to their ability, in half an hour or so at the Marienkirche organ, to impress old Buxtehude and the city fathers, would find themselves shivering and shaking when they presented themselves afterwards, hat in hand and with the keen wind of the Baltic whistling past their ears, at the master's door.

Two of these candidates had been invited to apply and came in the same carriage — an odd pair. They were from Hamburg.

The elder (he was twenty-two) was the director of the opera there, the composer of several works in the Italian style in which he himself took a leading part, since he was one of the city's most accomplished singers. His name was Mattheson.

The other, his colleague at the opera, and equally famous, though he was barely eighteen, was a pretty youth with golden hair and the complexion, the manners too, of a girl. He played second violin in the Hamburg orchestra, sometimes conducted from the harpsichord and already had a reputation as organist and improviser.

There was a good deal of gossip about the pair. They were inseparable and were renowned in Hamburg for their quarrels, which often took place in public; at rehearsals, in coffee houses, even once or twice in the street. These confrontations were extremely passionate, sometimes ending in blows and on one occasion, in the case of the younger, whose name was Händel, in tears. They had come to Lübeck to survey the prospects and to decide between themselves which, if either, would accept the post. They did not act like rivals. They sang and played together, praised

376

each other's performances, went boating on the Trave, at table kept up a constant mockery, one of the other, that was meant perhaps to keep their spirits up but was also, their hostess suspected, part of a private joke. The younger could scarcely contain his giggles. They were gallant enough — they had excellent manners — but they treated her, she felt, like a mere adjunct, a supernumerary chattel or comic codicil, and she was mortified to think what they might have to say to one another in a more unbuttoned state, when they had retired to the attic room that had been found for them; how they would pile up witticisms at her expense, going further perhaps than they intended in the attempt to outdo each other till they lapsed at last into crude hilarity. (She had seen enough of her father's choir boys to have no illusions about the nature of young men.)

What she found most insufferable was the camaraderie between them, which she could not help but feel was an alliance; that and the assumption, in their careless all-conquering manner, that the world was theirs by right, to be divided up just as they pleased. Well, not if she could help it!

But when young Händel seated himself at the organ one evening, and, high up in the familiar darkness, began to play, she was overwhelmed by the powers he called down, the light-heartedness and joy he could find among so much grandeur, the grace notes that really were a sign of grace. Her soul was touched. She shivered as if a finger had been laid directly upon her flesh. If he chose her she would have him — no possibility of denial. And how, she agonised, would she escape humiliation? She sat with her thin shoulders hunched, as pale as paste, while the great eddies of his breath, amplified a hundredfold by bellows and reeds and metal pipes, rolled out over her.

So when it appeared at last that they were not serious, these two, but were there simply to show off and amuse themselves, she was relieved, too conscious of a danger that had been averted to be angry with them, though she had every right to be.

He had been a fearful temptation, this brilliant youth. He might have destroyed her.

She had been let off this time, but she saw where her weakness lay. From now on she would be more wary.

She had a high opinion of what was owing to her father, and young Händel might have satisfied it to the highest pitch; but she had a high opinion as well of what was owing to herself.

Then one day (it was two years later and she was thirty-four) a young man called Bach appeared, that same Bach, Johann Sebastian, who later became so famous, but he was just twenty at this time and still unknown. A sturdy, thickset fellow, he had travelled all the way from Arnstadt, he told them; more than a hundred miles, and on foot. He had come to attend the concert week that took place each year at Christmas, and to sit at the feet of master

378

Buxtehude and learn. He did not mention the famous vacancy.

Margarethe was impressed. That he appeared ignorant of what had drawn so many others, caring only for music — that, for one thing. That he was rather shabby and had something of the Saxon peasant about him — that next. But most of all that he had come on foot: like a wandering apprentice, but like the hero too of the folk tale she had imagined herself part of, to alleviate a little the painfulness of her position, which she felt more keenly as she grew older and as the candidates, who got younger each year, came and went. Of course he knew of the vacancy, even if he did not allude to it. So she wondered if his coming on foot, which he quite insisted on, was not intended as a secret sign to her that he too had recognised the shape of an old nursery tale and was playing his part.

In fact no such thought had entered his head. He had come on foot because he was poor, but also because he was young, healthy and wanted the exercise; and further, as he hinted once or twice, because his duties at Arnstadt bored him, and having got permission to absent himself, he wanted to be away for as long as he could be. There was something of his Saxon nature in it too: he liked to approach things slowly. He stayed three months, and she, her father and the Lübeck councillors waited and waited for him to make his intentions clear. He studied, he attended concerts, played on the great Marien-kirche organ; nothing was said. He was, it seemed, occupied entirely with his art. It took up the whole of his nature. He was aware of nothing else.

Margarethe held her breath. He was the one who most nearly fulfilled all the conditions, not only of the post but of the story; he would be appointed, they would marry, all would be well. Except that it was not well, and she began to wonder if the tale she had been telling herself was the right one after all.

Music was the sphere he moved in. Everything outside it, the weather, a plate of steaming sauerkraut, the cleanliness or otherwise of the coarse stockings he wore, belonged to a world where, for all his stocky frame and the heartiness of his appetite, he had only the most shadowy existence. There was nothing boorish about him. It was a question of attention. He was fully attentive, his whole flesh and spirit were engaged, only in the one element of music. He would marry; he would get children, and they too, however many there might be of them, and whatever noise and disorder they might create with their messes, their coughs and croups, their little tantrums and temper fits, would be mere shadows for him till they too came into the element — that is, music — and began to be little practisers of scales, a pool of ready copyists, then followers of their father in the musical line.

Well, it was a great and noble craft and she too cared for it. Wasn't she too in the musical line, hadn't she too made a world of it? But the fact was, she had no wish to get her children, or have them begotten, in a shadowy way. When all was

380

said and done she cared less for music (this was blasphemy, she knew) than for life, by which she meant her own life, the life that was in her. So she gave him no sign, and was pretty certain that if she had he would have missed it. She let her prince go on sleepwalking, and when he had learned all he could, or began to worry that the patience of his employers back at Arnstadt might be wearing thin, he packed his bags, thanked them, and went away.

In later years, when the news of his greatness reached her, she remembered him with amusement but without regret. His works, and later the works of his sons as well, were performed at the Marienkirche music weeks, which continued after her father's death, but Lübeck was no longer a centre by then. The magic had moved elsewhere.

And she did marry. Three months after her father's death, at the altar of the Marienkirche, she married her father's assistant, Johann Christian Schieferdecker, a man of moderate talent but by no means incompetent, and he was at the same time confirmed in the vacancy. They had several children and she lived happily in Lübeck till the end of her days. As an old lady she liked to walk with her eldest daughter on the beach at Travemünde, telling her grandchildren of the famous men who had come to Lübeck to visit and pay their respects, and urging the smallest of them, as she looked across to Denmark where her father's people had come from, to listen for the song of the mermaids who lure sailors in the strait.

＊

*The Lord looseth men out of prison: the Lord
giveth sight to the blind.*

Psalm 146

Adam Thorpe

LOOK

Only the eye's lens does not age. Old as us,
it holds out gamely, gazing into time
as the rest remakes around it: skin,
nails, hair — every cell of their grounding,
every glistening hidden interior thing

repairing itself, rewiring to newness,
suckling on the protein of its own thrust
so nothing remains as it was for long

except the lens, the gaze of the iris,
the least impermanent thing about us,
subduing only to senescence
in the milky cataracts of my mother

the lasers seared from her, etch by etch,
delicately scouring the one part of her
unchanged from the womb, the diamond
hardness of the softest bit — the glance

of the newborn, the child, the lover;
the calm pool stormed by tears, the blusters
of growing; by those gritty mornings after
    bombs
when history hung to be blinked at,

the harmattan, the chlorine of the deep ends;
the salve of distress, grief's soft curtain
over the unbearable sights, the old sufferings
or the squeezed lemons of laughter;
and I think how fitting it is that the rest
falls away, endlessly remade, while a glance
remains immaculate — Donne's windows
of the soul, that gazed on the womb's red light,

admitting the permanence of unplumbed depths
others dive into, or query with leads,
shafted otherwise only by a life's daylight
or the serious dreams of the eyelid.

Author's note: my mother steadily lost her sight following a near-fatal attack of dysentery in Calcutta in 1961, during which she was given a medication that a Japanese pharmaceutical company were 'testing' in India (as is still the habit), and which was subsequently found to cause retinal deterioration. The cataract operation referred to above made no difference to her condition, and for the last ten years she has been totally blind.

ॐ

Writing turns terribly embarrassing to me, from the failure of eyesight. What a terrible thing blindness, or even extreme obtusity of sight would be to me! But God's will be done. I have had more service of my eyes than most people.

Sir Walter Scott, *Letters*

384

Elizabeth Berridge

LONER

The suburb lay, like others of its kind, poleaxed under the sun. Its absolute stillness was that of a man hit over the head, stunned, stupefied. It was not so much the silence as the absence of sound, of life. In this place everyone held his breath.

Mid-afternoon. Children in school and mothers given up to their beds, thrown down in clogging boredom, too tired, too hot to think. What was there to think about in this kind of afternoon? Heavy, the heat was heavy on their limbs, eyelids, minds. Fathers were 'in town' behind office windows where square feet of stale air were measured in money. All life in Giggs Green had withdrawn into the houses, behind curtains, like a beach at low tide, empty except for rock pools. Later, when the families reassembled and had been fed, life would retreat into back gardens, where scimitar-like flowerbeds slashed the tame lawns and neat sheds held the thousand and one implements needed to keep nature in check.

From the pavements, across hedges, one saw and smelt orange blossom, privet and roses. Earlier, rosebushes had stood, tortured and stunted among circles of dried blood. Now they obediently produced their disciplined blooms, well fed. Like the snakes on Medusa's head, another rose would grow in place of a lopped-off dead one. People in Giggs Green had a passion for lopping trees, especially limes, maybe because they smelt so sweetly of woodlands.

No tree in these pleasure gardens produced anything other than a show of blossom and a scant crop of inedible fruit or sharp, gaudy berries. Japanese cherries, mini-trees for mini-people, a showy celebration of sterility. Every tree tailored to requirements, no windows overshadowed; autumn leaves never allowed to lie among guardian gnomes. Indestructible, these gnomes. Also fishing cranes and stone corgis, concrete or wrought-iron poodles, and at least one basalt buddha smiling from among rock plants at the head of a fish pond made out of anchored plastic sheets.

The silence here was quite different from the silence of the country. There it was alive, fresh. Things happened secretly, wild flowers fell about in ditches and old wheels and sprouted from stone walls, birds sheltered in rustling hedges. Everywhere creation could be heard breathing: in the small nudging of grasses, the furtive creeping of an ant up a clover stalk, the unofficial landing of a butterfly on a petal.

Back in the suburb a sudden jangle broke the silence. An ice cream chime, like a cheap cinema organ on three notes. The blue and white van, decorated with pictures of cornets and giant iced lollies, lumbered up to the school gates to wait for its victims. Somewhere, far off, a thrush's unvarying song started, was cut off as a blackbird sounded the alarm note. Sparrows zig-zagged

386

across fences, uneasy.

For an entirely alien sound was cast suddenly into the air. Unbelievably, like a raspberry blown at royalty.

'Kah, kah, kah!'

And again, after a moment, loud and clear.

'Kah, kah, kah!'

One thought ran, like a perfect experiment in telepathy, through the houses, the gardens, across the streets. 'It's laughing at us. Look, it's a bloody great black crow, sitting up there — see it? There!'

There it was. Landed in the tallest elm (scheduled to come down before the autumn gales), looking about it with a bright yellow eye as if amazed at the neat gardens and the alarmed blackbirds and tamed sycophantic sparrows, the clipped hedges and regiments of earthed gnomes condemned to an eternity of fruitless fishing. It glimpsed limp women framed in their astounded windows, castrated roses, obedient shrubs, Tudor gables and stucco frontages, over-wrought iron and swinging name signs. At Kosikot and Toi-et-Moi the scarlet salvia shrieked against the red brick.

Mrs Tillett, at 16, Acacia Close, started off her bed in a frenzy of mauve nylon ruffles.

'What a cheek! What a row!'

The bird's harsh cries drowned the ice cream chimes, and Mrs Tillett's heart beat licketty-split in the hot silence — now splintered — of her bedroom. Mauve was a hot colour and nylon a fabric that refused to breathe. She slipped off the continental quilt on to the floor. She'd made a mistake over that new cover. Her nervous rash made her private parts pink and itchy, and she poked a furious face out of the window.

'You'll get yours!' she informed the cheeky bird, now sitting like a sniper in the doomed elm. But the sun flashed bright black chips from its sleek back and its tail feathers moved up perkily.

By the time the children came in for tea it had gone, only its mocking shout echoing back among the trees in Bushy Park. But she told her husband Dicky about it, that evening, over a tasty tuna salad.

Dicky Tillett was a bird lover most of the time. He had made a table for them, and regularly put out crumbs and fat in the winter.

'Get away,' he said, thinking of his work. 'Crows live in the country. What would an old crow want here?'

'What does it mean, Dad,' asked his son, butting in. 'Straight as a crow flies? We had it in school today. Mr Broom told us to find out.'

'Ah.' His father came awake. 'Straight as — yes. Why, that means that that old bugger can go straight as a die anywhere he wants. Nothing to stop him. A straight flight. He could go from here to Box Hill, say, in ten minutes. No traffic, see. No roads, no hold-ups.'

'Not like us trying to get to Brighton that Sunday, Dad!' said his daughter. 'It took us all day and then we had to have our sandwiches in that stinking old lay-by. Ooh, I do wish I was a crow!' and she flapped her hands like wings and sped round the room, calling, 'Caw, caw, caw!' until her parents told her to give over.

Dicky Tillett tried not to think about the country. He'd been brought up in it, masses of it. It had surrounded him as a boy. The Fens lying under that enormous sky, with Ely Cathedral the only real landmark for miles. His uncle had had a farm, and he'd seen crows there. And rooks. Hundreds of rooks, tossed up in the air at sunset like charred paper, calling and settling. Now he said to his children, 'Crows aren't like rooks. Crows are loners.'

'Turned me up,' said his wife. 'I'm glad there was only one.'

'Having a bit of a recce. Gone back to where it came from, I expect.'

But it hadn't. Every afternoon just before school came out, the crow flapped over all the gardens along Acacia Close, looking. What for? The edible cherries on a tree in the Tilletts' next-door neighbours' garden attracted it. It sat there and pecked and then flew off again in the direction of Bushy Park, with its harsh mocking voice forming a wake of noise, floating and sinking like the tail of a paper kite.

'Gets on my nerves, Dicky. It's just as if it's laughing at us,' complained Mrs Tillett.

'Well, we can't help living here! Not when I have to get to the bank — '

His wife looked at him in astonishment.

'We *chose* to live here! What are you on about?'

Dicky didn't reply. He didn't really know what he was on about. But after a whole week of it he looked out his air gun, the one he'd kept since he was a boy. He'd been a fair shot, picking off the odd rabbit or pigeon. He was keeping the gun for his son, when he was of an age, looking forward to taking him out to the country — see if his uncle was still alive — teach him how to use it.

That was Monday. All the weekend he'd listened to his wife's complaints, heard the crow twice on Sunday, watched his lawn grow steadily browner with the unremitting sun.

Even bowls of washing-up water didn't do much for it. He dared not hose it for fear of nosy neighbours.

Dicky longed for the country; a deep green wood, a liquid stream. Space.

Untrammelled by traffic, the crow could fly each afternoon back to where it most wanted to go. Straight as a die. Straight as — yes. A bitter envy settled on Dicky as heavily and blackly as the bird itself settled into the tree next door. The owner of the cherry tree didn't mind. He never hoped for any cherries, they were too high up, and what the crow didn't eat the starlings and blackbirds did. When he saw Dicky cleaning his gun he said, shocked, 'Oh, fair play, Dicky, if we don't mind it having the cherries, why should you? Anyway, it's not allowed by law, is it? To shoot in a built-up area?'

Dicky was evasive. 'Oh,' he said, smoothing oil where it was needed. 'Just scare the blighter, like. I'm used to birds. Born in the country, wasn't I?'

'Birds should know their place,' he told his wife as they lay apart under one sheet in the dark, baking night. If they touched, their hot skins might catch fire. 'Ungrateful, that's what

390

they are. Feed 'em through the winter and in the spring they tear your crocuses to bits, in the summer they eat your strawberries and blackcurrants, and in the autumn pigeons go for the greens — '

'We haven't got any greens.'

'We might have.'

'Oh, shut it, do! Go to sleep. How I hate this weather! Why doesn't it rain?'

Dicky got up at five the next morning. There was something private and pearly about this untouched time of day. He heard the dawn chorus from the paved terrace, holding the gun over his knee, watching the day break cleanly, like a great egg, and the sun come flooding out over the mysterious milky sky. Bloody marvellous, made you think. Made you remember mornings in childhood, the cold dawn wind over the Fens, the space, land and sky empty and waiting. No cars. No crowded trains. His anger, which had been seething for a week like porridge, subsided. What had he got up for?

Then he heard it coming straight over.

'Kah, kah, kah!'

It had never come so close. It was bending the branches of the laburnum near the trellis, sitting there with its bright despising eyes full on the prisoner of number 16. A quick dekko at all you lot in this built-up area and then I'm off, straight as a crow flies. I could be in Ely by teatime.

'Oh no,' whispered Dicky Tillett. 'Not this time, mate.'

He fired.

The bird seemed to spin and stagger, then it flapped from the tree to the trellis, its claws trying to clutch a hold. But its wing weighed it down. Clumsily it flopped, a thrown-out rag, on to the terrace at Dicky's feet.

Above Dicky's head a window was flung open and his wife's shriek broke his concentration. As he lowered the gun, his son came out of the back door, holding up his pyjamas and crying.

'I've winged it, great black booby,' said his father flatly. 'Ought to finish it off.' But he stood there, just looking.

'Don't finish it off, Dad, don't!'

Dicky watched the boy bending over it. He thought he detected a dying out of hostility in the bird's bright eye. It opened its beak but no sound came. 'I can mend its wing. I can. I'll have it as a pet. Let me keep it, Dad, and I'll put it in the shed, then it won't be all over the house, like cats and dogs and Mum won't mind — not out there — '

People were looking out of their windows. The man next door stared over the fence, shouted, but Dicky didn't answer. He went indoors, upstairs to the bathroom, had a shower and cut himself shaving. He'd never got on with his early morning face.

That evening he helped the boy make a cage for it. They put a clumsy splint on the wing, and the bird made only a half-hearted attempt to peck them as they lifted it in.

'All right,' he told his son, 'if it lives you can look after it. We'll tame it, that's what we'll do. Tame it. Clip its wings.'

His wife said, at the silent supper table, 'You ought to have finished it off, Dicky, kinder. I don't want it cawing at me every time I go down the garden to hang out the washing. Men!'

But the crow never bothered Mrs Tillett, although it made her uneasy in a way she didn't quite understand. It sat hunched in its cage as the wing healed, crookedly — the boy had done well enough, silly to waste money on a vet. Dicky never attempted to clip its other wing. There was no need. It ate worms and the things the boy and his friends brought for it. But you couldn't call it tame, not by a long chalk, not with that certain look in its eye cocked up at you, yellow and knowing. Or brooding on its special perch by the small window, dully watching the outside. Sometimes the boy sat it on his shoulder and they walked up and down the garden together in the hot dusk, with moths flying. The useless wing rose and fell, trailed along the burned-up grass when Dicky told his son to put it down and see what it would do. It ran along the ground, tried to take off like a faulty plane on a dicey runway, then crouched back on its long legs, and cawed loudly, twice.

'Fly, damn you. Go, fly. Go away.' The words echoed silently in Dicky's head as he turned and walked away up to the house for two quick, neat whiskies.

'Leatherjackets, that's what we ought to get for it, Mr Broom says,' the boy told his family. 'Crows are the farmer's friends.'

He took to looking sideways at his father and developed a crow-like hunching of his shoulders as he made his way back from shed to house, kicking at the dry tufts of grass.

Soon the weather broke and rain poured down on to the roof of the shed, on to the dried-up gardens, and grass began to grow again, weeds sprouted, flowers revived. Mrs Tillett's heat rash vanished. She would poke her head in at the shed door and say quite cheerfully, 'Not much to say for yourself, have you? Nothing to laugh at now. Taught you a lesson.'

The crow died as the first autumn winds blew in from the country outside Giggs Green. It keeled over one day and lay on its back, its claws curled. It had refused food for several days. At first Dicky thought it was shamming and said as much to his son, but when lice crawled out of its dulled black feathers the boy turned his head away from his father and put a fist across his eyes. He didn't reply when Dicky offered to take them all for a drive into the country now that the roads were clearer.

'Who wants to go now?' asked his wife reasonably. 'It'll be all mud. No, it's telly-time now, the serials are all beginning. We can switch on the logs in the lounge and be cosy and draw the curtains. Ooh, I'm glad this summer is over and done with. There's been altogether too much of it.'

Giggs Green went on being silent — apart from Concorde tearing open the sky twice a day — and, as the days grew shorter, the crow rotted in the grave by the compost heap and pyracantha grew its red berries up the brick walls of houses. Swallows and other wise birds fled the country.

Life went on and death went on, for it was die and let die in Giggs Green.

❧

Wise Nicodemus saw such light
As made him know his God by night.
Most blest believer he!
Who in that land of darkness and blind eyes
Thy long expected healing wings could see
When Thou didst rise!

Henry Vaughan, *Silex Scintillans*

Brian Thompson

HOW WE MET

When the junior Minister came to open
— well, of course, very few people can now
remember what he had come to open, in spite
of so much ink being spilt — he was ambushed
by June Walton. He had hardly started speaking
in his faintly goofy but good-humoured way
when this large woman in a fuschia pink
number barged forward and hissed, 'You are
talking total rubbish. You are a disgrace to your
calling.'

'My calling?' the Junior Minister murmured,
alarmed.

June said a lot more before she was bundled
away. There was a hurried consultation between
the Minister's minders and his hosts for the
day. It was agreed that the arrival, the welcome
and the ministerial remarks would all go for a
second take. It would be as though June Walton
and her intervention had never happened. That
was the bones of it. Outside in the car park, the
lady was being cautioned by the police and sent
home.

'Which is all very well,' Toby Walton drawled,
'but doesn't answer the main point. That he is
indeed a prat.'

Two days had passed. The Waltons were being
given dinner by the Tuckers. At one time the

Tuckers had been known as the Tucker-Tompkins until the arrival in the village of the Tilson-Tomkins, a ghastly family from Kidderminster. Ian and Jillie changed their name by deed poll to avoid the shame of it all.

Dinner had gone most extraordinarily well. Toby considered he had scored freely all round the wicket. His thing on the complete and utter impossibility of eating out in Paris produced gales of laughter. Ian Tucker was rather a good mimic and had a story about a Hertz girl in New Jersey that was well done. There was also some rather juicy local gossip. The vicar, who wore a beard, was almost certainly making a fool of himself with a girl from the village, causing his horse-faced wife to have some sort of nervous breakdown.

As if by prior arrangement, June's run-in with the Junior Minister had been saved for coffee and brandy in the Tucker's faintly chi-chi sitting room.

'I abhor the man,' she said. 'One can't open the paper without seeing his silly grin. He makes a great deal of his father having been a dustman or something. Well, all right, a railway porter. Same difference. Anyway, I'd simply had enough.'

Jillie Tucker's father had been the assistant manager of a furniture department and she was ever so slightly sensitive to these matters.

'I heard you were hustled away like a common criminal,' she said.

'My dear, I begged them to arrest me. I absolutely demanded it. But of course they are far too cunning for anything like that.'

'Spin,' her husband said vaguely.

Later that night, watching a naked June crash to and fro from the bed to the ensuite bathroom, looking for her ear-plugs, he rather wished his wife had been arrested, imprisoned, and deported. Only kidding, as a former mistress had the habit of saying, too often to be funny.

'A fine lot of support you gave me tonight,' June said, spitefully kicking away his paperback. 'I shouldn't wonder if there isn't something between you and that Tucker bitch.'

'My dear June,' Toby protested, feeling tiny icicles of fear clatter in his heart.

'Well, there's someone,' June said. It gave her absolutely no pleasure to see from his expression that she was right. She had not intended to be right.

* * *

Toby flew from this capital to that for a living, doing no one knew exactly what work, which explained his expertise on foreign foods and wine. Two days after the dinner party he was in Milan for three days, which gave June the idea of going to London and repeating her attack on the government. In order to strike fear in her particular opponent, she wore the same fuschia suit. They met as he left the ministerial car, eager as ever, his grin pasted to his lips.

'Remember me?' June bellowed.

'How very nice to see you again,' the Junior Minister began and then looked astonished as his Special Branch officer collared June and dragged her backwards through the photographers. She sat down heavily on the pavement, showing a lot of leg and knicker. She bit the young policeman on the wrist, was arrested and charged with assault. The photographs made the *Evening Standard*.

When she got home that night, released but charged to appear at Horseferry Road a fortnight hence, she got into the car at the station and drove straight to the Tuckers' house. Ian was eating a mournful plate of spinach.

'Bloody awful,' he said of the dish. 'I think you're supposed to add an egg or something.'

'Where's Jillie?' she asked with instant suspicion.

'Um? Torquay, I think. Until Thursday.'

'Has she taken her passport?'

'Really June, you say the funniest things.'

They drank two bottles of very good Muscadet and then June drove home. She was missing an earclip and her blouse was out at the back. She took off her shoes and began a flatfooted search of Toby's study. The phone rang three times. The first two calls were from newspaper diarists or their hacks. The third was from the Minister.

'I don't believe you,' June said darkly.

'I can assure you it's me. I was very sorry to hear you were arrested. You obviously have something you want to tell me.'

'Yes, that you're a disgrace. And an absolute waste of space.'

'Oh dear.'

'And don't try to ring off. I know where you

live, you horrible man. You have Cissie and Trevor Summerby's house, which happens to have very happy childhood associations for me.'

'It's still early. Come and have a look at the place. The gardens and so on.'

She was astounded. She sat down in Toby's captain's chair.

'Are you drunk?'

'Yes,' the Minister said. 'Well, no. Not yet. I've just been sacked. From the Government.'

'Not over me, I hope.'

'I don't think so.'

After she had agreed to go — a journey of forty miles — she had the almost impossible problem of what to wear. She rang him back.

'I don't suppose I can persuade you to come here?'

'I'm too pissed to drive,' he said in very unministerial language. She liked him for it.

They havered on the phone for a while. Next day he was clearing his desk, the day after she was having lunch with the directors of a charity. They settled on Thursday. His suggested venue was intriguing. It was a pub on the A34.

'I don't drink in pubs,' June said with a fine hauteur. 'And while we're on the subject, what does your wife have to say about all this?'

'She doesn't like me any more than you do,' he said.

★   ★   ★

They met at a butterfly farm, which had been June's suggestion. As soon as she got there she

400

realised it was a silly idea, for the highlight of the attraction was a walk through clouds of highly stupid insects who seemed to have been trained by the management to settle in the most unfortunate places. Never before had she flirted with a man whose fly was so shamelessly decorated. Various winged things clung to her cleavage.

'Well, of course much of the point of our quarrel has been lost,' she explained to Alan, as he asked her to call him. 'I mean since you have been dumped by your own crowd I consider victory has gone to me. Game, set and match sort of thing.'

Alan wore a cheap blue shirt over rumpled chinos. Stripped of his office, he seemed not smaller, but taller. With great gallantry he inclined his head to blow on the butterflies perched on June's breasts.

'I'm not sure one ought to touch them,' he said and though she looked at him very sharply he had spoken without innuendo. She stood on tiptoe and blew on a yellow and Amazonian something or other that was lodged in his hair. He held her gently by the forearms so that she could retain her balance. It was mildly dizzying.

'This is a ridiculous place,' she said.

He drove a Renault. June, who knew a thing or two about adultery, noticed the ghost of his wife compacted on the back seat, in the form of a crumpled cardigan and a red umbrella.

'I don't know what made me ring you,' Alan said, 'but I'm glad I did. Things have been bloody awful for a few months. I have not exactly been on-message. I mean, you know, everybody is supposed to be a manager, an executive or something nowadays. Bit of a salesman as well, I suppose. And as you noticed, that isn't exactly me.'

'Well, I wonder what is.'

His smile was ravishing. He took her hand in his, hanging on to it to change gear from time to time.

'Aren't you curious to know how I traced you?'

'Through the police, I suppose.'

'I didn't realise who you were to begin with. My wife's called Jane. Does that ring a bell?'

It didn't.

'She's a financial consultant,' Alan prompted. He named the firm.

'Oh my God,' June said as the penny dropped.

''Fraid so. She's in Milan. They're in Milan.'

He drew into a picnic area and June sat staring through the windscreen. Newly planted saplings had been bent and broken like matchsticks. The picnic tables were vandalised. Only the hills and the sky were out of reach.

'I wish you hadn't told me that.'

'Exactly. No judgement. I mean it would have come out sooner or later but I do have this completely inappropriate sense of tidiness. Life is not tidy.'

'Hardly,' June said. It was the first really political remark she had ever made. She let him hold her hand and kiss her wrist as if indulging a gangly child.

'Is this some sort of tit for tat thing?' she

402

demanded suddenly.

'No, this is me, this is you.' Alan said. He would have gone on to spoil the remark, she was sure, so she forestalled him by getting out of the car. Round her feet in the blond grass were all the signs of human happiness — crushed cans, cigarette packets, crown bottle tops, lolly sticks. She sat on the edge of a picnic table and stared out at the valley below her.

'I think you're supposed to feel young again and slim again when this happens,' she said. 'I actually feel like half a ton of condemned lard.' She turned to him. 'As a matter of fact I feel like bunking off down that path and never coming back.'

'Let me explain something,' Alan said. 'The very thing I don't like about it is the symmetry. He screws my wife, I screw you. I don't like that. I'm flying to see my brother tomorrow. He lives in Brisbane. He's a policeman. Okay, I jump in a plane and sit there reading for whatever it is — fifteen hours? — and then fall out at Brisbane. Suitably pissed. That's me. You could come with me. Or maybe you couldn't — no, cancel that. I go to Brisbane to make a futile gesture, come back and talk to you. You know, talk to you. Woo you. That's wrong too. Share with you.'

A dark blue and white butterfly from the farm crept out of her blouse, posed for a moment and then set off erratically as far as an elm.

'You don't know a thing about me,' June said, very shaken.

'That's how people meet.'

He kissed her on the cheek.

'You know,' he said, brushing her hair past her ear. 'They haven't the faintest idea what they're doing and then one day, bingo!'

'They were certainly right to sack you,' June said with the last of her common sense for many months to come. She searched the elm with her pale blue eyes. The escaped butterfly didn't stand a chance. On the other hand, she tipped nine stone on the scales and could read men the way other people read airport novels. Maybe.

'Buzz off to Brisbane, then,' she said and found herself being kissed for her impudence.

∾

So zestfully canst thou sing?
And all this indignity,
With God's consent, on thee!
Blinded ere yet-a-wing
By the red-hot needle thou,
I stand and wonder how
So zestfully thou canst sing!

Resenting not such wrong,
Thy grievous pain forgot,
Eternal dark thy lot,
Groping thy whole life long,
After that stab of fire;
Enjailed in pitiless wire;
Resenting not such wrong!

Who hath charity? This bird.
Who suffreth long and is kind,
Is not provoked, though blind
And alive ensepulchred?
Who hopeth, enduring all things?
Who thinketh no evil, but sings?
Who is divine? This bird.

Thomas Hardy, 'The Blinded Bird'

William Trevor

THE MOURNING

In the town, on the grey estate on the
Dunmanway road, they lived in a corner house.
They always had. Mrs Brogan had borne and
brought up six children there. Brogan, a council
labourer, still grew vegetables and a few
marigolds in its small back garden. Only Liam
Pat was still at home with them, at twenty-three
the youngest in the family, working for O'Dwyer
the builder. His mother — his father, too, though
in a different way — was upset when Liam Pat
said he was thinking of moving further afield.
'Cork?' his mother asked. But it was England
Liam Pat had in mind.

Dessie Coglan said he could get him fixed.
He'd go himself, Dessie Coglan said, if he didn't
have the wife and another kid expected. No way
Rosita would stir, no way she'd move five yards
from the estate, with her mother two doors
down. 'You'll fall on your feet there all right,'
Dessie Coglan confidently predicted. 'No way
you won't.'

Liam Pat didn't have wild ambitions; but he
wanted to make what he could of himself. At the
Christian Brothers' he'd been the tidiest in the
class. He'd been attentive, even though he often
didn't understand. Father Mooney used to
compliment him on the suit he always put on for

mass, handed down through the family, and the tie he always wore on Sundays. 'The respect, Liam Pat,' Father Mooney would say. 'It's heartening for your old priest to see the respect, to see you'd give the boots a brush.' Shoes, in fact, were what Liam Pat wore to Sunday mass, black and patched, handed down also. Although they didn't keep out the wet, that didn't deter him from wearing them in the rain, stuffing them with newspaper when he was home again. 'Ah, sure, you'll pick it up,' O'Dwyer said when Liam Pat asked him if he could learn a trade. He'd pick up the whole lot — plumbing, bricklaying, carpentry, house-painting. He'd have them all at his fingertips; if he settled for one of them, he wouldn't get half the distance. Privately, O'Dwyer's opinion was that Liam Pat didn't have enough upstairs to master any trade and when it came down to it what was wrong with operating the mixer? 'Keep the big mixer turning and keep Liam Pat Brogan behind it,' was one of O'Dwyer's good-humoured catch-phrases on the sites where his men built houses for him. 'Typical O'Dwyer,' Dessie Coglan scornfully pronounced. Stay with O'Dwyer and Liam Pat would be shovelling wet cement for the balance of his days.

Dessie was on the estate also. He had married into it, getting a house when the second child was born. Dessie had had big ideas at the Brothers'; with a drink or two in him he had them still. There was his talk of 'the lads' and of 'connections' with the extreme republican movement, his promotion of himself as a fixer.

By trade he was a plasterer.

'Give that man a phone as soon as you're there,' he instructed Liam Pat, and Liam Pat wrote the number down. He had always admired Dessie, the easy way he had with Rosita Drudy before he married her, the way he seemed to know how a hurling match would go even though he had never handled a hurley stick himself, the way he could talk through the cigarette he was smoking, his voice becoming so low you couldn't hear what he was saying, his eyes narrowed to lend weight to the confidential nature of what he passed on. A few people said Dessie Coglan was all mouth, but Liam Pat disagreed.

It's not bad at all, Liam Pat wrote on a postcard when he'd been in London a week. *There's a lad from Lismore and another from Westmeath.* Under a foreman called Huxter he was operating a cement mixer and filling in foundations. He got lonely was what he didn't add to his message. *The wage is twice what O'Dwyer gave*, he squeezed in instead at the bottom of the card, which had a picture of a guardsman in a sentry box on it.

Mrs Brogan put it on the mantelpiece. She felt lonely herself, as she'd known she would, the baby of the family gone. Brogan went out to the garden, trying not to think of the kind of place London was. Liam Pat was headstrong, like his mother, Mr Brogan considered. Good-natured but headstrong, the same red hair on the pair of them till her own had gone grey on her. He had asked Father Mooney to have a word with Liam

Pat, but the damn bit of good it had done.

After that, every four weeks or so, Liam Pat telephoned on a Saturday evening. They always hoped they'd hear that he was about to return, but all he talked about was a job finished or a new job begun, how he waited every morning to be picked up by the van, to be driven halfway across London from the area where he had a room. The man who was known to Dessie Coglan had got him the work, as Dessie Coglan said he would. 'A Mr Huxter's on the lookout for young fellows,' the man, called Feeny, had said when Liam Pat phoned him as soon as he arrived in London. In his Saturday conversations — on each occasion with his mother first and then, more briefly, with his father — Liam Pat didn't reveal that when he'd asked Huxter about learning a trade the foreman had said take what was on offer or leave it, a general labourer was what was needed. Liam Pat didn't report, either, that from the first morning in the gang Huxter had taken against him, without a reason that Liam Pat could see. It was Huxter's way to pick on someone, they said in the gang.

They didn't wonder why, nor did Liam Pat. They didn't know that a victim was a necessary compensation for the shortages in Huxter's life — his wife's regular refusal to grant him what he considered to be his bedroom rights, the failure of a horse or greyhound; compensation, too, for surveyors' sarcasm and the pernicketiness of fancy-booted architects. A big, black-moustached man, Huxter worked as hard as any of the men under him, stripping himself to his

409

vest, a brass buckle on the belt that held his trousers up. 'What kind of a name's that?' he said when Liam Pat told him, and called him Mick instead. There was something about Liam Pat's freckled features that grated on Huxter, and although he was well used to Irish accents he convinced himself that he couldn't understand this one. 'Oh, very Irish,' Huxter would say even when Liam Pat did something sensible, such as putting planks down in the mud to wheel the barrows on.

When Liam Pat had been working with Huxter for six weeks the man called Feeny got in touch again, on the phone one Sunday. 'How're you doing?' Feeny enquired. 'Are you settled, boy?'

Liam Pat said he was, and a few days later, when he was with the two other Irish boys from the gang, standing up at the bar in a public house called the Spurs and Horse, Feeny arrived in person. 'How're you doing?' Feeny said, introducing himself. He was a wizened-featured man with black hair in a widow's peak. He had a clerical look about him but he wasn't a priest, as he soon made clear. He worked in a glass factory, he said.

He shook hands with all three of them, with Rafferty and Noonan as warmly as with Liam Pat. He bought them drinks, refusing to let them pay for his, saying he couldn't allow young fellows. A bit of companionship was all he was after, he said. 'Doesn't it keep the poor exile going?'

There was general agreement with this

sentiment. There were some who came over, Feeny said, who stayed no longer than a few days. 'Missing the mam,' he said, his thin lips drawn briefly back to allow a laugh that Rafferty remarked afterwards reminded him of the bark of a dog. 'A young fellow one time didn't step out of the train,' Feeny said.

After that, Feeny often looked in at the Spurs and Horse. In subsequent conversations, asking questions and showing an interest, he learned that Huxter was picking on Liam Pat. He didn't know Huxter personally, he said, but both Rafferty and Noonan assured him that Liam Pat had cause for more complaint than he admitted to, that when Huxter got going he was no bloody joke. Feeny sympathised, tightening his mouth in a way he had, wagging his head in disgust. It was perhaps because of what he heard, Rafferty and Noonan deduced, that Feeny made a particular friend of Liam Pat, more than he did of either of them, which was fair enough in the circumstances.

Feeny took Liam Pat to greyhound tracks; he found him a better place to live; he lent him money when Liam Pat was short once, and didn't press for repayment. As further weeks went by, everything would have been all right as far as Liam Pat was concerned if it hadn't been for Huxter. 'Ah, no, I'm grand,' he continued to protest when he made his Saturday telephone call home, still not mentioning the difficulty he was experiencing with the foreman. But it had several times crossed his mind that one Monday morning he wouldn't be there, waiting for the

411

van to pick him up, that he'd had enough.

'What would you do though, Liam Pat?' Feeny asked in Bob's Dining Rooms, where at weekends he and Liam Pat often met for a meal.

'Go home.'

Feeny nodded; then he sighed and after a pause said it could come to that. He'd seen it before, a bullying foreman with a down on a young fellow he'd specially pick out.

'It's got so's I hate him.'

Again Feeny allowed a silence to develop. Then he said:

'They look down on us.'

'How d'you mean?'

'Any man with an Irish accent. The way things are.'

'You mean bombs and stuff?'

'I mean, you're breathing their air and they'd charge you for it. The first time I run into you, Liam Pat, weren't your friends saying they wouldn't serve you in another bar you went into?'

'The Hop Poles, that is. They won't serve you in your working clothes.'

Feeny leaned forward, over a plate of liver and potatoes. He lowered his voice to a whisper. 'They wash the ware twice after us. Plates, cups, a glass you'd take a drink out of. I was in a launderette one time and I offered a woman the machine after I'd done with it. 'No, thanks,' she said soon's I opened my mouth.'

Liam Pat had never had such an experience, but people weren't friendly. It was all right in the gang; it was all right when he went out with

412

Rafferty and Noonan, or with Feeny. But people didn't smile, they didn't nod or say something when they saw you coming. The first woman he rented a room from was suspicious, always in the hall when he left the house, as if she thought he might be doing a flit with her belongings. In the place Feeny had found for him a man who didn't live there, whose name he didn't know, came round every Sunday morning and you paid him and he wrote out a slip. He never said anything, and Liam Pat used to wonder if he had some difficulty with speech. Although there was other people's food in the kitchen, and although there were footsteps on the stairs and sometimes overhead, in the weeks Liam Pat had lived there he never saw any of the other tenants, or heard voices. The curtains of one of the downstairs rooms were always drawn over, which you could see from the outside and which added to the dead feeling of the house.

'It's the same the entire time,' Feeny said. 'Stupid as pigs. Can they write their names? You can see them thinking it.'

Huxter would say it straight out. 'Get your guts put into it,' Huxter shouted at Liam Pat, and once when something wasn't done to his liking he said there were more brains in an Irish turnip. 'Tow that bloody island out into the sea,' he said another time. A drop of their own medicine, he said.

'I couldn't get you shifted,' Feeny said. 'If I could I would.'

'Another gang, like?'

413

'Maybe in a couple of weeks there'd be something.'

'It'd be great, another gang.'

'Did you ever know McTighe?'

Liam Pat shook his head. He said Feeny had asked him that before. Did McTighe run a gang? he asked.

'He's in with a bookie. It'd be a good thing if you knew McTighe. Good all round, Liam Pat.'

Ten days later, when Liam Pat was drinking with Rafferty and Noonan in the Spurs and Horse, Feeny joined them and afterwards walked away from the public house with Liam Pat.

'Will we have one for the night?' he suggested, surprising Liam Pat because they'd come away when closing time was called and it would be the same anywhere else. 'No problem,' Feeny said, disposing at once of this objection.

'I have to get the last bus out, though. Ten minutes it's due.'

'You can doss where we're going. No problem at all, boy.'

He wondered if Feeny was drunk. He'd best get back to his bed, he insisted, but Feeny didn't appear to hear him. They turned into a side street. They went round to the back of a house. Feeny knocked gently on a window pane and the rattle of television voices ceased almost immediately. The back door of the house opened.

'Here's Liam Pat Brogan,' Feeny said.

A bulky middle-aged man, with coarse fair hair above stolid, reddish features, stood in the rectangle of light. He wore a black jersey and trousers.

414

'The hard man,' he greeted Liam Pat, proffering a hand with a cut healing along the edge of the thumb.

'Mr McTighe,' Feeny completed his introduction. 'We were passing.'

Mr McTighe led the way into a kitchen. He snapped open two cans of beer and handed one to each of his guests. He picked up a third from the top of a refrigerator. Carling it was, Black Label.

'How're you doing, Liam Pat?' Mr McTighe asked.

Liam Pat said he was all right, but Feeny softly denied that. More of the same, he reported: a foreman giving an Irish lad a hard time. Mr McTighe made a sympathetic motion with his large, square head. He had a hoarse voice that seemed to come from the depths of his chest. A Belfast man, Liam Pat said to himself when he got used to the accent, a city man.

'Is the room OK?' Mr McTighe asked, a query that came as a surprise. 'Are you settled?'

★ ★ ★

Liam Pat said his room was all right, and Feeny said:

'It was Mr McTighe fixed that for you.'

'The room?'

'He did of course.'

'It's a house that's known to me,' Mr McTighe said, and did not elucidate further. He gave a racing tip, Cassandra's Friend at Newton Abbot, the first race.

'Put your shirt on that, Liam Pat,' Feeny advised, and laughed. They stayed no more than half an hour, leaving the kitchen as they had entered it, by the door to the back yard. On the street Feeny said:

'You're in good hands with Mr McTighe.'

Liam Pat didn't understand that, but didn't say so. It would have something to do with the racing tip, he said to himself. He asked who the man who came round on Sunday mornings for the rent was.

'I wouldn't know that, boy.'

'I think I'm the only lodger there at the moment. There's a few shifted out, I'd say.'

'It's quiet for you so.'

'It's quiet all right.'

Liam Pat had to walk back to the house that night; there'd been no question of dossing down in Mr McTighe's. It took him nearly two hours, but the night was fine and he didn't mind. He went over the conversation that had taken place, recalling Mr McTighe's concern for his well-being, still bewildered by it. He slept soundly when he lay down, not bothering to take off his clothes, it being so late.

★   ★   ★

Weeks went by, during which Liam Pat didn't see Feeny. One of the other rooms in the house where he lodged was occupied again, but only for a weekend, and then he seemed once more to be on his own. One Friday Huxter gave Rafferty and Noonan their cards, accusing them of

416

skiving. 'Stay if you want to,' he said to Liam Pat, and Liam Pat was aware that the foreman didn't want him to go, that he served a purpose as Huxter's butt. But without his friends he was lonely, and a bitter resentment continuously nagged him, spreading from the foreman's treatment of him and affecting with distortion people who were strangers to him.

'I think I'll go back,' he said the next time he ran into Feeny, outside the Spurs and Horse one night. At first he'd thought Feeny was touchy when he went on about his experience in a launderette or plates being washed twice; now he felt it could be true. You'd buy a packet of cigarettes off the same woman in a shop and she wouldn't pass a few minutes with you, even though you'd been in yesterday. The only good part of being in this city was the public houses where you'd meet boys from home, where there was a bit of banter and cheerfulness, and a sing-song when it was permitted. But when the evening was over you were on your own again.

'Why'd you go back, boy?'

'It doesn't suit me.'

'I know what you mean. I often thought of it myself.'

'It's no life for a young fellow.'

'They've driven you out. They spent eight centuries tormenting us and now they're at it again.'

'He called my mam a hooer.'

Huxter wasn't fit to tie Mrs Brogan's laces, Feeny said. He'd seen it before, he said. 'They're all the same, boy.'

417

'I'll finish out the few weeks with the job we're on.'

'You'll be home for Christmas.'

'I will.'

They were walking slowly on the street, the public houses emptying, the night air dank and cold. Feeny paused in a pool of darkness, beneath a streetlight that wasn't working. Softly, he said:

'Mr McTighe has the business for you.'

It sounded like another tip, but Feeny said no. He walked on in silence, and Liam Pat said to himself it would be another job, a different foreman. He thought about that. Huxter was the worst of it, but it wasn't only Huxter. Liam Pat was homesick for the estate, for the small town where people said hullo to you. Since he'd been here he'd eaten any old how, sandwiches he bought the evening before, for breakfast and again in the middle of the day, burger and chips later on, Bob's Dining Rooms on a Sunday. He hadn't thought about that before he'd come — what he'd eat, what a Sunday would be like. Sometimes at mass he saw a girl he liked the look of, the same girl each time, quiet-featured, with her hair tied back. But when he went up to her after mass a few weeks back she turned away without speaking.

'I don't want another job,' he said.

'Why would you, Liam Pat? After what they put you through?'

'I thought you said Mr McTighe — '

'Ah no, no. Mr McTighe was only remembering the time you and Dessie Coglan used to

418

distribute the little magazine.'

They still walked slowly, Feeny setting the pace.

'We were kids though,' Liam Pat said, astonished at what was being said.

'You showed your colours all the same.'

Liam Pat didn't understand that. He didn't know why they were talking about a time when he was still at the Brothers', when he and Dessie Coglan used to push the freedom magazine into the letter boxes. As soon as it was dark they'd do it, so's no one would see them. Undercover stuff, Dessie used to say, and a couple of times he mentioned Michael Collins.

'I had word from Mr McTighe,' Feeny said.

'Are we calling in there?'

'He'll have a beer for us.'

'We were only being big fellas when we went round with the magazine.'

'It's remembered you went round with it.'

Liam Pat never knew where the copies of the magazine came from. Dessie Coglan just said the lads, but more likely it was the barber, Gaughan, an elderly man who lost the four fingers of his left hand in 1921. Liam Pat often noticed Dessie coming out of Gaughan's or talking to Gaughan in his doorway, beneath the striped barber's pole. In spite of his fingerless hand, Gaughan could still shave a man or cut a head of hair.

'Come on in,' Mr McTighe invited, opening his back door to them. 'That's a raw old night.'

They sat in the kitchen again. Mr McTighe handed round cans of Carling Black Label.

'You'll do the business, Liam?'

'What's that, Mr McTighe?'

'Feeny here'll show you the ropes.'

'The thing is, I'm going back to Ireland.'

'I thought maybe you would be. 'There's a man will be going home,' I said to myself. Didn't I say that, Feeny?'

'You did of course, Mr McTighe.'

'What I was thinking, you'd do the little thing for me before you'd be on your way, Liam. Like we were discussing the other night,' Mr McTighe said, and Liam Pat wondered if he'd had too much beer that night, for he couldn't remember any kind of discussion taking place.

★ ★ ★

Feeny opened the door of the room where the curtains were drawn over and took the stuff from the floorboards. He didn't switch the light on, but instead shone a torch into where he'd lifted away a section of the boards. Liam Pat saw red and black wires and the cream-coloured face of a timing device. Child's play, Feeny said, extinguishing the torch.

Liam Pat heard the floorboards replaced. He stepped back into the passage off which the door of the room opened. Together he and Feeny passed through the hall and climbed the stairs to Liam Pat's room.

'Pull down that blind, boy,' Feeny said.

There was a photograph of Liam Pat's mother stuck under the edge of a mirror over a washbasin; just above it, one of his father had begun to curl at the two corners that were

420

exposed. The cheap brown suitcase he'd travelled from Ireland with was open on the floor, clothes he'd brought back from the launderette dumped in it, not yet sorted out. He'd bought the suitcase in Lacey's in Emmet Street, the day after he gave in his notice to O'Dwyer.

'Listen to me now,' Feeny said, sitting down on the bed.

The springs rasped noisily. Feeny put a hand out to steady the sudden lurch of the headboard. 'I'm glad to scc that,' he said, gesturing with his head in the direction of a card Liam Pat's mother had made him promise he'd display in whatever room he found for himself. In the Virgin's arms the infant Jesus raised two chubby fingers in blessing.

'I'm not into anything like you're thinking,' Liam Pat said.

'Mr McTighe brought you over, boy.'

Feeny's wizened features were without expression. His priestly suit was shapeless, worn through at one of the elbows. A tie as narrow as a bootlace hung from the soiled collar of his shirt, its minuscule knot hard and shiny. He stared at his knees when he said Mr McTighe had brought Liam Pat from Ireland. Liam Pat said:

'I came over on my own though.'

Still examining the dark material stretched over his knees, as if fearing damage here also, Feeny shook his head.

'Mr McTighe fixed the room. Mr McTighe watched your welfare. 'I like the cut of Liam Pat

Brogan.' Those were his words, boy. The day after yourself and myself went round to him the first time wasn't he on the phone to me, eight o'clock in the morning? Would you know what he said that time?'

'No, I wouldn't.'

' 'We have a man in Liam Pat Brogan,' was what he said.'

'I couldn't do what you're saying all the same.'

'Listen to me, boy. They have no history on you. You're no more than another Paddy going home for Christmas. D'you understand what I'm saying to you, Liam Pat?'

'I never heard of Mr McTighe till I was over here.'

'He's a friend to you, Liam Pat, the same way's I am myself. Haven't I been a friend, Liam Pat?'

'You have surely.'

'That's all I'm saying to you.'

'I'd never have the nerve for a bomber.'

'Sure, is there anyone wants to be? Is there a man on the face of God's earth would make a choice, boy?' Feeny paused. He took a handkerchief from a pocket of his trousers and passed it beneath his nose. For the first time since they'd entered Liam Pat's room he looked at him directly. 'There'll be no harm done, boy. No harm to life or limb. Nothing the like of that.'

Liam Pat frowned. He shook his head, indicating further bewilderment.

'Mr McTighe wouldn't ask bloodshed of anyone,' Feeny went on. 'A Sunday night. You follow me on that? A Sunday's a dead day in the city. Not a detail of that written down, though. Neither date nor time. Nothing I'm saying to you.' He tapped the side of his head. 'Nothing, only memorised.'

Feeny went on talking then. Because there was no chair in the room, Liam Pat sat on the floor, his back to the wall. Child's play, Feeny said again. He talked about Mr McTighe and the mission that possessed Mr McTighe, the same that possessed every Irishman worth his salt, the further from home he was the more it was there. 'You understand me?' Feeny said often, punctuating his long speech with this query, concerned in case there was incomprehension where there should be clarity. 'The dream of Wolfe Tone,' he said. 'The dream of Isaac Butt and Charles Stewart Parnell. The dream of Lord Edward Fitzgerald.'

The names stirred classroom memories for Liam Pat, the lay teacher Riordan requesting information about them, his bitten moustache disguising a long upper lip, a dust of chalk on his pinstripes. 'Was your man Fitzgerald in the Flight of the Earls?' Hasessy asked once, and Riordan was contemptuous.

'The massacre of the innocents,' Feeny said. 'Bloody Sunday.' He spoke of lies and deception, of falsity and broken promises, of bullying that was hardly different from the bullying of Huxter. 'O'Connell,' he said. 'Pearse. Michael Collins. Those are the men, Liam Pat, and you'll walk away one of them. You'll walk away ten feet high.'

As a fish is attracted by a worm and yet suspicious of it, Liam Pat was drawn into

423

Feeny's oratory. 'God, you could be the Big Fella himself,' Dessie Coglan complimented him one night when they were delivering the magazines. He had seen the roadside cross that honoured the life and the death of the Big Fella; he had seen the film only a few weeks back. He leaned his head against the wall and, while staring at Feeny, saw himself striding with Michael Collins's big stride. The torrent of Feeny's assurances and promises, and the connections Feeny made, affected him, but even so he said:

'Sure, someone could be passing though.'

'There'll be no one passing, boy. A Sunday night's chosen to make sure of it. Nothing only empty offices, no watchmen on the premises. All that's gone into.'

Feeny pushed himself off the bed. He motioned with his hand and Liam Pat stood up. Between now and the incident, Feeny said, there would be no one in the house except Liam Pat. Write nothing down, he instructed again. 'You'll be questioned. Policemen will maybe get on the train. Or they'll be at the docks when you get there.'

'What'll I say to them though?'

'Only that you're going home to County Cork for Christmas. Only that you were nowhere near where they're asking you about. Never in your life. Never heard of it.'

'Will they say do I know you? Will they say do I know Mr McTighe?'

'They won't have those names. If they ask you for names say the lads in your gang, say Rafferty and Noonan, say any names you heard in public houses. Say Feeny and McTighe if you're stuck. They won't know who you're talking about.'

'Are they not your names then?'

'Why would they be, boy?'

Liam Pat's protestation that he couldn't do it didn't weaken at first, but as Feeny went on and on, the words becoming images in Liam Pat's vision, he himself always at the centre of things, he became aware of an excitcment. Huxter wouldn't know what was going to happen; Huxter would look at him and assume he was the same. The people who did not say hullo when he bought cigarettes or a newspaper would see no difference either. There was a strength in the excitement, a vigour Liam Pat had never experienced in his life before. He would carry the secret on to the site every morning. He would walk through the streets with it, a power in him where there'd been nothing. 'You have a Corkman's way with you,' Feeny said, and in the room with the drawn curtains he showed Liam Pat the business.

★ ★ ★

Sixteen days went by before the chosen Sunday arrived. In the Spurs and Horse during that time Liam Pat wanted to talk the way Feeny and Mr McTighe did, in the same soft manner, mysteriously, some private meaning in the words he used. He was aware of a lightness in his mood and confidence in his manner, and more easily than before he was drawn into conversation. One evening the barmaid eyed him the way Rosita

425

Drudy used to eye Dessie Coglan years ago in Brady's Bar.

Liam Pat didn't see Feeny again, as Feeny had warned him he wouldn't. He didn't see Mr McTighe. The man didn't call for the rent, and for sixteen days Liam Pat was the only person in the house. He kept to his room except when he went to take up the sawn-through floorboards, familiarising himself with what had to be done, making sure there was space enough in the sports bag when the clock was packed in a way that was convenient to set it. He cooked nothing in the kitchen because Feeny had said better not to. He didn't understand that, but even so he obeyed the command, thinking of it in that way, an order, no questions asked. He made tea in his room, buttering bread and sprinkling sugar on the butter, opening tins of beans and soup, eating the contents cold. Five times in all he made the journey he was to make on the chosen Sunday, timing himself as Feeny had suggested, becoming used to the journey and alert to any variations there might be.

On the Saturday before the Sunday he packed his suitcase and took it across the city to a locker at Euston Station, still following Feeny's instructions. When he returned to the house he collected what tins he'd opened and what food was left and filled a carrier bag, which he deposited in a dustbin in another street. The next day he had a meal at one o'clock in Bob's Dining Rooms, the last he would ever have there. The people were friendlier than they'd been before.

Nothing that belonged to him remained in his room, or in the house, when he left it for the last time. Feeny said to clean his room with the Philips cleaner that was kept for general use at the bottom of the stairs. He said to go over everywhere, all the surfaces, and Liam Pat did so, using the little round brush without any extension on the suction tube. For his own protection, that was. Wipe the handles of the doors with a tissue last thing of all, Feeny had advised, anywhere he might have touched.

Shortly after seven he practised the timing again. He wanted to smoke a cigarette in the downstairs room, but he didn't because Feeny had said not to. He zipped up the sports bag and left the house with it. Outside, he lit a cigarette.

On the way to the bus stop, two streets away, he dropped the key of the house down a drain, an instruction also. When Feeny had been advising him about cleaning the surfaces and making sure nothing was left that could identify him, Liam Pat had had the impression that Mr McTighe wouldn't have bothered with any of that, that all Mr McTighe was interested in was getting the job done. He went upstairs on the bus and sat at the back. A couple got off at the next stop, leaving him on his own.

It was then that Liam Pat began to feel afraid. It was one thing to have it over Huxter, to know what Huxter didn't know; it was one thing to get a smile from the barmaid. It was another altogether to be sitting on a bus with a device in a sports bag. The excitement that had first warmed him while he listened to Feeny, while he sat on the floor with his head resting against the wall, wasn't there any more. Mr McTighe picking him out felt different now, and when he tried to see himself in Michael Collins's trenchcoat, with Michael Collins's stride, there was nothing there either. It sounded meaningless, Feeny saying he had a Corkman's way with him.

He sat with the sports bag on the floor, steadied by his feet on either side of it. A weakness had come into his arms, and for a moment he thought he wouldn't be able to lift them, but when he tried it was all right, even though the feeling of weakness was still there. A moment later nausea caused him to close his eyes.

The bus lurched and juddered through the empty Sunday evening streets. Idling at bus stops, its engine vibrated, and between his knees Liam Pat's hand repeatedly reached down to seize the handles of the sports bag, steadying it further. He wanted to get off, to hurry down the stairs that were beside where he was sitting, to jump off the bus while it was still moving, to leave the sports bag where it was. He sensed what he did not understand: that all this had happened before, that his terror had come so suddenly because he was experiencing, again, what he had experienced already.

Two girls came chattering up the stairs and walked down the length of the bus. They laughed as they sat down, one of them bending forward, unable to control herself. The other went on with what she was saying, laughing too, but Liam Pat couldn't hear what she said. The conductor came for their fares and when he'd gone they found they didn't have a light for their cigarettes. The one who'd laughed so much was on the inside, next to the window. The other one got up. 'Ta,' she said when she had asked Liam Pat if he had a lighter and he handed her his box of matches. He didn't strike one because of the shaking in his hands, but even so she must have seen it. 'Ta,' she said again.

It could have been in a dream. He could have dreamed he was on a bus with the bag. He could have had a dream and forgotten it, like you sometimes did. The night he'd seen Feeny for the last time, it could have been he had a dream of being on a bus, and he tried to remember waking up the next morning, but he couldn't.

The girl next to the window looked over her shoulder, as if she'd just been told that he'd handed her friend the box instead of striking a match for her. They'd remember him because of that. The one who'd approached him would remember the sports bag. 'Cheers,' the same one said when they both left the bus a couple of stops later.

It wasn't a dream. It was the *Examiner* spread out on the kitchen table a few months ago and his father shaking his head over the funeral, sourly demanding why those people couldn't have been left to their grief, why there were strangers there, wanting to carry the coffin. 'My God! My God!' his father savagely exclaimed.

It hadn't worked the first time. A Sunday night then too, another boy, another bus. Liam Pat tried to remember that boy's name, but he couldn't. 'Poor bloody hero,' his father said.

Another Dessie Coglan had done the Big Fella, fixing it, in touch with another Gaughan, in touch with the lads, who came to parade at the funeral. Another Huxter was specially picked. Another Feeny said there'd be time to spare to get to Euston afterwards, no harm to life or limb, ten exactly the train was. The bits and pieces had been scraped up from the pavement and the street, skin and bone, part of a wallet fifty yards away.

Big Ben was chiming eight when he got off the bus, carrying the sports bag slightly away from his body, although he knew that was a pointless precaution. His hands weren't shaking any more, the sickness in his stomach had passed, but still he was afraid, the same fear that had begun on the bus, cold in him now.

Not far from where Big Ben had sounded there was a bridge over the river. He'd crossed it with Rafferty and Noonan, his first weekend in London, when they'd thought they were going to Fulham only they got it all wrong. He knew which way to go, but when he reached the river wall he had to wait because there were people around, and cars going by. And when the moment came, when he had the bag on the curved top of the wall, another car went by and he thought it would stop and come back, that the people in it would know. But that car went on, and the bag fell with hardly a splash into the river, and nothing happened.

O'Dwyer had work for him, only he'd have to wait until March, until old Hoyne reached the month of his retirement. Working the mixer it would be again, tarring roofs, sweeping the yard at the end of the day. He'd get on grand, O'Dwyer said. Wait a while and you'd never know; wait a while and Liam Pat could be his right-hand man. There were no hard feelings because Liam Pat had taken himself off for a while.

'Keep your tongue to yourself,' Mrs Brogan had warned her husband in a quiet moment the evening Liam Pat so unexpectedly returned. It surprised them that he had come the way he had, a roundabout route when he might have come the way he went, the Wexford crossing. 'I missed the seven train,' he lied, and Mrs Brogan knew he was lying because she had that instinct with her children. Maybe something to do with a girl, she imagined, his suddenly coming back. But she left that uninvestigated, too.

'Ah sure, it doesn't suit everyone,' Dessie Coglan said in Brady's Bar. Any day now it was for Rosita and he was full of that. He never knew a woman get pregnant as easy as Rosita, he said. He didn't ask Liam Pat if he'd used the telephone number he'd given him, if that was how he'd got work. 'You could end up with fourteen of them,' he said. Rosita herself was one of eleven.

Liam Pat didn't say much, either to O'Dwyer or at home or to Dessie Coglan. Time hung heavy while old Hoyne worked out the few months left of his years with O'Dwyer. Old Hoyne had never risen to being more than a general labourer, and Liam Pat knew he never would either.

He walked out along the Mountross road every afternoon, the icy air of a bitterly cold season harsh on his hands and face. Every day of January and a milder February, going by the rusted gates of Mountross Abbey and the signpost to Ballyfen, he thought about the funeral at which there'd been the unwanted presence of the lads, and sometimes saw it as his own.

All his life he would never be able to tell anyone. He could never describe that silent house or the stolid features of Mr McTighe or repeat Feeny's talk. He could never speak of the girls on the bus, how he hadn't been able to light a match, or how so abruptly he realised that this was the second attempt. He could never say that he'd stood with the sports bag on the river wall, that nothing had happened when it struck the water. Nor that he cried when he walked away, that tears ran down his cheeks and on to his clothes, that he cried for the bomber who might have been himself.

He might have left the bag on the bus, as he had thought he would. He might have hurried down the stairs and jumped off quickly. But in his fear he had found a shred of courage and it had to do with the boy: he knew that now and could remember the feeling. It was his mourning of the boy, as he might have mourned himself.

On his walks, and when he sat down to his meals, and when he listened to his parents' conversation, the mourning was still there, lonely and private. It was there in Brady's Bar and in the shops of the town when he went on his mother's messages. It would be there when again he took charge of a concrete mixer for O'Dwyer, when he shovelled wet cement and worked in all weathers. On the Mountross road Liam Pat didn't walk with the stride of Michael Collins, but wondered instead about the courage his fear had allowed, and begged that his mourning would not ever cease.

❧

Who saw no Sunrise cannot say
The Countenance 'twould be.
Who guess at seeing, guess at loss
Of the Ability.

The Emigrant of Light, it is
Afflicted for the Day.
The Blindness that beheld and blest —
And could not find its Eye.

Emily Dickinson

Doris Lessing

THE SWEETEST DREAM

(Extract from a novel to be published in autumn 2001)

Colin opened the door to a timid ring and saw what he thought was a mendicant child or a gypsy and then with a roar of 'It's Sylvia, it's little Sylvia,' lifted her inside. There he hugged her, and she shed tears on his cheeks, bent down to rub hers, like a cat's greeting.

In the kitchen he sat her at the table, *the* table, again extended to its full length. He poured a river of wine into a big glass and sat opposite her, full of welcome and pleasure.

'Why didn't you say you were coming? But it doesn't matter. I can't tell you how pleased I am to see you.'

Sylvia was trying to lift her mood to his height, because she was dispirited, London sometimes having this effect on Londoners who have been away from it and who, while living in it, have had so little idea of its weight, its multitudinous gifts and capacities. London, after the Mission, was hitting her a blow somewhere in the stomach region. It is a mistake to come too fast from, let's say, Kwandere to London: one needs something like the equivalent of a decompression chamber.

She sat smiling, taking little sips of wine, afraid

434

to do more, for she was not used to wine these days, feeling the house like a creature all around her and above her and below her, *her* house, the one she had known best as home when she had been conscious of what was going on in it, the atmospheres and airs of every room and stretches of the staircase. Now the house was populous, she could feel that, it was full of people, but they were alien presences, not her familiars and she was grateful for Colin, sitting there smiling at her. It was ten in the evening. Upstairs someone was playing a tune she ought to know, probably something famous, like 'Blue Suede Shoes' — it had that claim on her — but she couldn't name it.

'Little Sylvia. And it looks to me that you need a bit of feeding up, as always. Can I give you something to eat?'

'I ate on the plane.'

But he was up, opening the refrigerator door, peering up and down its shelves. And again Sylvia felt a blow to her heart, yes it was her heart, it hurt, for she was thinking of Rebecca, in her kitchen, with her little fridge, and her little cupboard which to her family down in the village represented some extreme of good fortune, generous provisioning: she was looking at the eggs filling half the door of the fridge, at the gleaming clean milk, the crammed containers, the plenitudes . . .

'This is not really my territory, it's Frances's, but I'm sure . . . ' He fetched out a loaf of bread, a plate of cold chicken. Sylvia was tempted: Frances had cooked it, Frances had fed her, with

435

Frances on one side and Andrew on the other, she had survived her childhood.

'What is your territory then?' she asked, tucking in to a chicken sandwich.

'I am upstairs, at the top of the house.'

'In Julia's place?'

'I, and Sophie.'

This surprised her into putting down her bit of sandwich, as if relinquishing safety for the time.

'You and Sophie!'

'Of course you didn't know. She came here to recuperate, and then . . . she was ill, you see.'

'And then?'

'Sophie is pregnant,' he said. 'And so we are about to get married.'

'Poor Colin,' she said, and then coloured up from shame — after all, she did not really know . . .

'Not entirely poor Colin. After all, I am very fond of Sophie.'

She resumed her sandwich then put it down: Colin's news had clamped her stomach shut. 'Well, go on. I can see you are miserable.'

'Perspicacious Sylvia. Well, you always were, while apparently little miss-I-am-not-here-at-all.'

This hurt, and he had meant it to. 'No, no, I'm sorry. I really am. I'm not myself. You've caught me at a . . . Well, perhaps I am myself at that.'

He poured more wine.

'Don't drink until I've heard.'

He set down his glass. 'Sophie is forty-three. It's late.'

'Yes, but quite often old mothers . . . ' She saw him wince.

436

'Quite so. An old mother. But believe it or not Down's syndrome babies — ever so jolly I hear they are — and all the other horrors are not the worst. Sophie is convinced that I am convinced she coaxed the baby from her reluctant womb, to make use of me, because it is getting late for her. I know she didn't do it on purpose, it is not her nature. But she won't let it go. Day and night I hear her wails of guilt: 'Oh I know what you're thinking . . . ' ' And Colin wailed the words with great effect. 'Do you know something? Yes, of course you do. There is no pleasure to compete with the pleasure of guilt. She is rolling in it, wallowing in it, my Sophie is, she's having the time of her life, knowing that I hate her because she has trapped me and nothing I can say will stop her because it's such fun, being guilty.' This was as savage as she had ever heard from savage Colin, and she saw him lift his glass and down the lot in a gulp.

'Oh Colin, you're going to be drunk and I see you so seldom.'

'Sylvia — you're right.' He refilled his glass. 'But I will marry her, she is already seven months, and we will live upstairs in Julia's old flat — four rooms, and I shall work down at the bottom of the house — when it's empty.' Here his face, reddened and angry as it was, spread into that exhilaration of pleasure that goes with the contemplation of life's relentless sense of drama. 'You did know that Frances took on two kids with her new bloke?'

'Yes, she wrote.'

'Did she tell you there is a wife, a depressive?

She is downstairs, in the flat where Phyllida was.'

'But . . . '

'No buts. It has worked out as well as might be. She has recovered from her depression. The two children are upstairs where Andrew and I used to be. Frances and Rupert are in the flat she always had.'

'So it has worked out?'

'But the two children reasonably enough think that now their mother has broken off with her fancy man, then why shouldn't their father and mother get together again, and Frances should just fade out.'

'So they are being horrible to Frances?'

'Not at all. Much worse. They are very polite and reasonable. The merits are argued out over every meal. The little girl, a real little bitch by the way, says things like, 'But it would be so much better for us if you went away, wouldn't it, Frances?' It's the girl really, not the boy. Rupert is hanging on to Frances for dear life. Understandably, if you know Meriel.'

Sylvia was thinking about Rebecca with her six children, two of them dead, probably from AIDS — but perhaps not — her usually absentee husband, working eighteen hours a day, and never complaining. She sighed, saw Colin's look. 'How lucky you are, Sylvia, so far away from our unedifying emotional messes.'

'Yes, I am sometimes glad I am not married — sorry. Go on. Meriel . . . '

'Meriel — well now, she's a prize. She's cold, manipulative, selfish and has always treated Rupert badly. She's a feminist — you know?

438

With all the law of the jungle behind her. She has always told Rupert that it is his duty to keep her, and she made him pay for her taking a degree in some rubbish or other, the higher criticism, I think. She has never earned a penny. And now she is trying to get a divorce where he keeps her in perpetuity. She belongs to a group of women, a secret sisterhood — you don't believe me? — whose aim it is to screw men for everything they can get.'

'You're making it up.'

'Sweet Sylvia, I seem to remember you never could believe in the nasticr aspects of human nature. But now Fate has taken a turn, and you'll never believe . . . Meriel went to see Phyllida who is quite a reasonable female after all — you are surprised — '

'Of course I am.'

'And she asked Phyllida to train Meriel as a counsellor, and she would pay.'

And now Sylvia began to laugh. 'Oh, Colin. Oh, Colin . . . '

'Yes, quite so. Because, you see, Meriel is quite unqualified. She didn't finish her degree. But as a counsellor she will be self-supporting. Counselling has become the resource of the unqualified female. It has replaced the sewing machine, for earlier generations.'

'Not in Zimlia it hasn't. The sewing machine is alive and well and earning women's livings.' And she laughed again.

'At last,' said Colin. 'I had begun to think you would never smile.' And he poured her more wine. She had actually drunk all hers. And he poured more for himself. 'And so. Meriel is going to move out to live with Phyllida, because Phyllida's partner is setting herself up as an independent physio, and our flat downstairs will be free and I shall use it to write in. And of course to evade my responsibilities as a father.'

'Which doesn't solve the problem of Frances being set up as a cruel stepmother. Apart from the children, is she happy?'

'She's delirious. First she really likes this Rupert, and who could blame her? But you haven't heard? She's back in the theatre.'

'What do you mean? I didn't know she was ever in it.'

'How little we know about our parents. It turns out that the theatre has always been my mother's first love. She is in a play with my Sophie. At this very moment the applause is ringing out for both of them.' And now his voice was slurred, and he frowned, concentrating on his speech. 'Damn,' he said. 'I am drunk.'

'Please, dear Colin, don't drink, please don't.'

'Spoken like Sonia. Well done.'

'Oh, Chekhov. Yes. I see. But I'm on her side, all right.' She laughed, but unhappily. 'There's a man at the Mission . . . ' But how was she going to convey the reality of Joshua to Colin? 'A black man. If he's not high on pot, he's drunk. Well, if you knew his life . . . '

'And mine doesn't justify alcohol.'

'No, it doesn't. So, you'd rather it wasn't Sophie . . . '

'I'd rather it wasn't a woman of forty-three.' And now a howl broke out of him, it had been waiting there all this time. 'You see, Sylvia, I know this is ridiculous, I know I am a sad pathetic fool, but I wanted happy families, I wanted mummy and daddy and four children. I wanted all that and I'm not going to have anything like it with my Sophie.'

'No,' said Sylvia.

'No.' He was trying not to cry, rubbing his fists over his face like a child. 'And if you don't want to be here to greet my happy Sophie and my triumphant mother, both high on Romeo and Juliet . . .'

'You mean Sophie is playing Juliet?'

'She looks about eighteen. She looks wonderful. She is wonderful. Pregnancy suits her. She is wearing white flowing robes and white flowers in her hair. Sylvia, do you remember her hair?' And now he began to cry, after all.

Sylvia went to him, persuaded him out of his chair, and then up the stairs, and where she had sat with Andrew, she held Colin and listened to him sob himself to sleep.

She didn't know where in this house she could find a bed. So she left a note for Colin. She told him she wanted him to 'write the truth about Zimlia'. Someone should.

She walked off into the streets and when she saw a hotel, went in.[1]

---

[1] This extract is from uncorrected proofs

Peter Porter

IN PARADISUM

The human body's a barometer
measuring the density of angels
and we who live in flats above the street
give readings of the preternaturally
miraculous. So many times I've listened
in the circling heat of Rome to the same
concise and consonant array of notes
from the piano in the neighbouring flat.
'Ah, Schumann's *Papillons*,' I've said,
and next morning with authority
'He's playing Schumann yet again'
and on the following day, 'Well, Schumann seems
quite at home in the Trastevere.'
My daughter's neighbour will never get to be
a virtuoso pianist however long
he practises: not up to speed, phrasing
ragged, confusion in his pedalling.
It seems as if this brave *Klavierkenner*
is pioneering Minimalism, his
repetitions and untidy sequences
the Ladder of Perfection's missing rungs.
Suddenly (*plötzlich* in Rilke's angels' way)
The Kingdom of the Equable appears,
and all the rubs of genius cease to count —
the being here, the doing that, the brain
which must abide the body — no, it's Spirit's
paradise, and through his tangled notes

we seem to hear the *chorus angelorum*
and the end of time, with pauper Lazarus
beyond need or call of resurrection.

OLD FRIENDS

Memory is an overcrowded party
where each face turns to leave
just as you come up to it.
Another beautiful anachronism —
this is punishment and benison,
anticipation of your Judgement
watching the sexual sins expand
until they are your only family,
seen in zones of pain and cleverness.

Caught by your trade — a specious memoir
elegant as Turgenev could be yours
to spike your life on — but you'd rather,
given the chance, put the thousand
anecdotal types back in their album
and scorch the world your helpless parents
and your early self served up as fate —
you know that Hell and Heaven must be
persons,
and love a promise lost in the palaver.

Old friends! Perhaps you really had the gift
of making friends. But long before you lost,
you doubted them. We're packed too tight
to trust ourselves in this existence,
our chafing neighbourliness,
our indiscriminate appetites,

our unposed innocence — and as they grow
they wave us on to nothingness,
these friends who stand between us and the
light.

This poem is for them, not lovers,
relatives or messengers of gods.
Friends are the ones who bear the scars
of work and disappointment. Their
martyrdom reveals us to ourselves
as poignant enemies. In wars
of self we have no allies; we know the light
inside our minds is not our own
but a brilliance unattainable like the stars.

❧

O dark, dark, dark, amid the blaze of noon,
Irrecoverably dark, total Eclipse
Without all hope of day!
O first created Beam, and thou great Word,
Let there be light, and light was over all;
Why am I thus bereav'd thy prime decree?
The Sun to me is dark
And silent as the Moon,
When she deserts the night
Hid in her vacant interlunar cave.
Since light so necessary is to life,
And almost life itself, if it be true
That light is in the Soul,
She all in every part; why was the sight
To such a tender ball as th'eye confin'd?
So obvious and so easy to be quench't,
And not as feeling through all parts diffus'd.

That she might look at will through every
pore?
Then had I not been thus exil'd from light:
As in the land of darkness yet in light,
To live a life half-dead, a living death,
And buried: but O yet more miserable!
Myself my Sepulchre, a moving Grave,
Buried yet not exempt
By privilege of death and burial
From worst of other evils, pains and wrongs,
But made hereby obnoxious more
To all the miseries of life,
Life in captivity
Among inhuman foes.

Milton, *Samson Agonistes*

Keith Ridgway

OFF VICO

(verum et factum convertuntur)

I sat there dozing, perplexed. Autumn is always a shock to me — all that greenery withering where it stands, failing; the dust of the black paths settling on my skin, the grass sickly, the air changing. Saint Stephen's Green in late September. Awful really.

It is my habit to sit and doze. I buy the paper and stroll from Baggot Street and set myself down and read a little. I have no opinions now; I just wade through the news and feel greatly sorry for myself, rambling as I am in small gentle circles, from home to park to home again, with treats pathetically feeble, such as trips on the train to see my niece, or a game of cards with an old friend in Donnybrook, which entails taking the bus — a great adventure. But the park is my favourite place now. It is easy to be there, because once there it is easy to imagine being elsewhere. I have of course my favourite bench, and regulars to nod to, and all that — the quotidian trivialities of my time of life, my decline, my slinking off. Usually I fall asleep, which is of course not advisable, but I carry a stick now, to help me walk, and I grip it always, ready, as I doze. And I try, in the sighing,

446

resigned way of men my age, to recall the sequence of the seasons, and the months that make them, and the numbers of the days.

This time anyway, this time I'm telling you about, this autumn, I was woken for some reason. A change maybe in the sound of footsteps, eyes on me, I don't know. I woke. And found myself stared at by a man not unlike myself, grey and slightly stooped, of my generation. He'd stopped in the path. He wore a coat like mine. His shoes were scuffed. No stick though. He stood there and looked at me. Pleasantly, with a half smile and a full head of hair.

'Hello.'

'Hello,' I said, squinting, trying to place him. It is a disturbing quirk of most people my age that they assume a familiarity based on shared decrepitude. This is something I discourage. However, I am hampered slightly by my own forgetfulness. I have to trawl, flustered, rushed, through half-remembered faces and lost names searching for a match. I have had so many conversations. He was distinguished-looking, despite the shoes. The hair was a good shade of silvery grey, very nice, hatless, unlike myself. His face was chalky and his eyes clear. He was a handsome man.

'You don't know me,' he said, obviously aware that the chirpy tone of my voice was a thin mask for my discomfort at believing that I might. I was about to become unfriendly when he added, 'Or at least, you won't remember me.'

I was inclined to agree. His tone of voice was

far too friendly. I remember people I dislike more clearly than the others. It's one of those gruesome little tricks that old age plays on you. This man rang no bells. Possibly he was a fan. It sometimes happens. Wretched old things that creep up to me and tell me how great I used to be and ask whatever happened.

He sat down, the cheeky bugger.

'It must be years,' he said, and laughed a choky laugh. Smoker. He continued to peer at me. I envied his hair.

'Since . . . ?'

'Since we met. At least forty. Forty-five maybe. I was about twenty, what, twenty-two. So it's more like fifty. Certainly before the millennium. Mid-nineties maybe.'

It was not going to be easy. If I had met him within the previous week, then, perhaps, there was a possibility. Even a month. If he was the best of company then I might stretch back as far as a year. But forty? Fifty? He was on to a loser.

'You were days before that prize,' he said.

'Prize?'

'You won some prize for your book. Your first book. About the boy growing up in Tramore.'

'Tralee.'

'Tralee, sorry. It was called . . . What was it called? *The Blue Beach. The Light.*' He was not very convincing as a fan.

'*The Bite of the Bright Sea.*'

'That was it. A bit of a mouthful. Your titles got better as you went on. *Shakers*, that's snappy. *The Island Square*, I liked that. My

448

favourite though was *The Height of It*. That's a marvellous book.'

'Thank you.'

Still he looked at me, examining my face.

'You've gotten older.'

It's a blunder I've often made myself. Telling people out straight the only thing they know for certain, as if it might be news. Standard rudeness really, I didn't mind, but he seemed disconcerted by it, embarrassed.

'I'm sorry. I have too. We both have. I was not . . . I was not accusing you of letting me down or anything.'

What a curious thing to say. Very sweet.

He looked at his shoes, tucked them out of sight. He sighed, folded his arms. I settled, got comfortable, waited for the anecdote. How he bought me a drink in the old days and I said something wonderful. How he used to do a bit of writing himself. Oh I don't mind. It beats sleeping.

'When we met I was just a boy. You had a few years on me. Seemed a lot then. Now of course you couldn't tell the difference.'

Huh.

'We met where . . . ?' I prompted. Less nostalgia I wanted, more fact. Facts are good, facts are funny. Facts you can argue about. Not much you can say to cheap little observations, wise words, sentiments — all that autumnal clutter.

He laughed. Looked at his hands, let them rest in his lap.

'You won't remember.'

Of course I wouldn't remember. That was the whole point. He wasn't very good at this.

'Try me.'

Go on for God's sake. Get it over with.

'Dun Laoghaire.'

'Yes?'

'I don't know what year. Fifty years ago. Maybe more. Before you won that prize.'

'Where in Dun Laoghaire?'

'Oh well. That'd be saying.'

He sighed again. Shifted a little. I thought he was going to get up and go. Seemed suddenly sad. His eyes lost focus. A woman passed us clicking heels. She coughed. He stared into space. I guessed that he'd realised his mistake, that he'd never met me at all, just knew who I was and thought he'd met me, and was trying now to get out of it.

It was colder than it had been. Is it not strange that your body becomes more sensitive with age and your mind more dulled? There I go, breaking my own rules. What I mean to say is that I was cold, and I wanted distraction. I wanted him to keep going. Who cares? Make it up. It wouldn't matter. Share a harmless piece of time, and part.

'We met by the pier. I wore my sports jacket and carried a bag. It was a Friday. I'd been out drinking with workmates. I told you that and you said 'Well that's always depressing' and I laughed.'

'By the pier?' He was making it up.

'Yes. There were other men there, the usual thing, late Friday night. You passed me and I saw you and I sat down on the bench. You went off

450

down to the shelter and I wandered around and when you came back, going towards the road, I sat down on the bench again. I was shivering. Cold. But it was August I think. Late August. Maybe September. You passed me and looked at me and sat down. It was a bench like this. Just like this. Near the cannon. You said hello, I said hello. I don't know what we said. You moved closer and touched my knee with yours . . . '

Well now. There's making it up and there's making it up.

'I certainly don't remember any such thing.'

'No,' he said quietly, eyes to the ground. 'You probably don't.'

I do believe I stared. Well, it's not the type of thing you expect to be confronted with, is it? Not at my age. Not in Saint Stephen's Green, out of the blue, one doddery autumn. Oh it was well known that I was queer, I never hid it, never needed to — I'd missed all but the tail end of the bad years. Half the bloody books were full of it. I was even notorious for a while, briefly had a lover in politics. We were much discussed. But what was this fellow saying? That I had tried to pick him up in Dun Laoghaire fifty years earlier? Not my idea of a funny story.

'You asked me did I want to go somewhere. I said yes.'

I squinted. Strange to say, I relaxed a little. He didn't fight me off then. Didn't call the police. This was not an accusation.

'Then we discovered that neither of us had a place to go to. I lived with my parents. I don't know why we couldn't have gone to your place,

451

but maybe you were nervous of me or something, I don't know.'

I had lived on the Northside then. Miles away. Fifty years, the nineties, early nineties, mid-nineties. I lived on Aughrim Street most of that time, lass of Aughrim, murder town, bus roars. What on earth would I have been doing at Dun Laoghaire Pier? I was intrigued now. It was not an accusation. And it was not true. Couldn't be. It was a story, and it would be fun to see how far he took it.

'You said we could go in your car and try and find somewhere discreet.'

I had to stop him.

'Ah well now there you're wrong you see. I've never had a car. It's someone else you're thinking about.'

I had to stop him. Had to. There's no point if suspension of disbelief is impossible, if it's lost. It's the first rule of story-telling. Believability. He'd have to go back a bit, redo it.

'No. It was you.'

He was very calm and certain. I frowned. He'd spoil it now, if he insisted on this car nonsense. I sighed. Disappointed.

'Go on.'

'We got into the car. It was . . . It was . . . Oh I don't remember what it was. I'd had a few drinks. We talked while you drove. You didn't know the area at all. I had to give directions. We drove through Sandycove and up into Dalkey and up the hill on the coast road towards Killiney. Wait . . . '

He held up a finger. Good nails.

452

'I'd forgotten. When we got into the car you held out your hand and told me your name was Ronan. Liar. I lied too — told you I was John or something. Don't know why. We shook hands. You said mine was cold. Every time you changed gear your hand brushed my knee.'

Ronan. Ronan. Ronan. The name ricocheted a little. I closed my eyes. When I was young I split things up. Ronan. Somewhere, in the furthest corner of my mind, I could dimly see, not see, remember, sense, sense a cold hand in a dark car and the sound of the sea. Could I? I was imagining it surely. I could not remember such things. That was a lifetime ago. I opened my eyes. Scratched my nose. He had stopped, was looking at me. His face.

'Did you wear glasses?' I said.

'My God.'

I raised my eyebrows. His mouth opened. Neat mouth, still some life in his lips.

'My God,' he said again, and smiled. 'Yes. Yes I did. God, you remember.'

'No I don't.'

'You do. You remember.' He laughed.

A boy with a beautiful face and a sandy sports jacket and glasses. Cold hand. Coughing. He had coughed a lot. Complained about cigarettes.

'I don't know,' I said. 'I have never owned a car. I do not know Dun Laoghaire. It's highly unlikely.'

He was excited now. He shuffled a little closer, put his arm up on the back of the bench. His smile was generous, happy, delighted.

'We went up those winding roads, you know,

453

and the bay was down below us and the lights all twinkled and you said you'd love to live there and I started telling you all the famous people who had houses there. Rock stars. What was his name . . .'

'It's left me.'

'Me too. And the racing drivers, and the actors. We talked like that. Up we drove, do you remember? Then I got you to stop on Vico Road, where there's that gap in the wall, and you were a little sceptical but you said okay, and I asked you could I leave my bag in the car, do you remember?'

Frank Conway had an old Japanese thing. I'd borrow it sometimes. When he went away. The sound of the sea. I shrugged.

'Fifty years ago?'

'Yes. And you locked the car and we went through the wall and down that sloping path to the bridge over the railway line, and all the time I was terrified that there'd be people there drinking, but there wasn't, there wasn't at all, and anyway, I'd had a few drinks, and I was — '

He looked at me, then glanced away, smiling.

I smiled too. I believed him. He had done this. But had I? There was no point, I thought, in gazing at his face, trying to find something that I might recognise. I looked slightly past him, and the out of focus perspective hinted at memory, at recollection, at the face of a boy with beautiful black hair.

Ach no.

The glasses though. I had remembered them. He had been small, or not small particularly, but

454

slim, and younger than me. The face. The hair. A lovely mop of black hair. His smell. I looked at him again, properly. Could I really remember the smell of a boy I was with fifty years before?

No I couldn't.

'We crossed that bridge,' he continued, 'remember? It makes an echoing kind of noise as you cross it. And then down steps. Steps and steps and steps. And I think I stumbled once or twice, because it was dark. Stars just, and the sea all the time, lapping the rocks below us. Lapping and rustling. And the grass rustling too. Long grass on each side of us. We went down, and turned a corner where the steps turn, and then I cut away from the path on to the grass where there's a bench. Another bench, just like this one. Do you remember now? Do you?'

I nodded. I did. I didn't. I shrugged. His hair.

'I sat down and you did too. We kissed.'

He stopped. Considered me. I knew what this pause was about. We are very old, past that now, through it and done with it and handed it over, a little shocked that we were ever in the midst of it at all. He looked at his hands. I wanted him to tell me though, to remind me if he could, word by word, for I was hanging on this now more than was healthy, and he must have seen that. Remind me. His eyes receded, lit an inner picture. He smiled.

'We kissed. We kissed and you took off your jacket and the bench was wet. Soaking wet. I could feel it though my trousers. I felt you. I ran my hands over you, over your arms, your chest. You kissed me. We kissed deeply, you ran your hands through my hair. You turned so that you half stood, and I lifted your shirt out of your jeans and I lifted it up over your chest and kissed you there, me and my mouth. You remember?'

'Yes.'

'And we fumbled. Fumbled and kissed.'

I could remember, couldn't I? High above the water. His jacket, light in the gloom. The rest of him black. His shirt black, showing the white of his skin at the neck where it opened. I remembered. Good God, I remembered it all. Didn't I? I fought for some detail of my own. A contribution. The things that came to me were of a sexual nature — my recollections all seemed below the belt. I was hesitant. At my age, at our age, talk is all that's left. Once you go there you can't really go any further. And there is the mundane question of embarrassment, to which we become increasingly susceptible I find, as we are less and less able to do what we say. As if words were ever linked to actions. In any case, I tried to remember something else.

'You were dressed entirely in black,' I ventured. 'Except for the jacket.'

He seemed bemused.

'Really?'

'Yes.'

'Are you sure?'

'Yes. Black. Black trousers, black shoes, black shirt, T-shirt. Underwear.'

He laughed, 'I was not.'

'You were. Black. All black.'

'They must have just looked black in the dark.'

'No. Well, maybe. I remember though. Against

456

your skin, all that black, it was . . . '

I trailed off. I did not know what I was trying
to say.

'I can only apologise.'

'No need. Really. Anyway . . . ' and I trailed off
again. It is damnable, it really is. What I wanted
to say to him was that I had slid them right off,
that I had stripped him bare in the moonlight,
that the colour of the things was not at issue, that
it was simply there, a detail, before the import,
pre-important, an earlier thing, a symptom of
recall, a hook in the myth of it, a toe-hold in
legend. I stripped him bare. True or not, it is
what I wanted to say. And yet, there I was,
staring at my crow hands perched on my stick,
mumbling nothing, no blood left for blushing,
never mind anything else, and I said nothing, I
told him nothing, I communicated nothing.
Nearly dead and still this stupidity.

'What is it?' he asked.

'It wasn't me. I wasn't there.'

He paused, and I sensed that he made a
movement, but I did not look up. Foul humours
take me very suddenly, very completely.

There was silence.

Abstractions by the handful, I grappled with
my history for a moment, as one will, must, will,
when confronted with a past which one had
imagined as a future, and one sees, again, always
recurring, that the bulk of things lies behind us,
done and dusted, used just once, through in an
instant. Abstract regret, abstract sorrow, abstract
life. That we discuss anything at all is a wonder
to me.

'I sat,' he said, and I closed my eyes and hoped he would go away. 'You stood in front of me. The bay at your back, the water glistening. I could hear the waves and the blood in your veins. I could taste the sea from you. The sea and the stars and the whole world.'

His voice was very light, catering for me, it seemed, making allowances. How many decisions is one supposed to make? Either I had been there or I had not. I opened my eyes. My hands were the same. What was the worst that could happen?

'You were naked,' I said.

'No. Was I? Maybe. Dishevelled certainly. Uncovered. I wanted you to lie on me.'

'I wouldn't. I didn't want to cover all of you at once, I wanted to cover you an inch at a time. I explored you.'

'Yes.'

'I remember your chest,' I told him. 'So neat. Your stomach. I remember your hair. Your hair was beautiful. The smell of your hair. So sweet. I wanted to do everything at once. I mean, at the same time.'

'I know. You would kiss my lips, and then you would be off somewhere else kissing, groaning, all that.'

Still we hesitated, the two of us. After all this time.

'And all the time I was stretched as if on a rack in the cold air, your hands on me like coals, wanting,' he dropped his voice, 'all of you inside me. But there was rustling.'

'Rustling?'

'Yes. We were looking for a condom. I had one. Just one. In my wallet. While I was searching for it you were looking around, being wary. You decided there was rustling in the grass and you didn't like it.'

'I remember. There was rustling.'

'It was probably the wind. The bay to our right. My right. Your left. The sweep of it off to Bray. The twinkling of lights in houses and on roads and by the water. The water. We stood there listening, pale bodies in the starlight. The security lights in a house in the distance kept coming on, and going off again a few minutes later. We watched and I stroked your body. You wanted to move somewhere else to use the condom.'

'I remember. More steps.'

'More steps. Down and down, diagonally, back and forth, until we came to a shelter on the rocks. Not a soul. Dark. The water louder. Wilder. You said, 'Maybe this was a bad idea,' then I kissed you, I remember that kiss so well, and you said 'Who cares' and we were there again, part of the sea and the air and the night, just the two of us. There was no one else on the planet. You put on the condom and you,' he searched for the term, 'made love to me. And I thought I had never been alive before.'

'Hold on.'

'What?'

'I made love to you?'

'Yes.'

'Translate that.'

'What do you mean?'

459

'I mean who did what to who?'

'You made love to me.'

'I, pardon me, fucked you?'

'Yes.'

'No no no. You made love to me.'

He stared. Scratched his head.

'No,' he said.

'Yes. I distinctly remember. Everything you said is right, but it was you who — I held the stone, a kind of bench, a seat, inside the shelter, and the sea was in my ears and you made love to me. Which does not cover it. You fucked me.'

He seemed concerned.

'And great it was too,' I added, thoughtfully.

He looked at his hands. Frowned. Shook his head slowly.

'No.'

A thought struck me, and perhaps it struck him at the same time, for he looked at me, embarrassed at last, letting it in, suddenly sheepish.

'How,' I asked, and carefully, 'do you know it was me?'

'I told you. Two days later, or three, or whatever, you won that prize for *The Bright Blue Sea*.'

'*The Bite of the Bright Sea*.'

'Whatever. Your picture was in the papers. I saw it, and I recognised you. I thought — thought it was hilarious. You were even on the radio about a week later and I knew your voice. I've kept an eye on you ever since. It was you.'

We had fluffed it. Only words to get wrong and we had got them wrong. Two old men telling each other such things, on a park bench, in autumn, in times like these. I shook my head. Two old vessels leaking fantasy, spilling out private little legends, mixing dreams with the truth, ending in confusion. A mist came down. I am old.

'It was you,' he said again. I shrugged. He was sure. So be it. Good for him. Why should I have any great urge for truth? Why should I feel possessive towards the events of my life? There are versions in every breath. Let him remember me like that if he wants. I'll be remembered worse.

We were silent for a while. He pondered the path. I affected a yawn. I wondered briefly whether we might not, despite the times we live in, despite the blunt doubt, slink off into the bushes and re-enact, reconstruct the supposed sequence of events. Try and jog our memories. Shake them up a bit. Put it to the test. But the bushes looked scrawny — awfully bare. I am past the point in my life where I might be mistaken for the fruit in such shrubbery, and am now much more likely to be confused with the branches. Except to the touch. I rejected the notion. Not in autumn.

In his face though, I could still see something (could I?) of youth. The ghost of it. Is that memory, or can that be seen in any face? And this notion I had, of the smell, the scent, of his hair. Young black fine hair, hair that slipped through my fingers. Clean hair. What was that? And the thought that he'd had glasses, which he had confirmed, as if . . .

'Where are your glasses?' I snapped, eureka-like.

'I had corrective surgery. My eyes are perfect now. It's the rest of me that's knackered.'

He could have made that up. Could have been thinking about it since I'd mentioned the bloody things. I was too slow.

What would it have been, on my part? A random lust, driven south of the city in Frank Conway's car, vented by the sea on the hill of Killiney with a black-haired boy in a sandy sports jacket and glasses. Would I not be sure of that? I had never been very good at cruising. Terrified always, half of being beaten up, half of being seen, caught by someone I knew. I was never happy. And I was fussy and slow. Not good with signs, looks, glances. I didn't do it often. I kept myself to pubs, to circles of friends, to socially acceptable predation. Not that I was very predatory. I waited, and had an awful habit of being grateful when someone showed an interest. When I did cruise, in the open air, in dangerous, public places, and got lucky (got lucky!) I would forget about it. Quickly. Why's that? Why?

'Did you . . . ' he started, and coughed. 'Did you go there with others?'

I frowned.

'Where?'

'That place.'

I didn't know that place. I had never been there.

'No.'

Which was why I must have been there with someone. With him, presumably. For I could remember it. I could remember that place. Not that place. That moment. I could recall it, independent of geography or time. That's imagination isn't it?

'Did you?' I asked.

'Yes,' he said. 'Once. I think.'

'With who?'

'I don't know.'

Something went bad inside me. Did mild, but sudden, jealousy prove anything?

'Maybe it was me,' I said.

'What?'

'I mean. Maybe it wasn't. Maybe you were with someone else, who you can't remember, and you think it was me. Maybe I'm not what you recall, I'm just, I don't know, woven in. Whimsy. Later. When you saw me in the paper.'

He smiled at me.

'You think I'd slip you into my fantasies?'

He had a point.

'Anyway,' he said. 'You remember it. You were there.'

'I don't know if I remember or imagine. I don't know.'

He moved closer to me. Our coats touched. He sat slightly sideways, looked at me.

'Imagine it,' he said.

'What?'

'Close your eyes. Let it come back to you. Imagine it. Tell me what you imagine. Tell me what happened.'

'But I can't remember.'

'So dream,' he sighed, sounding terribly like the man who cues in a song in one of those musical films my father loved. The orchestra creeps in.

I snorted, shrugged, demurred, didn't like it. But he leaned close to me, and our coats touched, and he insisted. He insisted.

At first I couldn't get away from where we were. Cold autumn afternoon, near death, but I drifted. I caught a scent and closed my eyes and drifted.

'The car borrowed from Frank Conway. I drove for the sake of it, loving the turning of corners. The long drive across town. I enjoyed going fast along the Merrion Road, taking the Blackrock bypass at speed, on my own in Charlie's car, turning the radio off, turning it on again. Dun Laoghaire. The night and the boats and the water and the pier and the men. I remember all of that, but, I don't know, it's a mess of different nights.'

'Me. See me.'

'You? I can't see you. Him, maybe.'

'Him then.'

'Him. I see him. I imagine him. I saw him. Sandy jacket. Glasses. Shivering. He . . . How strange. Shivering on the bench and I wanted to warm him. I mean that literally. I wanted him to be warm again. I was afraid to breathe, afraid he would disappear. He coughed in the car, told me that he smoked too much. He used his long hand to point the way. The stars played on his skin. I imagine that the stars played on his skin. We went through the gap in the wall, off Vico Road, and we walked into another world, or took another world with us, I don't know. Stepped

464

outside of things. There was only us, and it surprised me. We made love. It was part of the night. We were part of the night. We disappeared. We vanished. No one could see us. No one knew. We were together.'

For a moment I was stuck. His clothes had been smoky, his face pale. I had kissed his neck.

'I recall the afterwards. His coughing. The climb back to the car that he seemed not to notice but which had me breathless. The chill. The fear of meeting someone. I remember driving him as far as the dual carriageway, under his directions, and his insistence that I need not drop him home, that he could walk from there, and I remember the last look I had of him, a retreating figure in my rear-view mirror, that jacket, his bag slung on his shoulder. And I remember the regret . . . Am I making this up?'

'No. Go on.'

'Melancholy. It's a young man's thing. It came with the glancing at my watch and knowing that we'd spent little over an hour together. An hour. On the side of a cliff in the cold embrace of the Irish Sea. And that he was beautiful, and that we had been close, and that I would probably never see him again.'

I opened my eyes. I wanted to see him again. But he was not there. Just age and the withered world.

'We were not lovers,' I said.

'We were. For a moment.'

'A moment.'

I cleared my throat.

'Are you sure?'

'Yes.'
'It happened?'
'Yes.'
'It was you?'
'Yes.'

I chose to believe him. Why not? Perhaps he prowled city parks daily, and lit upon the bewildered and filled their heads full of foolish thoughts. Perhaps he was mad. A hypnotist. A subversive. Perhaps he was my boy. Perhaps it is I who am mad. But I think he remembers. I think I knew him, and he me, and I think we had met before, outside the history of our lives, off the standard story, as if we had dreamed the same dream. It pleased me to believe it.

'That night,' I said. 'That night. I kissed you, and I opened my eyes while I kissed you, because I was afraid, and when I opened my eyes I could see nothing but the sea and the lights of passing boats, and the waving grass and the stars, and I closed my eyes again, and there was only you, only you and your body and the sweet sweet smell of you, and then I looked once more, and I remember being surprised, astonished, that there was no one else but us. It seemed to me that the hill we were on, the steps, the path, the whole blessed place, the entire bay, should be covered with couples like us. Lovers. That the whole world should know the dark night and the embrace of skin and the taste of the sea and the kiss that we shared, that closeness, that moment. That moment. The joy of that. But there was only us. Us alone.'

He didn't move. He looked at me.

466

'Did you tell anyone?'

'No.'

'Nor did I.' He nodded, as if we had managed to keep some kind of promise.

He leaned towards me, laid a hand on mine. His hands, ghosts, were still cold. I dreamed of his shiver. He kissed me again, gently now, with paper lips, brushing my cheek. My dying skin. He stood and smiled and bowed a little and walked away.

I have not seen him since. I think of all the people in my life. All that love, pain, time. All the places where the people have been. I can count them and not stop. Year after year of writing it down, so that in the end, there is nothing of it kept. Gods, heroes, men. All that living. Telling.

And only one secret.

∾

I was standing at the door for a moment, full of sad thoughts about my father, when I saw someone drawing slowly near along the road. He was plainly blind, for he tapped before him with a stick, and wore a great green shade over his eyes and nose; and he was hunched, as if with age or weakness, and wore a huge old tattered sea-cloak with a hood, that made him appear positively deformed. I never saw in my life a more dreadful-looking figure. He stopped a little from the inn, and, raising his voice in an odd sing-song, addressed the air in front of him: —

'Will any kind friend inform a poor blind man, who has lost the precious sight of his eyes in the

gracious defence of his native country, England, and God bless King George! — where or in what part of this country he may now be?'

'You are at the Admiral Benbow, Black Hill Cove, my good man,' said I.

'I hear a voice,' said he — 'a young voice. Will you give me your hand, my kind young friend, and lead me in?'

'I held out my hand, and the horrible, soft-spoken, eyeless creature gripped it in a moment like a vice. I was so much startled that I struggled to withdraw; but the blind man pulled me close up to him with a single action of his arm.

'Now, boy,' he said, 'take me in to the captain.'

'Sir,' said I, 'upon my word I dare not.'

'Oh,' he sneered, 'that's it! Take me in straight, or I'll break your arm.'

And he gave it, as he spoke, a wrench, that made me cry out.

R L Stevenson, *Treasure Island*

Joanna Trollope

ON MY BEDSIDE TABLE

July, 2000

My grandmother's night table, I remember, was an intensely characterful affair. For her, being awake in bed wasn't just a peaceful matter of a book and a pair of spectacles: it was a chance to rev up into the intensity of activity that kept her buzzing through the day with hardly a pause. This chance required a minimum of the following beside her bed: lipsticks, apples, painting things, a selection of huge earrings, rose catalogues, toffees, writing things, powder compacts, dog biscuits, a novel from the travelling library (but never a crime story and never anything set in China), nail varnishes, a small coffee thermos, sewing, letters, photographs, Hobnobs, a copy of the *Daily Light*, and white seedless grapes. She slept in her rings (enormous) and her watch (minute), and would have despised the use of an alarm clock.

My bedside table, by comparison, is very dull. Apart from a small beanbag goose sitting on an unrelated tiny velvet cushion stuffed with lavender, given to me by a friend and my elder daughter as comforting accompaniments on an arduous American book tour a few years ago, and some scrumptious photographs of my granddaughter, there are no surprises. Specs, hand cream, water, books, clock and a small enamel box in which the friend who gave it to me cheerfully suggested I keep my glass eye. Instead, it contains airline earplugs, the foam kind that spring out energetically no matter how assiduously you try to stuff them in.

The books themselves are in two piles, and don't include the stack of newspapers, magazines, and lit. supps. on the floor. One pile is current, the second — larger — is of books that have somehow ground to a halt against the wall and have now been there so long that I've ceased to see them.

At the bottom of this second pile is a Guilt Book. A Guilt Book is one pressed into your hand by someone you like or admire (or both) with the words, 'I just *know* you'll love this.' The burden of being required to love such a book is often so great that I can hardly even *embark* on reading it . . . In this case, a much admired American account of life in a Benedictine abbey in Minnesota by the poet Kathleen Norris. The quotes on the cover are reverential, ecstatic, all from distinguished sources. I *ought* to read it. I know I ought. I tell myself that I loved Patrick Leigh Fermor's *A Time To Keep Silence*, so maybe I will love this. But I know I will simply leave it where it is, against the wall, at the bottom of the pile, exuding reproach.

Above it is a present from my younger stepson — Nicholas Albery's anthology *A Poem for the Day*. Despite my gloom about the poem chosen for my birthday, 9 December — Milton's seventh sonnet, 'How soon hath time' — I enjoy this collection which has some uncommon things in it (Thomas Flatman's 'An Appeal to Cats in the Business of Love') and some familiar treasures (Sassoon's 'Everyone . . . ' and Gray's 'Elegy' and Shelley's 'Skylark') and is interesting for testing one's capacity to learn something new by heart (moderate to disappointing).

Above the anthology is a handsome Bloomsbury paperback of Trevor Grove's *The Juryman's Tale*. I read this when I was researching *Marrying the Mistress* and thought it was not only excellent but a reassuring vindication of the jury system. Trevor Grove served on an Old Bailey jury in 1997 during a major kidnap trial, and this is his eloquent account of what went on, agony, ecstasy, absurd little details and all. It's only still by my bed because it has settled comfortably and invisibly into the pile like part of the wallpaper. It seems both arbitrary and a shame to move it. Books don't have to live in shelves, after all.

The next book was a present too, this time from the author. Charles Monaghan, a well-known American writer and journalist, and his wife Jenny, were extraordinarily kind to my younger daughter and her husband while the latter were their neighbours in Brooklyn. And then Charlie sent me his latest book, *The Murrays of Murray Hill*, one of those amazing histories of the entrepreneurs who, literally, *made* Manhattan. The Murrays' great family star was Lindley, a lawyer exiled to Britain in 1784 as a loyalist, who began there to write the school textbooks that made him the best-selling author in the world in the first eighty years of the nineteenth century — fifteen and a half *million* copies. And we're talking schoolbooks here, not Harry Potter. His *über* best-seller was *The English Reader*: Abraham Lincoln thought it was 'the best schoolbook ever put into the hands of American youth'.

On the top of the pile are two books for my granddaughter and me. One is Beatrix Potter's *The Tailor of Gloucester*. This is my choice, really, rather than hers, though she likes the mice ('Oh! Mouse! Hat! Shoes!') and will in time come to see, I'm sure, that even if this isn't the most accessible or immediately charming of the wonderful Potter canon, it is the best and the most poignant, and the illustrations are magnificent. Her choice is *The Very Hungry Caterpillar*. I am charmed that this — new when her mother was fairly new — is still such a favourite. And I am equally charmed that, just like her mother, she loves the page full of exotic American food — the pickle and the frankfurter and the cherry pie and watermelon. And the cupcake. 'Oh!' (lovingly) '*Cake!*'

In the front of this pile are the current books. There are three just now — a paperback of Alice Munro's latest short story collection, *The Love of a Good Woman*, a proof copy of the new Margaret Atwood *The Blind Assassin* and a treasure I found in a bookshop in North Carolina in June — an American classic, written in 1941, by W.J. Cash, called *The Mind of the South*. It's spellbinding, almost theatrically written, an analysis of the development of Southern personality, Southern attitudes, Southern convictions. As for the two Canadians — well, there are few contemporary writers in their particular fields to touch them. Alice Munro can't write a graceless sentence, and Margaret Atwood turns her steady, unflinching gaze on all sorts of human unpleasantness that we'd rather not confront, thank you — the treachery of women, for example — and then writes about them in clear, exquisite, candid prose. I read something last night that was pure Atwood. She's describing a marriage in which the wife, accommodating herself to a returning war veteran husband, behaves with unflinching and consummate selflessness. 'But of course,' says Atwood, almost carelessly, 'the other side of selflessness is tyranny'. *Brilliant.*

~

I do not live in a world of total blackness. I have already spoken of the part the imagination plays in re-creating the world it knows to be there, but there is something other than this, of which I have not been able to find an explanation. In front of my left eye I have a continual display of regular, rectangular patterns within a roughly triangular frame, somewhat resembling an heraldic shield. These shapes vary in colour from pale yellow, through golden-orange to red, or from green to blue, and at their brightest have a beauty and purity scarcely to be found in nature. They are always there, but are affected by my physiology. If I am tired or hungry they are much more vivid than if I am rested. They are not in any sense dream images, and have no symbolic content. Something is going on in the visual cortex of the right side of my brain.

John Heath-Stubbs, *Hindsights*

John Burnside

HEAVEN

Somewhere between the old kilns and the corner of Barton Street, Tom lost the little bag of coins he'd been saving to get him into the pictures. He retraced his steps, scouring the gutters and the narrow headlands of dirt and blown sweet papers along the fence, till his fingers were grimy from rummaging among the litter. Everything he touched was coated with a fine layer of soot and dust. The wind carried it in from the steelworks and left it everywhere, a pale grey powder, soft and fine, yet strangely persistent, like the residue from some huge chemistry experiment. Sometimes, when it rained, he would notice how the dock leaves and the privet hedges looked when they reappeared, impossibly green, like the bright shrubs and trees in the picture of heaven Miss Cameron had pinned on the classroom wall. It bothered him, thinking about that, as if heaven was really there all along, right there on earth, right under his nose, only it was covered with dust and soot, invisible and silent.

When he was sure he wasn't going to find the bag, Tom wiped his hands on the seat of his trousers and began walking away from town, towards the cemetery. He didn't want to go home — not yet: if she knew he'd lost the money, his mother would be annoyed, and, even though Tom could tell she was only being angry to hide her embarrassment, because she couldn't give him any more, he could never explain that he didn't mind, that he didn't expect more from her anyway. He was angry with himself — he didn't like losing things — but it was a vague, temporary anger, only half-meant, like a game. He didn't understand why his mother took everything so hard.

By the time he reached the park, the sky was beginning to darken. It was still afternoon, but it felt like evening already, and Tom half-expected to see the streetlights come on along Echo Pit Road. He liked this part of town best, this area on the outskirts where the lamps were yellow at night and autumn always seemed to be hanging around the next corner, waiting to slip in and powder the trees with frost. The houses were large and brightly lit between the park and the cemetery, and he'd walk by slowly, trying to see through the windows, catching glimpses of that richer world. People out here had pictures on their walls, and walnut tables covered in ornaments; at Christmas time they put their trees in the front windows, so passers-by could see how big they were. When his dad was still alive, they had come out here on Sunday afternoons, walking up through the park, then down the hill, past the big houses on Echo Pit Road to the cemetery then back the same way, looking at the wide, neat gardens of magnolia and lilies. The soot didn't seem to reach this far, and everything looked new, as if God had only just finished making it.

Now, with no money, and a couple of hours to kill, he decided to walk out to the cemetery and look at his father's stone. He'd been several times since the funeral, though always by himself: whenever he'd asked his mother if they could go, she'd put him off, saying she'd take him some other time, when she wasn't so busy. It was strange, as if she blamed Dad for the accident and didn't want to think about him any more. Tom knew it was upsetting for her; obviously she wouldn't want to be reminded of what had happened. But Dad was in heaven now: his wounds would be healed and it wouldn't be good if he looked down and thought that nobody remembered him.

Tom recalled every detail of the funeral, even though he'd only been a kid then, and didn't really understand what was going on. A boy in school had told him there wasn't a heaven, that dead people stayed in their coffins and rotted when they died, but Tom knew it wasn't so. He'd felt it that day: he had almost seen the blur on the air as his father's soul slipped away across the fields. The sheep had lifted their heads to watch him go — animals knew more about these things than humans did — and Tom had guessed that heaven wasn't very far away, not far at all, maybe as close as the next town, only in a different dimension. It was so close that the souls could walk there, meeting the others who had gone before them, a stone's throw from the streets and houses they had known all their lives. Sometimes he felt he was only inches away from that country for whole minutes at a time. Stepping outside to fetch coal for the fire, or crossing a street, his body would be drenched with cold, or wrapped in the fluttering of wings, and he'd imagine he was there, in heaven with Dad, for all eternity. One summer's afternoon he'd taken a short cut home from the river, plunging through a field of ripe barley, chest-deep in warmth and undertow, and he'd felt his body stray with each tug of the wind, as if something were trying to draw him in. For that one moment, he'd felt that it would be no great hardship to be absorbed into the darkness, and he'd imagined himself as a spirit, running free in the woods, or waiting to return to earth in a different form, subtly altered, forgetting the stillness of heaven as he was pulled back into the flow of noise and movement. This was called reincarnation: his dad had told him about it once, on their walk to the cemetery: how dead people lay waiting for a while, on the other side, then came back in new bodies, the same, only different. Tom wasn't quite sure if he believed in that: heaven sounded better, because you could do anything you liked there, and you only had to think of something, like an ice cream, or money for the pictures, and it would be there.

The cemetery was right at the edge of town. By the gates, near the older graves, there were flowerbeds and stands of rhododendrons, but at the far side, where his father was buried, it was almost bare. The paths were narrower — not tarmac, just dull, sand-coloured gravel. Most of the graves here had a jar of wilted carnations, or a bunch of plastic roses set beside the stone, but they still looked sad and forgotten. Tom wondered if the dead people minded. He knew they were happy in heaven, because they were with God; but they might still be sad, now and then, when they looked down and saw how lonely their graves looked.

He didn't notice the woman at first, and when he did, he was surprised. She was standing with her back to him, her head bowed, as if in prayer, but even from that angle, she looked out of place in her expensive clothes, with the large bouquet of red roses at her feet — a proper bouquet, wrapped in the crackly cellophane you get in florists' shops. It felt like an intrusion to disturb her, but Tom had no choice: the grave she had chosen to visit was his father's and, impelled by curiosity, he walked on till he was standing a couple of feet away.

She turned quickly when she realised he was there.

'God!' She gave a small, theatrical gasp. 'You startled me.'

She was more beautiful than any woman he had ever seen in real life, even Miss Cameron. She was like the women at the pictures, with her luxuriant, dark hair and bright blue eyes that seemed to look at him from some enormous distance. He felt embarrassed and foolish, standing beside her, grimy and uncombed, in his old jeans and his darned jumper. He hid his dirty hands behind his back.

The woman sensed his discomfort, and smiled. 'I didn't hear you coming,' she said. 'I was miles away.'

Tom glanced down at the flowers, then he read the carved letters, all lined with gold, on his father's headstone. David Mitchell, Rest in Peace was all it said, because that was all Tom's mother had wanted: just the name, no dates, no proverbs or messages. Tom thought there ought to be more, maybe something about the accident, some explanation of what had happened and who his father was. He looked at the woman again. He had never seen her before, but there was no doubting she had brought the flowers to this grave, and that her prayer had been for Tom's father.

'Is he a friend of yours?' Tom asked.

The woman nodded. 'Yes,' she said. 'He was a very good friend. Maybe the best I ever had.' She gazed down at the stone. 'A while back, we lost touch with one another,' she continued. 'I'm not quite sure how it happened. He just went away. All of a sudden.'

Tom could see that she wasn't really talking to him. She was saying the words in his direction, but really they were for someone else, or just for herself, something she wanted to say, to anyone. Grown-ups did that sometimes.

'It's taken me a while to find him,' she said.

She looked up. For a moment she seemed puzzled, as if she was only seeing Tom for the first time, and had started to wonder who he was. Then she smiled again, and turned back to the grave.

'We used to go to the pictures,' she said. 'He liked to stay on after the film, to see the credits, reading the names, making connections. He'd pay such close attention to detail, making stories out of everything: two brothers here, a man and wife there, a pair of twins playing the one child. Some names would come up again and again, and he'd be pleased to see them, as if they were old friends.' She picked up the bouquet of flowers and began peeling away the cellophane.

'He used to bring me fruit,' she continued. 'All kinds of stuff. We'd meet outside the cinema and he'd bring me something each time, exotic fruits, things I'd never seen before, never mind tasted. I never did find out where it all came from — mangoes, guavas, star fruits. Sometimes I didn't even know how to eat them.'

She laughed softly at the memory, and Tom began to feel even more uncomfortable. He thought the woman had come to the wrong place, because the man she was talking about didn't sound anything like his dad, but he was too embarrassed to say.

'I used to eat them the wrong way,' she said. 'He laughed when I told him I'd eaten the mango skin. I didn't know you had to peel them, you see. I thought they were like apples.' Her voice trailed away. Tom didn't know whether she was going to laugh again, or cry, and, despite his embarrassment, he wanted to reach out and comfort her. 'I don't understand,' she said, after a long silence. 'He didn't even write.'

She was talking to herself again. Tom was struck, once more, by how beautiful she looked. For a moment, he caught himself wishing that she was his mother.

'Maybe he couldn't,' he ventured.

'Maybe,' the woman agreed, but she didn't look convinced. She was smiling again, but Tom knew she wanted to cry. She turned to him and held out the bouquet of roses.

'What's your name?'

'Tom,' he said.

'Well, Tom, would you do me a favour?' She was putting him at his ease, trying to be friends, and he wondered if he should say who he was. It felt dishonest not to tell her — the trouble was, after all she had said, he didn't know how.

'I've brought these flowers for my friend,' the woman continued, 'but I haven't got anything to put them in. Could you find me something?'

Tom nodded. He knew exactly where to look, and he was glad of the opportunity to be useful, as if by performing this small chore he would belong to her in some way, so that, even when she was gone, there would still be a link between them. Without a word, he set off across the cemetery to the keeper's hut, selected the largest and cleanest jar he could find there, filled it with water from an old, coppery-scented tap, and carried it back to his father's grave. The woman cried a little while she was arranging the flowers, but she managed to hide it well enough for Tom to pretend he hadn't seen. Finally, she set the jar by the stone, stepped back, and gave an odd little bow.

'I don't suppose I'll come again,' she said. 'I just wanted to see.'

Tom couldn't tell if she was talking to him or to the headstone now, and he felt awkward again, as if he were intruding on a private conversation.

482

But, after a moment's silence, the woman gathered herself up and turned away from the grave.

'I have to go,' she said. 'Would you like to walk me to my car?'

Tom nodded and, as the light faded, they walked back together. The car was parked by the chapel of rest, a few yards from the gates. It was bright red, new-looking, with large, protruding headlamps, like the eyes of an insect, different from any car Tom had ever seen. The woman got in, then she rolled down the window and reached out her hand.

'Thanks for everything,' she said, and she slipped some coins into the pocket of his jumper; then, before he could say anything, she drove away, leaving him there alone, in the gathering twilight.

By the time he got back to town, Tom had made up his mind. He'd thought about buying sweets and a comic, or maybe keeping the money for next week's pictures but, after considerable thought, he decided to buy something for his mum. He felt a little guilty and he thought, if he brought her a present, and told her about the strange woman, it would cheer her up, to think that his dad had once had such an interesting friend. He'd considered buying her a magazine, or one of those romance novels she liked, but by the time he got back to town, all the shops were closed, so he stopped at the garage on Barton Road.

'Have you got any red roses?' he asked.

'There's only what you see,' the man behind

the counter answered curtly.

Tom picked through the bucket of ragged pinks and greyish-brown chrysanthemums. They weren't as nice as the roses, but he reckoned it was the thought that counted, so he pulled out the biggest bunch of red carnations he could find and the man bundled them up in old newspaper.

When he got home, his mother was sleeping in the armchair by the fire, so he left the flowers on the kitchen table and went to his room. Everything felt closer now: as he stood by the window, with his fingers pressed to the glass, he could see the light from the works, like a huge fire, just behind the houses, and he could taste the night air seeping through, touched with frost and tainted slightly with a faint, coppery sweetness. He gazed out into the dark, wondering where the strange woman was now, and whether his dad had looked down and seen them standing by his grave. Tom remembered how beautiful the woman had been, and he wondered who she was. He imagined her driving, in the cold night — driving for miles across open country, driving through silent villages and bright cities, stopping at service stations in the pale, gas-blue light from the pumps, then driving on, for ever, never stopping. He wondered what her house was like, and whether she had a husband, or a family of her own. Then he wondered if his dad still remembered her, or any of them, after all this time in heaven, or whether the dead forgot, on their way from one life to the next, leaving their

friends and children behind, in the difficult
world of the living.

∽

The hand of God directs me.
Follow, my children.
It is my turn now to be your pathfinder,
As you have been to me. Come. Do not touch
  me.
Leave me to find the way to the sacred grave
Where this land's soil is to enclose my bones.
This way . . . this way . . . Hermes is leading
  me,
And the Queen of the Nether World. This way
  . . . This way.
Darky day! How long since thou wast light to
  me!
Farewell! I feel my last of thee. Death's night
Now ends my life for ever.

Oedipus, Sophocles, *Oedipus at Colonus*

Douglas Dunn

THE HOUSE OF THE BLIND

I

When you sat on the upper deck of the bus
You could see the white metal bannisters
On the inclined stepped pathways.

Once, on a winter's morning,
I saw someone being taught to climb steps.
The rail would have been cold and wet on his
   hands.

That spring, a raincoated man in dark
   spectacles
Would have felt similar cold and wet,
But been refreshed by the scent of lilacs.

On a summer's day, I saw a woman
Instructed in the use of her first blind dog.
Even now the tug on her arm pulls at my
   heart.

After a catastrophe of spectacles,
This autumn I walk in a blur.
My daughter's nudge on my arm makes me
   think of her.

II

The coffee was good. I was on my third cup.
From opened windows across the street
Instrumentalists were practising —

Flutes, clarinets, trumpets, violins, several pianos.
In lulls for tuition or advice, a fine soprano
Stopped people in their shoes, listening.

A cellist surrendered to Bach with a passion.
I could imagine the genderless sway,
Planing the air, ironing sound.

I felt so glad to be in Prague, and free,
With time on my hands, and *Turandot* in the
    evening.
An oboe lingered, in love with Mozart.

Several students emerged with cased instruments.
They unpocketed, then unfolded, their white
    sticks.
I think the waiter was watching for my reaction.

His smile was benign, but proud, and defiant.
All day, every day, he listens to their music.
His smile broadened, and he nodded,

Approving my look of sympathetic surprise;
And, after three shots of strong black coffee,
    my cup
Was the more tremblingly lifted up.

III

After Louis Braille accidentally put his eye out
With an awl in his father's workshop,
And the other eye sympathised with its dead
partner,

A great kindness began in his darkness.
There was reading by raised dots before him,
Invented for French artillerymen to plan

The fall of shells in the dark without giveaway
lamps.
The gunners couldn't read, not even in daylight.
Braille refined and perfected and made a
    useful thing.

Thomas Edison invented the gramophone
To provide speaking books for the blind.
Tin Pan Alley and the entire repertoire

Recorded from a foundation in benevolence!
And then say it aloud, in perfect cadence,

Her voice delighting me. She's never seen
A poem, but she reads and hears. I write
To be read by eyes, and mind, and fingers.

IV

When you lose an eye, then you can lose the
    other,
Like Louis Braille, by 'sympathetic ophthalmia'.

It doesn't happen often. But you lose a
   dimension,

As my love discovered, hanging out the washing
On a line that felt uncertain, flat, and vague.
After that, I did it. Sympathy's mutual.

I hung the washing on a line that wavered.
That was as nothing to my love's nightmare —
Hanging washing on a line that wasn't there.

Michèle Roberts

SARDINES

I bought the tin of sardines in Borough market, the gourmet-food version held on the site of the ordinary fruit and veg one on the third Saturday of every month. Portuguese sardines, that I picked out from the surrounding jars of ground pimento, heaps of chorizos, and plump-hipped bottles of white wine scrambled together on the lace-covered trestle table. I chose them simply because the tin they came in was foreign and beautiful: not oblong but oval, labelled in scarlet and yellow, with swirly blue lettering in Portuguese and a picture of a booted and sou'westered fisherman holding up a monster fish by its tail.

The food sold in that market is all organic, farm-fresh, hand-reared and so forth, to show you what can be done if you take your eyes off the supermarket shelves for a second, but it is relatively expensive. The pleasure of wandering between the stalls resides mainly in looking and marvelling. You don't assume you're going to buy anything, necessarily, though you accept all the free tastes you're offered, shavings of Wensleydale or curls of honey-crackled ham. You hover over trays of smoked trout, imagine clotted cream and apricot jam sliding down your throat. You buy the Welsh goats cheeses, boxes of lamb's lettuce from Herefordshire, and flasks of Somerset cider vinegar mainly as Sunday treats, or as birthday presents for your friends.

So it did feel perfectly in order to select the sardines solely for their looks and take them home to display on the kitchen shelf next to the gaily coloured packet of couscous illustrated by a palm tree and a strip of beach, the two little pots of harissa flourishing red and green parrots, the camembert boxes showing buxom farm-maids in flowery meadows tending their cows, and the squat can of Spanish olive oil decorated with gold arabesques.

My appreciation of pretty packaging went back to when I was young, and wanted real paintings on my walls but could not afford them, and did not dare assume I could paint them myself. I used to pick up scrap wooden fruit trays and cardboard boxes chucked down by the Saturday traders in Portobello Road, selecting the ones whose labels and stencilled lettering I liked best, cart them home to the tiny flat I was illegally subletting in Powys Square from a housing-association tenant, reduce them down to single flat panels, and nail them up. They had been carefully designed, printed and put together, and I wanted to save them from going to waste. I cherished their beauty. They did not deserve to be so rapidly thrown away.

Likewise, one summer in Venice, when I was still young, and foolish too, I collected screwed-up and discarded orange wrappers from behind the fruit stalls where they were cast along with cabbage stalks and bruised plums, rolling in confusion with all the other fascinating litter of coarse lettuce leaves and broken, juice-stained redcurrant punnets and rotten courgettes, until the corporation men swept them into the rubbish barge, or the nuns, scavenging indiscriminately for their soup kitchens, scooped them up into their big wicker baskets, whoever got there first.

In those days Italian oranges were wrapped in pale yellow tissue paper printed with charming designs in two or three colours. Adam and Eve disported themselves among stags and unicorns; satyrs blew trumpets; volcanoes erupted; and suns blazed among the stars. Uncrumpled, wrinkles patiently smoothed away with a fingertip, so that the delicate paper did not tear, flattened out back into the original gold-rimmed squares, then carefully ironed, the little sheets of pictures could subsequently be framed and packed in my suitcase. I couldn't hang them up in the Contessa's low-ceilinged but chic garret. She would have thought they were out of place.

I had married an architectural historian at rather short notice two months previously, after he had taken me to visit Italy for the first time, and had accompanied him back out to Venice, where he was compiling a catalogue of architectural drawings for a forthcoming exhibition. As a result of visiting so many famous villas and writing about their doorways, or their porticos, or their colonnades, he had many grand acquaintances, which is why we were renting the attic flat at the top of the Contessa's tall house in a narrow *calle* off the piazza of Santa Maria del

492

Giglio, near San Marco. The architectural historian had a distinguished appearance; also he wore jackets of the finest herringbone tweed, trousers of the finest wool. All the lonely, bored contessas whose palazzi he visited loved the way he listened to them so intently, his head on one side and his fingertips pressed together. They invited him frequently to dinner and ran him about in their cars and lent him their summer houses on Capri.

To save him money during the four-month trip, because I did not have a job out here and we were living on his salary and travel and research grants, we never went out to restaurants. I cooked at home. Twice a week a few fruit and vegetable stalls set up in the piazza under striped blue and white awnings, and on those days I was able to do some of the shopping here, sparing myself a long walk back from the big Rialto market lugging heavy bags of food, wine and water, which had then to be humped up five flights of slippery marble stairs. It was the season of the aftermath of the Chernobyl disaster. *Carabinieri* patrolled the street markets enforcing the putting-up of posters warning the populace to be careful what they ate, but I bought oranges and picked up the orange wrappers regardless. They were too appealing to waste.

I was a collector of art brut in self-defence. I needed a tiny space of esoteric information that was exclusively mine, in order not to feel crushed by my inadequacies. The architectural historian was a renowned expert on the theory and practice of Renaissance building. When he took me out sightseeing he would linger for hours in cold churches (Renaissance churches only — I was discouraged from admiring the medieval or the baroque) in order to make ground-breaking discoveries: that a particular tomb might have been designed by Sansovino; that the style of a particular capital matched the details of one in a drawing by Palladio. Then he would disappear into the state archive near San Rocco for days to unearth the supporting documents.

In the face of this intimidating sharp-eyed expertise, I hastily learned to appreciate Renaissance notions of the beautiful, based on order, harmony and proportion, and to know my cornices from my architraves. At the same time I refined my connoisseurship as a collector of rubbish. I walked through Venice with my gaze swivelling down as well as round and up: I could spot an interesting brown paper bag, patterned with motifs of meringues and brioches, discarded outside a *pasticceria*, at twenty paces; I could penetrate at a single glance the bulky sacks of refuse toppling on the side of the *fondamenta* outside houses that were being done up, and know instantly whether or not it was worth sneaking back later to rootle through them for fragments of old tile or scraps of carved and gilded wood.

After two months in Venice, I had absorbed so much information about different ways of turning corners with pilasters, or methods of tucking farm buildings behind the wings of villas, that I was a less amusing companion than

I'd been at the beginning of our marriage. My initial patina of naive charm was wearing off. So new women, desperate to learn about architecture, began popping up, like capitals and tombs, each one more intriguing and appealing than her predecessor, in the archive, the university library, the *superintendenza*'s office, or simply in the the bar where my husband drank his morning cappuccino, and he felt obliged to pursue each fresh and delicious object of desire with all the single-minded passion of which a true scholar is capable. Long visits to churches would ensue. Then he'd return to our garret flat for lunch, accompanied by the latest wounded bird, who needed the friendship of a strong woman like me.

I was strong but unsatisfactory. I walked around the flat barefoot; I didn't bother wearing make-up because it melted off in the heat; I drank more wine than a decorous signora should; my clothes were not elegant; and I had been caught mopping up the sauce on my plate with a piece of bread stuck on the end of my fork. If you had to mop, my husband explained, then fingers were better than forks. But it was better not to mop at all, certainly at dinner parties, and it was also better not so often to accept second helpings.

It was in Italy that I first ate fresh sardines. Before that, in England, they'd come in tins, oblong ones, complete with keys. The key had a slit in its tail which corresponded with a flap of metal welded on to the underneath of the tin, at one end. You inserted metal tongue into key slit, gave the key one quick initial twist, flipping the tongue to bend over, the parts to catch and fit, until they gripped well together, without sliding away separate again; and then to unpeel the lid you turned the key, travelling it across from one ridged silvery end to the other, rolling up a long section of tin as you went. The opener cut along parallel to the tin's edge, most pleasingly, as your fingers worked it. The dangerously sharp-edged strip of metal finished up wound neatly on to your little implement, and the opened rectangular gap revealed the sardines, blackish blocks minus heads and tails, intimately packed in together under a quilt of oil. You ate them mashed on buttered toast, first lifting out, on a knife tip, their stretches of knuckled spine like decayed zips. Often, however, the key slipped on the tin's tongue halfway and its mouth refused fully to open, or the key would not engage, or got stuck, or broke off before you'd even properly begun, and then the frustration was extreme, and all you could do was hurl the tin away into the rubbish.

Fresh sardines I discovered at a neo-Palladian villa in the Veneto. We had been invited for dinner so that my husband could inspect our host's archive, in his pursuit of certain sixteenth-century documents relating to an attribution he was currently working on, and also the fine collection of antiquarian books that had been built up by the family over the centuries. Our aristocratic patron, who was related to our landlady in Venice, was an elderly bachelor who lived alone. Most of the villa was shut up, he explained on the telephone, to save money on heating, but nonetheless we were very welcome and he would do his best to give us something halfway decent to eat. We were to take the little local train, and then a taxi from the village, which he would order for us, and he would expect us at seven o'clock.

I had by now visited most of Palladio's villas, even the ones not open to the public. Some were lived in by rich people, and had been sumptuously restored; others got by as best they might. One, for example, was currently a lamp and striplight shop jostled by the factories and bleak housing of an industrial zone, its farm and gardens long gone; another, encroached on by rolling fields of towering maize, was furnished with nothing but iron bedsteads in its shabby, vast rooms, and had chickens pecking about over its tesselated floors. Our host's villa, having been built fifty years too late, and being somewhat over-ornate, lacked the austere grace of the true, original Palladian style, and so my husband did not bother hovering about too long outside admiring its façade. He contented himself with pointing out the number of columns cluttering up the loggia on the top storey, and the slightly awkward sweep of the stable block.

Our host turned out to live in the right-hand wing, opposite the stables, in a lofty-ceilinged and frescoed interior which was stuffed with decaying antique furniture and gloomily lit by gilt chandeliers. In between the painted panels hung worn tapestries and the heads of dead animals. On arrival we had deposited our coats in a marble-floored vestibule off the imposing circular entrance hall, and now we followed the young black-haired retainer, dressed in a peculiar, tight-fitting brown jacket, who had opened the door to us, through three interconnecting saloons, each one darker and chillier than the last.

Our host was finally run to earth in a shadowy drawing room, whose shutters, he explained, were kept closed to stop the sun fading the carpets by day and the mosquitoes entering by night. He was a small man wearing brown shoes that gleamed in the twilight. Like my husband, he was faultlessly dressed in an immaculately cut suit. He kissed my hand, pretending not to notice the short black denim skirt and long-sleeved striped Breton T-shirt I was wearing, which had caused my husband such grief five minutes ago when he realised what I had on under my raincoat.

A very simple dinner, our host warned us: you'll have to understand, an old bachelor like me, I'm not used to entertaining. I hope you'll make allowances for the primitive fare I'll be offering you.

We were not the only guests. In my husband's honour our host had also invited the director of the local museum, and one of his curators, who specialised in Renaissance ivories and faience. She was slender, and very smartly dressed in a calf-length pleated green silk suit with silver and diamanté buttons. Her nails were painted pale pink, her hair subtly blonded and swept up in a chignon, her face expertly made up. Her feet were expensively shod in crocodile. She had a sweet, vulnerable look, and I saw my husband spot this and smile encouragingly at her.

The introductions made, the sips of prosecco taken, the Japanese crackers nibbled, we were ushered through double doors into the dining room. The table bristled with elaborate settings: arrays of cut glass goblets and frilly-edged white porcelain plates, ranks of silver cutlery, two tall candelabra, and mounds of enormous starched white napkins. How sensible these were; you could wrap them around yourself, like the towels hairdressers swathed you in before they brandished the scissors, and then you did not splash embarrassing drips of *pastasciutta* sauce down your chin or front. I lifted and shook out my vast linen bib and tucked it into the neck of my T-shirt. I hastily untucked it again, lowered it, and smoothed it over my lap, as all the others were doing, as soon as I saw my husband glare at me. I glared back, and he turned his head and began to talk to the well-groomed blonde lady, who was sitting next to him.

I cheered up when I was given a small glass of pale gold wine. A white-gloved hand came from behind me and poured from a decanter. I had not seen white gloves since my convent-school days. I twisted round in my delicate eighteenth-century dining chair and glanced at the owner of the hand. I had never seen a man in white gloves in my entire life. This one was the young retainer with curly black hair who had shown us in earlier. He still wore his tightly buttoned brown jacket, that I now saw simulated a livery of some kind, but to serve the dinner he had added the white gloves and a white cloth folded over one arm. He smiled at me as he tilted out the wine without spilling a single drop, then twisted his wrist and spun the decanter away.

Dinner began with *pappardelle* in hare sauce, the wide noodles delicate and light as could be. I was impressed with our host's skill. Next came the sardines, much longer and fatter than they looked when tinned, resplendent and blackly shining on a big antique majolica plate. I speculated as to whether our host had a special fondness for the south, for he had cooked the sardines *alla siciliana*, stuffed with chopped sultanas, anchovies, black olives, and garlic, a sliver or two of lemon peel, and some minced parsley. They had been brushed with olive oil and then grilled. I ate my portion of delicious scented fish as slowly as possible, trying to work out the recipe, wondering whether it was the same as the one given in my Italian cookery book.

I used to read the cookery book at night, after my husband had fallen asleep, savouring its poetry, its precise vocabulary. Recipes were indeed like poems, compact with carefully chosen words. You were supposed not to overdo it, not to stuff in too many words, too many ingredients. Subtlety and finesse mattered; you left out anything that wasn't strictly necessary. Change the ingredients, just a couple, and one regional dish slipped into the version made in the village next door, the village on the other side of the hill.

There were various ways, for example, of making lamb stew with dried haricot beans, tomatoes, and white wine; it all depended on which part of Tuscany your mother had come from, what the source of her particular recipe was, and whether or not she included rosemary. Italian cooking was not indiscriminate; you never threw black pepper into your *ragu* just because you felt like it; you included it only if the recipe traditionally called for it. I, who had prided myself in my art school days on my bolognese sauce made with whatever I could find in the cupboard, now learned to simmer the best beef and tomatoes and onions with good red wine and proper meat stock, to adjust its fragrance with a clove or two, some salt but no black pepper or garlic, to finish it, after a couple of hours, with a ladleful of cream, and never, under any circumstances whatsoever, to let the green peppers so beloved of student cooks in the early seventies anywhere near it.

These musings got me through the rest of the excellent and elaborate dinner over whose preparation our host must have toiled all day. Boiled meats with pickles, then green salad spiced with rocket, then cheese, and finally cold caramelised rice cake flavoured with nutmeg, lemon and cinnamon.

I couldn't have drunk too much even if I'd tried. The decanter appeared briefly with each successive dish, then vanished. Half a small glass of wine at the beginning of each course, for me, served by the smiling footman, and one glass apiece, lasting the whole of dinner, for my four

501

companions. They did not discuss what they ate, which would have been, I had learned by now, bad manners; they were embroiled in a passionate and complex discussion of architecture that I couldn't join in. My Italian was not yet good enough. Quite soon, in any case, my husband shifted his exclusive attention to the blonde signorina. He bent his head towards her and looked at her from under his eyelashes. He listened very attentively to her as she spoke, as though they were the only two people in the whole of creation. She appeared to be telling him all about the villa's beautiful gardens, and the shell-studded eighteenth-century grotto which had recently been opened up at their far end. Completely out of my husband's period, of course, which was why our host had been too modest to mention it. My husband murmured excitedly and intimately. The signorina glanced at him shyly. As soon as we had finished our coffee, served in tiny espresso cups, he led her from the room, explaining gaily over his shoulder that he simply had to go and see the grotto before it grew too dark to appreciate it properly.

The rest of us lingered on at table, drinking more coffee, then toying with thimbles of *grappa* and *amaro*. Half an hour passed. I made stilted conversation about the beauties of Venetian painting and architecture. Fired, finally, by the *grappa* which I knew ladies were not supposed to drink, I expatiated on the talents of Tiepolo and Titian, the purity of Palladio, the sensitive severity of Sansovino. My two companions, somewhat embarrassed by my eloquence, let alone by my husband's prolonged absence from the party, began yawning discreetly and glancing at their watches. The last train back to Venice left quite early, and we had not yet been shown the library and our host's collection of incunabula, which was supposedly the whole purpose of our visit.

I got up and excused myself, muttering something about wanting to go and admire the stables. My host stood up and bowed, waved a courteous hand.

'Please. Wander wherever you like. We shall go and begin to look at the books in the library.'

I wanted the lavatory, but was too timid to ask for it. I presumed it was one of those words not spoken in polite dining rooms. I hurried out, and circled the suite of saloons several times, avoiding the now empty dining room and what I guessed must be the library, backing away every time I approached the tall, double wooden doors and heard the men's voices behind. I looped back and forth, constantly returning to the circular entrance hall. Six sets of doors opened off it. It was just a question of choosing correctly. All the doors looked identically handsome, rather forbidding; you couldn't tell what was concealed behind them.

I caught a whiff of sardine and turned round to peer into a dark corner behind the wide stone staircase. Ahead of me was a single, narrow door which I guessed might give on to the kitchen. I pushed it open, went down a short corridor, opened another door, and entered a cave of heat and commotion. In here the blackened, vaulted walls were hung with copper pans and cake moulds like big rosy-gold blooms. A radio hummed in one corner. Around a wide old sink thronged at least half a dozen aproned women busy washing-up amid clouds of steam, clattering dishes and saucepans, all energetically talking at once in deep contralto voices as they scoured and wiped.

The kitchen opera ceased as I came in. The women all spun round and looked at me in a friendly way. They showed no surprise at my abrupt entry. They seemed to have comprehended immediately that I was one of the dinner guests. Now, their affable faces told me, I was their guest also, and they were waiting to see how they could offer me hospitality.

'*Mi dispiace di disturbarvi . . . ma . . . il gabinetto, per favore?*' I tried: 'WC?'

The young footman with curly black hair had thrown his brown jacket over the back of his wooden chair. He was wearing a white, short-sleeved T-shirt. When he pushed away his empty plate and sprang up from the table, I saw that he was wearing jeans, and sneakers just like mine. The large flat dish in front of him held a second lot of sardines, a discreet orgy of fish beautifully arranged head to tail, their shining silver-black skins scattered with parsley and garnished with slices of lemon.

Now I realised that it was of course this team of sturdy women, presumably recruited from the local village, who had cooked all the delicacies we had eaten earlier on, not our host with his manicured politeness and his trousers falling in exquisite pleats over his well-polished shoes. How foolish I was. I fished up my best Italian. I thanked the smiling ladies for dinner. I complimented them clumsily but sincerely on the excellence of their cooking, particularly their sardines. I apologised for disturbing their supper.

They exclaimed and scoffed at this. They were not yet ready to sit down and eat, not until they had finished all the clearing up. In the meantime, Federico could show me to where I needed to go. They waved me off and turned back to their work.

The young man, armed by the cooks with a basket containing a clean towel, a bar of soap, and a bottle of eau de cologne, escorted me up two flights of stairs without fuss. He opened a door and arranged the contents of his basket on the washstand within, made sure there was a brush and comb to hand, and showed me how to flush the antique cistern. He closed the door, waited for me to emerge, then showed me downstairs again. Our sneakers squeaked on the stone steps as we tramped past the masks of foxes and hares.

In the hall he paused. He spoke slowly so that I would understand.

'Would you like a cigarette?'

We went out through a small side door into pitch blackness. I stumbled, and Federico caught my arm. He steered me over cobbles, round a corner. Now a lantern gleamed from its hook on a post, and we were approaching the kitchen from the yard. Under the lighted window a bench stood on the gravel, flanked by pots of

505

laurel and oleander. The pale flowers glimmered in the darkness. The air was warm on my neck and face. It smelled aromatic, as though cedars grew nearby.

We sat in silence for a while, smoking the ferocious cigarettes Federico produced from his jeans pocket. Then he pointed towards the low wall of the yard, the semi-invisible garden beyond.

'That's the terrace, over there, you can just see the statues along the balustrade, and below that the steps leading to the cypress walk. Your husband is down there somewhere, with the blonde lady.'

'I know,' I said.

Federico shrugged.

I didn't know how to explain I had stopped minding. Instead I asked Federico if he was related to the women in the kitchen.

'My mother,' he said, 'and her sisters-in-law. My aunts by marriage.'

His father's family, he told me, was from the south. Life being so difficult down there, his father had come north to find work, as a young man, had married a northern girl, had stayed. So Federico's mother had learned to cook certain southern dishes, to remind her husband of home. Like the stuffed and grilled sardines, which had become one of her specialities, and which were now a favourite with our host.

My marriage had been a version of coming north, I thought. My husband had seemed so glamorous at first.

I felt like crying, and took a deep drag on my

506

cigarette to stop myself.

'I thought I'd fallen in love with my husband,' I said to Federico, 'but of course it was Italy I'd really fallen in love with, not him at all.'

I thought I'd better change the subject, in case I did indeed start crying.

'In England,' I said, 'in my childhood, we used to play a game called sardines.'

I wished I could speak Italian well enough to describe it, as a way of trying to thank him for his company, and for the cigarettes. I wanted to convey how the house was plunged into darkness and so transformed into a mysterious new landscape, how the point of the game was hiding yourself, in an impossible place no one normally ever went to or would ever dream of finding you in, and then waiting for someone to discover you. Of course you hoped it would be the person you loved the most, the person in whose presence you were speechless and clumsy and weak at the knees. You dreamed how he would approach you in the darkness, unsure whether you were really there or not, how he would stand still, and listen for your breathing, sniffing you, but not touching you, and the air between your skin and his would grow warm then ignite with your longing. Perhaps, still saying nothing, he would stretch out a hand and trace with his finger the outline of your face and guess your identity. Perhaps you would kiss and caress each other, your hands plunging under the layers of your clothes to find the warm reality underneath. Then, if you were unlucky, all too soon, one by one, the others would find you, and pile in, giggling and whispering, which was when the game became truly sardines. But the best was to be the first two sardines alone in the dark and not speaking and just beginning to dare to touch.

We smoked a final cigarette and then Federico went back to the kitchen, and to his supper, and I returned to the library and to the incunabula session. Afterwards the blonde lady drove us back to the village just in time for us to catch the last train.

Shortly afterwards I returned to London and to the single life. I was penniless and homeless all over again, but at least my suitcase was full of art brut, cookery books and drawings, and my imagination crammed with ideas for all the painting I wanted to do. Prowling Portobello Road once more, on the lookout for interesting junk, I was intrigued to perceive how the neo-classical architecture of the Notting Hill streets sprang freshly alive at me now that I knew the names of all the different parts of the houses and could recite those classifications, that poetry.

∾

The most important fact about Milton, for my purpose, is his blindness. I do not mean that to go blind in middle life is itself enough to determine the whole nature of a man's poetry. Blindness must be considered in conjunction with Milton's personality and character, and the peculiar education which he received. It must also be considered in connexion with his devotion to, and expertness in, the art of music.

Had Milton been a man of very keen senses — I mean of all the five senses — his blindness would not have mattered so much. But for a man whose sensuousness, such as it was, had been withered early by book-learning, and whose gifts were naturally aural, it mattered a great deal. It would seem, indeed, to have helped him to concentrate on what he could do best.

T. S. Eliot, *On Poetry and Poets*

Richard Holmes

DREAMING, SAILING, WRITING

They say that most Englishmen fall in love with sailing boats in their baths. The little cockleshell that coasts round your knee, makes fair-weather passage southward towards the archipelago of your toes, and then heads undaunted into the awful squall of the cold water tap, is a type of everything to come. It is, I think, the characteristic of all boats to be freighted with their owners' dreams. But sailing boats, with their peculiar combination of sturdiness and fragility, somehow give those dreams wings from earliest childhood. They are borne on heaven's breath.

My first real sailing boat was a beauty. She had a red wooden hull, a tin keel, and two white cotton sails with black stitching round the edge. Both sails could be adjusted with small metal sliders. She was about two foot long, and clearly capable of cruising round the world.

One breezy August afternoon, my grandfather and I launched her ceremoniously off the shingle at Folkestone. She bobbed briefly around in awkward circles, rolled over flat when the wind blew, and then somersaulted back to my feet in a breaking wave.

'Let's ease the mainsail,' said my grandfather. He let out the boom with the little slider, and the big sail with its lovely black stitching swung in the wind and pulled sharply against my hand. 'Wait for the next wave. Put her in gently. Let's see how she rides.' The moment I let her go, the boat came alive. She swung her prow away from the beach, heeled over, steadied herself at a racy angle, and bolted straight out to sea. My grandfather reached out with his stick, but she was gone in a moment. After she had bucked over the first few waves, there was nothing but her flickering white sail getting smaller and smaller.

My grandfather and I climbed slowly back up the Lees Cliff in gloomy silence. We borrowed the deckchair man's binoculars, and scanned the immense sea. No sign. 'Well, she'll come back one day,' said my grandfather unconvincingly. But of course, he was right.

That night I lay in bed, tossing in my hot summer sheets, utterly bereft. But then as I fell asleep, I found myself back on board sailing towards the horizon. I have never quite lost that feeling of mingled terror and exaltation, as I leapt from wave to wave. And that's how my dream sailing began.

★　★　★

I have been a late starter in all things, except writing and dreaming. It was not till the age of forty that I took my dreams to water and made them drink. I enrolled for a week at the Emsworth Sailing School on the Chichester Estuary. I took my RYA Basic Seamanship qualification in the classic sixteen-foot dinghy known as the Wayfarer.

This is a big, powerful, general-purpose dinghy, with lovely simple lines, stable in rough seas, and with a breathtaking turn of speed when close-hauled, like a carthorse suddenly breaking into a Newmarket gallop. 'In the right hands,' said my eighteen-year-old instructor, 'this boat can be sailed across the North Sea.' This is literally true, and some years later I met the woman who had done it, the famous small-boat sailor from Norfolk, Margaret Dye, author of the classic study, *Dinghy Cruising*. She was a compact little woman of sixty, sitting cross-legged on the foredeck of a Wayfarer wearing a blue knitted cap, with a faraway look in her eyes. The fact that the Wayfarer was in the centre of a stand at the Olympia Boat Show, surrounded by glistening new power-boats and enormous catamarans, only added to her mystique. 'Not much breeze in here,' was all she said to me. But it was all I needed to know.

At Emsworth, I was twice the age of all the others, slow-witted in manoeuvres, and hopeless at knots. But I proved very good at the man-overboard exercise. This involved throwing a pink plastic buoy off the back of the boat, howling 'man overboard,' and tacking the Wayfarer briskly round on a triangular course. The aim was to bring the prow round to a dead halt alongside the bobbing pink head, as rapidly as possible. I empathised so vividly with the drowning man, 'not waving but drowning' as Stevie Smith says, that I always flew to his side with unerring accuracy. I began to show off, flicking the helm into the wind, and scooping him from the water in one easy, practised motion.

One afternoon our Wayfarer grew impatient with this display, and as I leaned gracefully over the transom, gave a little roll and tossed me over the side. As I spluttered to the surface, I saw her racing away, with my fellow crewmen calling out languidly, 'Oh, man *really* overboard.' They took a long time to complete the triangle.

On the last day we had to carry out an exercise which involved deliberately capsizing and righting the boat three times in succession. The trick is to swim beneath the mainsail, find a particular rope (rather confusingly known as the 'windward jib-sheet'), and to walk up the keel or centreboard from the other side, while pulling in the rope hand over hand. As you walk and pull, the boat swings up out of the sea, and with correct timing you can step straight off the top of the keel on to the side of the boat and (as it continues to swing upright) back into the boat itself.

As with nearly all sailing manoeuvres, there is a subtle gap between theory and practice. On the first capsize I got dramatically tangled beneath the mainsail, and had to be pulled to the surface myself. On the second, just as the boat became upright, I fell backwards off the centreboard. On the third time, I swung up over the side with perfect timing, and found myself standing triumphantly on board with my swimming trunks round my ankles. 'I think perhaps you should try yachts,' said my instructor as he initialled my RYA logbook.

★ ★ ★

The next summer a long-suffering friend agreed to go halves on a second-hand Mirror dinghy. The Mirror is the Morris Minor of the marine world: small, old-fashioned, oddly plump and probably indestructible. Tens of thousands of them have been mass-produced since the 1960s. But to me she was unique. I think it was the shocking red sails, bright as a boiled sweet, with the serial number 59-429 stencilled on them in piratical black, which cast the spell.

There was, however, the problem of her name. It had been firmly painted on the bow by the previous owner, a hairdresser's assistant. The name was *Sea Fairy*. It is traditionally bad luck to change a ship's name, but this was too much for us. We argued that the hairdresser was dyslexic, and with a little paint-brush editing she became the *Sea Flea*. This turned out to be true to her character: both sprightly and mischievous. She was all of twelve foot, with a little squared-off prow, and sailing her was like sitting in a wooden hip-bath with your knees constantly hitting your chin.

The Emsworth Sailing School had been bracingly athletic in tone. But I now entered what the Germans would call my *aesthetic* phase. We kept the *Sea Flea* at Apuldram, and skittered about the estuary with a small picnic basket containing cold chicken and half-bottles of champagne.

514

For all her prosaic limitations, the little *Sea Flea* introduced me to the poetry of sailing. She took me into a new world, governed by wind and tide. The moment that we cast off from the rackety wooden pier, the world spun slightly on its axis and all physical objects settled themselves into a new order of being. The sights and sounds of the land fell back, the motion of the water rose up seductively through your legs and stomach, the boat came alive in your hands through the ropes and helm.

Her best sailing was in a light wind, maybe Force 3, just enough to ripple the water into little chuckling wavelets and set the tops of the distant birch trees flickering on the shore. On a broad reach, when the wind is coming over the side of the boat and talking steadily into the place just behind your windward ear, the clinking boom would swing out over the water and the red sails swell into two fat voluptuous curves, thrumming slightly like a drum.

It is an intriguing fact of marine physics that on this heading the boat is propelled by two quite different forces. It is partly blown along by the wind pressing directly on the inside of the sails; and partly drawn along by the low-pressure curve created on the outside of the sails. So on a broad reach a boat is simultaneously pushed and pulled by the wind, both cajoled and tempted. This seemed to me a perfect expression of the *dialectic* of maritime adventure. (As I said, it was my aesthetic phase.)

This sort of sailing is a kind of trance, and it produces a peculiar, hypnotic music under the bow as the water breaks and parts steadily along the hull. Every sailor hears this sound in their dreams, but it has rarely been conjured into words. One of the best I know comes in Coleridge's poem *The Ancient Mariner*. Amid all those scenes of nightmare terror, there is a single stanza which captures it almost perfectly. The Mariner's ship has been haunted by the song of unearthly and often vengeful spirits, but there comes a brief moment when Nature kindly reasserts her powers.

> It ceased; yet still the sails made on
> A pleasant noise till noon,
> A noise like of a hidden brook
> In the leafy month of June,
> That to the sleeping woods all night
> Singeth a quiet tune.

That was exactly the sound of the bow wave of the *Sea Flea*, heading for one of our picnic islands in the drowsy early afternoon off Birdham Creek. It is odd to think that at the time he wrote it, Coleridge's only experience of sailing was a crossing of the River Avon on the Chepstow ferry.

After our epic passage of at least two hours, we would lie beached on some small foreshore within sight of the real ocean, vaguely planning circumnavigations of the world. If we were not exactly Ancient Mariners ourselves, we did gain a satisfactory *castaway* sensation, feeling wonderfully 'far and few', like Edward Lear's Jumblies who successfully went to sea in a sieve.

Sailing home, always a little late, we tacked back on the ebb tide, the centreboard half-raised to slip us back through one or two feet of departing water, scuffling over gravel bars, and threading the invisible narrow channel by lining up two trees on the distant top of the South Downs, still lit by the setting sun. We rolled into the local pub, our life jackets hung casually on our arms, like a couple of sea-salts who had just navigated the North West Passage.

★ ★ ★

But even here, on this idyllic estuary, there were moments of terror too, which seem inseparable from sailing. One late autumn morning, we were caught in a squall, which swept in suddenly from the west, mournfully rattling the halyards of the safely anchored yachts a mile away from us. Turning to run for home, I gybed the boat in the rising wind behind us, and the *Sea Flea* became a Sea Demon.

The involuntary gybe is a classic piece of panicky seamanship, for which no Elmsworth graduate can be forgiven. It is achieved by a landlubberly misreading of a following wind, and the effect is instantaneous and spectacular. The boom swings furiously from one side of the boat to the other, usually cuffing heads like a demented schoolmaster, and the craft plunges viciously on to the opposite tack with all balance and order gone. In a small dinghy, capsize and even dismasting frequently follow.

For thirty seconds we spun helplessly on the

waters, suddenly black and menacing, with a chaos of snapping canvas and stinging ropes above our heads.

I have since been in rather worse situations. I have even gone so far as to be plucked from a life raft in the North Sea by an Air-Sea Rescue helicopter. But the first time you utterly lose control of a boat has a humiliating, comic horror that never leaves you. I clung obliviously to the helm like a beetle clinging to a twig in a typhoon. It was my patient friend, lying on her back in the bottom of the boat, who finally caught the mainsail rope, and slowly brought us back on course.

We dropped the mainsail, and ghosted back to the pier on the jib, in sepulchral silence. The *Sea Flea* was ankle-deep in water. 'On the whole, I don't think I'll ever sail with you again,' said my friend cheerfully, rolling the sails back into their bags in the dinghy park under the soughing trees. For at least half an hour I thought she meant it. Then we went to the pub and began to talk about bigger boats.

★ ★ ★

It was the next year that my time with the *Pentoma* began. She was a 28-foot wooden sloop, built just after the war, larch on oak, heavy and solid as a maritime grandmother who still remembers the coquettish days of her youth. Her dark blue hull, with an exquisite upward curve, lay low and sleek in the water with a deep open cockpit sheltered behind a little flat doghouse.

518

Her four oblong portholes, edged in brass, whispered of adventures like some seagoing gypsy caravan.

She was berthed at Pin Mill, on the River Orwell in Suffolk, one of the legendary moorings of English sailing, where Arthur Ransome's *Swallows and Amazons* once set sail. She belonged to the equally legendary publisher, James MacGibbon, whose family had sailed her for twenty-five years to all points round the Channel and the North Sea, from Gothenburg in the Baltic to Roscoff on the coast of Brittany.

It was James, and his son Hamish, known respectively as the Admiral and the Captain, who really made sailing dreams part of my life. For five unforgettable summers they taught me what makes a happy boat, a good crew, and a heavenly sail. They also taught me how to make a pink gin in a gale at sunset, how to engage in amorous radio badinage with Dover Coastguard, and how to behave when you think you are going to drown.

James's rules of sailing, first announced on a blind sailing date off the Isle of Wight, were memorably simple and quite as important as those taught at Emsworth. First, remember that sailing is a very odd activity, and friends, spouses, lovers, cannot be expected to like it, and they are quite right too. Second: no decent captain will ever shout at his crew. Third: if you're fed up, say so. Fourth: no female crew member should ever have to cook, unless she resolutely insists upon it. Fifth: the true art of sailing is friendship.

Our voyages were still small on the chart, but now genuine seafaring. From Pin Mill we sailed to a fish restaurant in Orford, a public baths in Ramsgate, a pub in Poole. We sailed to Amsterdam and Boulogne, and Dieppe. We sailed for six hours, and we sailed for six days, but always we sailed to some magic place, and told increasingly wild stories about it when we came back.

The essential difference between yacht sailing and dinghy sailing is that things happen more slowly on yachts. But they go on longer, and the transformation of the physical world is more extreme. Sailing out of sight of land, your whole past seems to drop away. Your worldly belongings are reduced to what will fit into a small canvas kitbag. My basic list of life requirements was soon reduced to ten items: jersey, cap, binoculars, sea boots, toothbrush, razor, book, biro, pipe and hand-held compass.

In contrast, the personalities of fellow crew members — sometimes as few as two, sometimes as many as eight — seemed to flower and expand in the intimacy of the boat. Entire life histories would be narrated in the course of a single night watch. Elaborate games, jokes, songs, even dances would develop with arcane and baroque complications that became quite impenetrable to any outsider.

On several trips the crew even changed their actual names, inventing whole new identities for themselves, with long and ludicrous autobiographies attached. I have sailed with a nuclear physicist who delivered Shakespearean soliloquies to a raging

520

sea. I have sailed with a doctor who wrote me a NHS prescription for 50 milligrams of Bollinger champagne every twelve hours. I have sailed with an accountant who composed recipes in rhyming couplets.

Yet the strange and even surreal social life aboard the *Pentoma* was always set against a physical world of extraordinary beauty. I remember waking up in a bunk at dawn, and hearing the marsh birds calling across a mist-laden creek in Vlissingen, while a tea kettle hissed just above my head, and thinking I had been reborn into a kind of paradise. I remember crossing the Channel one fog-bound night, from Dieppe to Rye Harbour, on a blind compass course of ten degrees; and then as I sat alone in the cockpit, seeing the fog lift and finding that I could steer by the north star which sat bright and exact at the point where the port shroud met the mast tip.

* * *

And all the time, through the quiet influence of the Admiral and the Captain, I was learning an entirely new art: navigation. There is something infinitely satisfactory about a yacht's chart table, where the whole contingent, tossing world of the sea is reduced to a series of pencilled triangles and fixes on a flat blue map. With the simplest of tools, a 2B pencil, a brass calliper, a protractor, a ruler, and some tide tables, you bring a kind of alchemical order and stability to your own bit of the universe.

521

The satisfaction of predicting the exact arrival of a distant buoy off the port quarter, or the precise appearance of an unseen landfall after many hours' sailing, is a peculiar delight. And I may add, a peculiarly rare one. It is perhaps the nearest I have ever come to understanding the pleasure of pure mathematics. Yet at the same time, navigation is an art of approximation, and requires a kind of philosophy. Theory must meet practice, Classical order must cope with Romantic chaos. This, I suspect, lies close to the heart of sailing.

The Admiral particularly encouraged this philosophic approach, and he introduced me to one of the great classics of modern sailing, the *Glenans Sailing Handbook*. This is a practical guide produced by the world-renowned French Sailing School on the Glenans Isles, off the western coast of Brittany near Quimper. It is one of the most detailed and severely practical marine guides ever written, and yet being French it manages to rise to passages worthy of the eighteenth-century *philosophes*. Here is what the *Glenans Handbook* says of the navigator:

Correct assessment of the observable facts is the heart of Navigation, and it presupposes unflagging attention, and a highly developed sense both of the sea itself, and of life aboard the ship. This is the time when the personality of the Navigator comes into its own. On the deck he must be a reserved kind of type, but at the same time constantly on the alert. His kingdom is the chart table (the ship's nerve centre) but nothing that goes on on board escapes his notice. He sees everything, records everything and says little about it. He establishes facts, but passes no judgements.

Psychologist as well as technician, he has summed up every helmsman skill, and knows what to expect from the boat's performance at a given speed, or under given sails. The state of the sea, changes in the wind, movements of the barometer, the weather forecasted — everything interests him. It is as if he were conducting a continual experiment, and considering every incident from a viewpoint all his own. At table, when a sudden lurch sends the crockery flying, he draws different conclusions from the rest of the crew. When he urinates leaning out between the shrouds, he uses the opportunity to observe the second bow wave. Back in his bunk, he still listens and ponders.

Finally, when the moment arrives, summing up all his observations, calculations and reflections, he puts the point of his pencil on the chart and says, 'We are here.' Navigational science is learned in books, but a good navigator has to be something of an inspired artist as well.

These, of course, are counsels of perfection. But I have to add, they also speak to me as a literary biographer. All lives have something of the quality of a sea voyage, and I must confess that in describing and analysing the long storm-tossed course of artists like Shelley or Coleridge,

I have often tried to imitate that ideal, invisible, Glenans Navigator silently observing his captain and crew at work on the long, unpredictable passage, and saying finally, 'Look, I have plotted their course, they are here.'

This perhaps is the lasting gift of sailing. It takes childlike dreams, tosses them robustly against the physical realities of another life, and then gives them back miraculously refreshed and renewed into your own. Every summer my thoughts still migrate to the water's edge. And when I can, I slip away with the beloved novelist Rose Tremain to a little boat called the *Jocunda*, anchored off one of the Ionian Isles, in waters the colour of lapis lazuli.

I still cannot see the smallest sail on a local pond, the tattiest dinghy on a river, or the most glamorous three-masted schooner far out at sea, without the same surge of longing like a tide-turn in the heart. Oddly enough, it was that most landlocked of English poets, William Wordsworth, who best captured that simple, inexplicable compass-quiver of delight in a sonnet he did not even bother to name.

With Ships the sea was sprinkled far and nigh,
Like stars in heaven, and joyously it showed;
Some lying fast at anchor in the road,
Some veering up and down, one knew not why.
A goodly Vessel did I then espy
Come like a Giant from a haven broad;
And lustily along the Bay she strode,
Her tackling rich, and of apparel high.
This Ship was nought to me, nor I to her,

Yet I pursued her with a Lover's look;
This Ship to all the rest did I prefer:
When will she turn, and whither? She will brook
No tarrying; where She comes the winds must
  stir:
On went She, and due north her journey took.

I would hazard the guess that even Wordsworth
once had a sailing boat in his bath.

Fay Weldon

EYES IN THE DARK

Cats have souls. You know, because they haunt houses. For a time after a cat dies you see movements out of the corner of your eye. A flash of a tail disappearing round the door, a kind of shifting blur under the table where it used to eat, yet when they were alive you got the feeling they didn't really care for you one bit, they wouldn't acknowledge you at all. I've known cats hang around the living for years, and a canary once — but that's another story. Dogs don't normally haunt: when they're dead they lie down: their graves are quiet. They're such bundles of emotion in life, they've none left. The effort of communicating without words for a lifetime has altogether exhausted their spirit. Enough of that, they say, that's enough, I've failed, I'm off, sorry and all that but goodbye. Finish.

This is the story of Galway, our yellow Labrador, who did stay around. I don't know if he exactly had a soul or not, but his spirit certainly outran his death. He was a sturdy, grave animal, affectionate but somehow distant, slightly disdainful, as if Olive the cat had had rather too much influence on his growing years. Olive, golden eyed and silky black, would box his ears when he was a puppy and misbehaving, a quick one-two with either paw, and then Galway

526

would remember his canine nature and chase her up the apple tree outside the back door, and she would sit up there and sneer down at him, and he would sit and gaze up at her with doleful, rather envious eyes, as if he wanted to be like that, to be able to impose swift and just retribution, and then leap up a branch and be superior. We lived in the country then, on a smallholding: those were the good days.

In the winters Olive would sleep leaning up against Galway in his basket in the utility room and once in the morning I found my two-year-old in there as well, all three lying in a warm sleeping breathing heap, Galway, Olive and Mark. I was too exhausted to worry about parasites, or fleas, I was just grateful for a happy, sleeping child. His younger twin sisters were only six months old: if the animals would give a hand so much the better.

We had four Soay sheep in the field, what gluttons for punishment we were. Soays are a rare breed, accustomed to hardship: they have long stringy legs, they startle like deer, for which they are sometimes mistaken. Their natural habitat is the rocky Scottish coastline, their proper diet is seaweed and scrub. We gave our small flock, or herd, three ewes and one ram, lush southern grass to graze, and they took it in their stride. The ewes stopped being all rib and scrag, and turned quite plump and rounded and velvet coated, if never tranquil, and the ram's horns grew strong, curved and proud; he learned to stamp his foot. They had an acre field to themselves, with a gate that led from our vegetable garden, and even a high point to stand on, in place of a cliff, for all it was only a grassy hump: an old burial mound, it was said. But they were always nervous of us, though we were their benefactors. We'd take them out their sheepnuts and fill their trough with water every morning and they'd dart away and stand at a distance, on their mound, staring, ready to bolt. The ram would place himself in front of his two wives and his old mother, and lower his curly horns and do a bit of stamping. But as with so many animals, they went through their rituals of flight, defence, attack, more for form's sake than out of any urgency. I never thought they took us really seriously.

And when one night unexpectedly the youngest ewe gave birth to twin lambs they were there waiting for us in the morning, the four of them, proud and pleased to show us what they'd done, waiting for our acknowledgement, our oohs and aahs, before affecting to be terrified and leaping off to their mound to view us askance, the two curious, skinny-legged lambs, born ready for flight, tottering up the slope, legs tangling, following after.

The sheep fascinated Galway: he'd wriggle under the gate and lie just the other side of it watching them, while they ignored him — rather insultingly, I thought — grazing right up to inches from his nose, in sheer defiance of his canine nature, which was, quite honestly, to chase them from here to kingdom come. You could see his ears twitching from the effort of not.

One day when I was putting the washing on the line, Mark — he must have been just over two at the time — let himself out through the gate and sat cross-legged and peaceful next to Galway, sheep-watching. Olive, black and sinewy, stalked through patches of nettles — they never ate nettles — to join them.

It was the first day of spring after a long hard winter; the sky was washed and beautiful: you know that line in the psalms when it says 'and all the valleys shall be exalted' and you wonder what it means? One of those mornings. Our robin sat on the clothes-line and said 'Well, spring's here at last!' or would have, I was sure, if he only had the power of speech. As it was, he just looked at me, head on one side, eyes glittering, for a full four beats longer than usual before flying off to the apple tree.

And I stood where I was, amazed. Because one of the lambs, dazzled perhaps by the sudden glittery sunshine, and all normal wintry rules of engagement deferred, had joined Galway, Olive and Mark. Sheep, dog, cat and child sat in a circle and stared at one another, and from one to the other, for all the world as if they were trying to decide who they were, what they were, which was the one they were like. The twins started crying in the house and I moved suddenly and the spell was broken, and they dispersed, but I think from that day on Galway decided he was a sheep; certainly after that he was forever trying to be one of their number. The sheep didn't want that, and when he ran up to join them ran off in the opposite direction in apparent distress and panic, and Galway would run after. A process known by the local farmers as 'running the profit off 'em'. So it became our function to try and keep Galway out of the field while he tried to get in. Animals can be a terrible nuisance.

Oh, they were mischievous, those Soays, those dancing, prancing, nervy sheep from the Orkneys. Once a year we had to round them up and take them to the livestock centre to be dipped against scabies. We humans would start from the corners of the field, and move in upon them from every angle, and Galway was allowed in because clearly he had the heart of a sheepdog in the body of a Labrador; he'd race round, knowing instinctively what to do, driving back any who ran for cover, and Mark at three joined in and waved his little arms in the air in the right place at the right moment, and between us we managed it. It was one of those days you don't forget, such a mixture of joy and dreadfulness. My husband fell and drove a stick into his knee and simply pulled it out and carried on. On a normal day it would have meant doctors and stitches and anti-tetanus jabs, and all that other human ritual to do with survival.

And then that autumn when Mark turned five, Galway was run over and killed. They'd built a new bypass at the end of the lane and he was sensible enough in many ways but his life experience had not included a six-lane highway, and we had failed to protect him. The grown-ups cried, the twins howled, Mark went and lay in Galway's basket and I had to drag him out. Later, while he wailed, I swore never, never to have another animal. It was unendurable. The robin had gone, too. Some bird of prey, no doubt, or even Olive, I wouldn't put it past her. She was upset too: she marked Galway's absence by sitting in the apple tree long after dusk, waiting. Mark had screaming fits in the admission class at school; they sent him home for a psychologist's report. He wouldn't let me out of his sight, or only at dusk, when he'd go out on his own to feed the sheep.

A week after Galway's death he came back, smiling, and said, 'Galway's in the field with the sheep.'

'That can't be so,' I said.

'I am not in error,' he said, his spirit back, and his colour, and with it his five-year-old pomposity. 'Galway's got into the field again. I saw him. You'd better do something.'

I went out to look and there were the sheep, five ewes and a ram lined up, standing as usual on the burial mound staring, their background a red-streaked but darkening sky. No Galway. Well, of course not. We'd buried him under the mound. I went back in.

'Mark,' I said, 'I'm sorry but he's not.'

'Yes he is,' he said firmly, but happily, and went to bed on his own, refusing my assistance.

I took my husband out to the field just to check. It was almost dark by now. We had a torch with us. I could only just see the blackish blurs that were the sheep so I shone the torch and devil's eyes glittered back at me, slit eyes, yellow and gleaming, Satan's eyes, spooky but expected. Shine a torch at a sheep or a goat in the night

531

and that's what you get. I counted. Fourteen eyes. So many eyes are hard to count but they remained remarkably steady, lined up. I tried again.

'How many sheep?' I asked my husband. 'Quick, before the light goes altogether.'

'Six, of course,' he said, beginning to count. 'Five ewes and a ram. Why?'

'Because there are fourteen eyes,' I said.

'Oh come on now, that's impossible. They must be moving round.'

But they weren't, they were just standing there staring, as if they knew something was up.

The pair of eyes in the centre of the group were not so slit as the others, more rounded, the iris a white rim round deep green pools. Dog's eyes in torchlight in the dark, Labrador's eyes. I wondered if the sheep could see Galway too or if it were only Mark.

'Fourteen,' my husband said. 'Can't be.'

Now the Soays were making things difficult, they took to turning and tossing their heads, or who knows, perhaps they were winking; at any rate checking was impossible. And then they were off: the whole lot of them took flight, and we heard the swift clippety-clop of cleft hooves and then a short sharp cheerful bark as well, but you can imagine things.

I don't know. Did we count wrong? I don't think so. Mark went out alone into the field early the next morning — I couldn't: fear had caught up with me — and came back to say firmly that Galway had gone off now but he'd be back by sunset. We stayed out of the field and let matters take their course. You could just about trust Galway to do the right thing. Olive took to sitting in the nettles the Galway side of the gate instead of cursing us all from the apple tree. Mark was taken back into the admission class and forgot about it being his job to feed the sheep, and cheered up. And little by little there was less evidence of Galway being around, the movement in the corner of the eye ceased happening, the blurred flurry at feeding time, just so long as you didn't go shining torches into dark corners at night. But I do think he came back, or at any rate stayed around. It suited us all, didn't it? Galway got his way and into the sheep field, where he'd so insisted he belonged, and the sheep accepted him, and Mark was healed, and we stopped feeling guilty about his death, because really you know there isn't any such thing.

&

Aye on the shores of darkness there is light,
And precipices show untrodden green,
There is a budding morrow in midnight,
There is a triple sight in blindness keen.

Keats, 'To Homer'

Susan Wicks

WHEN I AM BLIND I SHALL

paint pictures: take a step backwards,
point my brush like a knife and dare
the canvas to come closer, all my creations —
fruit, flowers, fields, clouds,
nudes — stippled all over
with wet sunlight pungent as leaves,
as I touch here, and here, and here, as we
    used to
pin tails on donkeys.

WHEN I AM BLIND I SHALL NOT

write in colours. As I come down
over the headland, the bay's silver
surprises me, and the blue mountains,
the white-rimmed clouds, the black
of high fir-trees, the road-signs
like mustard. I shall write sun
and shadow by the sweat on me,
hills by my heartbeats, the angle
at my ankles, write this other landscape
by smell, the taste of
salmonberries, hearing the birds
and the wind always, the shriek
of a July firework echoing on a barn,
the   beep-beep-beep   of   something   heavy
reversing.

536

Other titles in the
Charnwood Library Series:

THE POPPY PATH

T. R. Wilson

It's 1920 and, the years of wartime rationing over, the inhabitants of the seaside resort of Shipden are turning again to the good things of life. The hottest news is that a new doctor has arrived in town: a handsome young man who would sweep any one of Shipden's many hopeful females off their feet. So when James Blanchard decides to marry pretty Rose Jordan the community is both shocked and outraged. Like many of the 'war widows' around her, Rose is an attractive, highly intelligent, single mother. But the scandalous difference is that Alec Taverner — the father of her four-year-old daughter — is still very much alive.

FALSE PRETENCES

Margaret Yorke

When her goddaughter is arrested during an anti-roads protest, Isabel Vernon is startled to discover that the fair-haired child of her memory has become a shaven-headed environmentalist and that Isabel herself is now regarded as Emily Frost's next of kin. Emily, released on bail to the Vernons, takes up a job as home help to a local family and forms an instant attachment to Rowena, the four-year-old girl in her charge. Emily's presence in the Vernons' house proves troubling, and is deepening the profound tensions within Isabel's marriage when the arrival of someone else threatens the safety of both Emily and the child, Rowena.

STILL WATER

John Harvey

The naked body of a young woman is found floating in an inner-city canal. Not the first, nor the last. When another woman disappears, following a seminar on women and violence, everyone fears for her safety — especially those who know about her husband's controlling character. Is this a one-off domestic crime or part of a wider series of murders? What else has been simmering beneath this couple's apparently normal middle-class life? As Resnick explores deeper, he finds disturbing parallels between the couple he's investigating and his own evolving relationship with Hannah Campbell.